PRAISE FOR ERIN LITTEKEN

"A beautiful, hard-hitting tribute to her own family's history and to the people of unbowed, unbroken Ukraine." **Amanda McCrina, author of** *The Silent Unseen*

"Litteken's compelling, well-researched and moving storytelling soars as it brings to life a harrowing slice of history while intricately highlighting the past that echoes to the present day." **Marina Scott, author of** *The Hunger Between Us*

"A multi-layered saga woven with history and heart... An unforgettable gem of historical fiction." **Paulette Kennedy, bestselling author of** *The Witch of Tin Mountain*

"Erin Litteken gives voice to WWII Ukraine with gritty authenticity... The Lost Daughters of Ukraine is a broom to sweep out Putin's propaganda." **Marsha Forchuk Skrypuch, author of** *Making Bombs for Hitler*

"A powerfully moving debut . . . Ukraine's tragic history painfully echoes its current crisis, and on every page the Ukrainian spirit shines out, unbowed, unbent and unbroken." **Kate Quinn, author of *The Diamond Eye***

"A compelling and intimate story of love and survival. Harrowing and haunting . . . yet, at the same time, it is sensitive, beautiful and inspiring. Everybody should read this story, especially now. I cannot recommend it highly enough." **Christy Lefteri, author of *The Beekeeper of Aleppo***

"A stunning portrait of Ukraine and its people, of strength, of endurance, of the fight for survival during the forced famine, the Holodomor, but also a tender story of Katya, a grandmother whose hidden history holds the power to guide her granddaughter through the darkness of loss and grief, toward life and a limitless future. A remarkable read not to be missed." **Lisa Wingate, author of *Before We Were Yours***

"This beautifully written snapshot of Ukraine's history is both timely and heart-rending, sensitively bringing to life the culture of a nation devastated by an enemy invader. How shocking it is that it's a history that's being repeated today. And how important a reminder that where there's life, there's hope." **Fiona Valpy, author of *The Dressmaker's Gift***

"*The Memory Keeper of Kyiv* is a meticulously researched novel . . . depicting a country whose people managed to dig deep enough to find the strength, determination and heart to survive." **Deborah Carr, author of *An Island at War***

THE LOST DAUGHTERS OF UKRAINE

ERIN LITTEKEN

Boldwood

First published in Great Britain in 2023 by Boldwood Books Ltd.

Cover Design by Head Design Ltd

Cover Photography: Shutterstock

Every effort has been made to obtain the necessary permissions with reference to copyright material, both illustrative and quoted. We apologise for any omissions in this respect and will be pleased to make the appropriate acknowledgements in any future edition.

A CIP catalogue record for this book is available from the British Library.

Paperback ISBN 978-1-80415-772-5

Large Print ISBN 978-1-80415-773-2

Hardback ISBN 978-1-80415-771-8

Ebook ISBN 978-1-80415-775-6

Kindle ISBN 978-1-80415-774-9

Audio CD ISBN 978-1-80415-766-4

MP3 CD ISBN 978-1-80415-767-1

Digital audio download ISBN 978-1-80415-769-5

Boldwood Books Ltd
23 Bowerdean Street
London SW6 3TN
www.boldwoodbooks.com

For Bobby

HISTORICAL NOTE

To better understand the setting of this novel, one must be somewhat familiar with the history. On the heels of World War I, the 1921 Treaty of Riga ended the Soviet-Polish war, and in Ukraine, it ended several years of multi-front fighting to create an independent country. Ukraine was divided between Poland and the Soviet Union, and Volhynia, a historic region located in what is now western Ukraine and comprised primarily of Ukrainians, fell under Polish rule.

During this interwar period, Poland wanted to assimilate their newly acquired territory into their way of life. Polish authorities closed Ukrainian schools, destroyed Orthodox churches, and arrested Ukrainian leaders, teachers, and priests. Polish veterans of WWI were given prime land in Volhynia in a colonial attempt to strengthen the Polish grip there. In return, Ukrainian nationalists assassinated Polish leaders and attacked Polish landowners. Poland then opened what is now recognized as a concentration camp, Bereza Kartuska, where Ukrainian nationalists were imprisoned without trial and tortured and abused.

In 1939, the Soviet Union and Nazi Germany started World War II by invading Poland and dividing the country between them. In the east, the Soviets occupied Volhynia until 1941, when Hitler broke his pact with Stalin and attacked the Soviet Union. Under German occupation, Volhynia became a part of the newly formed *Reichskommissariat* Ukraine. Both regimes devastated Ukraine and Poland, destroying villages and cities and arresting, deporting and murdering millions. During this upheaval, the historic tensions between the Poles and Ukrainians erupted in a series of violent clashes and brutal massacres of innocent civilians. Whole villages were decimated and the sheer brutality of these deaths—often executed with farm implements—contrasted directly with generations of intertwined families and friendships between Poles and Ukrainians. It is an ugly, nuanced history that even today is hard to comprehend.

My grandfather was born in Volhynia. He and his family lived through this turmoil. Much of the following novel is inspired by their experiences.

PROLOGUE

Halya unfolded the weathered paper—the most important personal possession she had left in the world—and stared down at the sketch of her parents. Innocent and young, they had no idea what troubles their daughter would face one day— no idea that their likeness, drawn with such remarkable precision, would be a salve on their daughter's soul as she struggled to survive this war. But then, who could have anticipated this horror? Who could have dreamed up such a nightmare?

She flipped the paper over, the roughened skin on her fingers catching at the jagged edges as she wrote, carefully listing the names just like Mama did in her paper prayer booklet from the church. Mama had two lists in her book—one for the dead and one for the living. Halya only had this single page to document both.

She let the names pass by her lips silently as she transcribed them, breathing them into the night air and invoking their memories, letting the solace they provided seep into her.

Alina

Katya

Kolya

Slavko

Liliya

Vika

Maksym

Bohdan

Sofia

Nadya

Some dead. Some alive.

Some, the family she'd found; some, the family she'd lost.

Like the scars on her body, they would forever be a part of her.

Her father's words pulsed in the evening air as if he were there, whispering in her ear, his arms wrapped tight around her. She could almost feel the stubble on his jaw tickling her cheek.

Promise me you will be brave and always fight, no matter what happens. Fight, because life is always worth fighting for.

"I fought, Tato," she whispered. She brushed a tear off her cheek with the back of her hand before it could fall and smear the names. "And I will keep fighting. I promise."

1

LILIYA

June 1941, Volhynia Oblast, Soviet Ukraine

Liliya recognized her brother's body by the jagged scar under his right eye. She'd given him that wound eight years ago, when she was seven and he was ten, swinging a bucket at his face after he'd snuck up behind her while she fed and watered the chickens. Her brother, always a prankster, had laughed at her reaction, even as she'd cried over his spilled blood.

Now that seemed such a foolish thing to cry over.

A strangled sob escaped her lips and drew her father near as she fell to her knees. Half of Mykhailo's face was missing, his body bloated. A villager from Lutsk had told them the NKVD—the Soviet police force—had dragged the first round of inmates into the courtyard and unleashed a volley of hand grenades and tank fire on the prisoners. They'd forced the remaining prisoners to bury the dead before killing more and fleeing the advancing Nazis, leaving those bodies out to rot in the sun.

The prisoners. Enemies of the people. Intelligentsia. Nationalists. Anyone who didn't support Stalin.

Her brother.

As hard as it was to see Mykhailo's one lifeless blue eye staring up at her, it was better than never knowing what had happened to him. Uncertainty would have left room for hope, and hope had no place here.

Mykhailo—her big brother, her idol, her biggest supporter. When they were young, when Poland ruled Volhynia, he'd earned money to buy her a sketchbook like her mother's. Mama thought Liliya too young, but he saw the way her eyes followed the swallows as they swooped around the barn, the way her fingers traced their movements in the dirt.

"Here, Liliya," he'd said, handing her the pad and tugging her braid. "Start now and you'll be as good as Mama in no time. Maybe even better."

Liliya still had that sketchbook, tucked away under her clothes in a trunk back home. Filled with rudimentary drawings and childish notes, it was almost laughable compared to the detailed sketches she did now. Still, she didn't think she'd ever be as good an artist as their mother, who, despite lacking a formal higher education, had taught herself more about shadows and light while drawing wildlife and family members than many professional artists.

"It's time, Liliya." Her father, his face drawn and gaunt, touched her shoulder. "We're burying them together. Here. The Germans are close, and I want to get home to your mother before they arrive."

Liliya stepped back as the men moved her brother to a mass grave, but she didn't turn away. She would bear witness to this, to everything the Soviets had done to them during their two years of occupation. The blood-soaked earth of this courtyard would be cleansed by rain and time, but the red stain of the Soviet invasion would never be scrubbed away. Two years of horror and suffering had scorched a permanent mark on Volhynia.

Mykhailo's loss was not the first, only the most recent. Most raw. She shuddered, remembering the villager the Soviets had tortured last month, peeling back the skin on his chest and pouring salt on it as he watched them execute his wife and children. They killed him afterward, branding him a thief and saboteur, but not before making him suffer.

Another atrocity on her list.

The men set Mykhailo's body in the grave with the other prisoners, then shoveled dirt on top of him.

"Goodbye, Mykhailo," Liliya whispered. She crossed herself, then kissed her fingers before pressing them into the ground covering him. "Fly high with the birds."

A soft breeze swirled through the pasture, pulsing against the cornflowers and making them brush against Liliya's arms. Ignoring the sensation, she propped the sketchbook on her lap and angled the pencil to shade in the scruff her brother always had on his jaw. Drawing his face as she remembered it before his arrest helped buffer what she'd witnessed at the prison.

Her mother hadn't uttered a word since they'd arrived home

late last night, her normally merry eyes stretched wide and vacant as Tato pulled her close and whispered the news. Mama had wanted them to bring Mykhailo back, dead or alive, but Tato had decided Mykhailo should rest with his OUN brothers, the other members of the Organization of Ukrainian Nationalists the Soviets had captured and killed.

Mama sat mute at the table, not offering food or drink when Nina, Liliya's oldest, dearest friend and her mother had come to pay their condolences early that morning, so Liliya had filled the role, setting out a jar of plum preserves and bread, knowing her mother would normally never let anyone leave her kitchen hungry or thirsty.

"Give her time," Nina had murmured as she hugged Liliya. "She's still in shock."

Liliya had wanted to scream, "So am I!" but sweet Nina didn't deserve her anger. The Soviets did. So, she bit her tongue and nodded dumbly, letting Nina's warm embrace dull the chill that hadn't left her bones since seeing her dead brother.

Liliya glanced up at the cow grazing next to her, oblivious to the muffled explosions and rumbling tanks that had almost become commonplace. After the Germans had breached the Soviet line near Volodymyr-Volynsky a few days ago, they'd poured into Volhynia with a barrage of tanks thundering through the countryside and airplanes buzzing overhead. Liliya and her father had twice rerouted their trip home to avoid them, and after they'd climbed into the loft above the barn and seen the line of stalled Soviet tanks south of the village, he told her to graze the cow in the long grass just outside their orchard instead of going all the way to the normal pasture.

Liliya paused as a nightingale swooped past, heading toward

the brushy thicket at the edge of the nearby woods. In a few minutes, his song echoed through the pasture, the sweet beauty of it sending a rush of emotion through Liliya so strong and bittersweet that she had to brace her hands against the ground so it didn't wash her away.

"Some people think they only sing at night because of their name," her mother had told her when she first taught Liliya how to draw them. "But they'll sing night and day, these sweet harbingers of spring."

Mama called Liliya her little *soloveiko* because she never stopped chattering, just like a nightingale, when she was young, but Liliya never minded. She thought it a great compliment to be likened to such a beautiful little bird.

A low hum, different from the sounds of the tanks, forced its way into Liliya's consciousness. Looking back at her house, she saw her mother standing in the road, watching the sky. Behind Mama, two Luftwaffe planes appeared on the horizon. Moving fast, they swooped low over the stalled Soviet tanks in the distance, releasing a burst of bullets before angling upward and circling wide around Liliya's house so they could approach the tank line from the other side. Liliya jumped to her feet, the sketchbook sliding to the ground.

"Mama! Get down!" Panic set Liliya in motion. Her bare feet pounded into the dewy ground, the wet morning grass sticking to her legs until she hit the dirt road.

"Get down, Mama!" Liliya waved her arms as she ran, but her mother wouldn't move. She stared at the planes, frozen—stuck in her grief, paralyzed with her fear, Liliya didn't know which. She kept running as the planes appeared behind her mother on their flight back to the tanks, loud and low, but Liliya felt as if she was slogging through honey.

Sharp, staccato bursts, like the sound of a spoon banging on a metal bucket, punctuated the din of the motors.

Mama pitched forward, falling into Liliya's arms as they finally met, knocking Liliya to the ground. She landed hard on her back, the air rushing out of her lungs with a sharp exhale, her mother limp on top of her.

The planes flew past, their fading drone replaced by Liliya's screams. Shock rendered her motionless as she clutched her mother. Blood seeped out of Mama's body, saturating Liliya's shirt. She squeezed her eyes shut as she felt Mama draw one last shuddering breath. Minutes passed, or maybe hours. Liliya couldn't tell which anymore. It wasn't until her friend Oleksiy cupped her cheeks with his big hands that she opened her eyes.

"I'm here now, Liliya," he crooned as he gently pulled her away from her mother's lifeless body. Oleksiy, already as big as an ox though only a year older than Liliya's fifteen, picked her up as if she were a baby. Cradling her close to his chest, he carried her into her house, then walked back and carried her mother's body home.

For two days, while her father grieved, Oleksiy sat with her. His was the first face she saw when she woke screaming and the last before she fell into a fitful sleep full of blood and bullets and disfigured faces.

"I will always take care of you, Liliya," he'd promised over and over, until she finally believed him. She had nothing else to believe in anymore.

* * *

"I don't want to leave, Tato." It wasn't the first time she'd told her father this in the weeks since her mother's death, and he gave her the same answer he'd given every other time.

"We cannot live under this roof right now." He set his mouth in a hard line and picked up the reins. "Maksym and his wife, Vika, need a bigger home, and we need to get away. The parish in the Kholm district will be a welcome change. You're all I have left, daughter, so you're coming with me. There's nothing more to be said."

"We're very grateful for your generosity," Vika said from the doorway. "We'll take good care of your home, and you'll always have a place here."

Liliya liked her uncle Maksym, her mother's younger brother, his wife, Vika, and their children. Slavko, the eldest, was only a few years younger than her, and his charismatic personality had been a welcome contrast to her own dark moods of late. When he sashayed into their somber house, swooping her up in a big hug just like Mykhailo had always done, the sting of familiar tears swelled in her throat. But before they could fall, he pulled a piece of chocolate out of his pocket. "Here. I saved this for you."

His smooth words made him seem far older than he was, but his silly antics revealed a boyish side to him that had brought a smile to Liliya's face for the first time in weeks. Still, that didn't mean she wanted to leave her home to them.

Liliya set her trunk in the back of the wagon and climbed up next to her father. She didn't look back as the wagon rolled down the road, but she could feel Oleksiy's eyes on her from where he stood next to Maksym.

"This will be better, you'll see," Tato said. "I'll have more time to work on languages with you, which will be very helpful for you when you attend university. I can teach you some basic German, and as our new village has a large Polish population, you'll be able to practice your Polish as well."

"I don't want to learn German and I don't need to practice Polish. I prefer to speak Ukrainian, and I want to stay here. Where I grew up. Where my friends are. Where my mother and brother lived. We can't just run away from our emotions, Tato," Liliya said. "Mama and Mykhailo will be just as dead in Kholm as they are here."

Tato flinched, and a pang of guilt ricocheted through her.

"I'm sorry, Tato. I didn't mean it that way."

Tato smiled sadly and patted her leg. "We will heal together, Liliya. I will take care of you, and you will take care of me, just as your mother and Mykhailo would have wanted. But it will be easier in a new place. You'll see. And when the time is right and this war settles down, I will get my bright girl to a university, just like we always planned."

Her father picked up the reins and Liliya gave one last look at her home. Mama's treasured poppies had exploded with color overnight, blossoming for the first time this summer— their vibrant red petals like drops of blood splattered against the stark, whitewashed walls of the house.

Liliya jerked her head away and leaned on Tato's shoulder, praying that he was right, because she didn't know what else to do about the pain and anger tangled so tight inside it made her heart ache.

2

HALYA

August 1941, Kyiv Oblast, Soviet Ukraine

Halya never intended to eavesdrop on her parents, but when she heard them talking in low voices inside, she paused at the door and pressed her back against the wall of the house. At almost ten years old, she wanted to know more about what was going on, even if they didn't think she was old enough to understand.

"The Reds are fleeing," Tato said, "but Stalin is calling for a scorched earth policy. He wants everything destroyed—the crops, the livestock, the farm implements—so the Germans can't get it. And he's conscripting all the men."

"Not you, though?" Mama said.

"Not with my bad leg, Katya," Tato said. "I'm of no use to them if I can't walk straight."

"You walk just fine, Kolya."

Halya couldn't see them, but she figured Mama was probably rubbing Tato's shoulders like she always did when he got sad about his leg. He'd broken it in a farming accident with a plow a few years back, and it never healed properly. The collective leader had whipped him for ruining the plow and "sabotaging state property."

"We need to hide food and whatever we can, starting tonight," Tato said. "The Germans are only a few kilometers away."

"Maybe they won't be so bad," Mama said. "Compared to Stalin, this might be a welcome change."

"I'm not hopeful," Tato said. "I think it will be more of the same."

Halya didn't want to hear any more. She slipped away and climbed up into her favorite place in the yard, a brambling cherry tucked in the small orchard behind the house. Ensconced in the bony arms of the tree's embrace, the green leaves rustling in her ears, she felt safe. She didn't have to think about the Red Army soldiers and their scorched earth plans or the advancing German tanks. Up here, with her book of Lesya Ukrainka poems—a very special book her father had gotten for her, then insisted she hide every night in a hole in the barn wall—she could retreat from the world and just be herself.

She lost herself in the words, letting the worry and fear that had gripped her since overhearing her parents fall away as the beautiful poetry soothed her. Thirty minutes later, when her father tapped her foot, she jumped.

"Are you building a nest up there? Shall I have your mother send up your supper?"

Halya closed her book and tucked it into her pocket. "You shouldn't sneak up on people like that."

Tato laughed, the same deep, rolling sound Halya had loved her whole life. "I lumbered up to this tree like a pig loose in a grain bin. If you didn't hear me, it's because your head is in the clouds."

"Well, I am in a tree," Halya said. She held her arms out to him, and he swung her down from the branches, giving her a hug before he set her on the ground. He smelled of the outdoors: wind, sunshine, and earth, and Halya loved it. She placed her hand in his. "I was reading the poetry book you got me."

"Ah, and which is your favorite?" Tato asked.

"'Against All Hope, I Hope'" Halya answered without thinking. That poem spoke to her like nothing else ever had.

"What's taking so long out there?" Mama poked her head out the door. "I sent you to get Halya, not hide out there with her."

"I wasn't hiding, Mama." Halya skipped forward and planted a kiss on her mother's flour-dusted cheek. "I was reading."

"Of course you were." Mama smoothed Halya's loose hair. "And were you reading so hard your braids fell out?"

Halya grimaced. "Sorry. They must have snagged on the tree branches."

"Come, let me fix it for you while Tato cleans up for supper."

Halya sat down at the table. She knew her parents wouldn't say anything else about the invasion in front of her. They liked to protect her as much as they could. Normally, it made her crazy, but today, she was glad to ignore the war looming outside her door.

Mama took up the brush and ran it down the length of Halya's hair. Halya sat back in the chair as little tingles of pleasure danced across her scalp. She'd seen her friend's mother yank the brush through her hair, but Mama was always gentle.

"Your hair is so long now. It reminds me of your mother's." Mama's throat hitched on the word "mother," and it took every ounce of control Halya had to keep from turning around and gaping at her.

"It does?" Halya whispered. Her mother rarely talked of her sister, Halya's birth mother, Alina. She'd died when Halya was a baby, and Katya, the woman Halya now called Mama, had raised Halya as her own.

"Yes." Mama spoke loudly, as if forcing out cheer. "She had beautiful thick hair, dark and shiny."

"Like yours?"

"Much prettier. Like yours."

Halya swallowed hard and pushed out the words fast before she lost her courage. "Do you think I look like her?"

The brush stilled for a second, then resumed its downward motion slower. Halya heard Mama take a deep breath.

"Yes," she finally said. "You look a lot like your mother."

Something inside Halya shifted into place, filling in a hole she hadn't realized existed. A smile trembled on her lips, composed of equal parts relief and trepidation. "Which parts?" She forced out the question she'd always wanted to ask.

"Well, your eyes and the shape of your jaw are very similar. Your nose, too. But I think the thing that reminds me the most of her is your hair." Mama set the brush down. "We used to brush each other's hair and braid it, just like I do for you." Her mouth curved up, and she stared outside in the way adults did when they weren't really looking at anything, when they were picturing something else in their mind. "I was always so jealous of the way her hair shimmered in the sun. She loved putting bright red poppies in her vinok and weaving them into her braids."

Mama sighed, and Halya held her breath, waiting for more. She finally turned her eyes toward Halya. "Sometimes, if I close my eyes, I can almost imagine it's her hair I'm brushing, and we're young, happy girls again."

Mama reached down and pulled her into a tight hug. "She lives on in you in all the best ways, Halya. Never forget that."

Halya pondered those words later as she stood next to the fence in their yard, staring out at the line of Soviet tanks moving east past her village. Their stark metal forms cut across the beauty of the fields like an ugly scar. She didn't want to think about them or the Germans, so instead, she knelt next to the poppies, plucked a blossom, and tucked it in her braid, just like her mother used to.

3

VIKA

December 1941, Volhynia, Reichskommissariat Ukraine

Vika covered her eight-year-old son's eyes as the SS officer sliced off the partisan's ear.

"This is what happens to those who fight against Germany! And remember, if you aid the partisans, you'll share their fate!" The Ukrainian auxiliary policeman translated the SS officer's words as he went to the next man and did the same thing. He repeated the action for all four captured partisans for both ears, then moved to the noses.

Blood ran in rivers down their pale faces. The youngest one, who couldn't have been more than seventeen, cried and begged for his mother. By the time the SS officer finished, Vika wanted to throw up. The whole village, forced to gather to witness this, had gone completely silent. When the four shots rang out in quick succession, ending the partisans' misery, Vika murmured a prayer, then grabbed Bohdan's hand and hurried away, past the low fences and dead plants hugging the thatched roofed houses and down the dirt road that led to their home. Her other children, Sofia and Slavko, too old at ten and twelve respectively to have their eyes shielded from the horrors of their everyday lives, followed. Her husband, Maksym, stayed back with some of the men to talk.

Vika's thoughts strayed to Liliya as she paused and brushed the snow off the *kalyna* bush Liliya and her mother had planted next to their gate. It had been nearly two months since Liliya's last letter, and she wondered how they were doing under Nazi rule in Kholm.

Vika had scoffed six months ago when the other villagers had welcomed the Germans with bread and salt. Of course, she'd been glad to see the Reds go back to Russia as they fled the Germans, but she didn't trust this new invading force, either.

"They're promising us a free country," Maksym had said.

"They want our land, just like everyone else. The Poles. The Russians," Vika had retorted. "Why should we trust them?"

"It won't be as bad," he'd said. "You'll see."

And she had. She'd seen that her instinct was right and the Germans cared nothing about Ukraine or her people. Even the news that the Americans had entered the war hadn't tempered the Germans' erratic tempers. Today's events highlighted that perfectly, and it made the news she had to share with Maksym that much more difficult.

* * *

That night, when Maksym slid into the bed next to her, she rolled toward him. He smelled like the *horilka* he'd been drinking. "Where have you been?"

"Talking," he mumbled.

"I hope you're being careful. You have a family to consider."

"I always consider my family," he said. "The people I was with tonight have Ukrainians, including our children, foremost in their minds." He turned onto his back and closed his eyes. "Besides, you're one to talk."

"What do you mean?" Vika sat up and glared at him, even though she could barely make out the outline of his face in the dark, moonless night.

"When you brought home that little Jewish boy last month, did you stop to think what would happen if the Germans found him here? You helped him at great risk to our children."

Vika's breath caught as she pictured the little tear-stained face. "I couldn't turn him away. I had to help him."

"I know. That's why I love you. You're fierce and brave." He pulled her to his chest and stroked her hair. "Don't you see? I'm only trying to help how I can, too."

Vika stared out the window at the black sky. Yes, they'd helped one Jewish boy, rescued from the side of the road where his mother must have hidden him when she realized the finality of their march, but they'd watched so many more walk to their deaths. Was that the moment she'd grasped the futility of her life? Or was it further back, when she'd lost her sisters, her brothers, her parents to Stalin?

At some point, she'd recognized she had no control over the fate of the people she loved. They were flowers struggling to grow under the constant stomping of military boots, and she couldn't save any of them. So, she pulled away. Closed down. Grew hard and didn't allow herself to feel. But asleep, she couldn't control her emotions.

She would dream of the Jews again tonight. The long rows of terrified people moving down the road in front of her house. Men, women, children. Generations of families marching to their deaths. The empty pit next to the Jewish cemetery, filled with bodies, the earth shifting for weeks as they settled and decomposed—a grim reminder of the atrocities hidden beneath the soil.

Maksym never shot a gun, never joined the Ukrainians who worked as auxiliary police for the Germans and assisted in this murder, but he saw, just like she did, what was happening and didn't stop it. They couldn't, unless they wanted to join the Jews in their mass grave. And how did one person make a difference against an army?

"One child at a time," Maksym had told her as she cried in his arms that night. "You are making a difference right now."

But she couldn't stop asking herself what level of complicity was enough to be damning when it meant saving your own family? She would do anything for her children, but didn't every mother feel that way? How could she save her children at the cost of other mothers' children?

Maksym propped himself up on his elbow and looked down at her. "What did you need to tell me, Vikusia?"

Vika flinched at the reminder of her news, then took his hand and placed it on the slight bulge of her belly. "I'm pregnant."

4

HALYA

June 1942, Kyiv District, Reichskommissariat Ukraine

Halya grimaced as Mama rubbed the cut garlic cloves onto her arms and neck. An old woman had told her it would leave a harmless rash that would deter the Germans from selecting them as laborers, and ever since, Mama had employed the practice with a religious fervor.

So much had changed since the Germans arrived last fall. Gone were the days when Halya could roam the woods or wander the fields on her own. Now, she was restricted to the yard, and each day started with a garlic rubdown.

"Be still! Just a bit more. You should be grateful we have enough garlic stored away to use for this. There was a time not long ago where this wouldn't have been possible."

"I know, Mama, but it burns!" Halya clawed at the red streaks on her forearm.

"It's not supposed to feel good," Mama said as she paused to scratch at the rash she'd given herself to prove to Halya that it worked. "The Germans are rounding up people to send to work in their factories, and I promise you, this garlic rash is far better than being taken by them. Besides, you're a big girl. Almost eleven years old now. You can be brave."

"Yes, Mama."

The pungent, peppery scent tickled Halya's nose, and she sneezed as soon as Mama released her. So far, Halya's skin hadn't responded to the garlic treatment as much as Mama would like, but it wasn't for lack of trying.

"Stay close to the house. No wandering," Mama instructed as Halya grabbed her coat. "They've taken thousands of people from the district already and hundreds of thousands across Ukraine. It will only get worse!"

Halya nodded at the familiar warning and escaped outside to her cherry tree, grateful that it sat close enough to the house to fall within Mama's approved area. She pulled herself up into the familiar branches, then took the picture out of her pocket.

She scrutinized it, searching for pieces of herself in the woman who looked back at her. Her mother. Not Katya, who she called Mama, but her real mother. The woman who'd carried her, birthed her, and left her.

Alina.

She whispered the name, letting it linger on her tongue, tasting the longing, the grief, the missed opportunities like the bitter *kalyna* tea Mama made her drink when she was sick.

My real mother's name was Alina.

Last month, she'd found her father going through old pictures. One showed Alina and Katya, arm in arm, smiling in front of a field of sunflowers, but Halya only glimpsed it for a moment before Mama snatched it away and clutched it to her chest, tears trembling on her lashes as she marched out of the house.

"This is still hard for her," Tato had said apologetically as he pulled out another picture. In it, Tato and Alina, dressed in Western-style clothes—her mother in a fine white hat and dark blue overcoat and her father in a suit, tie, and black overcoat— leaned close, their heads tilted toward each other, small smiles dancing on their lips. Tato had held it up to Halya like a talisman, offering her a piece of her history she hadn't realized she missed.

"My God, I knew you looked like her, but to see you next to this picture . . . it's uncanny," he'd said. Tears had welled in his eyes, and it terrified her. Her father was big and brave—a strong man who worked hard all day, then came home and greeted her by tossing her in the air until she shrieked with joy. He didn't cry or get sad.

"I'm sorry, Tato." Her hands instinctively covered her face in an attempt to shield him from the pain of seeing her, but desperate, unspoken questions stuck in her throat.

How? Which parts?

He'd pulled her hands down and gently gripped her chin. "Don't ever be sorry, my love. Your mother was a beautiful, wonderful woman. It is a gift that you resemble her."

Halya didn't think it was that great a gift, because after that day, her father grew quiet whenever he looked at her.

She ran her finger down her mother's picture. She loved her mama, Katya, so much, but she couldn't deny her fascination with her mother, Alina. High cheekbones, perfect arched brows, huge eyes, and a smirk on her lips. Yes, her mother was beautiful, but when Halya looked in Mama's small hand mirror, all she saw was a scrawny girl with blue eyes too big for her peaked face, gaunt cheeks and dry, gnawed-up lips. She was certain her father was wrong.

Still, she tucked the photograph into her skirt pocket, just like she did every morning, hoping one day her mother's beauty would somehow seep into her, like the garlic soaking into her bruised skin.

5

LILIYA

December 1942, Volhynia, Reichskommissariat Ukraine

Ice-covered branches whipped into Liliya's face, but she had no tears left to spare for the pain. Her bare feet scrabbled along the frozen ground, numb and clumsy as she left the woods and stepped out onto a dirt road. The cold air pierced her lungs with each breath, and her father's last words played on a loop in her mind.

"Go home!"

She'd known instantly what he meant, though their current home was on fire.

Home was Maky, the small village in Volhynia south of Kovel. Where she'd grown up. Where she'd fallen in love with nature and birds. Where they'd buried her mother on a hot summer day nearly a year and a half ago.

Every morning, as Liliya made breakfast for the two of

them, her father asked her the same thing, though he liked to mix up the languages—Ukrainian, Polish, German, Russian—to "keep her sharp," as he put it.

"Did you soar with the birds in your dreams, daughter?"

Before tonight, she'd thought he meant to encourage her to have high goals for her life, to dream of more than a life in a small village, which was what he and her mother had pushed her to do—sending her to school in the city before her mother's death and encouraging her scholarly pursuits and dreams of university. But now, after traveling dozens of kilometers through the dark in her nightclothes, his words conveyed a far deeper insight than she'd previously imagined. She had flown with the birds. Through fields, woods, and even across part of the iced-over river, miraculously not running into any partisans or soldiers demanding paperwork.

And now, she'd arrived.

She gripped the fence as she stared at the house. Her house. The one she'd grown up in. Whitewashed walls glowed pink in the new light of the rising sun. Outbuildings huddled close to it, as if trying to conserve warmth together. The starkly dormant garden, normally riotous with blooms and vegetables, slept through the winter. She hadn't seen it in so long, but it looked the same.

She pushed open the gate and took an awkward step forward, her trembling muscles barely supporting her after hours of travel.

The door opened and Liliya froze. Tall and broad shouldered, a man stepped out onto the path, then halted as he took her in.

"Who are you? Where are Maksym and Vika?" Using her

voice, broken and raspy from the screams, made her throat ache, and her hand moved unconsciously to clutch her neck. Fear or common sense should have prevailed—instead, she took another step forward and peered up at him. Maybe she'd never had much common sense. Maybe all her fear had disappeared as she watched her father being murdered. Or, and this seemed the most likely to her in this moment, maybe after losing everyone in her family, she didn't care if she lived or died anymore.

Her traitorous body chose that moment to finally give out, and she sank to the ground.

A strong hand cupped the back of Liliya's neck and pulled her forward.

"Drink this," a voice ordered as a bottle was placed against her lips.

The smell of *horilka* made her eyes flutter open as a swig of the fiery liquid poured into her mouth. She choked it down, then coughed and let her head fall back onto the bed.

"It will warm you up. You're half dead from cold," the voice said.

Relief coursed through Liliya as she finally recognized Vika next to her. "I thought you were gone."

"Of course not. We're right here where you left us. Now, let's see to these wounds."

Vika pulled a chair up next to the bed and splashed the alcohol over the sores on her feet. Liliya stifled a groan and wished for the numbness she'd worried about earlier to return.

Desperate for a distraction, she turned toward the table where Maksym and the stranger sat staring at her.

"Uncle Maksym, it's good to see you."

"I agree, but what happened, niece?" Maksym asked. "Where is your father?"

Liliya's eyes flickered to the stranger, unsure how to answer that question with his penetrating gaze on her. Maksym must trust him if he'd asked the question in front of him. But then, her father had trusted the wrong people, too.

She flinched as Vika dabbed at a particularly nasty gash on the sole of her left foot. "Dead," she finally said. "The Polish Underground killed him and burned down our house."

Maksym straightened in his chair. "Why?"

"Why do you think? He was the priest in the Orthodox church. A driving force in promoting cultural awareness among the Ukrainians in our village. They're getting rid of everyone like him across the river."

"Like some Ukrainians seek to do to the Poles here!" The words snapped out of the stranger's mouth as he stood, his hat knotted in his fist. His voice was low and melodic, but slightly stilted, as if Ukrainian wasn't his first language. He glanced at Maksym, his cheeks red. "I should go."

Maksym's eyes flickered over to the man, as if he'd forgotten he was there. "There's no need, Filip."

Not Pylyp, a Ukrainian name. Filip. Polish.

The man raised his hand. "We'll talk later."

As the door slammed shut, Liliya pushed herself up. "Who is he? Why do you have a Pole here?"

Maksym leaned forward and rested his elbows on his knees. "Filip works with me at the stable, and he's been sleeping in our barn ever since his mother was killed by Ukrainian nationalists last month."

Liliya's jaw clenched. "It seems your house is a wayward home for orphans of all types, then."

"I will never turn away someone who needs help," Maksym said, his voice tight. "No matter who it was. And neither would your father."

"My father is dead," Liliya said flatly. She leaned back into the pillow and closed her eyes, letting exhaustion finally overcome her.

* * *

Vika held out a thick shawl. "Go outside, go see the animals, go do something. You can't sit there forever."

Liliya glared at Vika. "I don't want to."

Vika shook the shawl at her. "Go on. Some fresh air will be good for you."

Liliya sighed as she stood from the chair she'd perched in for the last three days and took it. Vika was easier to appease than fight.

Wrapping it around her shoulders, she made her way into the barn, then reached into the stall and scratched the horse's neck. It stuck its muzzle in the air and stretched forward so she could reach it easier.

"Are you feeling better?"

She whirled, startling the horse. Filip stood in the doorway, an apple core in his hand, watching her. Liliya frowned. She didn't want to talk to him. Maybe it was because he'd witnessed her at her lowest, hobbling to the house on bloody feet and drowning in a pool of despair. Maybe it was because he was the first Pole she'd talked to after watching other Poles shouting as they beat her father and burned their home.

Maybe it was simply because he was Polish.

"No," she barked. "I don't feel better. What are you doing here?"

Filip stepped inside the barn and closed the door behind him, his words calm and slow, as if he were talking to a fiery young horse. It only made Liliya angrier.

"Maksym lets me sleep here."

"Because you have nowhere else to go?" Liliya should have regretted the harsh words as soon as they left her mouth—it was a low blow even for her—but she couldn't bring herself to care.

"I suppose we have that in common, don't we?" Filip fired back, his facade cracking. He cleared his throat, as if surprised by his own outburst, and moved toward the horse. "He likes you."

Liliya recognized the olive branch he was offering, then snapped it in two, her voice tight.

"Of course he does. I helped raise him."

Who did this man think he was? Didn't he realize this had been her farm? Her horse? Her life?

Filip reddened as he held out the apple core. The horse plucked it off his hand with its dexterous lips, chewing and swallowing the treat in a few short, noisy bites.

"I'm sorry about how I reacted to you the other night. I still get emotional about my mother," he said, his eyes meeting hers. "And I'm sorry about your father."

A lump stuck in her throat, a sudden swell of emotion she

hadn't quite processed. She pushed it down with a cough, surprised at the tears pooling in her eyes. She hadn't let herself cry about her father yet, and she wasn't about to start now in front of this man.

Filip fished a handkerchief out of his pocket and held it out, but she shook her head and wiped the back of her hand across her eyes.

She should have offered her sympathy for his loss in return —she'd been raised well-enough to know that—but her wounds were too fresh, too raw for her to see past their sting. And she didn't want to link herself to him in any way through their shared grief. Their losses alone pitted them against each other, not together, so why see him as something more? Something real. It was futile.

"I'm fine."

Filip lowered his hand, his fingers closing tight around the handkerchief. "I'm sure you are. You seem quite resilient."

Liliya grimaced. "One must be to survive here, don't you think?"

He started to speak, then stopped himself. She waited, watching his mouth work as he chewed on his thoughts. He didn't spew them out before thinking like she so often did and, despite herself, a spark of admiration for him flared in her chest.

"I won't apologize for being Polish, though," he said. "I'm proud of who I am."

Heat flooded her cheeks, and she whirled to face him, all thoughts of admiration gone. "And I won't apologize for being Ukrainian."

"But I never asked you to, did I? That's the difference

between me and you. You see me the same way you see your father's killers, but I'm not them."

"I didn't say that!"

"You don't have to. I was just like you after I lost my mother. Angry at all Ukrainians for something a small group did. Maksym helped me get through that. Helped me see the shades of gray."

"I am not just like you." Liliya shoved her hands into her pockets to hide their sudden trembling. His words hit too close to home, but she would never admit that. "And I don't need your advice."

Filip nodded once, a sharp jerk of his head. "Right. I should let you get inside," he finally said, but it came out in Polish. He scowled at the slip before he started to repeat himself in Ukrainian, but Liliya held up her hand.

"I understand you and your language just fine," she said stiffly in Polish, then slipped out of the barn.

6

VIKA

February 1943, Volhynia, Reichskommissariat Ukraine

Kneading bread soothed Vika. The rhythm, the familiarity. The promise of food in her children's bellies. It helped her think. It helped her forget.

Push. Fold. Push. Fold. The dough came together in her hands, soft and pliant. A stark contrast to the rough hands working it. She sprinkled more flour on the table then continued.

Push. Fold. Forget. Push. Fold. Forget.

Forget that she and Maksym were now responsible for his seventeen-year-old niece, Liliya, who'd lost her parents and brother in this bloody war already. Forget that the Nazis were forcing people, even children, to go to Germany to work in their factories or on their farms. Forget that her family lived under the constant threat of danger and only a few months ago she'd brought a new baby into this broken world.

"Mama! They're taking people right off the street!"

Vika glanced up at Sofia, her golden-haired eleven-year-old daughter, as she ran in. Her big brown eyes trembled with tears, and Vika's heart constricted at the sight. "What are you talking about? Who took people?"

"They rounded up a group of teenagers to send to Germany." Slavko came in behind Sofia and pulled the door closed. At thirteen years old, he knew far more than he should on the dangers this world had to offer, and the effects of that knowledge stained his countenance. Still, he forced out a smile for his mother, but his eyes, once quick to crinkle in laughter, didn't follow suit.

Sofia shifted from one spindly leg to the other in her unease at being the bearer of such bad news. "They said if the village elders don't turn over the workers, they'll just take what they need."

The semantics weren't lost on Vika.

What they need.

Not *who*. Not people with families who loved them.

Just eastern workers, or *Ostarbeiters*. Slave labor.

"Is that true, Mama? Can they just take us?" Sofia asked.

Vika's hands went back to work.

Push, fold, forget. Push, fold, forget.

Rhythm. Regularity. Control. These things were non-existent in the rest of her life, but here, with the dough, in her home, they were her constant. She didn't answer Sofia's question but asked her own. "Who are they taking?"

"Everyone. Even younger children. Like me and Slavko."

Sofia's normally sunny face clouded with worry, and her eyes darted to Slavko. "Do you really think they'll take people that young?"

Sofia's hands twisted in her skirt as she waited for Vika's promise that everything would be all right, but Vika remained silent. She wanted to reassure her children; she wanted to find the perfect words to make them feel better, but she couldn't. The truth was, nothing about the Nazis shocked her anymore. She'd seen them march the Jewish population to a ravine and heard the gunshots marking their demise. She'd smelled the charred flesh and acrid smoke from the village they'd burned to retaliate against Ukrainian partisan strikes on German supply lines. She'd been forced to watch them whip her neighbors for infractions such as keeping too many of the vegetables from their garden or hiding a milk cow in the woods.

In the last year and a half, it had become abundantly clear that the Germans the villagers had initially welcomed, bread and salt in hand, as liberators from the brutal Soviet regime were no better than the Soviets and were, perhaps, far worse.

"No, of course not," Maksym answered for Vika as he came in the door. Apprehension pinched his handsome face, and, like his son, his smile didn't reach his eyes.

Vika exhaled slowly. *He's lying.*

Sofia ran to him, and he wrapped her in a hug. "As long as we stay together, we'll be all right," Maksym said. He scooped up Bohdan, hugging him against his chest before setting him back down and picking up the baby. A calm child, little Nadiya had arrived one hot summer night, the quickest and easiest of all of Vika's labors. Maksym had wanted to name her after the virtue of "hope," and Vika acquiesced, though she'd never felt more hopeless in her life.

Despite that, the whole family adored their "Nadya," as they called her affectionately, and there was no doubt her sunny demeanor brought joy to the house. It just couldn't compare with Vika's fear every time Slavko and Sofia tended the animals in the barn or Bohdan fetched vegetables from the garden. Any time they were outside, out of her sight, she worried.

Maksym snuggled Nadya close, his gaze wavering as his eyes fell on Vika. She forced her face into an impassive mask. Staying together hadn't saved her family when Stalin's men sent her older brothers to the gulags and starved her parents and sisters to death. In fact, leaving had been what saved her. At her parents' insistence, she'd abandoned most of her family. Taking only her youngest sister, Maria, she'd followed Maksym, left the devastating hunger gripping the countryside, and moved in with his family in Volhynia just before the borders closed. So, she and Maria survived while their entire family perished in Stalin's famine. That guilt pulled at her every minute of every day.

Vika stared out the window at the land. "Maybe we should have left long ago."

"Leaving would have been useless." Maksym came up behind her and kissed her cheek. "War is raging all over, and Stalin may be retreating now, but that's because Hitler is advancing. And Stalin will be back. He always comes back. What's important now is that we're together. Together, we can take on the Soviets and the Germans. This land will thrive again, and we will be here to raise our family on it."

She swallowed down the empty promise and wrapped it

around the ball of fear that writhed constantly in her stomach. She had to believe him, so she forced herself to. If she didn't, she'd have given up on life long ago.

"Where is Liliya?"

She should have been home helping Vika with the house chores and staying close so Vika could keep an eye on her, but instead, drowning in grief, Liliya floated around the countryside like a wraith.

As if she was the only person in the world who'd ever lost someone they loved.

"Liliya is out drawing her birds," Sofia said.

Slavko elbowed her. "You shouldn't tell on her!"

"I can't lie," Sofia said, her expression aghast at the idea of such a travesty.

Vika gave a tight nod and deftly shaped the dough into a neat loaf before placing it into the oven. Deportations or not, with the German food quotas taking the sustenance from her house daily, she couldn't afford to let anything go to waste. She wiped her hands on a cloth and looked up at her children. Uncertainty made their faces both hopeful and afraid, and Vika knew she should comfort them like Maksym had. But constant worry had worn her down to a withered shell, her denial an intricate web holding her body together. If she opened her arms to them, let them breach her fragile exterior, she'd crumble under their weight.

"Slavko, take the children and go check on the chickens." Maksym touched Vika's arm gently, as if she were a delicate flower, and Vika wondered if she didn't do as good a job as she thought of hiding her weaknesses from him. Instead of leaning into him like she wanted, she stiffened her back and shook off his hand.

Slavko ushered everyone outside, and Maksym set Nadya back on the bed as he went on. "I sent Filip to find Liliya. I've heard they're doing roundups all over the countryside now. Everyone needs to be aware of what's going on."

"Filip's not exactly her favorite person," Vika said.

Maksym rubbed the back of his neck. "Does she think it's easy for any of us? Her father was like a brother to me, and I can't help but think about the men that killed him every time I see Filip or the other Poles at the stable. But, then I remember that Filip is a good man, and he lost his mother at the hands of some Ukrainians. There is no black and white here, Vika, and the only thing I've learned from any of this is that a person can't be judged by who their parents were or where they were born. Liliya must learn to see the man, not the uniform or nationality."

Vika shook her head. "That's not always easy here, but I don't want to talk about that now. I want to know what is going on with labor deportations."

"The Germans surrounded a theater full of young people in Kovel, rounded up everyone inside, and put them on a train west. Nobody was notified, no parents had a chance to say goodbye or bring supplies." Maksym sat at the table and started shoveling in spoonfuls of borsch from the bowl Vika set in front of him. "One girl managed to escape and tell everyone what happened. I've heard similar tales from local villages as well. Now that no one is volunteering, the Germans are ordering the village elders to turn over lists of people for each shipment, but people are refusing to go. So, the Germans are taking any young person they can find by force and punishing those who disobey. Liliya must be very careful."

"But we don't really need to worry about our children, right? They're too young?" Vika grabbed a cloth and began to wipe the table as Sofia and Slavko's words echoed in her mind, but surely they were wrong. The Germans wouldn't want to bother with such young children as laborers.

Maksym paused, his spoon suspended in the air, and met her gaze. "Ivan Schimansky said they took his cousin's two daughters. The youngest is twelve."

7

LILIYA

February 1943, Volhynia, Reichskommissariat Ukraine

Liliya still hadn't found a way to fill the holes in her heart in the two months since her arrival in Maky. Her emotions vacillated between all-consuming anger and morose apathy, but rarely fell in between. Drawing, once her escape, now carried so many painful memories she could hardly make herself drag her favorite pencil—a gift from Oleksiy—across the paper. Still, she persisted in trying every day, telling herself she'd give up sketching people and only draw birds to make it more tolerable, but it still hurt.

The Bohemian waxwing froze, its beady black eye assessing the danger of Liliya's presence. When it spread its wings and tore away from the bare *kalyna* bush, Liliya groaned and dropped her pencil. Maybe it was better this way, the bird preemptively ending her self-inflicted torture before she lost her mind.

After her father died, and she'd truly become an orphan, the blackness of those holes slowly enveloped everything else, like a gangrenous limb poisoning the rest of the body, but from the inside out. She couldn't eat, she couldn't sleep, she couldn't function.

It had taken a firm hand from Vika, scolding and cajoling her to get moving, because, as her aunt said, "The cows don't care if you're sad. Their udders fill with milk whether your parents are alive or not. Life goes on, Liliya."

Vika believed in burying your feelings in hard work, and while Liliya could appreciate that perspective, she much preferred trying to lose herself in her art like she once had. She liked to sit at the memorial Maky had erected for the victims of the NKVD prisoner massacres. Her brother wasn't in the symbolic mound with the cross on top of it, but she felt closer to him whenever she read the words, "To the Memory of Those Who Fell for the Freedom of Ukraine."

"What are you doing?" Oleksiy's lumbering footsteps approached, and Liliya glared up at her friend.

"What are *you* doing?" She turned his question back on him. "I can't believe you're actually here. You've been so busy lately that I was beginning to wonder if you'd joined the resistance and left us."

His face reddened and, not for the first time, Liliya wondered if Oleksiy was involved with the UPA, the *Ukrayins'ka Povstans'ka Armiia*, the partisan military arm of the OUN. She hadn't come out and asked him yet because she wasn't sure she wanted to know the answer. She and Vika, along with the other village women, helped the UPA members living in bunkers out in the woods—doing their laundry and preparing food for them—as they waged guerrilla warfare against Reds and Nazis, and the lives they led weren't easy. Liliya had been toying with approaching them about helping more. Maybe that could be the new direction her life needed. Maybe, if she could move past the all-consuming sadness and channel the anger burning in her core, she could do something useful.

Oleksiy ignored her question and picked up the pencil she'd dropped. "Is this the same one I got you all those years ago?"

"Yes." Liliya let him deflect, too drained to get into that conversation now, and took the proffered pencil. "It's my favorite. Draws smoother than any other, so I ration its use."

"I still have the drawing of us you made me." Oleksiy smiled and patted his pocket. "But right now, it's not safe for you to be out here alone."

Liliya waved a hand. "Let the partisans and soldiers find me. I don't care."

"We care. As good as you are, drawing birds is not worth risking your life."

She ignored him. How could she explain that in drawing the birds, she was attempting to escape this pain and reclaim a small piece of her old life? To reconnect with her mother, her brother. With every curve of a beak and shading of a feather, she felt them there with her, by her side. Teaching her. Guiding her. Encouraging her. And with every completed drawing, as painful as it was, she was making her father proud. Pursuing the path of study he'd always pushed her toward. "I just needed a few more minutes."

His eyes widened. "A few more minutes? Slavko said you've been out here for hours."

Liliya squinted as she took in the position of the sun, now low in the sky. "I didn't realize it had been so long."

"You never do." Nina smiled as she stepped out from behind Oleksiy's bulk. "How are you today?"

Nina treated Liliya as if she were made of glass, and Liliya tried not to hold it against her.

"Fine. It's good to be out in the sunshine, even if it is cold." Liliya flipped her long honey-colored braid back over her shoulder and hugged her friend.

She'd fallen back into her easy friendships with Nina and Oleksiy when she came home, as if the year and a half she spent in Kholm never happened. Her oldest friends, they were the only friends she still talked to who knew her before. That's what she called her life when she had a family. The before.

Before she lost hope.

Before she was alone.

They knew her before, and they still wanted to be with her after. That said a lot about their loyalty, for Liliya realized she was as fickle as the weather and her company wasn't always easy. She forced a smile. "Thank you for checking in on me so often, but you really don't have to. I'm fine."

She pursed her lips and whistled the same song the waxwing had just warbled, trying to lure it back. It flew closer and responded in kind, until the sound of approaching hoof-beats caused the bird to take flight again. A lone rider stopped and shielded his eyes from the sun as he stared at them, then he let the horse gallop across the field.

"Who is that?" Oleksiy shaded his eyes with his hand as he squinted.

"Who cares?" Liliya blew out an exasperated sigh. "I'll have to come back later to sketch her."

"I think it's Filip Nowak. No one else can ride like that," Nina said as the rider approached.

"He's nothing special," Oleksiy muttered as he shoved his hands into his pockets.

"I agree," Liliya said. "Maksym loves him because he's such a good horseman, but I don't see the appeal." She hadn't seen him much since their fight in the barn several weeks ago, and Liliya suspected he'd been doing his best to avoid her.

"I think he's quite handsome," Nina said with a shrug. "And very kind. He helped my father with his horse when it took ill."

Oleksiy shot a glare of disapproval at Nina and stepped forward as Filip halted in front of them. "What brings you out here, Filip?"

Filip's serious expression never wavered as he ignored Oleksiy, then nodded at Nina before looking at Liliya. The intensity of his gaze pierced her, and she crossed her arms against it.

"I needed to exercise this horse, so Maksym sent me to get you. He asked that you come home right away." Filip held out a hand. "I can give you a ride, if you'd like."

"I'll walk home with her." Oleksiy put his arm around Liliya's shoulders.

Liliya, who, up until Oleksiy's proprietary statement, had every intention of doing just that, stiffened and threw off his arm. "I can speak for myself."

She turned to Filip, ignoring Oleksiy's obvious displeasure. He may have been her friend, but she was tired of people telling her how she should feel or what she should do. Maksym and Vika were bad enough. She wouldn't take it from Oleksiy, too, and she'd even get on a horse with Filip Nowak to prove that point. Besides, a horse this beautiful would make it much easier to overlook the rider. "I'll take that ride, Filip. Thank you."

Surprise, presumably at her sudden willingness to be in his company, flickered over Filip's face, but she couldn't change her mind now. She hated backing down more than she hated Filip. No, that wasn't quite right. She disliked Filip, but she didn't hate him any more than she hated her Polish friends who lived next door to her old house, or Nina, whose mother was Polish. She hated the animosity festering between so many in Volhynia. She hated her conflicted feelings about her father's death. And she hated being the only one left in her family. Alone, any one of those would have been enough to leave her struggling. Together, they made her head spin.

Swinging her bag onto her shoulder, she gripped his hand as he pulled her up behind him on the sleek chestnut horse. He rode bareback with a bridle, but Filip moved like the horse was an extension of his body. Vika had told her his father had been a groom at one of the premier Polish Arabian stud farms before the Soviets arrested him. Now, Filip, along with Maksym, worked at that same stable, but under Nazi rule.

"I guess you haven't heard the news," Filip said as Liliya settled in behind him. "The Germans just hit Kovel and are expected to head this way next to gather up people for a big shipment of laborers to send west. They're taking them right off the streets, now."

Amid Nina's gasps and Oleksiy's swearing, Liliya felt Filip's thighs shift, and the light-footed Polish Arabian took off. She wrapped her legs around the horse's belly and gripped Filip's narrow waist. His hips rocked with the motion of the cantering animal, and she moved hers along with his to avoid bouncing. Pressed so close to Filip, her arms clamped around him and her body in sync with his as they raced through the fields, she shivered with a startling thrill of excitement—the first emotion besides anger or grief she'd felt in weeks.

It seemed wrong.

"Stop!" Liliya ordered suddenly. She forced her arms to unlock from his waist.

He sat back, never pulling on the bridle, and the horse slowed to a stop almost immediately. Liliya glanced back, making sure they were out of sight of her friends, then swung her leg back and over the horse's rump before popping down.

"I'm sorry," Filip said. "Did I ride too fast?"

"No. You ride like the wind. When I closed my eyes, I imagined we were flying."

Her thoughts tumbled out of her mouth before she could stop them, and she bit her lip to hold the rest back, finishing in her head. *Away from here. Like the birds.*

"You have a fanciful way with words." His tone was neutral, guarded, and she didn't blame him. The last time they'd conversed, she'd yelled at him. Still, the corners of his lips lifted at her compliment. "Then why did you want to stop?"

Liliya straightened her skirt and readjusted her bag. "This is far enough."

"But you're not home yet."

She started walking down the road. "I don't need you or Oleksiy to get me home."

"Why bother riding with me at all?"

Liliya refused to look over at him. "It's more of a reflection of the horse than you. This is by far the fanciest, most beautiful horse I've ever had a chance to ride. I wanted to see how she moved."

"And what did you think?" He nudged the horse into a walk next to her.

Liliya spared a glance at the majestic creature, then stroked her glossy shoulder. "She's perfect."

"I won't disagree with you there. So that was your only reason? You didn't want to use me to annoy your boyfriend?"

"Don't give yourself so much credit," Liliya scoffed. "Besides, he's not my boyfriend."

Filip laughed. "Right. You might want to tell him that."

"I don't need your advice, and I don't need your help," Liliya said, her annoyance growing by the second. Why did this man persist in harassing her? Hadn't she made it abundantly clear she wanted nothing to do with him? She walked a little faster, trying to get ahead of him, but the horse adjusted her pace to stay in line with Liliya. "What are you doing?"

"I'm escorting you home like I told your uncle I would."

"You don't have to do that." Liliya pushed her chin in the air. "I can see the house. I'll be fine."

"I have no doubt you'll be fine, but this isn't about you. I always keep my word." He scratched the horse's neck. "Besides, she likes you. She's walking with you all on her own."

As they approached the yard, Filip clicked his tongue at the horse, and she picked up a light jog and pulled ahead of Liliya. He stopped her in front of the gate and jumped down. Pushing it open, he held out his arm as if ushering Liliya through it.

"There. Now, I've seen you home."

"I'll be sure to let Maksym know," she said dryly before giving the horse one more pat. "Thank you for the ride."

She met his eyes as she stepped past him into the yard, and he stared at her, probing, as if he were searching for something, looking deeper than the facade she put on every day. "It was my pleasure."

Liliya blinked away the intrusion and squared her shoulders, pushing her guard back up. "I was talking to the horse."

Filip laughed softly. "Well, it was still my pleasure." Now low and gravelly, his voice sent pinpricks of awareness over her body and, despite herself, Liliya glanced back up at him. For the first time, she took in his shaggy dark hair, high cheekbones, and dimpled chin.

He hesitated, looking down at the ground before meeting her gaze again. "It's good to see you out and about."

Liliya opened her mouth to reply, uncertain what would come out, but before she had to decide, Sofia ran around the side of the house, a book clutched to her chest.

"Liliya! Mama wants to see you!" She stopped short at the sight of them. "Oh, hi, Filip. I didn't think you and Liliya were friends."

It was as if someone had poured a bucket of cold water over her head.

"We're not," Liliya snapped as she jumped back.

Filip's lips quirked into a small grin again, apparently nonplussed by her reaction. She could feel his eyes still on her as he addressed her young cousin in Ukrainian.

"*Dobriy den*, Sofia."

"More like, 'Good day, busybody,'" Liliya grumbled. She

cleared her throat before forcing out the required nicety. "Good-bye, Filip."

Filip swung onto the horse in one fluid motion and nodded at her as he nudged the mare forward.

"Is Filip your new boyfriend? He's very handsome." Sofia propped her elbows on the fence and rested her chin on her hands, staring after him as he rode away.

"He's not my boyfriend." Liliya glared at her young cousin. "I don't have a boyfriend, new or old."

"I thought Oleksiy was your boyfriend." Sofia's face wrinkled in confusion. "I like Oleksiy."

"Oleksiy is a boy, and he is an old friend. Just like Nina is an old friend. That is all. No boyfriends for me."

"I don't know if Oleksiy knows that." Sofia frowned.

"Of course he does. And why is everyone suddenly so concerned with my love life?"

Sofia sighed, a dreamy look on her face. "When I'm seventeen, the war will be over, and I'll have lots of boyfriends."

Liliya patted Sofia's shoulder. "Hopefully by then, you'll realize that there's far more to life than boys."

Liliya slid the heavy stall door open and stepped inside. The smell of horses—sweat, manure, hay—all mingled together with the leather tack and saddle oil. Liliya took a deep breath and sighed. She loved horses, though she didn't get to spend near enough time with them. Offering to drop off her uncle's forgotten lunch gave her the perfect excuse to not only see them, but to get away from Vika, who'd kept a tight rein on all of them since the news of the increased labor transports got around the day before.

"Stay to the woods and off the roads. Come right back," she'd instructed Liliya.

Liliya had acknowledged her with a forced smile and a wave of the hand. She knew Vika was only trying to take care of her and fill one of the missing parental roles in Liliya's life, but she wasn't stupid. She could be discreet when necessary.

"Hello, beautiful," she crooned as she stroked the mare's silky neck. "Do you remember me? I got to ride you yesterday."

The horse chuffed and nuzzled Liliya's free hand with her velvety nose.

"I'll bring you a treat next time, girl," Liliya said. "I promise."

Voices echoed down the long aisle, and Liliya ducked behind the horse's neck, grateful she'd left the stall door cracked just enough for her to escape fast if need be. Her uncle had explicitly told her not to wander, but she didn't think stopping to pet a horse really counted. Still, she didn't want to get caught and get him or herself in trouble.

Three men came inside, leading their horses into their respective stalls. She didn't recognize the first two, but the third was Filip.

She moved to the edge of the stall and sank down so only her eyes peeped over the top board, listening to the scrape of leather and jingle of bits as they began to untack.

"I don't know why you continue to stay at Maksym's sometimes," the first man said. His voice, high and reedy, grated on Liliya's ears. "It doesn't look good for you to be associated with any Ukrainians."

"Maksym is a good man," Filip said. "He took me in after my mother died, no questions."

"Yeah, maybe he's the exception," the second man said. "But don't forget, it was Ukrainians who killed her."

Filip paused, his hands poised to pluck the saddle off the horse's back, his voice cold. "You needn't remind me about my own mother's death."

"Well, maybe I should remind you that this is our land anyway, or it should be, at least," the younger man said. "The *Kresy* is a part of Poland, and it wouldn't be what it is without Polish culture and education. We're bringing western civilization to them. We gave them schools. We gave them democracy. We gave them Catholicism."

"It's not that simple," Filip said as he lifted the saddle.

"It's simple enough. Ukrainians have been attacking our politicians and leaders for years when they should be grateful to Poland," the older man said. "These poor, uneducated peasants have no idea how difficult it is to run a modern country, and they're not utilizing this rich land to its full potential."

"Hitler has similar thoughts," Filip said. "And I'm wary of any line of thinking akin to his."

"You're all missing the point," the younger man chimed in again. "We Poles have to unite against Nazis and fight for Poland. The Ukrainians want to fight for their own nation, so they won't fight with us. That means it's up to us to save Poland. We don't have time to worry about Ukrainians and their attempts at sovereignty. They've tried before and it's never worked out. Why would it now?"

Filip turned his back on the two men and slammed his

saddle on a rack. "You're both needed back in the arena, so I suggest you get moving."

Liliya's legs shook with fury, and she recognized that if she didn't remove herself from this situation, she'd do something stupid. She didn't wait to hear any more. Moving past the horse, she slid between the narrow opening she'd left between the stall door and wall and slipped out the side entrance.

Hours later, as she went out to feed the chickens, she still couldn't stop thinking about what she'd heard earlier at the stable—Filip pushing back at the anti-Ukrainian sentiments his friends spouted, even though Ukrainian nationalists had killed his mother.

Maybe he wasn't as bad as she thought.

And maybe she wasn't as open-minded as him.

The thought needled at her. She'd written him off so quickly because he was Polish, but she'd had plenty of Polish friends before. This hatred between Poles and Ukrainians, this animosity over the land, ran as deep as the marriage, familial, and neighborly bonds between them. So, why did she take out all her anger about her father on Filip?

Liliya stopped by the barn and grabbed a handful of corn. Kneeling near the chickens, she held it out, and they rushed at her, pecking at the food and watching her with cocked heads.

"Don't worry, my friends. Nobody is destined for the soup pot tonight. We're just happy no Germans have come to take you away from us yet." Like they had everything else. The cow. The crops. The preserved food Vika had put up for the winter. A large portion of the pig Maksym butchered. "I only wish I could tame the wild birds like I have you."

"Liliya?" Oleksiy's deep voice made her jump.

"Have you come to chase away these birds, too?" She stood and brushed off her hands.

Oleksiy's normally cheerful face sagged, and Liliya tensed. "What's wrong?"

"I wanted to tell you yesterday, but then Filip showed up and I didn't get the chance."

She ignored the sour way he said Filip's name, her own feelings about the Polish boy still a tangle of confusion. "Tell me what?"

He pulled off his hat and twisted it in his hands, dropping his gaze. "I'm joining the *Schutzmannschaft*."

Liliya's stomach dropped. "No! You can't join the Schuma!"

She couldn't even say the word without shuddering. "You'll be working for the Nazis! The men who killed my mother, who killed all the Jews, who take young people for labor and murder partisans and their families. I thought you were going to tell me you joined the UPA. Not the Nazis. How could you do this?"

He ran his hand through his blond hair. "My mother is begging me to join to protect my sisters. If I'm in the auxiliary police force, they won't get sent to Germany as laborers. Since my father died, she's not been the same. I'm afraid that if she loses one of the girls, she won't recover."

Liliya frowned. Like her brother, Mykhailo, Oleksiy's father had been executed by the Soviets in the mass prisoner executions. His mother, one of the kindest people Liliya knew, hadn't handled the loss well.

"She's not a strong woman," Vika scoffed after Oleksiy's little sister had come to tell them her mother wouldn't get out of bed. "Women must bear such loss and keep everything else going. It's not easy, but it's what we do." Still, she'd sent borsch and bread along to help them and promised to walk over to check in the next day.

Oleksiy continued. "I'm hoping I can help. Maybe subvert their efforts while I'm there. I won't truly become one of them."

"You're one man. How do you think you can stop their army?"

"I can't stop it, but maybe I can help people escape transports. Look the other way. Things like that."

"That's very dangerous." Liliya softened slightly, a flicker of concern for her old friend forcing its way up through her anger. "They'll kill you if you're caught."

He shoved his hat back on his head. "They could kill me right now or on my walk home. Nobody is safe here, Liliya. Look, I don't want to join the Schuma, but I will for my mother and sisters. It won't be for long, and if I can do a little good while I'm there, maybe it will be worth it. It doesn't mean I'll become a Nazi, but it does mean I'll have access to weapons and training that could be useful later."

"What do you mean, 'useful later'? Are you planning on using the Schuma for weapons and training, then leaving? Joining the resistance then?"

Oleksiy's jaw flexed as he looked away from her. "No. Of course not. I only meant it might be useful to have those skills after the war."

Liliya searched his face for traces of the boy she'd grown up with, the boy who'd taught her how to fish and spent hours trekking through the woods with her looking for birds, the boy who'd held her hand through her mother's funeral and who'd cried on her shoulder when his father died, but this Oleksiy was all sharp angles, wiry muscles, and barely contained frustration.

"It seems as if your mind is made up, then."

"It is. I don't like it, but it is."

"Then I wish you well." She took her basket and walked past him toward the house, hating the finality in her words, but just as unable to stop it as she was him.

"Wait. I can protect you, too." He grabbed her arm, his cheeks flushed with emotion. "Marry me, Liliya. My name will keep you safe while I'm in the Schuma and keep you out of the labor transports."

She tugged away from him, surprised at the emotion rising in her. "And what about after? What would happen to me and your family after you leave the Schuma or if you die? Now isn't the time for love, Oleksiy. We can't even promise each other tomorrow."

"We should look for happiness where we can find it. This war will end and we will rise again. Imagine a free Ukraine, where we don't have to bow to Russian or German invaders or speak Polish in our schools. Where we rule ourselves."

"You don't still believe those German lies, do you?" Liliya scoffed. "You know they never planned on giving us our own country. They only said that to placate us."

"I know that, but that doesn't mean we can't fight for it." He took her hands and squeezed them. "For us. For Ukraine."

Liliya stared up at the first stars peeking through the dusky sky. How often had she dreamed of attending university and making something of herself? But that wasn't what Oleksiy wanted. They'd spoken of it so many times, lying in the field under the big linden tree. He wanted a houseful of children and a doting wife. Plum and cherry trees scenting the air with their blossoms before their boughs dipped low, heavy with fruit.

Fields rippling with healthy crops. Grassy hills dotted with happy cows grazing to produce rich milk. He wanted the life he knew in Volhynia before the war touched them, but that life was dead, just like so many people Liliya knew.

"You should marry Nina," Liliya finally said, her voice wavering. "Protect her. She wants the same things in life as you. I don't. I will never marry, and I wouldn't make you happy."

Oleksiy's face crumbled as her words sank in. His hand dropped, and for one brief second, Liliya's already broken heart splintered even more as the sweet innocence of her old friend broke through his tough facade. There he was. *Her* Oleksiy.

"I thought you loved me." His voice cracked on the word "me," sending a jolt of pain through Liliya's chest.

She balled her fists and blinked back the tears in her eyes. "I'm broken, Oleksiy. Everyone I love dies, so I won't love anyone. You'll be better off for it."

He swayed back with the quiet force of her words and shook his head.

"You're a terrible liar, Liliya."

* * *

Liliya sat with her back against the barn after Oleksiy left, staring out into the approaching darkness. How had her world gotten to this point of confusion and violence? How could there be so many different warring factions in one place?

A board creaked in the loft overhead, and Liliya scrambled to her feet. She grabbed the shovel propped against the wall and held it up, her gaze trained on the door.

A few seconds later, Filip stepped outside, then took an

immediate step back, his eyes widening at her choice of weapons. "Are you that angry with me?"

"I don't know. I'm just a 'poor, uneducated peasant,'" she quipped. "What do I know? Thank goodness you and your Polish friends are here to help us."

Filip had the grace to flush. "You were at the stable today?"

"Seems like we're all butting in on conversations we shouldn't." Liliya exhaled a shaky breath, wondering how much Filip had heard of her exchange with Oleksiy. "What are you doing here? I thought Maksym said you were visiting an uncle."

"I had to come back for tonight, but I'll be leaving again soon. Don't worry."

She lowered the shovel. "You don't have to leave on my account."

"I have other places I can stay. I didn't want to make things harder for you." He fiddled with the latch on the door. "I don't agree with them, you know."

"What, you don't think Ukrainians should be grateful to only speak Polish in school and convert to Catholicism?" She thought of her gentle father, and a flash of fury surged through her so fast she almost picked the shovel back up.

A muscle jumped in his cheek. "I think the whole situation is far more complicated, and I think you know that, too."

Liliya clenched her jaw. "I know I didn't hear you disagree."

"But you didn't hear me agree," he said. "There's a time and a place to be true about my thoughts."

"And what are your true thoughts? Please, enlighten me."

Filip sighed. "Maybe someday I'll tell you. When you don't hate me quite so much."

Liliya thought of all she'd lost in her young life, all the

senseless death, then answered softly. "There's too much hate in this world already. I don't hate you."

His mouth quirked on one side. "If you like me, you have a funny way of showing it."

Liliya's lips compressed. "I didn't say I liked you. I said I don't hate you. There's a difference."

"Well." Filip tilted his head, appraising her. "I don't hate you, too, Liliya."

His hand lifted, shifted forward, as if he wanted to touch her, but then it dropped, sending a surprising wash of disappointment over her. She clasped her hands together, staving off the sudden urge she had to trace his sharp cheekbone with her fingers.

He went on, oblivious to her inner turmoil. "I think we've been through a lot of similar things, and in another world, we could be great friends."

A current of vulnerability charged his words, but Liliya ignored it.

"I don't know you!" she exploded. Her frustration with Oleksiy, her grief over her family, her confusion about her feelings, all of it erupted toward him. "Why should I like some stray my uncle took in who will most likely be dead before the year is out, just like every other person involved in this godforsaken war? It's better we stay distant, no matter what kind of made-up connection you think we may have."

Filip stood, unflinching, as her verbal blows struck him, then smiled sadly. "Oleksiy was right. You're a terrible liar, Liliya."

He melted back into the darkness of the barn before she could respond, so instead, she kicked over a bucket and swore.

8

HALYA

February 1943, Kyiv District, Reichskommissariat Ukraine

Halya skirted around the back of the Melnyks' house and ducked behind a tree. Mama would be furious if she knew Halya had taken a walk down the road after she'd been forbidden to leave the yard, but she couldn't spend another minute stuck there. Besides, she'd heard that the Melnyk family had been forcibly evicted last night, and she wanted to see the *Volksdeutsche* family, a mother and two young children, who'd moved in.

Germans brought in to farm the fertile soil when Ukraine was still ruled by Russian tsars, the *Volksdeutsche* kept mostly to themselves even now, generations later. Germany still considered them coveted members of the Aryan race, and they allowed them to requisition homes in German-occupied Ukraine. Sometimes the homes were already vacant, and sometimes, like in the Melnyks' situation, they were made to be vacant for the incoming settlers. Mama said they were leeches sucking the life blood out of Ukraine and Halya should not associate with them, but that only made Halya want to observe them more. Besides, Halya had also seen Mama give a small loaf of bread to a young *Volksdeutsche* woman and her baby as they traveled through their village, so Halya had decided that interacting with them could be considered on a case-by-case basis.

A woman shrieked in German, the harsh words filtering out of the house and silencing the birds. Suddenly, the door flew open, and someone threw an armful of books out into the yard. Halya gasped as the door slammed shut again. Feodosia Melnyk would have been horrified to see her cherished books lying on the ground like this.

Halya crept closer, hoping to grab a few since the new resident didn't seem to want them. Just as her fingers closed around the nearest book, the door opened again. The woman started yelling, but this time in the oddly accented, German-influenced Ukrainian Mama said most *Volksdeutsche* spoke.

"Get out of here, you little thief!" She ran at Halya, wielding a frying pan like a weapon. "Go on! Get out of my yard!"

Halya grabbed the book and bolted, but not before a burst of courage had her shouting back, "It's not really your yard, you know!"

When she was far enough away to slow down, she sat against a tree and opened the book clutched in her sweaty hand, reading the title out loud.

"*Kobzar* by Taras Shevchenko."

Another book of poetry, and this one from her father's

favorite poet. She flipped through the pages and began reading, so absorbed by his lyrical words that she didn't notice Mama stomping over.

"What are you doing so far from home?" Mama's lips pressed into a tight line, an expression Halya recognized all too well as one of disapproval.

"I'm sorry. I wanted to go for a walk. Look what I found!" Halya held up the book of poetry like a prize, and Mama's face softened a bit.

"Where did you find that?"

Halya lowered the book. "At the Melnyks' place. The *Volksdeutsche* woman who moved in didn't want any of their old books."

Mama's lips pressed even tighter, and her eyes narrowed to match. "A book of poems is not worth risking your safety. I thought I taught you better than that." She grabbed Halya's arm and pulled her along. "Come home with me now."

* * *

"Your mama was sick with worry when she couldn't find you today."

The chickens scratching at their grain near Halya's feet clucked in sympathy at his stern tone.

"I'm sorry, Tato. I didn't mean to do that." She stared at the stork sitting in her nest on top of their house. Every year, the same stork returned and laid her eggs. Halya recognized her from the deep notch cut out of her left wing. She liked to think about what happened to the stork. Maybe she scared off a predator to save her babies, but not before the attacker took a bite of her wing. Maybe she was born that way. Or maybe a cruel person ripped it away in a fit of anger, scarring the bird forever. Now, missing a piece of herself, she could never be whole.

Halya felt a kinship with that stork.

Tato chuckled softly. "Your mama just wants you to stay safe. That is her sole mission in life, do you understand? She gives you her all because you must never give up on family, no matter what the circumstances. Family is everything. Staying together is everything, and it's always worth fighting for."

Halya bit her lip, but the question tumbled out of her anyway. "Why didn't my mother try harder to stay with me? My real mother, I mean. Alina."

Tato's shoulders slumped, and his words came out in a breathy sigh. "Oh, Halya. She did. She tried so hard to be there for you. You meant so much to her. But in the end, some things are out of our control. Like what happened to the Melnyks."

"Then why even try?" Bitterness laced Halya's words. "Why try if what we do doesn't matter?"

"Trying always matters, Halya. Trying is fighting, and fighting is what we must do now. There are many people here who would rather see us gone and take this land for themselves, but we are Ukrainian. We are strong, and we rise up again and again, like the *kalyna* bush growing up in the marsh where the young maiden sacrificed herself to save her village. Even when the odds are stacked against us, we fight for our land, for our families, for our way of life, because if we don't, we will always lose."

He ran a rough hand down her hair, smoothing it back from her face. "I need you to promise me something, Halya."

She nodded, unable to speak past the lump in her throat. The conversation had shifted away from her mother to something she didn't quite understand, an intangible concept tinged with heaviness. The somber tone in Tato's voice made her sit up straighter.

"Promise me you will be brave and always fight, no matter what happens. Fight, because life is always worth fighting for."

She swallowed hard. "I promise, Tato."

"And promise me you'll look out for your family. Family may not always be who you expect, but it is everything."

Halya's face burned with shame as she thought of all the times she'd tried to evade Mama's garlic cloves or hidden up in her tree to avoid chores. How much worry and grief had she caused this woman who had dedicated herself to Halya? Who had taken Halya in and loved her without question? Maybe Mama had imagined a life with a different husband or a different child when she was younger, but she and Tato loved each other now. And Mama loved Halya like her own, raised her like her own. There was never any doubt about that.

She was Halya's mother, just as much as Alina was, and Halya loved her with her whole heart.

Family may not always be who you expect, but it is everything.

She repeated Tato's words in her head several times, committing them to memory until she could write them on the blank pages of one of her books later.

9

VIKA

Vika looked up from the onions on her cutting board and watched as Liliya, sketchbook tucked under her arm, stepped out of the chicken coop into the morning light.

As much as Vika loved Liliya, she remained an enigma. Her smiles were rare, her joy nearly non-existent. With so much loss in her early years, sometimes Vika wondered if Liliya had absorbed those heavy feelings the way plants soak up water—pulling in the sorrow and grief and making them an integral part of her makeup. A young girl embodying the sum of their collective pain.

In the months since Liliya's return after her father's death, Vika had tried to bring Liliya out of her shell, coaxing laughter and smiles, but Liliya always reverted to her regular mode of quiet indifference. Nothing affected her. Nothing moved her. Nothing compelled her except drawing and her study of birds.

Slavko ran across the lawn, laughing as he and Sofia herded the geese back into their pen for the evening, and a smile cracked open Vika's drawn expression. With Slavko, she never doubted herself. She knew how to encourage him as needed and rein him in when necessary. Slavko's impulsive kisses and endearing efforts around the house made him a joy to be around. He was the complete opposite of Liliya, all sunshine and exuberance, where Liliya was cloudy and morose.

"Here are your eggs." Liliya's dust-streaked face bore the smears of wiped-away tears. She set the basket down and sat at the table. "How do you know when you are making the right decision?"

Vika almost laughed at the absurdity of the question. Indecision plagued her like a swarm of locusts, constantly needling her and casting doubt over everything she did, so she barreled through life not making decisions, but doing what was necessary. There wasn't thought or desire involved. She was the last person anyone should ask for advice on the topic, so she hedged the question. "I suppose it depends on the decision."

"It doesn't matter." Liliya stood as quickly as she'd sat. "My mind is made up."

"If your mind is made up, then why are you asking me about it?"

Liliya continued, as if Vika hadn't responded. "I'm writing the letter tonight."

"Letter to who?"

Liliya's head snapped around to stare at Vika, her eyes now clear and focused. "The Ukrainian Free University in Prague."

"Prague?" Vika couldn't hide her incredulity.

"Well, I always wanted to go to L'viv University. I knew it would be a long shot since the Poles limited Ukrainian attendance to 15 percent, but things changed with the war."

"Do you mean first the Soviets and then Germans slaughtering the professors and students?" Vika asked dryly. "Yes, that's much better than limited attendance. We're in the middle of a war, Liliya, and the Germans won't even allow Ukrainians to attend school past year four. How can you even think of something like this?"

Liliya crossed her arms. "I know I can't go right now, but we won't be at war forever. When it's over, I want to go to university."

"Fine. Plan for the future, but why send a letter now?" Vika asked. She scraped the onions into a frying pan and added a dollop of precious butter. "You can hardly go to the village safely, let alone all the way to Prague. Besides, the Nazis are there, too."

"It won't be that way forever," Liliya repeated. "And that university was founded there by Ukrainians to avoid Soviet influence. I think they'll be up and running again sooner, and it's going to be far more stable than anything here. I want my name to be at the top of their admittance list."

"Nothing is stable, and it won't be for a long time." Vika shook her head. "I wish I were as optimistic as you."

"I have to look ahead," Liliya insisted. "I want to be ready."

Vika stirred the contents of the pan, and the scent of fried onions and butter filled the room. "If that's what you want."

"It is." Liliya gave a decisive nod. "It's what I've always

wanted. To go to university and study art and wildlife. My parents and I talked about it often."

"What about a husband and children?"

"I don't want either of those things," Liliya said. "A husband and children will tie me down here, and I want to see the world."

"Love isn't something you always choose. Sometimes it chooses you. Besides, you're only seventeen. You might change your mind if you meet a strapping, handsome young man who sweeps you off your feet." Vika offered a new direction for the conversation, hoping Liliya would open up to her about Oleksiy. Sofia had told Vika after breakfast that she'd overheard the proposal the night before.

"No." Liliya gave a nonchalant wave of her hand. "I will never love anyone enough to marry. Besides, the men here are too busy fighting each other to do any sweeping."

* * *

"I'm worried about Liliya," Vika said.

Maksym stood in the wide aisle between the stalls, grooming one of the Polish Arabians. He didn't look up as he slid his hand down the back of the horse's leg, then gave it a little squeeze to signal it to pick up its foot. The horse complied, and he gripped the hoof and picked it clean. "Liliya is fine. What is there to be worried about?"

"She's lost her whole family." Vika nodded to Filip as he led another horse past them, looped its lead rope through the ring next to her, and began brushing it.

"We're her family, too," Maksym said. "We'll take care of her."

"Yes, but it's not the same, and you know it." Vika bit her lip and lowered her voice. "She has delusions of being able to go to university soon, but it's crazy to think of right now."

"Maybe so, but it can't hurt her to have dreams," Maksym said.

"And Oleksiy asked her to marry him."

Maksym finished picking the front left hoof and straightened. "Did she accept? I always thought those two would end up together."

Filip dropped his brush, and it clattered toward Vika. He didn't meet her eyes as he swooped down and grabbed it, his face bright red at being caught eavesdropping.

Understanding dawned on Vika, and she spoke louder than normal, watching Filip as he ran the brush through the horse's mane with sudden, ferocious intensity. "No. She said she doesn't love him."

Maksym moved to the back of the horse and repeated the process with the left hind leg. "It takes far more to build a marriage than love."

Vika stiffened, thoughts of Filip's feelings for Liliya vanishing from her mind. "Most people say love is the most important part of a marriage."

"Most people are fools," Maksym grunted as he held firm while the horse shifted and tried to pull its hoof away. "We both know it takes more than just love."

The specters of their fragile beginnings reared up in front of Vika. Usually, she kept those memories at bay, along with her doubts about Maksym's true intentions in marrying her, but when he made comments like this, it wasn't easy to forget them.

He'd been a broken shell of a man, his grief over losing his wife and young child to tuberculosis apparent, when he appeared on her doorstep fifteen years ago, asking to work on their farm.

"My father knows your father," he'd said, his hands twisting his hat. "He wanted me to come give his regards and see about a position in the grain mill."

He'd exuded a sadness so palpable she could almost taste the salt of his tears, but she opened the door anyway, inviting him into their home and her heart.

Most days, she thought he'd done the same—offering shattered pieces of his soul with each tender glance or gentle kiss he gave her. But sometimes, he'd make a comment or give her a look, and the ugly doubt she kept tucked away in the dark recesses of her mind poked up, needling into the small cracks in their relationship.

Who did he see when he looked at her? A woman thrust upon him while he was at his lowest, or a woman he truly loved? Her parents had pushed for the marriage, especially as Stalin's collectivization plan started, seeing Maksym as a way out for Vika, and she let them.

"Marry him and move to Volhynia. Life will be better there," her father had told her.

But what had Maksym really wanted? In his fragile state, could he have said no to her bossy parents while he lived in their house? Vika had fallen in love with the handsome, quick-witted Maksym almost instantly, but it had taken him years to speak words of love to her. Even now, he kept his feelings mostly to himself so much that when he showed her any love or affection, she consumed it like a starving person, swallowing it down fast for sustenance, but losing the flavor and beauty in her desperation. She hated herself for that.

She gritted her teeth, banishing the ugly thoughts back deep inside where they wouldn't hurt her so readily. This was why she kept her emotions in check and chose instead to focus on practical matters. Feelings only muddied the waters of life, and she needed a clear head to keep her family alive in this war.

"Of course you need more than love," she finally managed. She forced herself to lean close so Filip wouldn't overhear. "He's also joined the Schuma. She won't tolerate that."

Maksym met her eyes, but she didn't see surprise there, and she wondered if Oleksiy had already shared his plans with him. "No. I expect she won't, but maybe there's more to that story."

"Maybe. I just want her to be happy. I've always loved her, but now, it's hard not to think of her as a daughter." Vika patted the horse's rump. "I should get home to the children. Slavko is there now but getting him to stay in one place is nearly impossible."

Maksym chuckled. "He has a soul for adventure, that son of mine."

"It will get him killed," Vika retorted. Slavko was a good boy, but his free spirit, so different from her own, made her sick with worry now that danger lurked around every corner. "I'm afraid he'll be snatched up and taken to Germany."

"He's smart," Maksym said. "He won't put himself in danger."

"It doesn't always matter how smart you are," Vika said. "You, of all people, should know that."

10

LILIYA

March 1943, Volhynia, Reichskommissariat Ukraine

"Do you think Oleksiy is making a mistake?" Liliya asked Nina as they walked to the village one evening after work. With all the turmoil over the recent labor deportations, Liliya had strict instructions to stay with Nina, pick up the items on Vika's list, and return home straightaway.

"He's doing what he thinks he must. It can't be easy to work for the Schuma." Nina hesitated. "I think you are the one making a mistake."

Liliya laughed. "I can't marry him. I don't want the life he wants, so it wouldn't be fair to either of us."

"But you love him?"

Liliya stared down at the dirt road stretching out before them, so much like her relationship with Oleksiy—long and sometimes rocky, winding so far forward and backward she couldn't find the beginning or imagine the end. She didn't remember her life without him in it.

"I love him," Liliya said. "Maybe not in the way he loves me, but he's a part of me. A part of my family. I'll always love Oleksiy."

"Then would it be so bad to be married to him? He's a good man."

Liliya touched the letter to the Ukrainian Free University in Prague tucked safely in her pocket. She planned on dropping it in the mail today, and she'd mail another one next month, and over and over until she got through to someone who could help her. It might take years for her to find her way there, but taking this small first step, as futile as it was, made her feel better.

"It's not the life I want," Liliya repeated. "Marriage is not the answer to everything."

"What's so wrong with having a home of your own, filled with children?" Nina's gaze floated up to the sky as if she were imagining her own future family written in the clouds.

"I know it's what you want. It's what most people want, but I don't want a family. I've already lost one; I don't need another. I want to get out of here. See the world. Study the birds and wildlife in different lands." Her fists balled at her sides as the truth of her words resonated within her, filling the empty places inside her heart with longing and purpose. She was alone now, but she still had her dreams. "Oleksiy can't give me that. Only I can give myself that."

Nina grinned and elbowed her. "I'm sorry if our peasant dreams don't align with your lofty life goals. I hope you can tolerate existing with us in the meantime."

Liliya kicked at the ground. "You know it's not like that."

"I know. I'm just teasing." Nina linked her arm through Liliya's. "Was his proposal romantic, at least?"

Liliya shrugged. "Noble, maybe. Not so much romantic. I told him to ask you to marry him."

Nina gasped. "You did not!"

"I did. You both want the same things, and if his name could protect someone, I'd rather it be someone I care about."

"But I don't love Oleksiy like that," Nina said. "I've had my eye on the baker's son for some time now but he's disappeared. I think he's living in the woods with the UPA."

"I hope it's that and not that he's been taken to Germany," Liliya said. "But that's another thing. You and I have talked before about doing more to help the UPA besides making food or doing laundry—maybe becoming nurses or couriers. We'll be pitted against Oleksiy now and—"

"Liliya," Nina interrupted. "I received my notice yesterday."

Liliya stopped walking and grabbed Nina's arm "For labor transport? Why didn't you say anything?" She would never forget the images of the first labor shipment from their village: mothers and fathers wailing and throwing bundles of food and clothes toward their children as they were forced out of the village at gunpoint; Schuma officers and Wehrmacht soldiers beating parents with clubs and allowing snarling dogs to lunge at them. She tried to picture Nina lost in that crowd, leaving Liliya, leaving her parents, leaving her home. She shuddered.

Nina gave a slight nod, but her gaze remained fixed on the ground. "What is there to say?"

"When are you supposed to report?"

"Tomorrow," Nina said. "It's supposed to be everyone born in the year 1926. You'll probably be getting one, too."

Anger flashed through Liliya like a fire igniting dry kindling, and she shook her head. "I won't go. I'll run and hide if I have to, but I won't go. You shouldn't either."

"If we don't go, they come after our families."

Liliya could hear the sob hovering on the edge of Nina's words, so she fell silent and took her friend's hand as they started walking again. The homes grew closer together, and the fences ran into each other, bordering the road on either side. A lone dog ran down out of a yard, barking, but nobody else was out.

Suddenly, the hairs on the back of Liliya's neck popped to attention, and every instinct in her screamed that she should run. She jerked Nina back just as a Schuma officer, his rifle brandished in front of him like a shield as if he were the one needing protection, stepped out from behind the church in front of them.

"Papers?" he barked.

They dug out their identification papers and presented them to the man. As he flipped through them, Nina's fingers squeezed into her arm. Liliya quelled the stir of fear in her gut and squared her shoulders. She'd seen this man around her village. He was close to Vika and Maksym's age, but his pockmarked face made him look older.

"You don't have essential jobs. Come with me," he ordered.

Liliya bristled. Her father had always warned her to "temper her temper," but he wasn't here now to remind her, and she no longer saw the point.

"We do have essential jobs. We work at the collective farm. If you'd look closer, you'd see our work cards are in order and stamped with our current labor status. Our families rely on us to provide food, as does the German army."

His upper lip sneered into a half-smile. "Well, don't you think highly of yourself! But it doesn't matter. You're born in 1926, so you have to go now. Move!"

"Wait!" Nina tried to pull away. "I'm supposed to report tomorrow. I must say goodbye to my parents!"

The guard ignored her as he forced them into the field next to the church where a clutch of people pressed against the confining border of soldiers, the scent of fear and sweat thick in the air. Schuma officers and German soldiers patrolled with their rifles in hand, ready to shoot anyone who tried to get away. Snarling dogs lunged on the ends of leashes, snapping and spraying drool while mothers around the perimeter begged for their offspring to be released. Young children, some no older than Slavko, cried on each other, and the older teenagers tried valiantly to look brave.

Liliya and Nina huddled together near the edge of the group as Liliya took slow, even breaths and searched for any way to extricate them from this chaotic mass of people. All around her, others did the same, and despite the brave front she wore like an armor, she wondered if her fear was as obvious as theirs. She only recognized a few people; it appeared to be a random assortment collected from the neighboring villages as the group moved toward the train station in the next town.

"Liliya," a soft voice whispered in her ear. She jumped and whipped around to see Filip's earnest face inches from hers.

His appearance sent the familiar prickles of unease swirling in her stomach, but her relief at finding someone she knew usurped them.

"What are you doing here? You work at the stable. You should be exempt."

"They grabbed me in the village. I didn't have my work card on me."

Liliya eyed Filip. His expression gave away nothing as he scanned the landscape, then assessed the guards. There was no fear in his eyes; only restless energy crackling off him, reminding Liliya of the stallions pacing their stalls at the stable.

"I see Oleksiy," Nina whispered.

Liliya stood on tiptoe to see where Nina pointed and spotted Oleksiy, standing at the front of the group with a gun.

On her other side, Filip grunted. "Yes, your friend is one of our escorts."

Nina glanced at Liliya, but Liliya only pressed her lips tight, keeping the bitterness of Oleksiy's betrayal bottled inside. He'd made his choice, and it had led them to this moment—him with a gun herding up his friends to send to Germany.

"He doesn't want to be a part of this," Nina finally said.

Liliya remained silent as guilt twisted through her, but she still couldn't bring herself to defend Oleksiy, no matter his reasons.

"He didn't seem to mind having to haul me in." A muscle jumped on Filip's cheek as his eyes fell on Oleksiy.

"Maybe he'll be able to help us," Nina said.

Liliya recalled her conversation with Oleksiy, his desperate words. *"I'm hoping I can help. Maybe subvert their efforts while I'm there. I won't truly become one of them."*

As if her thoughts drew him in, Oleksiy's eyes suddenly met hers, widening in surprise as he registered her and Nina's presence in the group. Emotion arced between them over the crowd before he dropped his face in shame, and Liliya swallowed down her disappointment.

"I'll take my own chances," Filip said bitterly.

As night fell, an additional group of deportees joined them, and they set off down the road. Five people walked abreast with armed guards and dogs patrolling their perimeters. The whole time, Filip scanned his surroundings. Liliya expected him to bolt at any minute, but he stayed next to her, trailing her as they were herded into the train station in the next town.

The mothers and fathers who had followed behind screamed and cried as the young people filed inside a cattle car. As the door closed, Liliya saw a Schuma beating back two women with his baton. Undeterred, they tried to throw themselves at the train.

In the velvety darkness, packed like sardines in a can, Liliya swayed against Nina on one side and Filip on the other, her back pressed against the wooden boards of the car. It took her eyes some time to adjust to the pale shaft of moonlight streaming in between a cracked board, but even then she could hardly make out Nina's face.

Liliya's thoughts sharpened with a fierce intensity. She had to focus; she had to take care of Nina.

"Do you think we'll travel all the way to Germany like this?" Nina asked.

"No," Filip answered. "They'll want to do medical inspections. I've heard they have transit camps along the way where they process us."

"Like we're livestock," Liliya said.

Filip chuckled. "Well, we are in a cattle car."

"How can you joke at a time like this?" Nina asked, her voice shrill.

He shrugged, his shoulder moving upward and the back of his hand rubbing against Liliya's. He turned his palm and squeezed her hand for one brief second, then let go. "If we don't laugh, what do we have to live for?"

Liliya tensed at the contact, surprised at the jolt of comfort his touch gave her. She flexed her fingers before clenching them into a ball, savoring it. "That's wildly philosophical of you," she rasped. "But that doesn't really help us now, does it?"

A loud explosion cracked through the night air ahead of them, and the train jerked, throwing Nina into Liliya, and Liliya into Filip. He caught them both, and Liliya found herself sandwiched between them, pressed against Filip's broad chest, his heart racing under her cheek as the weight of all the people in the car surged forward.

A burst of light, followed by another deafening explosion, flashed through their car. Filip pushed them both down, covering their heads with his torso. Screams rang in Liliya's ears as the acrid smell of smoke filled her nose, and for the first time in a long time, fear broke through her bravado, surprising her with its familiar intensity. After everything she'd seen, everyone she'd lost, she'd thought herself long past such a base emotion, but as sweat prickled on her neck, she wondered if maybe that was just another lie she'd told herself.

"The partisans bombed the train!" someone shouted.

Liliya straightened, looking around, surveying the scene. The front half of their car was gone, along with the people who'd been standing there. Twisted metal and broken boards jutted up through the tendrils of smoke while the now visible moon and stars twinkled down on them.

"What do we do?" Nina asked.

Liliya ripped her eyes away and shoved the fear back down inside. She had no time to think or worry now. She had to react. She had to protect Nina. "We run!"

Nina hesitated. "What if they catch us?"

"Liliya's right," Filip said. "We need to go now while it's still chaotic."

"This is our only chance!" Liliya said. "Come on, Nina. We'll be fine." She didn't really believe the words any more than she'd believed Oleksiy when he'd told her he could protect her, but she wasn't going down without fighting.

Other people had the same idea, and soon, anyone left standing was pushing forward to the open end of the car. Adrenaline surged through Liliya, and she grabbed Nina's hand and pulled her along as they climbed over the mangled wreckage. As they picked through it, Liliya realized not everyone was completely gone. A severed arm dangled from a jagged piece of metal, and someone's headless torso poked from underneath the front wheel of the car. Jerking her eyes away, Liliya ignored Nina's cry of distress and jumped off the train behind Filip, pulling her friend with her. They ran as fast as they could from the train wreck, Liliya's feet pounding against the uneven dirt and her pulse throbbing in her ears, but it felt as if she moved in slow motion, hampered by gravity and the daunting impossibility of their escape. Broken corn stalks from last year's harvest scratched at her legs and made finding good purchase difficult.

Filip ran deftly next to her, but he slowed to keep their pace. "Come on, girls. Faster!"

A scream rang out, and a guard shouted into the night. "I've got one!"

The nearness of the voice inspired a fresh burst of speed, but Liliya didn't dare look back, her eyes fixed on the forest just ahead.

As they took their first steps into the cover of the woods, more shots cracked through the inky night air. Nina fell forward silently, her arms striking Liliya and her body landing hard on the ground. The fear that Liliya had so neatly boxed away burst open, and this time, there was no holding it back because it wasn't for her. It was for Nina. It throbbed in her head, marking the cadence of her panic. She didn't stop to think but grabbed her friend under the arms and took a few steps backward, dragging the still body.

"Come on, Nina! Get up!" Liliya whispered at her friend. "You can walk! You just tripped!"

Liliya pulled at Nina, but something warm and wet made her hands slip. She fell backward, then jumped up and stared at the dark, viscous liquid on her hands.

She bit back a scream, wiped her bloody palms on her skirt, and tried again.

"I won't leave you, Nina. You'll be just fine." Liliya squeezed her eyes shut as she pulled, her mind flashing back.

"Get down, Mama!"

The staccato shots from the plane.

The blood.

A wave of dizziness washed over Liliya. She opened her eyes and swallowed it down, then dragged Nina several feet further. If she could just get Nina hidden, she could stanch the blood flow until the guards gave up.

"I won't leave you, Nina." Her voice was stronger, surer. She would die here with Nina before she left her. "I won't leave you."

"I've got her." Filip appeared out of nowhere, bending to grab Nina. He grunted as he hefted her over his shoulder. "This way!"

Liliya stared, shocked at his reappearance. He pointed to a low ravine covered in brush and pulled her along a few steps before her feet began running on their own, Nina's extra weight barely slowing him.

"We can hide in here. Help me clear it out." He scooped out leaves and old snow from a hollow under the far edge of the ravine with his free hand, and she did the same, her movements quick and measured, like the thoughts in her mind.

"Liliya!"

Liliya's head jerked up at the strangled whisper, and she spotted Oleksiy entering the woods.

"Get in!" Filip nudged her toward the hiding spot.

Oleksiy paused, his gaze probing the dark shadows, and Liliya pushed Filip. "No, you go in first and hide behind me. He won't hurt Nina or me, but he might take you." That realization stung, and doubt pressed down on her as she watched Nina's blood drip down Filip's torso.

Filip shook his head. "No. I don't want to put you in more danger."

She pushed him again, her hands small but strong against his chest. "I'll be fine. Trust me. Now go! We don't have time!"

Filip carefully set Nina down in the hollow, then crawled in next to her, hiding her from view. Liliya scrambled in and spooned her body against his, trying in vain to cover his large form with her own. They pulled the loose leaves and branches back in place as Oleksiy's footsteps approached.

Nausea rolled through her, and her hands, sticky with dried blood, clenched and unclenched as she held her breath and tried to fade into the ground, invisible.

"Liliya!" Oleksiy's quiet, anguished voice cut through the night air. "Where are you?"

As his eyes scanned the forest, she snapped hers shut, severing the invisible tie that a lifetime of friendship had created. Still, his footsteps advanced. He would find her. Oleksiy moved through the forest like a fox, and he knew her well. This chase of cat and mouse was only a continuation of the games they'd played together their whole life.

"Stay here," she whispered to Filip, then before he could reply, she scrambled out of their hiding spot and took a few steps away from it so Oleksiy wouldn't notice Filip and Nina.

Oleksiy's gaze locked on hers, his face softening in relief, his body so close she could touch him. His rifle, a stark reminder of their differing positions in this situation, pointed up at the sky. "Are you hurt? Where's Nina?"

Liliya fought back the simultaneous urges to either hit or embrace Oleksiy. A dozen unnamed emotions fought to gain hold in her brain, but they all flitted away, scattering in the wind like a flock of birds.

A man's voice, far too close to their hiding spot, rang out. "Oleksiy! Any luck?"

"No!" he shouted back. "Still looking!"

"How could you do this?" She finally gave voice to the one coherent thought that had taken hold.

Oleksiy shook his head, disgust written on his face. "You

have to believe me—I'm trying my best. I help people on every transport escape. This bombing was the Soviet partisans' work. We had no idea they would hit this train now."

Images of the mangled wreckage flashed through her mind. "People are dead because you put them on that train."

"I'm sorry, Liliya. I only want to take care of you. Now hide like we used to when we were young. Don't let them find you." He cupped her cheek, his thumb brushing against her lips, and for one second, Liliya wasn't in the woods with her wounded friend, running from a forced transport. She was young, mourning her mother, cradled in Oleksiy's warm, safe embrace.

Before she could reply, Oleksiy melted back into the darkness, yelling, "It's clear over here!"

Liliya climbed back into the hollow with Filip. "We can't wait too long. We have to get help for Nina."

Filip's hand found hers once again and squeezed, but this time he didn't let go, and their bloodied fingers stuck together. "Liliya, that shot hit her in the head. I'm sorry, but she died instantly."

Liliya twisted around so fast she knocked him in the jaw with her elbow. She didn't apologize. "You're lying. You carried her out! You saved her!"

He bowed his head, pressing his forehead to hers. "No. I knew you wouldn't leave her. I saved you."

11

LILIYA

March 1943, Volhynia, Reichskommissariat Ukraine

In the early hours of dawn, through woods and fields to avoid roads and Schuma patrols, Filip carried Nina home. Liliya's feet moved alongside his, but her tongue was still, her mind numb. She watched when he set her cold body on a bed in her parents' house as her mother keened and her father swore.

Filip filled the void and explained what had happened. How sorry they were. How hard they'd tried to keep her safe. Filip did everything necessary while Liliya shrank away to nothing, curling up within herself, small and taut, sure that she would splinter into a thousand pieces if anyone touched her.

When Nina's mother screamed, "Why her? Why my Ninka?" Liliya couldn't answer, but she wondered the same thing. Why had the bullet found Nina and not her? Nina, who still had parents to mourn her and dreams of a beautiful future. What would have happened if she hadn't dragged Nina along? Forced her to run?

Nina would still be alive. If she hadn't followed me, if I hadn't made her run, she'd still be alive. Just like my mother. If I'd reached her in time, she'd still be alive, too.

Bile gorged in her throat, and Liliya clapped a hand over her mouth and ran outside. The coppery smell of Nina's blood on her fingers made her gag, and she fell to her knees and heaved the scant contents of her stomach into the yard.

Gentle hands pulled her braids and their loose tendrils back from her face. When she finally stopped retching, someone offered her a handkerchief.

Filip.

She stared up at him with his kind eyes and gentle touch, and confusion twisted inside her. This man, this Polish man she'd been so rude to initially, had done so much for her and Nina in the last few hours. He held out a hand to help her up. Her gaze skittered away as shame filled her; she couldn't look him in the eye now while everything was so tangled up inside, but she took his hand, Nina's blood binding their fingers together, and didn't let go. They walked to her house as the sun rose, the blood on her clothes now stiff and scratchy against her skin, keeping to the woods and fields and away from the roads.

"We should stay out of sight for a while," Filip said.

He watched her, waiting for a response, but she clenched her jaw and let go of his hand.

He caught her arm and turned her toward him. His brown eyes, fierce and sad, bored into hers. "I'm sorry for what happened to Nina. But I'm not sorry we got away."

Liliya wrenched her arm away from the comfort he offered. "I am! I should have been the one shot! I pushed her to run. I took her hand and dragged her along. This is my fault!"

"No." Filip's voice was strong, like the hand he placed on her shoulder. "This is the Germans' fault. Make no mistake about that. Her death is on them."

"And me," she whispered. "Nothing you say will change that fact."

She didn't want to go in the house and face Vika and Maksym yet, to hear the story of Nina's death again, so she let Filip lead her up into the loft above the barn. Exhaustion tugged at her limbs. She longed to close her eyes and pretend this had all been a bad dream, but the coppery red streaks on Filip's face screamed the truth.

"Let's rest for a few hours until everyone wakes. Then we can clean up and figure things out." Filip moved stiffly as he took off his jacket and laid it out for a pillow, then lowered himself into a pile of hay.

Liliya nodded as she swayed at the top of the ladder, but when she couldn't bring herself to take another step, Filip pushed himself back up and came to her. He ran his hand down the side of her head, smoothing her hair and cupping her cheek, his eyes searching hers like they always did. She wanted to tell him he was looking for something in her that didn't exist. She was empty inside. Devoid of anything. But she couldn't even muster the strength to do that small task.

He bent over and scooped her up, as if she were nothing but a feather. She wished she were, so she could blow away on the wind, away from this wretched war. His arms quivered under her, strained from carrying Nina so far, but he never wavered as he walked to the hay and placed her in it. Liliya pressed her face into his rough jacket and curled into a ball. Filip lay down a few feet away, but when the silent sobs she'd held in for so long finally overwhelmed her, racking her body, he scooted close, wrapped his arms around her, and held her as she cried.

12

VIKA

March 1943, Volhynia, Reichskommissariat Ukraine

Vika moved methodically, trying to keep her mind off her missing niece. Her ears strained, listening for the sound of Maksym's return from his search for Liliya. She spooned out a small dish of the cooked *kalyna* berries and honey to each child before sitting at the table to eat her own. The sweet honey was almost necessary for the tart, red berries, even though she'd left them on the bush past the first frost to dull their bitterness. Her precious *kalyna* bush, now almost as tall as her, provided flowers and bark for medicinal teas on top of the berries she used for treating anything from sore throats to stomach troubles. The berries also made an excellent jam.

No other plant had more folk songs about it than the *kalyna*. In an attempt to drown out her worries, Vika hummed her favorite, the one her father had learned from his days with the

Sich Riflemen, *"Oy U Luzi Chervona Kalyna,"* as she stepped outside to check on it. The first few warm spring days had encouraged its growth, and she could see the start of the leaves and buds emerging from the branches. She would have a good harvest this year if all went well.

"Have I ever told you the story of how the *kalyna* bush came to be?" Vika asked as Sofia walked up holding an armful of firewood. She pulled away some dead leaves and old twigs from the base of the bush.

"Tell me, Mama," Sofia said as she set her logs down. Her pinched countenance betrayed her need for a distraction, too.

Vika put her arm around Sofia's shoulder. "Long ago, but much like now, invaders arrived here, coming to take our land. A young woman named Kalyna saw them before anyone else, and she led them away from her village and out into the swamp, where they all drowned, Kalyna included. She sacrificed herself to save Ukraine. Where she died, the first *kalyna* bush sprouted from the ground, with white flowers representing her hope and purity, red berries signifying the bloodshed Ukrainians always face in defending our homeland, and green leaves for the constant renewal of our people. The *kalyna* bush is a symbol of Ukraine in every way, and that's why we cherish it still with songs and poems."

"And in our embroidery," Sofia said, holding up her arm and showing off the sleeve of her embroidered vyshyvanka. "I love that story. I hope I can be as brave as Kalyna."

"I hope you never need to, but I'm sure you would be if the time came," Vika said as Slavko ran out of the barn.

"Mama!" he shouted. "Come quick! I found Liliya and Filip!"

* * *

Vika knew grief. She had dived into its depths, languished in its waves, and somehow emerged each day, battered and scarred but also wiser and more cautious. Stronger, her spine now forged of steel, not bone. But it was still hard to see Liliya like this. The girl moved like she was asleep, suspended in a dream-like fugue. She'd have to wake up eventually, have to let the pain pierce her fully before she could heal, but for now, Vika left her alone. You couldn't throw a rope to someone who hadn't yet realized they were drowning.

Maksym returned soon after Slavko discovered Liliya and Filip sleeping in the barn, and Vika sent him and the boys outside with Filip while Sofia filled a small tub with water heated on the stove. Tenderly, Vika peeled the stiff, crusty clothes from Liliya's body and helped the girl wash away her best friend's blood. She scrubbed and rinsed Liliya's long blonde hair until the water ran clear as Sofia and Nadya watched from the bed, all the while tempering her shock and focusing on the task at hand. All night, she'd lain awake worrying after Liliya didn't come home. She'd prepared herself for Maksym to return and tell them Liliya had been taken to Germany. While she was relieved that wasn't the case, she didn't know how well Liliya would handle another devastating loss like this.

"All she wanted was a house of her own and a family," Liliya said, her voice low and raw from her sobs.

"There's nothing wrong with that," Vika spoke softly as she began brushing Liliya's hair.

"I thought it was silly. I thought she was silly. To want so little when there was a whole world out there to see. Just because I wanted something different." Liliya whipped around, her wet hair smacking against her neck. "But she never judged me for what I wanted. When we were young, she saved scraps of paper for me so I could practice my sketching. She hiked all over the woods with me, looking for birds. She checked on me every day after my father died. She supported me and loved me no matter how different I was from the other girls."

"And you loved her, too," Vika said as she straightened Liliya's head and began braiding her hair. "She knew that."

"I'm done loving people! Everyone I love dies!" Liliya ground the heels of her hands into her eyes.

"What kind of bird was she?" Sofia's little voice piped up from the bed.

They'd played this game long ago when Liliya was younger and first discovered her passion for birds. She'd likened her uncle Maksym to an owl, always watching over her. Vika had been a sparrow, constantly busy at work and never sitting still. As the children got older, Liliya taught them the game and assigned them birds—Slavko, a sparrowhawk, wise and coura-geous, Sofia, a nightingale, always singing but shy around strangers, and Bohdan, a barn swallow, noisy and fast. Everyone they met became a type of bird.

Liliya gave Sofia a tremulous smile. "Nina was a dove. Generous, kind, and sweet. And so very gentle."

"I like that," Sofia said. "Nina the dove."

Liliya's jaw clenched. "But like a dove, she wasn't fast enough to evade the hunter's bullet. She wasn't a quick sparrow or graceful swallow. She was naive and good, and they took advantage of her trust, of her inability to fly quickly away." Her voice wobbled as she trailed off. "I took advantage of her trust."

"No, Liliya." Sofia crept closer and took Liliya's hand. "Filip told us what happened. You didn't take advantage. When you left your hiding spot to talk to Oleksiy, you protected her, like Kalyna from the legend. You put yourself in danger to lead the Schuma away from her and Filip. I think you're brave."

Liliya snatched her hand away. "I should have done more. I should be working with the resistance, fighting back against our oppressors."

The surprising heat of Liliya's words stoked an old fire in Vika. She'd once had the same passion to do more. To fight back. But when mere survival had become a struggle, she'd given up fighting for anything more than another day for her family. She'd learned to be content with the little joys in life. Food on the table. Her children nearby. Long visits with her sister, Maria, when she could travel to her village. These things sustained her. These things were all that mattered.

"You did everything you could," Vika said.

"I could have done more," Liliya said. She glared at Vika. "We could all do more!"

Vika bit the inside of her cheek until the tang of blood reached her tongue, fouling her mouth like it fouled her land. She leveled her gaze at Liliya and gave a final sharp yank on the wet braid as she tied it off.

* * *

In the following days, Liliya and Filip stayed hidden away in the barn while Vika and Maksym let it be assumed that they'd been taken to Germany. For a short time, they had a reprieve as the chaos of the train wreck left the Nazis scrambling to find out who was dead and who had run away from their transport.

But that didn't assuage Vika's fears. If the Nazis caught them harboring Liliya and Filip, the repercussions would be devastating. That knowledge sat in her stomach like a rock all day long, but Liliya was like a daughter to them. No matter the risks, they would do whatever they could to protect her. Vika only prayed Liliya's safety didn't come at a higher cost for all of them.

13

LILIYA

March 1943, Volhynia, Reichskommissariat Ukraine

"It's not proper," Vika admonished when Liliya came down on their sixth day of hiding to retrieve her books and personal items from the house.

"Nothing is happening between us," Liliya insisted, her voice dull. How could Vika think she could feel anything but despair? Filip was her link to Nina's last minutes, her tenuous thread to the moment she'd lost her. That grief mixed with the pain of losing her father, her mother, her brother, had swirled together into a torrent of misery she couldn't escape from. "I don't even like him, remember?"

It wasn't a lie. She didn't like him. She never had. His existence was a reminder of her father's death, and now, Nina's. But it didn't matter how much she liked him, because the more time she spent with him, the harder she found it to breathe without him. As unlikely as it was, he'd become her one source of solace in this sea of grief. But it wasn't romantic.

Maksym narrowed his eyes. "I'm not so sure he feels it's nothing. I've seen the way he looks at you."

"Don't be ridiculous. We are grieving."

Maksym's concerns seemed silly when she was lying next to Filip in the dark, pressed close together to fight the chill of the cool spring nights. Filip had never made untoward advances or given any inclination that he cared for her in any way other than as a friend.

Earlier, he'd listened to her talk for hours about Nina and Oleksiy, about her parents and brother. In turn, he'd shared that his mother had named her only child Filip because it meant "lover of horses."

"Was she right? Do you love horses?" Liliya propped her head up on her elbow and stretched her legs out, welcoming the diversion from the images of Nina's last moments that constantly assaulted her brain. The newly risen full moon illuminated the loft with a calming light, and in its glow, she lost count of Filip's smiles as he talked about the Polish Arabians.

"Those horses are my family; I would do anything for them. My grandfather, and his father before him, worked with the Polish Arabians there. I was raised in those stables; I learned to ride before I could walk."

"Your whole demeanor changes when you speak of them." Liliya marveled at the way his eyes brightened and the little scar under his lip creased into a dimple when he smiled.

"They remind me who I am and where I come from. They're a piece of Polish history, and it makes me proud to know I'm doing my part to ensure their survival through this war."

"Did your father love them, too?"

Filip drew his long legs up and rested his arms on his knees. "Yes, but the Soviets arrested him and my uncles and sent them to labor camps in the north. He hid me in the woods before they came. Saved me."

"So that you could now hide in a barn loft, wasting your days away."

He smiled. "Well, we can't hide in the loft forever, can we?"

"Sometimes it seems far preferable to the outside world. But no, I suppose you're right. We'll have to come out sometime. Maybe sooner than later."

"Maybe," Filip said. "Maksym is talking to the men at the stables to see if I can get a pass to come back, but it's a tricky business since I didn't have my work card and ran from the Schuma. He said it may be several more days until we know for sure."

Liliya rolled a piece of hay between her fingers. "He and Vika are worried about the properness of the two of us up here alone so much."

Filip's face reddened. "It's a normal concern. I should have spoken to Maksym."

His lack of denial surprised her, and she hurried on. "Don't worry. I reassured him that nothing will happen. It's not like that between us."

He jerked his gaze away from hers, then blinked hard. "No, of course it's not. Still, it might help if I talk to him, too." He said the words louder than normal, as if he were trying to convince himself of their truth. He patted her hand reassuringly, but his hand lingered half a beat too long, the warmth of his fingers heating her blood, pulsing it upward until she felt it staining her cheeks. She clenched her fingers, trying to brush off the heat of his touch, then cleared her throat.

"Maybe, but I don't see how they can care. There's no room for normal concerns these days. Besides, they know I have no desire to settle down and marry."

Filip rubbed the dark scruff on his jaw as he scrutinized her. "What do you desire of life, Liliya? You've told me much of your past, but not any of your dreams for the future."

She shrugged. "It doesn't matter now."

"What if it did?" He leaned forward.

Liliya hesitated. Her dreams seemed so ridiculous now, but this was a far safer topic to discuss. "I always wanted to go to a university and study art and biology. Birds, flowers, plants. To see the world. To move out of this small village and make a life for myself that's more than marriage, babies, and constant work."

She finished her thoughts silently. *To escape. Leave behind the sadness and loss. Start fresh.*

She grabbed her sketchbook and flipped it open to a page overflowing with information about nightingales and showed him. Last year, she'd drawn the bird from three different angles, made notes about its habitat and feeding customs, and sketched a nest she'd found.

"For as long as I can remember, I've loved to draw. Especially birds."

"These are really good." Filip looked at her with new appreciation. "I had no idea you were so talented."

"The talent part is up for debate, but I was driven, and that's what mattered. I've studied all the local birds. I can cite their

Latin names, tell you their migration habits, and list their favorite foods and nesting habits."

"Who taught you?"

She closed the book. "My mother. She loved nature."

"Do you still draw?"

Liliya hesitated, then shoved the book behind her. "No. It was a silly dream and I need to let it go."

"I don't think anyone should ever give up on their dreams." He paused, as if choosing his next words carefully. "I've seen you sitting out in the fields, writing in your book. I wondered what you were doing."

She cocked her head. "You noticed me out there?"

He fiddled with the chunk of wood he'd been whittling. "I always notice you."

Something small and sweet unfolded within Liliya then—a surprising sensation, different than the grief she'd been swimming in for so long. She couldn't put a name to it, but she clung to it, digging her fingers in and savoring the unexpected swirl of hope it brought.

14

HALYA

April 1943, Kyiv District, Reichskommissariat Ukraine

"They're starving in the city," Tato said. "No one is allowed into Kyiv to trade. It's the opposite of what happened in 1932 and 1933. Then, we starved, and they wouldn't let us in the city to work or trade for food. Now, we have the food, and they won't let us bring it to the city dwellers."

Halya tried to look busy working on her embroidery so her parents wouldn't notice her listening. They never openly talked about the hunger when she was around. She knew her mother and grandparents had perished, but she didn't know all the details. Whenever she asked, Mama hushed her and said, "The walls have ears, Halya. We can't speak of such things."

"It's a bitter irony that here, on some of the richest soil in the world, Ukrainians starve so often," Mama said. She unfolded her special *rushnyk* she kept hidden away with her prayer books and icons and took out a small paper booklet.

"Irony isn't the word I'd use," Tato muttered. "I'm going to hitch the horse."

When the Germans first arrived, they'd allowed the churches to re-open, and Mama had gone almost daily. "We have a lot of lost time to make up for," she'd told Halya.

But, as things got progressively worse under German rule, Mama resumed praying at home. When she murmured the names of their relatives who had passed away, going down the long, handwritten list she'd added to her little paper booklet, Halya always listened for her mother's name.

"Katya!" Tato called from the yard. "Can you come help me load the cart?"

Mama rushed outside, leaving her things out on the table. Halya inched closer, letting her hand reach out and touch the fine paper. She found her real mother's name immediately. Written in spidery letters, the name "Alina" drew her eyes in like a magnet. She traced the letters, sounding out each one, letting the flow of the word roll off her tongue.

Halya flipped through the book. Her own name appeared a few pages later, under the prayers for the continued health of the living. She turned back to the dead.

"There are so many more dead," she murmured. "Hardly any living."

"Come, Halya." Mama bustled back into the house. "Put that away. We must make a trip to town. We need to get a few items from the market before they won't let us trade there like in Kyiv."

* * *

At the market, Mama kept a tight grip on Halya's shoulder as Tato broke away to talk to some friends and try to trade. Before, the bustle of the market—the people, the stalls, the goods—intrigued Halya. She enjoyed getting lost in the crowd and soaking in the chaos, but today, the mood felt different. Everyone seemed nervous and wary, like her mother.

Suddenly, a scream pierced the air, followed by an angry shout. A dog barked as a rush of people pressed against Halya, ripping her from her mother's side. She stumbled and fell, scraping her knees on the packed dirt, then scrambled to her feet before the crowd trampled her.

As soon as she stood, a hand clapped on her shoulder and spun her around. Terror paralyzed Halya as she stared up at a stern-looking man in a Wehrmacht uniform. Next to him, a police officer tapped a baton against his open palm.

"Papers!" His spittle flew in her face.

Halya looked around, desperate for her mother. "My mama has them."

"Here!" Suddenly her mother's voice rang out, and she was at Halya's side again. "We have papers. I'm employed at our collective farm."

The man flipped through their papers, then nodded at the man with the baton. "Take them." He said it with such cold indifference, as if he were selecting apples at a food stall. He waved a man forward and turned his back, moving on to the next person.

As the man took Mama's arm, she erupted in a wild frenzy

of flailing limbs and shouts. Halya stood, stunned. She'd never seen her mother so angry, so shrill.

"No! I have a job! And she's just a child. We won't go!" she shrieked. "You can't make us go!"

Mama wrenched free and grabbed Halya, but another officer came up from behind holding a snarling dog tight on a leash. Bits of slobber flew off the dog's lips and tongue, sprinkling Halya, and she huddled close to her mother.

"You go, or my friend and I make you go," the man said. His scratchy voice made the hairs on Halya's arms stand on end.

The blood drained from Mama's face as if someone had flipped a switch. Then, she took a deep breath, forced a tight smile, and gripped Halya's hand. "Come along, Halya. We'll get this straightened out. Don't you worry."

They moved with the crowd as the officers herded everyone toward a large van. Around them, overturned baskets of root vegetables and broken jars of honey and preserves littered the ground. So much wasted food, Halya thought dully. She looked for her father's tall shape, but the people pressed so close around her she couldn't see past their torsos. What if he didn't realize they'd been taken? What if she never saw him again?

Panic surged in her chest, making her heartbeat echo in her ears. She pulled back against her mother's fierce grip, but Mama was stronger, and she tugged Halya along, away from the snapping jaws of the dog.

"Where's Tato?" Halya shouted. "I don't see Tato!"

"Just stay close to me," Mama said, but she too was searching the crowd for Tato, standing on tiptoe and scanning frantically. Her hand squeezed Halya's so tight it ached, but

Halya didn't pull away again—she squeezed back as they stepped into the van.

* * *

Halya had always wanted to visit Kyiv, but not like this.

She tucked her knees into her chest and shivered. After spending most of the day huddled in the yard between several houses used as a holding point, her earlier terror had faded into a dull, throbbing fear, but she couldn't shake the chill in her bones. All around her, children cried, and mothers tried to soothe them. Men paced back and forth like caged animals. Teenagers huddled in groups, talking in low whispers. And Mama stared at the door, as if willing someone special to walk through it. Halya didn't know who her mother expected could help.

"Do you think they'll feed us?" Halya asked.

Mama tore her gaze away from the door and smoothed back Halya's hair. "What? No. This is a temporary place. I don't think we'll get any food, but I have these." She fumbled in her pocket and pulled out two wrinkly apples. "If you can, always have food on you, Halya. You never know when you'll need it. Let's eat only one now."

This wasn't the first time her mother had doled out that piece of advice. Halya took a bite and chewed slowly, letting the sweet juice soak into her tongue. Around her, people made makeshift beds with bundles of clothes on the floor of the building they'd finally been placed in as they prepared to settle in for the night. Halya didn't want to think about staying here long enough to sleep, but soon there wouldn't be much of an option.

"Do you think Tato will come for us?" She finally asked the question that had been on her mind more than any other, but she dreaded the answer. If Tato came, he would be in danger. If he didn't, she might never see him again.

Mama attempted a smile, but it fell flat. "He'll try to come, but we can't get our hopes up. We need to be thankful that we're together, at least."

"But Tato is alone," Halya said. She thought of her dear father, with his kind eyes that crinkled into crescent moons when he laughed, all by himself at their house. Who would read him poetry or "pepper him with endless questions" if she wasn't there?

"Tato will be fine." Mama spoke in clipped tones as she smoothed her skirt over and over.

"Where will they take us?" Halya asked.

"Nowhere!" Mama finally snapped. "I have a work card, and you're too young. When the officials realize that, they'll send us home. Now, no more questions, Halya."

"You don't really think they care about that, do you?" a woman sitting next to them asked. "Who are you trying to convince? Yourself or the kid?"

Mama's eyes spat fire at the woman until she finally moved away from them, then Mama opened her arms. "Come, Halya. Lean against me and try to get some rest. Everything will look better tomorrow."

Tucked safely against her mother, Halya slept until the early morning hours when a guard came into the room and shouted,

"Come along! We're going across the street for the medical inspections."

As they stood, Mama fussed with Halya's neck. "You still don't have a good rash."

"It never took, Mama. The garlic didn't bother me longer than a few minutes."

Mama pressed her lips together like she always did when she was upset. "Don't worry, you're too young. They won't want you."

"What about you?" Halya asked. "What if they want you?"

"I have a job already. Remember?" Mama said. She pulled the embroidered neckline of her vyshyvanka down, revealing a red, bumpy rash. "Besides, even if that fails, they won't want me either. Apparently, the garlic bothers me more than it does you."

Outside, Halya sucked in deep breaths of the damp spring air—the smell of wet dirt and budding flowers was far more pleasant than the stink of human sweat and fear that had soured Halya's nose inside the crowded room they'd slept in.

Throngs of people waited for them. Mothers shrieking and throwing coats at their children, fathers surging forward, trying to break the barrier of guards escorting them. Some guards lashed out, their batons singing through the air as they connected indiscriminately with the heads and shoulders of parents wild with grief, and other guards used their whips to propel the crowd of detainees forward. Halya nearly had to run to keep up with the group.

"Katya! Halya!"

Halya recognized his voice instantly. "Tato! We're here!" She waved her arms, jumping up to try and see her father over the sea of people. He pushed toward them, his face drawn and weary, and Halya wondered where he'd slept, or if he'd slept at all.

"Kolya!" Mama cried as he tried to slide in between two guards. The rear guard noticed and swung his baton at Tato's head, connecting with a sickening thump. Tato's eyes locked with Halya's for one brief second before fluttering closed as he slid to the ground. Bile rose so fast in Halya's throat she couldn't hold it back, and she bent over and retched onto her bare feet.

Mama yanked Halya upright, her gaze flickering to Tato before boring into Halya's. "You mustn't stop, Halya, or they'll do the same to you. Tato will be fine. He's strong." Then Mama turned her head, jutted her chin forward, and pulled Halya along, not looking back at Tato again.

Inside the next building, a doctor gave them a cursory perusal, scanning their bodies and looking in their mouths briefly before marking them off on a checklist and pushing them to another holding area. Halya went first, and the doctor barely glanced at her before nodding at the nurse. She pushed Halya through to the next room, but Halya braced her hands on the doorframe when she heard the doctor say, "Stop. This one can't go through with this rash. She'll just be sent back."

Halya whipped around in time to see the doctor inspecting the garlic-induced rash on her mother's neck. He motioned to a guard stationed at the door, and he came forward and took Mama by the arm.

"No! I'm going with my daughter!" Mama shrieked as she swung out at the guard. "I want to go! Let me go!"

"You can't go!" the guard said. He tried to wrap his arms around her to stop her flailing, but her fist connected with his jaw. He roared in rage and hit her back, knocking her to the ground. She pushed herself up immediately, her eyes wide and wild, her cheek already angry and red where he'd struck her, and flew at him again. This time, he used his baton, cracking it against her skull, just like the other guard had done to Tato. But he didn't stop. He swung his baton again and again, beating it against her shoulders and back. Mama curled into a ball, covering her head with her hands, her angry shouts morphing into cries of pain before fading away as her body went still.

Someone else was still screaming, though, and it wasn't until the nurse dragged her to the next room and pushed her outside that Halya realized the primal sound was coming from her. She paused to suck in a breath, and in that moment of cavernous silence, a brass band jumped to life, serenading the prisoners on their march toward the train station as if they were leaving on holiday. Halya was so shocked at the audacity of the lively music that she didn't scream anymore; she only stared in disbelief as the mass of people propelled her forward, past the band, away from her parents, and onto a train car.

15

LILIYA

April 1943, Volhynia, Reichskommissariat Ukraine

"What are you making?"

Filip stayed silent as he methodically shaved off a few more curls of wood. Liliya leaned close, peering down at the form. Cleared by his German boss, he'd gone back to work since they'd escaped the forced laborer shipment three weeks before, but he still came to visit often and sleep over when need be.

Liliya was grateful for the company. Vika and Maksym thought it best that she remain hidden in the loft, out of sight of prying eyes who might turn her in to the authorities, but Liliya didn't know how much more she could take. She felt like a bird in a cage, uselessly beating her wings against the bars of her prison when she could be of more use fighting back. She wanted to join the UPA as soon as she figured out a way to do so without alerting her uncle, who, though not a member himself, kept in regular contact with many of them.

"Oh," she gasped as Filip held up the small wooden bird for her appraisal. "It's a nightingale! A perfect nightingale!"

He frowned. "It would be better with paint, but this will have to do for now." The pink in his cheeks surprised Liliya as he placed it in her hands. "I made it for you."

"For me?" Liliya touched the smooth surface, her lips curved into a rare smile. The careful marks of his knife had uncovered an astonishing depth and beauty from a rough piece of wood. "I can't believe you made this. I've never owned anything so fine."

Filip shifted uncomfortably, a self-conscious grin brimming on his pleased face.

Without thinking, she bent and kissed his cheek. "Thank you, Filip. I will treasure it always."

He stilled at her touch, as if he were the real version of the wild bird he'd just carved, frozen with terror and uncertainty at a human's nearness, and Liliya found herself unable to move back, her lips hovering inches from his face. The raw yearning in his eyes pulled at her. His hand, rough and calloused, slowly slid up her neck, his fingers twining in her hair, and for one glorious moment, Liliya forgot everything else.

A shout in the yard broke the spell, and Liliya heard a familiar voice talking to Maksym. She pulled away and leaned forward, peering through the crack.

"Who is it?" Filip stepped close behind her.

"It's Oleksiy." She met his gaze and marveled at how quickly he masked the disapproval that flashed across his face. "I have to see him. I have to know if they'll come after Maksym and Vika because of me."

"Of course." Filip moved aside and held an arm out toward the ladder.

She scrambled down and ran out into the yard, trying not to think about the moment she'd just shared with Filip.

"Liliya!" Oleksiy caught her in a hug and squeezed her so hard he didn't seem to notice her lack of reciprocation. "I've been going crazy wondering if you made it home or not."

She extracted herself from his grip and stepped back. Dirt caked his boots and covered his weary face. His once-sharp green uniform was now ragged and dusty.

He faltered for a moment at her lack of response, then forced a grin that didn't quite reach his eyes. "You shouldn't be out here in the open. If anyone sees you, your whole family will be in danger."

"I know. I stay hidden. I only came down when I saw it was you. Where have you been?"

"They sent us on roundups in neighboring villages. And to retaliate against those who don't come in when they receive notice."

Liliya took another step back, her stomach rolling. "Will they come here? Will they go after Maksym and Vika because I ran away? And the children?"

Oleksiy rubbed his scruffy jaw. "Maybe. I don't know."

Liliya stared at him. "What do you do to the families who wouldn't give up their children? I've heard stories. People getting their homes burned down. Being beaten."

Oleksiy's mouth tensed, accentuating his hollow cheeks. He

didn't reply, but his tormented eyes locked on hers, pleading for understanding, for atonement.

Her heart sank as she realized she already knew the answer. "Oh, Oleksiy. How could you? How could you do this to your own people?"

"I'm doing it for the greater good. Once you know everything, you'll understand."

"Then tell me! What don't I understand?"

He looked away, then stiffened, ignoring her question. "How's Nina?"

Liliya's head snapped back as all the emotions of that horrible night came rushing back. "You don't know?"

"Know what?" Oleksiy's grip tightened on his rifle, and he took a step forward.

"Someone shot her as we ran. Nina is dead." She spoke slowly, watching pain ripple across his face as the horror of what had happened sunk in.

He shook his head. "No, not our Nina."

But Liliya couldn't stop as the anger she'd sat on for so long bubbled to the surface.

"Was it you, Oleksiy? Did you pull the trigger that killed her?" Her voice was soft, but razor sharp with its precision, and Oleksiy flinched as her words cut him. A tiny pang of regret stabbed through her, but she shoved it down and didn't take the accusation back.

"I never shot my gun. I tried to help our people get away when I could." Oleksiy covered his chest with his hand. "You know that. You saw that!"

Liliya's body thrummed with a barrage of emotions. "I don't know what to believe anymore."

"You know me." He gripped her chin and made her look at him in the eye. "You know I loved Nina. And I love you."

She stared into his blue eyes, and a thousand memories pulsed through her veins. Oleksiy helping her up after an older boy pushed her down in the schoolyard. Oleksiy dunking her in the creek when they went fishing. Oleksiy tagging along on her bird-watching expeditions, but always scaring the birds away.

And now, Oleksiy, in the green German uniform of the Schuma. Holding a gun like the one that had killed their friend.

When he surged forward and pressed his lips to hers, she reacted without thinking, slamming her hands into his chest and pushing him away.

"What are you doing? You don't get to come here and tell me these horrible things and then kiss me!" She pushed him again. "I told you no, Oleksiy. You asked me to marry you, and I told you no."

He stepped back, his face still so close she could count each dark eyelash framing his blue eyes, and his voice cracked. "I'm sorry. I thought maybe you finally felt the same."

Liliya crossed her arms over her chest. "I don't know what I feel, but it isn't this."

"I know what I feel, Liliya, and I love you. I need you."

She shook her head. "You need me? Or you need someone to absolve you of your sins?"

He winced. "I need you. I need to feel something other than pain again."

Liliya's lips curled into an ugly grimace. "I don't think there's anything left in our world besides pain."

"That's not true." He hesitated, then leaned in closer. "I left the Schuma. I couldn't tell you before, but I'm a member of the

UPA. I have been for some time now. My commander wanted me to join the Schuma to get weapons and access to information, and we all left together to fight for a free Ukraine. It was a mass exodus of Ukrainians, but it didn't take long for the Poles to fill our roles."

She looked down at his jacket, finally noticing the missing patches—a Schuma uniform stripped bare. "I knew it," she breathed.

"Some men joined the Schuma early because they thought Germany would help us in our fight for independence, but it became clear pretty quick that wasn't the case. Since I joined later, I knew that. I knew what I had to do for the long game. Does that change how you feel about me? Realizing that I was always fighting for you? For us? For Ukraine?"

"No. I love you as a friend, nothing more. You being in the Schuma didn't change that, and you being in the UPA doesn't change what you did for the Nazis while wearing this uniform." Liliya rubbed her temples in an attempt to thwart the dull ache growing there. "What will you do now?"

"Fight the Germans. Fight the Soviets. Fight the Poles. Fight whoever we need to in order to gain our freedom. Can you imagine?" A hopeful smile flashed across his face. "An independent Ukraine with our own schools and churches. A government of Ukrainians, not Polish landlords or Soviet collectives or Nazi brutes."

"But what about your mother and sisters? Aren't you worried the Germans will punish them for your desertion? They persecute UPA members and their families."

The dreamy look fell off Oleksiy's face. "They'll have to be careful. I built them a hiding place—a bunker in the woods behind our farm. You could join them there."

"If I'm any part of this, I wouldn't want to hide," Liliya said. "I'd want to help."

Oleksiy's jaw tightened. "There are some women involved. Nurses, couriers. Spies, even, but it's not for someone like you."

"What does that mean?" Liliya snapped. "I am capable of all of those things."

"Of course you are, but what about your dreams? What about your plans to leave here? I wasn't enough to make you give them up, but the UPA is? Living in a dank bunker in the woods, fighting for our cause but hidden from your birds, your studies, from everything and focusing only on the missions at hand?" The hurt on Oleksiy's face needled at Liliya's conscience.

"That's different, and you know it."

Her dreams seemed so ridiculous considering what was happening here. She thought of the letter she'd written to the Ukrainian Free University on the day Nina died, now soaked with blood and stuffed under the hay in the loft. How naive to think that simply writing a letter would change her dire existence. But without those goals, who was she? For so long, they'd been such an integral part of her makeup. Her life plan had become almost tangible, a fruition of hopes and wishes longed for so hard that they'd nearly been willed into reality.

But the truth was, as much as she didn't want to admit it, those dreams had died with the Red Army invasion, and the Germans had put the nails in the coffin.

And where did that leave her? What did she dream of now? Survival? The opportunity to live another day? Paltry dreams in comparison to the unrealistic longings of her youth. Or did she dream of fighting back? Of channeling her anger and frustration toward the enemy?

A board creaked in the barn, and Liliya saw a flash of movement against the crack in the wall.

Filip.

Did she dream of him? A type of life she told herself, and Oleksiy, that she never wanted—a life filled with love and commitment instead of education and escape or fighting for freedom?

Oleksiy followed her gaze. "Who's up there with you?"

She jerked her eyes away from the loft. "No one. It's probably a barn cat."

He relaxed. "I thought maybe it was Filip. He got away too, you know."

"I didn't know he escaped," she lied, surprised at how easily the words rolled off her tongue. "But would you promise me something, Oleksiy?"

"Anything. I would promise you anything." He took her hands and pressed them to his lips, but she pulled back. His touch, normally reassuring, now chilled her. Deep down, she wondered if she would ever be able to forgive him for his role in Nina's death.

She pushed those thoughts aside. "If you do come across Filip, promise me you won't hurt him. I care about him, just as I care about you, and I couldn't stand to see either of you hurt."

Oleksiy's eyes narrowed, jealousy glinting in their blue depths. "Do you love him?"

"I've told you before. I love no one, but that doesn't mean I want to see my friends suffer."

"I didn't realize you were so close to him." Bitterness twisted his handsome features into something Liliya barely recognized.

"I'm not. I've already lost Nina and my whole family. I don't want to see anyone else hurt. I feel the same about you."

Oleksiy shook his head. "We go back much farther than that, Liliya. I'd hope you'd feel more for me than you do some stranger."

"Oleksiy, I'll always care about you. You're one of my oldest and dearest friends, and I worry about you too. What you're doing with the partisans, what you've done with the Germans, it's all dangerous."

"And necessary."

"Perhaps some of it. Not all." A harsh, bitter laugh erupted from her mouth, surprising her and startling the evening birds chirping around them into silence. "Aren't you glad I didn't marry you? It would have only made things more complicated for you now."

"No." Oleksiy's answer was swift, sure. "We could have fought for a free Ukraine together. We still can." He took her hand again, and this time, his passionate words weakening her resolve, she let him. "You and me, together all the time, just like it used to be. Think about it, Liliya. If you really want to help, meet me tonight after dark where the creek behind Nina's house curves, and join us. Join the UPA."

* * *

Filip looked up from his new whittling project as Liliya climbed into the loft, and her heart somersaulted in her chest, matching the turmoil in her mind after her conversation with Oleksiy.

Filip schooled his face into an impassive mask as he attacked the wood in his hands with sharp, angry slices.

"So, he wants to marry you."

Liliya stepped toward him. "You were listening. Just like last time."

He stopped whittling and tightened his grip on the rough piece of wood. "Not to all of it. Only that part. Oleksiy is very loud when he professes his love."

"Did you hear my response?"

"Yes, but he would treat you well and keep you safe. That's what's most important. You should reconsider."

If Filip thought Oleksiy could still keep her safe, he hadn't heard everything, but it wasn't her place to share Oleksiy's secret about leaving the Schuma and joining the UPA. She took another step closer to him. Heat radiated off his body.

"Oleksiy can't protect me. No one can."

A muscle in Filip's cheek twitched. "At the very least, you love him as a friend. Successful marriages are often built on the foundation of friendship, and you've been friends for years."

She stared at him, the soft curl of his dark brown hair, the adept strength of his hands gripping his knife, the wide angle of his jaw flexing as he ground his teeth. Her hands tingled with the sudden urge to touch him, and her feet moved of their own volition, drawn to him like a bee to a poppy. "If I do ever marry, which I don't plan on, I'd want a marriage based on romantic love, not some archaic sense of duty."

Filip tensed, as if prepared to jump away from her. "Not many of us are getting what we want these days, are we?"

"And what do you want, Filip?" She hated her desire to know almost as much as she hated the inexplicable attraction she felt for him. Her whole life, she'd sworn she wouldn't be tied down without following her dreams. But the losses they shared, the terror they'd lived through, the three weeks they'd spent locked away together, had created an intense intimacy between them that she both craved and feared. She needed him like she needed water, but he was pulling her under, drowning her.

"You've asked me. Now I'm asking you." She held herself back, moving slowly as she would with a wounded animal, and reached out and traced his jaw. Coarse stubble pricked her fingertips.

He jerked back from her touch. "It doesn't matter what I want, Liliya."

She held out her hand, an open invitation. "It matters to me."

"I want you to live!" Filip's tone was low and guttural, as rough as his skin. He grabbed her hand and placed it over his racing heart. "I want you to survive this any way you can, and if that means I lose you to another man forever, then so be it. I can live with that, but I can't live in a world where you don't exist."

She pressed her palm harder against his chest, synchronizing her breath and heartbeat with his. The torment in his eyes shredded the last strands of resolve she possessed, and she lurched forward into his arms, propelled by a dozen near misses, a hundred lost opportunities.

He groaned, and suddenly he was kissing her all over. Her cheeks. Her neck. Her lips. And she was kissing him back, her hands shaking as she clutched him close, pressing tight against him as if she could meld into him. Become one.

All the emotions she thought she lacked bubbled to the

surface of her skin, reawakening her dulled senses and she realized this was what Oleksiy wanted her to feel.

And she did; just not with him.

Filip wrenched away, and Liliya nearly cried out as cold desolation ripped through her at the sudden loss.

He pushed his hand into his hair. "We shouldn't be doing this. I'm leaving, Liliya."

She swayed, the floor unsteady beneath her feet as she fought to regain hold of logic. What had just happened? This was not who she was. This, he, was not what she wanted.

Was it?

"Where will you go?" She pushed the words out in a shaky jumble and took a step back.

"I'll keep working at the stable. The officer in charge there likes me. He knows my skill with the horses, my familiarity with them. He won't let me be sent to Germany again."

"And?"

He glanced sharply at her, and she took another step back, her clarity increasing the further away she moved from his intoxicating presence.

"I'm no fool. What else will you do?"

His gaze dropped. "Does it matter?"

"It matters to me."

He moved toward her as if he wanted to grab her hands, but she crossed her arms, and he froze, resignation written on his countenance.

"I pass on information."

Liliya's breath hitched. "To who?"

Filip's beautiful mouth twisted into an ugly smile. "How lucky are we to have so many options? Soviet partisans.

Ukrainian partisans. Polish partisans. The Polish Home Army. The German army. The Schuma. The Red Army. The possibilities for us to join a group and kill each other are endless."

She swallowed hard. "Are you with the Polish Underground?"

He gave one tight nod. "A local partisan group. A Peasant Battalion. We haven't joined up with the Armia Krajowa yet, but it's only a matter of time. All my group has done up until now is fight back against German confiscations and deportations. And I swear, I've never hurt any Ukrainians. But I can't sit here while Germans and Soviets, and now Ukrainians, try to destroy us. I have to do something."

I have to do something. Such a familiar chorus these days. Hadn't it inspired her?

"You have to fight," she whispered.

We have to fight. The words danced on her lips, but she couldn't say them, couldn't tell him of her plans to join the UPA now.

He reached out and grazed his fingers against her cheek. "If I must. It's not my goal."

"What other way is there to do things here?" She didn't try to hide her bitterness. How could it be that Filip worked with the same group, albeit in a different area, that had killed her father? And now, he'd be fighting against Oleksiy as well. Against her. She pressed her fist into her stomach, willing it to stop twisting.

He hurried on. "It's not what you think. I'll work at the stable, just like before, gleaning information when I can, and I'll pass it on. When we know when the supply trains are coming through, we strike. When we hear about possible attacks, we defend."

"And if you're caught?"

"I won't be. I've been doing it for some time."

"Does Maksym know about this?"

"Nobody knows. I don't want to put him in a difficult position."

"But you're here so often. Isn't that already putting him in a difficult position? And you told me. Why would you tell me?"

"I don't know. Maksym is like a brother to me. Our love of horses bonded us long ago. He and Vika treat me like family and continuing to come here gives me the opportunity to see you. I can't pass that up." Filip locked his gaze on hers. "When I'm around you, I feel different. More alive than I've ever felt. Up here, with you, I can almost forget what's happening out there. Everything is colorful and vibrant in this miserable, gray world."

"Filip, I'm not . . ." Liliya choked on the words she intended to say, the words she'd said to him and everyone else so many times. *I don't want to be tied down. I can't risk caring about anyone else because everyone I love dies. I want to leave, to study, to see the world, but if I can't, I want to help. I need to do something.*

But this time, they all stuck in her throat like wheat chaff, because when she stared into his earnest brown eyes, they didn't matter. Nothing else mattered.

He took her hands. "I want to come see you again. May I?"

She nodded, still unable to speak. Filip raised her hands to his lips and kissed each of her palms, then pressed them to his heart. "Then this isn't goodbye, Liliya. I'll be back for you."

The warmth of his breath on her skin rushed through her,

honing her thoughts until everything sparkled with a stark clarity. She loved him. No matter their past, no matter their future, she loved him.

But would that be enough?

"I'll be here," she promised, praying it would be true, praying that in this bleak, miserable war, she would be able to keep this piece of happiness for herself.

She watched him walk away through the fields, peering out a crack in the barn wall, swallowing down the despair washing over her in waves. Her eyes followed his every movement, from the long-legged strides he took to the way his left hand swung more than his right, until his form was a tiny dot, far off in the distance. Still, she kept watching, oblivious to anything else, even the German army truck roaring down the road until it stopped in front of the house. Now, Liliya, like a bird perched in a tree, watched it and the two men who went to the door. Liliya strained to hear what Vika was saying, the tension in her voice traveling all the way up to the barn loft, but the man's words were loud and clear.

"We're looking for Liliya Shums'ka."

And just like that, she knew her promise to Filip would be broken.

16

VIKA

April 1943, Volhynia, Reichskommissariat Ukraine

Slavko pulled a cluster of poppies and cornflowers from behind his back. "Here, Mama. I saw these and thought of you."

Vika took the flowers and smiled at her eldest child. He'd been bringing her bouquets since he could walk—from grubby handfuls of dandelions proffered by dimpled hands to artfully arranged medleys like this one. Slavko may have had a smart mouth and impish nature, but he was sweetness through and through. She prayed the war wouldn't change that, wouldn't destroy his kindness, but it seemed inevitable. Nobody would come out of this unscathed.

"Thank you, Slavko. They're beautiful." She poured water from the pitcher into a cup and set the flowers on the table. "Have you seen your father?"

"No, he's not home yet."

The roar of a motor in the front yard paused their conversation. Vika ran to the door and peered out as an Opel Blitz truck pulled up. Two men got out and marched toward her, a Wehrmacht officer and a Schuma.

Vika gripped Slavko's arm. "Take your brother and sisters and hide. Keep them quiet."

"But Mama—"

"Now, Slavko!" Vika pushed him behind her and stepped outside to meet the men.

"We're looking for Liliya Shums'ka," Yevheniy said. A vile man who'd worked for the Soviets when they'd invaded, he now wore the German Schuma uniform proudly. A traitor to his people every time the opportunity arose.

Vika fought the urge to spit on his shiny black boots. "She's not here. She was taken to work in Germany."

Yevheniy translated her response, then the German's reply.

"She escaped, so we need someone from this household to go in her place."

Vika's heart stopped beating. She felt it, suspended in her chest, then it crashed into her ribcage so violently she thought it would burst out of her. She pressed her palm against her breast to keep herself together as she thought of Liliya hiding in their loft, unaware of this threat she'd brought down on their heads.

"But she went. It's not our fault she escaped. Perhaps you should have guarded her better."

Yevheniy hit her, so quick and hard her neck cracked as her head jerked sideways, but she didn't stumble. She straightened and glared at him.

"What would you have me do? I can't change what she did."

The German officer spoke, and Vika recognized one word. *Kinder.* Children. Her vision tunneled.

"You have children," Yevheniy translated. "Your eldest will come with us in Liliya's stead."

"No!" Vika's fists balled at her side. "My son is only fourteen. You will not take him. I had no control over what happened with Liliya, and neither did he."

The German officer gave a slight nod, then put his hand on his pistol. At his signal, Yevheniy pushed past Vika, knocking her into the doorframe as he barreled into her house.

She ran in behind them, trying to place herself in front of the children, but they weren't there. Only Slavko stood at the table, opposite the bed where the younger children normally slept, his face calm, his hands loose at his side.

"Can we help you, gentlemen?" His steady voice didn't betray the flash of fear Vika glimpsed in his eyes. He shot her a reassuring grin.

A distraction. He's using himself as a decoy like the tale of Kalyna, she thought. Her brave, strong boy, always there for her, always thinking of others over himself.

She moved to his side, praying the other children would be quiet. Nadya was too young to be taken for labor, but Vika had heard stories about young Aryan-looking children kidnapped and adopted out to German families. And Sofia and Bohdan weren't much younger than Slavko. These men could take them, too.

"We cannot help them." Vika kept her voice steady. "They want Liliya, but as I've told them, she never came home. As far as we know, she's in Germany."

"And as we've told you, we'll need someone to go. This boy

will work." Yevheniy snaked out a hand and gripped Slavko's arm. "Come along nicely and there will be no more trouble for your family."

"No!" Vika shouted. "He's not going with you." Her eyes locked on her eldest child—his sun-kissed golden hair, his freckled nose, his mischievous green eyes. She wanted to swoop him up into her arms and rock him like she had when he was a baby, but he wasn't a baby anymore. He was nearly a man.

"I'll be fine, Mama. It will be an adventure." Slavko touched her shoulder. "I'll write to you, and we will see each other soon."

The cord tethering Vika to common sense snapped. She flew like a wild woman at Yevheniy, pummeling her strong fists into his face and chest. Startled, he dropped Slavko's arm and raised his own up as a shield against her before regaining his wits and executing one sharp backhand to her cheek. This time, she went flying, crashing into the table and knocking over the dishes on it.

"You crazy *suka!*" Yevheniy shouted. "I think you broke my nose!" Blood streamed out of it, and he grabbed a towel from the tilted table and pressed it to his face with one hand and seized Slavko again with the other.

Slavko wrenched away, pushing at Yevheniy as he tried to get to Vika, but Yevheniy gripped him tight with one hand and slammed his fist into Slavko's eye with the other. Slavko sank back against the table, and Yevheniy leaned close to Vika, still on the ground, and growled, "I know you have more children. That pretty little daughter of yours—if I looked hard enough, I could probably find her right now. You and the boy keep fighting, and I will."

Vika pushed herself up, but the room spun, and vomit rose in her throat. She dropped her head, willing her body to steady itself as the hopelessness of the situation struck her. They would take Sofia. If she fought for Slavko, they would take Sofia and Slavko. Two of her children, gone to work as slaves in another country. But what if they had Liliya? What if she gave them the person they originally wanted? Could she do that? Trade one life for another?

Slavko straightened, his eye already puffy and swelling. "Mama! Please, stop. Liliya is gone, and I will go instead. There's nothing more to be said." He spoke as if reading her mind, shutting down her thoughts of turning in Liliya to go in his place— his voice, harsh and sharp, sounded just like his father's. She raised her head, half expecting to see that Maksym had walked through the door. But it was her son, making decisions about his own fate to help others. How could she go against that? Especially if it meant sacrificing another one of her children?

"I'm here!" Liliya ran through the door, her wild hair tangled in a golden halo around her head. "I'm here. Take me and leave the boy."

For a moment, relief coursed through Vika, followed quickly by admiration for Liliya's bravery. The girl was made of sterner stuff than Vika had given her credit for.

"So, you were hiding her?" Yevheniy said.

"No." Liliya stepped inside. "They didn't know I was here. I hid on my own."

Yevheniy conferred with the Wehrmacht officer briefly in a mix of German and Ukrainian, then turned to Vika. "We've decided to be generous today, since the girl turned herself in.

Luckily for you, we won't burn your house down or arrest you, but we will take both of them."

Vika sucked in a ragged breath.

Slavko closed his eyes and bit his lip for one moment, just as he had when he was a small boy and nervous about going to school or riding a horse. Then he smiled widely at her as they dragged him and Liliya out of the house, reassuring his mother while he buried his own fear.

A deep sob tore from her throat, and her eyes fell on the bouquet Slavko had brought her, the flowers scattered and trampled on the floor by the ugly black boots. She let only one tear flow into that spilled water before she pulled herself up and told Sofia to stay hidden with the younger children. Then, she prepared a parcel of food and extra clothes and followed them.

* * *

When Maksym came home late that night, after the other children had gone to sleep, he found Vika scrubbing the table, blood leaking out of the cracks on her knuckles as she rubbed the rag over the wood over and over. The left side of her face, puffy and sore, had enclosed around her eye, leaving her blind on that side.

"What happened?"

When she ignored him, Maksym took her by the shoulders and made her look at him. "Vikusia, what happened here?"

"They took Slavko and Liliya." It hurt to say the words, to push them out into the world as a spoken truth when she wanted to deny the fact with every fiber of her being. But she couldn't. He was gone, and there was nothing she could do.

"Who?" Maksym tensed, his hands tightening on her shoulders, and she shrugged him off.

"Who do you think? The Germans! They took him to go in Liliya's place, and when she came out to rectify the mistake, to go so he wouldn't have to, they took them both."

After returning from unsuccessfully trying to bring Liliya and Slavko a bundle of extra clothes and food—the guard had taken it, but she didn't have high hopes he'd pass it on—she'd expended all her tears, a devastating breach in her normally impenetrable walls. Now she was a hollow husk of a woman. Dried up and squeezed out like an old washcloth.

"The other children are safe for now, but they threatened to take Sofia if I kept fighting them." She paused. Each breath she took made the ache in her chest sharper, as if her lungs were jagged pieces of glass pressing into her heart, twisting with all the emotions she'd denied for so long. She dropped the rag and slumped into a chair. "So, I stopped. I let them take our son."

Maksym's jaw twitched, and his gaze fell on the bundle of flowers Vika had set on the table. She couldn't bring herself to get rid of them—her last gift from her sweet boy—so she'd picked each one up, straightening the bent stems and removing loose petals, then filled another cup with water, and put them back out.

"Today? How long ago?" Maksym asked.

"Four hours."

"Did you go up there? See if anything could be done?"

"Of course I did!" Vika snapped. "I prepared a package of food and clothes, followed them, and watched as they were shoved into a truck and driven out of our village. I don't know where they went after that or if they even got the supplies I gave a guard."

"Maybe I can find them and do something."

"What would you be able to do? You won't be able to stop them. No one but the village elder could have possibly stopped this, and he can't be trusted. He makes most of the labor lists in the first place."

Maksym sat down next to her and took her hand. "I'm the new village elder, Vika."

She froze. Pinpricks tingled in her fingertips where her skin connected with her husband's, tiny fissures in the bedrock of their connection, and she jerked away from him. "What are you saying, Maksym?"

Maksym ran his hand through his hair, making it stand on end. "I'm saying they arrested our village elder today and informed me I'm to be the new elder, which means now, when they demand a labor list, I have to make it."

"No." Vika shook her head. "You can't help them send our children away! You can't."

He slammed his fist on the table, and in the corner of the room, the sleeping children shifted in their beds. "Do you think I want this job? Do you think I want any part of creating lists of people for the Germans to steal away from our village?"

"There must be another way."

"I can tell them no and they can arrest me too. Then they can send my whole family to Germany. Nadya can hang on your skirts while you work in one of Hitler's bomb factories, and I'll rot in a jail or a grave from a bullet to the head. Is that what you want?"

"Of course not," she replied. "But they could have found someone else. Someone who wanted to be village elder. Why didn't they pick them?"

"Would that have really been better for our village? For our family? This is not my choice, Vika, but maybe it will save Sofia and Bohdan from Slavko's fate."

"What about Slavko? Does this change things for him and Liliya?"

Maksym sighed. "Maybe. If this had come one day earlier, then yes, they might have been safe."

Vika's breath caught. One day. One short day could have kept her boy and her niece here. But at what cost?

"What about our friends? Our neighbors?"

Maksym dropped into a chair, leaned forward, and let his face fall into his hands. "I don't know yet."

17

HALYA

April 1943, German General Government of Poland

Halya sat alone in the train car, moving further away from her mother and father with each second. It had only been a few hours since she'd left Kyiv, a few days since she'd last seen her home, but it felt like forever. She pinched the skin between her thumb and first finger until it hurt. If she concentrated on that pain, she could almost forget Mama on the ground, still and lifeless.

Almost.

Something had broken inside Halya in that moment, squelching her will to resist. She'd moved passively down the street to the train station—not fighting like she'd promised her Tato. *Not even being brave*, she thought, as she stood in the corner and tried not to cry.

The train chugged along, its rhythmic lurching almost

comforting despite the fact that it was stealing her away from her home. They'd stopped twice already through the night to pick up more people, and Halya had no idea how far west they'd traveled. Had they reached Poland? Was she still in Ukraine?

She pulled out her poetry book and pressed her palm into it. Hidden away in her pocket through the day and night spent huddled on the ground with her mother and the other women and children in Kyiv, this and the picture were all she had left of her old life. Light filtered in through the boards nailed haphazardly over the upper window of the car, but it wasn't enough to read by, so Halya closed her eyes and recalled the poems in her mind. The familiar cadence of the words flowed through her like a prayer, each clever turn of phrase imbuing strength into her as her lips moved along with the prose in a whisper. Suddenly, the train jerked as it began to slow, and Halya pitched forward, the book sliding out of her hands.

She dropped to the floor, feeling around, desperate to touch the reassuring heft of the pages, the soft worn cover, but the people were packed in so tight she could barely move.

"Please, I dropped a book. Has anyone seen it?"

No one replied, and her voice grew shrill. "Please! Just look down and see if it's at your feet!"

Most people were asleep, and a few mumbled, half-hearted responses trickled back. Nothing helpful.

"It couldn't have gone far," Halya murmured. She squatted down and pulled her legs to her chest, tucking her quivering chin into her knees. "I'll find it when we get off."

Something poked into her arm, and she looked up. A boy, not much older than her, held out her book.

"It hit me on the head." He smiled, his teeth a shocking jolt of white across his dirty face. His eyes, one so brilliantly green it sparkled even in the dim light, and the other, swollen nearly shut, shone with compassion as he held out the book.

"Thank you." She took the tome, its weight once again a calming presence in her hands, and flipped through it until she found the picture. A sigh of relief escaped her lips.

"What's that?" The boy leaned close, and Halya jerked back. She tried to decide whether she should lie or slam the book shut and ignore him. She didn't think she'd ever show anyone the picture.

"Nothing," she finally said, pulling the book to her chest. "Just some poems I love."

The boy cocked his head, then nodded. "All right. When you're ready, then."

Halya stared at the strange boy. A purple bruise colored his swollen eye, and Halya wondered if he'd fought back like her mother had. Like she hadn't. She shuddered.

"Slavko! Don't do that again! We need to stay together!" A girl, maybe seventeen or eighteen, with long blonde hair, whacked the back of the boy's head.

"Hey!" He ducked away from her as best he could in the tight quarters. "She dropped something, and I was returning it."

The girl glanced over at Halya, her eyes distant. "Fine."

"This is my cousin, Liliya, and I'm Stanislav. You can call me Slavko, though," the boy said, smiling. "I have a feeling we'll be great friends, so we may as well skip the formalities."

"I'm Halyna." Halya plucked at her thin dress nervously. "But you can call me Halya."

"Where are you from?" he asked.

"Sonyashnyky. Kyiv Oblast."

"We're from Maky, in Volhynia." He jerked a thumb at the older girl, who seemed reluctant to be drawn into their conversation. She shifted away from them, her gaze dancing over the other people in the train car as if she were looking for someone.

"Are you alone?" Slavko asked.

"Yes." Halya spoke so softly she barely heard herself. Answering the question made it a truth she didn't know how to accept. She was alone. Completely and utterly alone.

Slavko scooted closer, and his shoulder bumped into hers as the train swayed. "We'll be with you then. So, now you're not alone. Right, Liliya?"

The older girl's head snapped around, and she gave a half-hearted nod. "Of course."

Warmth blossomed in Halya's chest, and she blinked back tears at their kindness, though Liliya's seemed less natural. But Halya wasn't in a position to be picky about her friends now.

"Thank you." She forced the words out around the lump lodged in her throat.

"How did they get you?" Slavko asked.

Halya squeezed her eyes shut, trying to block out the image of Mama covering her head as the guard beat her, but even after she opened her eyes, she still saw it.

"Maybe she doesn't want to talk about it," Liliya said. This time, there was understanding in her words, and Halya wondered what Liliya had endured.

"They got me at my house. I put up a fight, though." He winked at her with his good eye.

"Slavko!" Liliya elbowed her cousin. "What's the matter with you? Don't bother this poor girl with all your chatter."

"It's fine. I don't mind him talking," Halya said. Slavko's nonchalance distracted her from the ache in her chest. If he talked, she wouldn't have to think. "What happened?"

Liliya glared at Slavko while he answered Halya's question. "Liliya escaped this fate once already, but they came looking for her. I tried to go in her place, keep her hidden, but she wouldn't have it. So, they took both of us."

Halya glanced at Slavko's black eye before she could stop herself, and he gave a wry grin. "Courtesy of a Schuma."

"I'm sorry," Halya said, but Slavko waved it off.

"This is nothing. You should have seen—"

"They should have let Slavko go," Liliya interrupted, her jaw clenched. "They had me. They had who they came for."

"And leave me behind to miss this whole adventure?" Slavko said.

"Aren't you afraid?" Halya asked, surprised at how her voice came easier this time, how comfortable it felt to talk to him.

"Only a fool isn't afraid when it comes to Nazis," Slavko said. "But I know how to work hard, and I figure I'm pretty tough, so I'll be fine. Liliya, too." He gave Halya a once-over with his good, bright green eye. "How old are you?"

Halya straightened under his perusal and added a year to her age, though she wasn't sure why. "Twelve. Almost thirteen."

"Hmm. I would have guessed ten or eleven," Slavko said.

A flush of anger reddened her cheeks. "I may be small for my age, but I'm strong. How old are you?"

"Fourteen." Slavko's scrawny chest puffed up.

"That's not much older than me," Halya scoffed.

"Fourteen is a man!" he said. "Twelve, if that's what you are, is still a child."

"That's ridiculous," Halya said. "Fourteen is not a man, and I could do anything you do."

A broad smile flashed across Slavko's face again, and it made Halya think of the way the sun could blind you when it suddenly peeked out from behind a cloud.

"Ah, there it is. I could see you had a fire in you, even through your sadness," he said. "Better keep it burning if you want to make it through this."

Halya stared at him, her mouth hanging open. Had he only been teasing to get a rise out of her? "I'll have no trouble, you'll see. And I won't need your help."

"I expect not," Slavko agreed. He leaned his head back against the wall of the car and closed his eyes. "But either way, you shall have it. Liliya's too, because despite all her moodiness and scolding, she's quite nice. Now, we should try to rest and be glad that we sat away from the hole in the floor people are using for an outhouse."

Liliya gave Halya an apologetic shrug. "Slavko has always been a handful. I'd apologize for him, but then I'd never be able to do anything else."

Slavko's lips quirked at the commentary on his personality, but he didn't open his eyes to respond.

Halya sat back, both annoyed and pleased to realize how easily Slavko's ridiculous comments had taken her mind off the situation for a few brief moments. But when she closed her eyes, she still saw Mama, screaming and reaching out for Halya as the guard brought his club down on her head over and over.

18

LILIYA

April 1943, German General Government of Poland

The girl Slavko had found looked even younger in repose. Liliya dragged her eyes away before she developed any futile attachments, and, in the dim light of the moving train, searched the scared faces around her for anyone she recognized.

For a moment, when she spotted a tall, dark-haired man in the far corner, her heart leapt into her throat. Then, the man turned his head, and she realized it wasn't Filip. He hadn't been captured, and she should be glad for it, but she couldn't forget the sense of calm he'd given her when they'd been taken the first time.

Do you trust me?

His question to her then had opened a door she didn't want to go through, but she couldn't close it.

She trusted him. She loved him.

She could easily admit that with a clear mind now, far away from his intoxicating presence, but how could she have fallen in love with someone so quickly?

Either way, it didn't matter. He was fighting with the Polish resistance, and she was on her way to Germany as a forced laborer. Even if they both managed to survive somehow, the odds were she'd never see him again. Their fleeting connection would have to remain a part of her treasured memories, like those of her family. Something she took out and mulled over when she felt alone, like a pebble worn smooth from rubbing.

It would do no good to dwell on it, or him. She had to put on a brave face and take care of Slavko.

"Lean against me and try to sleep." Liliya poked at Slavko, and he opened his eyes and glared at her.

"I was already almost asleep."

"Fine." She pulled her bag to her lap and dug through it. In her hurry to turn herself in, she'd grabbed the few closest items in the barn loft and shoved them in without thought, so she wasn't sure what she'd taken. She pulled out a tin cup, a shawl, and a chunk of bread. All useful, but none of her books or sketchbooks or pencils. Not that she'd even drawn anything worthwhile lately. With a sigh, she dropped the bag next to her, and something rolled out.

Slavko picked it up and inspected it. "Where did you get this?"

Liliya snatched the wooden nightingale from his hands and clutched it to her chest, emotion overwhelming her. She still had a piece of him with her. Opening her hands, she admired the detailed beauty of the piece.

"A friend made it for me."

"Filip?"

Even hearing his name shot longing through her, but now it was tinged with regret. What would he think when he came back and found her gone? What a fool she'd been to let herself fall for a man during this war. But she couldn't give voice to any of that now, so she only said, "How did you know?"

"I didn't until I saw your expression just now. It's the same one you get whenever he walked into a room." Slavko fluttered his eyelashes and put on a silly smile, and Liliya barely resisted the urge to hit him in his good eye. She closed her hands over the bird and shoved it back into the bag.

"I'm sorry. I'm just teasing." His lighthearted expression slipped away. "Why did you come down, anyway? They would have taken me and been satisfied."

"I didn't ask you to take my place," Liliya snapped.

"It would have been fine if you'd stayed hidden like you were supposed to." Slavko crossed his arms and sat back next to her.

"I couldn't let them take you instead. You shouldn't even be here." Liliya scooted down so she could lean back against the wall of the train car. "This is all my fault. I never should have run the first time. It led to Nina's death and you being here now."

And it led to her falling for Filip. All mistakes she couldn't rectify.

"At least we're together," Slavko said. "Now we can look out for each other."

Liliya ruffled his hair. "Yes, I suppose we can. But that means staying close to me. No mouthing off to the guards again."

Slavko touched his swollen eye, an ugly match to the one Liliya assumed Vika now sported. "I can live with that."

Liliya hugged Slavko close—and surprisingly, he let her.

"But I want you to help me with Halya." Slavko glanced at the little girl, asleep with her head tipped sideways and pressed against Slavko's opposite shoulder.

"Don't ask that of me," Liliya said. "How am I supposed to help? I have no control over what's happening now."

"I know that, but she's so young. You should have seen the way she held that book to her chest, just like Sofia always does. Anyway, I keep thinking about how Sofia would do if she were here on this journey alone, and I could only hope someone kind would look after her."

Liliya frowned as she took in the girl's pale, pinched face. Something flickered in her chest, but she ignored the sensation. She didn't have the capacity to take on caring for anyone else now. It only ended in more pain when she lost that person, and Slavko had to be her sole focus if she wanted to get him safely back to Maksym and Vika.

"Do you promise, Liliya?" Slavko stared at her, his one good eye boring into hers. "She needs us. She needs you, especially. I know you've not been yourself since, well, since you've lost everyone, but you're so strong. You can help us get through this."

Liliya's head jerked back at Slavko's assessment. Was that what he saw when he looked at her? Strength? But, even if that was his false perception, he didn't understand what he was asking. He hadn't lost what she had. He hadn't had his heart shattered into a million fragments over and over. He hadn't had to piece it back together and encase it in stone just to make it through the day.

But he wasn't wrong either. This little slip of a girl could be washed away so easily by the tides of war, slipping underwater into the darkness without a second thought.

Nina would have never let something like that happen. Neither would her mother or father. A tendril of guilt pierced a crack in her hardened soul, and against her better judgment, she nodded.

"I'll try."

And she would. She would look after the girl and keep her safe, but she'd keep her at arm's length. Slavko might have hope, but Liliya knew the impossibility of saving someone in this war.

19

VIKA

April 1943, Volhynia, Reichskommissariat Ukraine

Vika tucked the blanket around her sleeping children. The morning light illuminated the room, chasing away the darkness of night, but not the darkness hanging over their lives. No matter what Vika did, there was no escaping that.

Bohdan stirred, then threw his arm over Nadya and sighed. Vika waited for the feelings of maternal yearning to tug at her heart, but they couldn't compete with the ragged edges of fear that pierced everything she did and felt these days. That fear tainted her love, overshadowing the joy that was the fundamental basis of a mother/child relationship. It festered in her mind, driving her mad with worry.

She'd already lost one child and a beloved niece in this war. Losing another person she cared about would kill her.

"Mama?"

Sofia's soft voice broke into her thoughts, and Vika dragged her eyes away from Bohdan and Nadya.

"Yes?"

Sofia crawled up into Vika's lap, something she hadn't done in years as part of her quest to be considered mature like her big brother.

"I miss Slavko." Sofia's big brown eyes brimmed with tears. "Do you think he's all right?"

Vika swallowed hard. She didn't want to lie to Sofia, but she also didn't want to scare her daughter. Or did she? Would a healthy dose of fear help her children stay aware and smart? Every day she walked on a tightrope, navigating a delicate balance between protecting and preparing her children as they grew up in a war zone.

"Slavko is strong and smart. He can take care of himself. And Liliya is there with him, too."

"Who will take care of Liliya?" Sofia asked.

"They will take care of each other," Vika said. "That's what family does. That's why Liliya went with him."

"He saved me, Mama. I tried to follow him, but he pushed me back under the bed and told me to be still. Slavko was like Kalyna, but I wasn't."

Vika clenched her jaw. The balance had to fall on the side of preparation. The harsh reality was she couldn't protect her children. She'd seen that firsthand two days ago. But she could prepare them.

"Slavko did that because he loves you. He saved you at the cost of his freedom, and to honor that sacrifice, you must be doubly careful so that you aren't sent to Germany, too. No wandering around the village, no leaving my sight. These are dangerous times, and we are all at risk, Sofia. You must understand that and be smart."

Sofia's shoulders hitched as she swallowed a sob. "Yes, Mama. I understand, but does any of it matter? They took Slavko from our house. We aren't even safe here."

Vika ran her hand down Sofia's soft curls and said nothing, because Sofia was right. They weren't safe anywhere.

*   *   *

Vika left Sofia with strict instructions to stay in the house with the younger children and went out to the barn to do the chores. Maksym had left early to go to work, so when a man's figure stepped inside the barn, she jumped to her feet, nearly knocking over the milk bucket.

"It's just me, Vika." Filip walked toward her with his hands in the air. "Is it true then? Is she gone?"

Vika dropped back on to her stool. "Yes. Slavko, too."

"What happened?" Agony twisted his handsome features.

"They came to find her, since she'd escaped." She recited the story woodenly; she'd revisited the experience so many times in her mind, but saying it out loud still hurt. "She was hidden in the barn, so Slavko offered to go in her place. Liliya must have overheard, because before they could take him, she ran into the house and turned herself in."

Filip's fingers curled into the barn door, his knuckles white. "It must have been right after I left. And they took them both?"

Vika nodded.

Filip paced. "Did Maksym go after them? Was there nothing to be done?"

"No." Vika swallowed her pain and resumed milking the cow. Even in her grief, she still had children to feed and chores to do. "They've already been sent out on a train. Maksym couldn't help."

Filip swore under his breath and ran his hand through his hair as the barn door swung open again. This time, Oleksiy stormed in. He was leaner than the last time she'd seen him, and his severe cheekbones highlighted the dark hollows under his eyes.

"She's gone?" His gaze danced over Filip and narrowed before resting on Vika.

She pursed her lips. Bad enough that she couldn't erase the image of her eldest being taken away from her mind. Now she had to relive all of it for Liliya's suitors.

"Yes, Liliya and Slavko are gone. Nothing can be done. I don't want to talk about it anymore."

"Were you on duty for this transport, too?" Filip snapped at Oleksiy.

Oleksiy whipped around, his teeth bared in a snarl. "I fight for Ukraine now, not the Germans, but I do find it interesting how quickly the Poles filled all of our spots in the Schuma when we left."

"You seemed pretty vested in the German war effort when you dragged me in," Filip said.

"Maybe that was more personal! You tried stealing my girl!" Oleksiy yelled. "Liliya loved me long before she knew you."

"Liliya can make her own decisions about who she loves, and if you recall, she never said yes to any of your many marriage proposals." Filip's fists clenched at his sides.

"And did you actually think you had a chance? A Polish

boy?" Oleksiy growled into Filip's face. "After all the Poles did to her and her family?"

"And what about what the UPA does to the Poles? Do you think she supports that?"

Throughout their bickering, Vika milked until the cow's udders emptied, observing their passionate exchange blandly. When she was finished, she picked up the full water bucket meant for the cow's trough and threw it on the two men standing nose to nose, dousing them with the cold well water.

"You're both idiots. Liliya committed to neither of you, and she's gone, so she certainly wouldn't want you here fighting about her and bothering me. Now get out! I have things to do, and I can't moderate your stupidity now."

Filip and Oleksiy spluttered and wiped their faces, muttering their apologies shamefacedly as they left the barn. Vika didn't care if they fought elsewhere. She'd seen enough young men fired up by war and love to know they probably would do just that somewhere down the line, but she didn't have to witness it.

She had to think. She had to plan. She had to figure out how she was going to get her family back.

20

LILIYA

April 1943, German General Government of Poland

The people on the train had gone silent by the time it stopped rolling along the tracks. A soldier flung open the door and waved his arms, shouting, "*Raus! Alle raus schnell!*"

Thanks to her father's tutelage, Liliya had picked up a great deal of German since the invasion in 1939, but none of it was necessary to infer the soldier's meaning. She pulled at Slavko and Halya. "Come on, we've got to get out."

On the platform, armed guards, some holding snarling dogs, ushered them down the street into a barbed wire fenced complex. The large building inside the fence looked like it had once been a factory of some kind, but the first room they entered was empty of any machinery. A few people huddled in makeshift beds made from low boards partitioned off into boxes along the aisles, and empty "beds" revealed the piles of dirty straw used as mattresses. Something moved in the straw next to Liliya. She leaned closer to inspect it, then jerked back when she realized it was bed bugs, writhing and wriggling as they searched for a host.

"You will stay here until we are ready to inspect and clean you dirty Russians before you go any further into Germany," a German woman told them in clumsy Polish.

"I'm Ukrainian, not Russian," Slavko said.

The crack of her hand across his face silenced the crowd. "Even worse."

Slavko glared at her. He started to reply, but Liliya grabbed his arm and pulled him back.

"Stop drawing attention to us," she hissed in his ear.

"I won't be called a Russian." Slavko spat on the ground. Blood tinged his saliva.

The German woman went on for a few more minutes, rattling off instructions before dismissing them. Liliya kept a tight grip on Slavko's arm as the group broke apart and everyone found a space to sit. She threw her small bag of belongings down on the floor. "What were you thinking back there, Slavko?"

"I was thinking exactly what I said. I'm Ukrainian, and I won't be called a Russian," he repeated.

"You can't say whatever you want to these people," Liliya said. "The next time, you might not get lucky enough to only get a slap."

Slavko pushed the dirty straw aside and patted the ground next to him, ignoring his cousin. "Here. Sit, Halya. Liliya won't be able to stomach being next to me until she cools down."

Halya stood back, shifting from one foot to the other as she glanced between the two of them. "I don't want to be a bother. I can find my own bunk."

Liliya wanted to agree and send the young girl on her way. Looking out for Slavko was proving to be a bigger job than she had anticipated, and she didn't want to be responsible for someone else. But Halya's forlorn expression made Liliya wince. She rubbed her face with her hands and forced a smile. "Don't be silly. Stay with us, Halya. Slavko won't change, no matter how much I yell at him, but maybe you can help me talk some sense into him."

Halya twisted her hands and stared at the ground. "It was dumb to talk back to that woman, but I think it was also very brave to say you're Ukrainian."

Liliya stifled a surprising smile. Perhaps the girl had more grit in her than she suspected. "That's not quite what I meant, but I suppose you're not wrong."

Slavko laughed. "Of course she's not. Now come help me feed these bed bugs, Halya. The Germans expect us to be filthy and vermin-ridden, so we may as well accommodate them."

They dozed on and off until a guard roused their row and took them to another room in the back of the building. After standing in line there for nearly an hour, Liliya finally gave her name, age, religion, and place of birth as they rolled her fingers in ink and stamped her fingerprints onto a work card. Then, they pushed a cardboard panel with numbers written on it at her.

She took it, her hands shaking. Her life had been reduced to a series of numbers identifying her in the German labor force. They wouldn't remember her name or her village. They didn't know that she used to love drawing and birds. They didn't care that her favorite meal was her mother's green borsch and that no matter how many times she'd tried since her mother died, she'd never been able to replicate the sorrel-based soup.

She was number 68410 to them—nothing more.

A man instructed her to hold the panel up as he took her picture for her identification papers, then they were shoved back into their vermin-ridden bunks and left alone for the night.

Despite her exhaustion, sleep didn't come quickly for Liliya. Thoughts of Vika assaulted her—the desperation and agony on her face as they'd taken her son, the anger she had to feel toward Liliya for causing all of this. How would her aunt ever forgive her?

Liliya shook her head and tried to think of Filip instead. His easy smile, his kind eyes, his gentle, work-roughened hands. Her face flushed, but not with shame, as she remembered the way he'd touched her. No, she would never be ashamed of that. Being reduced to a number instead of a person, that was shameful. But the love-fueled caresses they'd shared were some of her most beautiful memories. They, like nothing else, would sustain her until she saw him again.

If she ever did.

21

HALYA

April 1943, German General Government of Poland

The next morning, Halya started the day like she always did—looking at the picture of her parents. She concentrated on her mother's steady gaze, searching for advice, for guidance on what she should do. But this time, she also stared at her father's image—his strong jaw and warm, open expression. She'd grown used to the ache that came with her mother's absence, but not the fresh pain of missing her father.

"What are you looking at?"

Liliya's voice made her jump, and Halya dropped the picture. Liliya reached over and picked it up, studying it. "Are these your parents?"

Halya's first instinct was to snatch the photograph out of Liliya's hands and hide it, saving it for her own eyes only. But she surprised herself by turning to Liliya instead. "Yes. My mother died not long after I was born, though, so I don't remember her. My aunt and my father raised me."

"Your mother was beautiful." Liliya leaned closer, studying the photograph. "You look just like her."

Halya looked at her mother again—the high cheekbones and twinkling eyes, the curve of her lips in a half-smile, the thick hair tumbling out of her hat. Tears brimmed on Halya's lashes. "Do you really think so?"

Liliya hesitated for a moment, then pulled Halya into an awkward side hug. "I really do."

Halya swallowed hard. "Thank you for saying that, though what I really hope for now is to be strong like my mama. My aunt, I mean. She's the toughest woman I know, but still the best mama I could have asked for. I wish I had a picture of her, too."

"If she raised you, then I'm sure you've got her strength," Liliya said.

Slavko rolled over and groaned. "What are you two going on about so early in the morning?"

"Halya's parents," Liliya said as she turned the picture so it faced Slavko. "See? She looks just like her mother."

Slavko propped himself up on an elbow and peered down at the picture, then glanced up at Halya. "Is this what you were looking for in the book the other day on the train?"

She nodded, the lump from Liliya's kind words still stuck in her throat.

Slavko leaned back and scratched his head. "Yes, they could be twins. Now, can we go back to sleep? These bed bugs kept me up all night with their voracious appetite."

Halya and Liliya left Slavko and made their way to the bathroom line, where they waited for almost an hour to use one of the three filthy toilets and sinks for the hundreds of people there. By the time they walked back to their spot, Slavko had woken up and now stood talking to a group of teenagers clustered together on the far side of the room.

"He's always been a charmer," Liliya said.

Halya's face flushed at having been caught watching Slavko. She'd never met anyone like him, so self-assured and confident. She envied his effortless manner and the way he carried himself. He talked to everyone as if they were an old friend, and people responded to him just that way.

"I wish I was as outgoing as your cousin. Even in this horrible situation, he's so at ease."

"He's more like a little brother than a cousin," Liliya said. "He has a heart of gold, but he's still a pain in my rear."

Halya surprised herself as a laugh bubbled from her lips. "That's all siblings, I think. I don't have any, but my neighbors used to fight all the time."

Slavko walked over. "The word is you can only get some soup if you have a cup or bowl to put it in. Do you have anything like that?"

Halya shook her head, but Liliya dug through her bag and pulled out the small tin cup. "We can share this."

Slavko took it and returned after a few minutes with a watery broth. "I don't think we got any actual meat or vegetables in this scoop, but I suppose it's better than nothing."

He passed it to Liliya, who took a drink, then gave it to Halya. Between the three of them, the cup emptied fast.

"I can go try to get more," Liliya offered, but before she could leave, a guard entered the room.

"Line up for your medical inspections. Men this way and women that way! Bring your clothes and personal effects!"

"I'll find you once we're done," Liliya told Slavko. "Just keep your mouth shut, all right?"

Slavko, silent for once, only nodded as Halya and Liliya followed the other women down a narrow hallway that opened into another large room. In the front of the room, five men sat at a table covered with paperwork. Large baskets lined the back wall. Two armed men stood at the door, and another walked up and down the line of women and girls as they filed in.

"Take off your clothes and put them in the basket behind you for delousing," he instructed. "Your things will be returned to you after your shower. You may keep any identification papers you have with you."

A ripple of unease moved through the group as the women glanced around nervously. No one wanted to undress in front of men.

"Now! Or we will undress you ourselves." The guard cocked his rifle. The clicking echoed through the room for a moment before everyone began to move at once.

Some women cried as they stripped off their clothes. Others clenched their teeth and stared straight ahead, as if their avoidance of the guards meant they weren't there. Halya did the latter. She was more concerned with her book and photograph. She didn't have her papers with her, and they hadn't issued her new ones yet, so she couldn't tuck the photograph into those. And she didn't want to carry both together. Someone might deem the book unnecessary and confiscate it, but she also didn't know what the delousing process entailed. What if she left both with her clothes and it damaged them? Could she slip the slim photograph past the guards? She had to try.

She tucked the photograph under her armpit, pressing it tight between her arm and ribcage. Her skin covered nearly all of it, but a small corner peeked out. Reluctantly, she pushed the book into the pocket of her skirt and prayed that it would still be there, and still be whole, after her shower.

The first woman approached the table, and a collective gasp of horror flowed through the group as one man, presumably a doctor, ran his hands up and down the woman's limbs and torso. Another man held a flashlight in one hand as he used a stick in his other to inspect her scalp and pubic area for lice. A third man asked questions while the first two worked, and the fourth took notes, then announced the verdict.

"Healthy. Lice. Shave and delouse."

Someone behind Halya translated their words as the woman up front was pushed through a doorway to another room, and the next person in line was forced to stand in front of the table. The whole ghastly process took no more than one minute, but Halya knew the shame of that inspection would live on in all of them forever.

Suddenly, Halya was next. She tried to step forward, to get through this horrifying degradation that was so much more invasive than the medical inspection her mother had failed, but her feet wouldn't move. A guard shoved her from behind, and she stumbled to the ground.

She pushed herself to her knees, glancing up at Liliya standing behind her. The older girl was frozen, indecision rippling across her features. Humiliation tore through Halya as she realized the position she'd put Liliya in. Halya didn't want her to feel responsible or have to intercede. She had to learn to take care of herself now and babyish actions like this only weakened her precarious position with her new friends. She straightened and steeled herself for the task ahead, but before she could move, Liliya clenched her jaw and stepped forward.

"I'll go first," Liliya said firmly. "You'll see, Halya, it won't be so bad."

Halya watched, trembling, as Liliya squared her naked shoulders and strode forward, her chin so high in the air she was staring at the ceiling. One of the guards leered, but Liliya didn't miss a step. Halya didn't know if it was kindness toward her or sheer stubbornness that compelled Liliya.

The men went to work, and even as the man with the flashlight paused longer than normal as he inspected Liliya's pubic area, her spine stayed ramrod straight.

"Healthy. No lice or nits. Cut and delouse," the man with the clipboard announced.

As she walked away from the table, Liliya turned and spoke in fast Ukrainian, a light Halya hadn't seen before sparkling in her eyes. "Take heart, ladies. This is the only way most of these fools will ever see a naked woman."

Some of the women cheered, and though the Germans seemingly didn't understand the full weight of her insult, it was hard to misinterpret the response it drew from the women. A guard strode forward, grabbed her arm, and dragged her to the next room.

Liliya's courage had the intended effect, and Halya moved forward easier, thinking that despite Liliya's annoyance with her cousin Slavko's outspokenness, maybe she wasn't so different from him after all. In fact, she was just as feisty as him.

Halya flinched as the men began their inspection, pulling open her mouth to look at her teeth and combing through her hair to check for lice. Her face burned, but like Liliya, she kept her head high and stared straight ahead. When the man checking her limbs tugged at her left arm, she resisted, keeping it pressed tight against her so the photograph wouldn't fall.

He swore and pulled harder, wrenching her arm up. She cried out, not from pain but from distress, as the photograph fell to the ground.

"What's this?" The man spoke in stilted Ukrainian as he grabbed the picture and peered at it, disdain twisting his features into an ugly mask.

"A picture of my parents," Halya whispered. Her bravado fled and she crossed her arms over her chest.

The guard stared at Halya, then held up the photograph and slowly ripped it in half. He smiled as he turned the halves and ripped it again, then again, until all that remained of her parents were scraps of paper. An eye. Half of an ear. The top of a hat.

"Identification papers only. You are all *Untermenschen*." Spittle from the guard's mouth hit Halya's cheek. He crumpled the pieces in his fist, then let them fall to the floor as he stared at her. "Subhuman. Remember that."

The man with the clipboard announced her results. "Number 68411. Healthy. Nits. Shave and delouse."

They pushed her into the next room where, still naked, the women were lined up behind four chairs, each manned by a person with shears. As soon as they'd chopped off the hair of one person, another took her place, and the process began again.

Halya touched her mahogany braid with trembling fingers, Mama's voice whispering in her ear.

I think the thing that reminds me the most of her is your hair.

She'd lost the picture, and now, she was losing her hair.

Halya sat in the chair and closed her eyes, unwilling to witness them cutting away the part of her most like her mother. Each snip of his scissors made her wince, like a physical blow, hurting even more than when he nicked her scalp.

When he finished, she opened her eyes and touched her head. Uneven chunks of hair stuck up all over, shorn nearly to the skin in some spots and left a bit longer in others. Her fingers came back red and damp with blood from the wounds, then the man pushed her hands away and slathered a thick, tarry substance on her head.

She stared at her hands, trembling in her lap, and thought of the way Mama had fought back, fierce and brave, against men with weapons to try to save her. Mama had fought for family. For her.

Halya drew a shuddering breath and looked up. Maybe she looked like her mother, Alina, but in this moment in her life, Halya needed to be like her mama. Katya.

She didn't remember moving to the next area, but suddenly shower heads above her turned on, dousing them with cold water.

Liliya, again at her side, gave her a gentle nudge with her elbow. Because she didn't have nits, her hair hadn't been shorn like Halya's, but her beautiful golden braid had been hacked off at its base, leaving her hair to fall in loose waves around her jaw line.

"Try to rinse off, all right?" Liliya followed her own advice, then leaned over and helped Halya scrub the black goop from her head as best she could. The water shut off after only a few minutes, and they sat wet and shivering until they dried. Two men dusted them with a powder as they left the showers and entered a room filled with the baskets of their freshly deloused clothing. Hands shaking, Halya numbly dug through them, searching for her own shirt and skirt with the hidden book.

"Do you see our old clothes?" she whispered to Liliya.

"Here's some of mine." Liliya held up a dress, then dug into the pocket and pulled out a small wooden bird. "My dress is discolored, but my bird is still there." She clutched the bird to her chest for a moment, then resumed digging. "Here, isn't this yours?"

Halya took the misshapen skirt and ripped through the pocket, searching for the book, but it was empty. She turned the skirt inside out, then plunged her hand back into the basket, groping each piece of clothing before turning the whole thing upside down.

"It's gone," she whispered, devastation sucking the air out of her lungs as she finally accepted the futility of her search. "They took my photograph, and now, my book is gone."

Grief pulled her down, the weight of her losses too heavy for her narrow shoulders. Her legs buckled, and she dropped to her knees. She'd lost everyone she loved, she'd lost her photograph of her birth mother, and now, she'd lost her poems.

"I have nothing," she cried. Her head dropped into her

hands as tears rolled out of her eyes. "And I don't know how to be brave like my mama."

The large cafeteria, filled with other workers, droned with the quiet hum of hushed conversation. Halya poked at the one piece of rutabaga in her watery soup. A small chunk of black bread sat next to it. It had been hours since her hair had been shorn and she'd lost her picture and poetry book, but her eyes were still swollen from tears. Her stomach growled, empty like the cavernous hole in her chest, and despite the poor quality of the food, Halya shoveled it into her mouth.

"Thank you for helping me earlier," Halya said. "I'll try to be stronger. I promise."

Liliya nodded as she continued her constant scanning of the crowd. "I still don't see him."

Halya wiped her mouth with the back of her hand. All around her, quiet, scared people hunched over and ate, just like her, but she didn't recognize anyone.

"Do you think he's all right?" Liliya whispered. Worry creased her brow.

Halya swallowed a mouthful of bread. She may have only known Slavko a few days, but he'd already made quite an impression. "Of any of us, he's probably doing the best."

Liliya gave her a weak smile. "You're right. He always comes out fine, but he has such a mouth. I'm afraid he'll get himself in trouble."

"There he is!" Halya straightened and pointed as Slavko came out of the food line. Liliya stood and waved, and he sauntered over and sat down as if they were having a comfortable family meal at home.

"Quite the cuisine we have, isn't it?" Slavko quipped as he dunked his bread into the soup.

He looked odd with his newly cropped hair, but then Halya touched her own clipped locks, and her face flushed. She hadn't seen herself yet, but she was sure it wasn't pretty.

As if he were reading her mind, Slavko grinned. "Who would have thought you two girls could pull off short hair so well?"

Liliya let out a half cry, half laugh and threw her arms around him. "I've been worried sick about you," she cried.

"Don't be silly." Slavko gave Halya a wink across the table. "You know I always take care of myself."

After they ate, they were shown to new, cleaner barracks to wait in until they shipped out. Halya and Liliya chose a low bed near the door. She thought of Slavko, alone in his barracks without anyone to look out for him or talk to.

"Do you think Slavko is lonely without you?" she asked.

"Slavko makes friends wherever he goes," Liliya said. "I worry more that he'll speak his mind to a guard again and get in trouble, but he probably already has a group of boys following him around. People are attracted to him like flies to honey."

A female guard came in and addressed them in slow Ukrainian mixed with Polish. "Lights out in thirty minutes. Tomorrow, you will be shipped west, where you will be assigned to your posts." She pulled small square badges out of a bulging envelope. "In the meantime, you're to take these and sew them to the top right side of all your clothing. Line up and get yours, and remember, you must wear it always," she instructed as she handed Halya two.

White with dark blue letters, the badge read: OST.

"What does it mean?" Liliya asked.

"You are *Ostarbeiters*," the guard said. "Eastern workers traveling here to help the German war effort."

"Not by choice," Liliya muttered.

Despite herself, Halya smiled. Yes, Liliya wasn't so different from Slavko at all.

22

VIKA

April 1943, Volhynia, Reichskommissariat Ukraine

Vika handed Nadya to Sofia and braced herself as Lyubov Yuriivna marched toward them, eyes crackling and skirts snapping, then grabbed Lyubov's arm before it could connect with her cheek.

"How dare you show your face here!" Spittle flew from Lyubov's mouth as she wrenched away from Vika's grip.

Vika stepped back and pulled Bohdan closer. A line of sweat trickled down her back, making her shirt stick to her, but it wasn't the warm spring day making her perspire. She hated confrontation, but she wasn't going to let this woman scold her, especially in front of her children. "I shop here every week. I live in this village. Where else would you have me go when I need something?" She kept her voice even, but her heart pounded in her ears.

"Your husband thinks he's so high and mighty, doesn't he? Making the forced labor lists?" Lyubov's mouth twisted, and for a moment, Vika softened as she glimpsed the grief hiding below the anger boiling at Lyubov's surface.

"He doesn't enjoy it, if that's what you're suggesting." Vika pulled herself up to her full height. "He doesn't want to be a village elder, and he certainly doesn't want to send our young people to work in Germany. He's doing everything he can to keep people from going."

A strangled cry rushed past Lyubov's lips. "Well, it's not enough. They took my nephew yesterday because your husband put him on the list. My sister is out of her mind with worry."

Vika drew a shuddering breath. "I'm sorry."

What else could she say? Maksym had quotas to fill. The Germans wanted more *Ostarbeiters*, and the means by which they procured them were only getting more violent. Maksym didn't want to help them, but he had to choose: find people to send to Germany to work on their farms and in their factories or be shot.

He chose to make a list, and that choice was killing him. Maybe not as fast as a bullet to the head, but the effect was nearly the same.

"You are collaborators! When Stalin comes back, you'll be lucky if he lets you live long enough to make it to the gulags!"

"Might I remind you, my own son and niece are there." Vika struggled not to scream at the woman. Every minute of every day, she worried over Slavko and Liliya's safety.

Lyubov dropped her face into her hands and wailed, so Vika

stepped around the woman. "Please give my apologies to your sister," she murmured.

Vika hurried her family down the dirt road that led to their home just south of the village. Green wheat fields flanked the road on one side, and woods hugged the other, shading them from the warm sun. Newly awakened bees happily buzzed through the spring air, hopping from flower to flower as they drank from the vast bounty of Ukraine's flora. But even with the picturesque scenery along this stretch of road, Vika couldn't stop thinking about what had just happened or scanning the area for soldiers or resistance fighters.

"What's a collaborator?" Bohdan asked, breaking into her thoughts. At nearly ten years old, he was far too serious for his age. But then, growing up in the middle of a war didn't make for an easy childhood.

"Nothing for you to worry about," Vika said.

"It's someone who helps the enemy," Sofia said. She'd been silent since the exchange with Lyubov, but Vika wasn't surprised. Her sweet chatterbox of a daughter had dimmed since Slavko and Liliya left, and now anger fueled her words. In years past, Sofia would be filling her arms with the copious flowers growing along the fields, but now, she walked by them without even looking their way.

Bohdan's mouth dropped open. "Is that what Tato is? Is that what we are? We're helping the Germans?"

"No! Of course not." Vika's fingers involuntarily tightened around Bohdan's shoulder as they stepped into their yard. He whimpered and slipped away from her grasp. "Your father hates the Germans as much as anyone else. He's just doing what he must to keep us safe."

"Then why did that woman call us that? Will Stalin really send us to the gulags?" Bohdan pushed the gate open and stepped into their yard.

"Enough questions for now. Sofia, bring Nadya inside, please." Vika saw words forming on Sofia's open lips and raised a hand. "Without comment."

"Why is Sofia so grumpy all the time now?" Bohdan whispered to Vika as Sofia and Nadya went in the house. "She never plays with me anymore."

Vika thought about her own brothers, arrested and sent to the gulags only months after she'd married and moved to Maky. When they were young, they'd fought more often than not, but now, years later, Vika would give anything to see them again.

"Brothers and sisters aren't always sunflowers and poppies, Bohdanko. Like any garden, there can be rough patches, but it doesn't change her love for you."

Bohdan pulled his coat tighter and sighed. "I think she's so angry about Slavko and Liliya leaving that she doesn't know how to love us anymore."

Vika blinked as she struggled with an appropriate response, but luckily, Bohdan walked off to the barn, leaving Vika wondering how her young son had so eloquently summed up in one sentence all the concerns she had for Sofia.

* * *

"I have no choice, Vikusia," Maksym said as Vika relayed Lyubov's story to him later that night while they whispered in bed. "You know that. If I don't make a list of workers to send, they'll do the same to me as they did to Danylo when he was in this position before me."

Vika flinched, the same way she had at the sound of the Wehrmacht officer's pistol firing into Danylo's head. The whole village had been forced to witness his execution, and after that, nobody, not even the few villagers still enamored with the Germans, had stepped up to take his place.

"But they shot him for stealing, too. It wasn't just the missing labor lists. He wasn't turning all the food he collected in to the Germans," Vika said.

"It doesn't matter. They're unpredictable and they don't care about any of us. Besides, as much as you hate this job, it's keeping our family together here. You or I could be called up, and now that the required age of laborers is only ten, so could Sofia. And soon enough, Bohdan."

"I know, and I'm grateful you're able to do that for us," Vika said. "But it doesn't make this easier on you, and it doesn't make it easy for us in the village. People are angry. I don't feel safe going there anymore."

Maksym rubbed his face with his hands. "I didn't want to be a village elder, and now I'm trying to choose the most appropriate people I can for the labor lists. Communists, criminals, but sometimes I have to send people I don't want to . . ." he trailed off.

Vika squeezed the knot of tense muscles clumped at his shoulder, and Maksym sighed and rested his cheek against her arm. "Her nephew was put on the list because he's been helping the Soviet partisans. The UPA keeps tabs on these things, so Oleksiy passed on the names of some known communist collaborators. We've seen what Stalin and his ideals did in your old village and in this village before the Nazis invaded. Anyone who supports that isn't someone I want around when this godforsaken war finally ends."

"All right, but what will you do when they want another list in a few weeks?"

Maksym pursed his lips. "I have a plan."

Vika snatched her hand away, but it was anger, not fear, that fueled her words. "What plan could you possibly have that won't get you killed?"

"I talked to the raion chiefs at the meeting last night. We've already filled over seventy percent of the labor quota before I came on. As you know, anyone working on the roads, in the fields, and at the sawmill is exempt. We're going to try to place more people in jobs there so they can stay in the village, and in turn, try to get the Germans to lower the quota since we don't have the means to fill it."

Vika propped herself up on an elbow and stared down at him in the darkness. "And you don't think the Germans would notice a bunch of extra workers milling about in the fields and come to you to find out why?"

"We heard of another raion that did it and the district commissar eventually lowered their quota. Our raion chiefs think we can try the same thing here."

"Even if your quota is lowered, you'll still have to send people. You can't avoid it altogether."

Maksym shook his head and set his hand on her arm. "No, I can't."

"Will your numbers game save Sofia now that they've lowered the ages?"

"Right now, the biggest thing protecting her is me. As unfair as it is, as long as I am a village elder, my family is safe."

"The family you have left." Vika closed her eyes and pictured Slavko's sweet face.

Maksym jerked his hand back. "There's more going on than that. The UPA is clearing the countryside of Germans in some areas, pushing them back into the cities. Oleksiy thinks it will happen here soon. If it does, I won't have to make any lists, no matter what the quota is."

Vika's eyes flew open. "That's all fine and good, but they'll still want laborers. We'll have to worry about raids."

"Maybe. Maybe not. If the UPA does well enough, maybe they can drive the Germans out completely," Maksym said.

A glimmer of hope kindled inside Vika. "Do you really think that?"

"I hear things, but I'm not in the UPA, so I don't know everything," Maksym said. "I do know they're taking out German supply trains regularly and attacking the German raiding groups when they come out of the cities."

Vika looked over at her sleeping children. Bohdan, with his arm flung over Nadya's face, and Sofia, curled in a ball facing the wall.

"Whatever happens, we can't let them take anyone else we love."

23

LILIYA

April 1943, German General Government of Poland

Liliya stared at the deep purple bruise on her arm where the guard had jerked her forward after she'd mouthed off. She was lucky to only have that mark on her and lucky that none of the Germans seemed to have understood her. She poked it, cringing as a wave of pain radiated from the center where his thumb had pressed the hardest. Slavko was right. She did still have her fire, and she didn't regret any of it. She was tired of living in fear all the time, moderating her words and actions to appease one of the many aggressors around her. Let them do what they wanted, but she wouldn't take it lying down. She didn't care anymore, and she would have done a lot more if she didn't have Slavko, and now Halya, to worry about.

Perhaps she shouldn't have given Slavko such a hard time about his smart mouth. A smile played on her lips as she remembered the shock on everyone's faces, Halya's in particular. Her gaze dropped to the small form sleeping next to her, and the anger that had flowed through her like a raging river for so long slowed. Halya was tough, there was no question about that, but she was also terrified. Liliya didn't know what it was about her, but despite what she'd told Slavko about wanting to keep her distance, the little girl brought out a maternal instinct in her.

Slavko was reminded of Sofia when he saw Halya, but Liliya saw something else. Maybe it was the determined set of her jaw despite the terror shining in her wide blue eyes, but Halya's naiveté and innocence reminded Liliya of Nina when they were young—always trusting and optimistic, willing to follow Liliya to the ends of the earth. Liliya had failed Nina, but maybe she could save Halya.

Halya shifted restlessly in her sleep next to Liliya, and Liliya fought the urge to draw the little girl close and tell her to be brave, that everything would be all right.

She didn't want to lie.

She didn't know if everything would be all right. They were hundreds of miles from home. They had no idea if their families were safe and if they'd ever see them again. And poor Halya had lost the last connection she had with her dead mother. Liliya knew that pain, and her heart ached for the younger girl.

Maybe Halya reminded Liliya of herself.

Moonlight filtered into the room through a dingy window, illuminating a woman in the next bunk scribbling furiously with a pencil. Liliya leaned toward her.

"Do you have any more paper?"

The woman looked up, her pursed lips highlighting the gauntness of her cheeks. "Why should I share it with you?"

Liliya reached into her pocket and pulled out the crust of bread she'd saved from their meager supper. She'd learned quickly to always keep back a bite or two for later. "I'll trade you. One piece of paper and the use of your pencil for this."

The woman's eyes glittered as she nodded, her hand snaking out to snatch the bread from Liliya. She shoved it into her mouth and closed her eyes, chewing slowly. Liliya wondered where she'd been before arriving here because she'd clearly been starving for a long time. Was this what her future looked like?

Liliya kept her hand extended until the woman placed the pencil and a piece of paper in it. With a nod of thanks, she lowered her eyes and began to draw.

At first, the pencil moved in jerks as she fought to find her rhythm. Each stroke was hard fought and painful, threaded with memories, but it helped that she didn't know these people. She focused on remembering the angle of their faces, the tilt of their eyes.

By the time she finished, she was emotionally exhausted. She shoved the pencil back at the woman.

"You're pretty good," the woman said. She leaned over and eyed the sketch. "Were you an artist before you came here?"

"No," Liliya said shortly. "I don't draw anymore."

She put the paper in her pocket where she wouldn't have to look at it. She'd only done this for Halya, and she'd never do it again.

* * *

Before dawn, they were ushered onto another train without breakfast. Thankfully, Slavko was able to squeeze into the same car as them. The slatted rails allowed a breeze to move through the stagnant car, carrying away the smell of the slop bucket in the corner where everyone relieved themselves.

"Why did they bother cleaning us if they were just going to throw us on another dirty train?" Slavko asked, but no one answered.

Darkness had crept in on the day by the time the train finally lurched to a stop. Halya dozed on Liliya's shoulder, but Liliya couldn't sleep.

The door whipped open, and a man in a Wehrmacht uniform set a bucket and a large loaf of bread on the floor, then without a word, slammed the door shut again.

Everyone stared in shock for a moment at the first food or water they'd seen since leaving the transit camp, then an older boy grabbed the bread and began breaking off pieces and passing them around. Others, jerked into motion by his actions, swarmed the bucket, using their hands to scoop water into their dry mouths. Slavko scrambled to the bucket, dragging Liliya by the hand behind him.

"Come on! You too, Halya. Get up here!"

Liliya plunged her hand into the bucket and grimaced when the tepid, foul-tasting water splashed her lips, but she swallowed down the liquid greedily.

She reached into the crowd and grabbed a hunk of bread from the boy dispersing it and divided it up between the three of them. "Here. It's not much, but at least everyone got some."

"I think you're the youngest one here, Halya, but not by

much." Slavko ripped a piece of bread off and chewed with his mouth open.

Liliya glanced around as she gnawed on the stale bread. Slavko was right. Most of the people crammed into the car were teenagers, but none seemed as young as Halya. The little girl stuck her hand in her pocket, then winced. Liliya knew she was looking for her poetry book and photograph, and she vowed to give Halya the drawing as soon as they were settled and the risk of it being taken or lost while they traveled lessened. It wasn't the same thing as having the photograph, but maybe it would help.

Slavko turned and pointed, his finger slipping into the wide cracks between the boards behind them. "Look! That one is headed home."

Liliya peered through the gap at the other train parked a few tracks over. As they watched, a door slid open, revealing a mass of people lying on the floor of the car. Two skinny men dressed in rags came to the entrance, dragging another body. A soldier covered his face with a handkerchief as he bent over to assess it. He waved a few more men over, and together, they pulled the body from the car and slid it to the ground.

The first soldier pointed and gave instructions in German, then the other two soldiers dragged the body over to the ditch alongside the tracks and dumped it there.

"They're just leaving him there like that?" Halya whispered.

A woman came to the door of the car, her face red and puffy from tears, holding a tiny bundle. The soldier held out his arms, but she hesitated, shaking her head and backing away. He yelled at her and poked her with a club, then gave her a sharp smack. She cried out, then passed the bundle over.

"It's a baby," Liliya breathed.

The tiny, still form flopped like a rag doll in the soldier's hands. He held it out far from his body, a grimace of disgust on his face, and walked over to the ditch and dumped it by the other body. The woman screamed and tried to jump out after him, but another soldier pushed her back with the end of his rifle and slammed the door shut. The soldiers ambled away as the mother's wails filtered through the thin walls, echoing around them.

Liliya shuddered, her eyes still on the baby lying in the ditch. Halya's small, cold hand slipped into hers, and Liliya squeezed it, surprised at the comfort it gave her.

Slavko pressed his lips to the crack in the rail car and called out over the tracks. "Hey, where were you? And where are you going?"

Across the way, a man pushed his face against the interior of his own car, his fingers snaking through to grip the board as he shouted, "We were in Germany. Slave laborers. But we're too sick to keep working so they're sending us home."

"Those of us who survive the trip!" someone on the other end of their car yelled, then coughed. "We've got typhus in here."

"They starved us, beat us, and left us with no shelter from the elements, then got mad when we fell ill. They're evil. Pure evil," the first man added.

An officer walked up to the other car and banged his truncheon against it. "Shut up! No talking!"

The man slipped back into the darkness of his car, and Liliya sat down and hugged her knees to her chest.

A hushed conversation filtered in between the cracks, and

Liliya peered out and saw the two men who had thrown the bread and water into their car smoking just outside where she sat.

"Those fools should be grateful. They're the last shipment the Führer is wasting money on to send home. After this, useless laborers will go to the death camps."

"I'm surprised he didn't do it sooner," the other man said. "This is such a needless use of time and resources."

"What are they saying?" Slavko dropped down next to her and leaned in. His German was rudimentary at best, and Liliya had never been more grateful for that.

"Nothing much, just talking about their families," she lied.

Slavko frowned as their train car jolted back to life with a lurch, but he didn't press her. They began to move down the tracks again, the momentarily grateful chatter at receiving bread and water now replaced with the silence of abject fear.

24

HALYA

April 1943, Germany

At the final stop, they were ushered out of the car, through a large brick building, and into the open yard behind it. Surrounded by a brick wall, they filed in and filled the space. After nearly two full days in the cattle car, the smell of sweat and fear clung to them in a dirty fog.

"You will sleep here overnight," the guard announced. "In the morning, you'll receive your work assignments. There are toilets inside for your use, but only two, so don't all rush in at once."

"He didn't mention food," Slavko said.

"I still have a bit of bread left from earlier." Liliya held out the crust, but Slavko pushed it away.

"You eat it. I'll be fine."

Halya's stomach growled as Liliya ignored him and split the bread into three even bites, then forced it into their hands.

"Eat it," she ordered.

Halya complied, letting the dried bread linger until saliva pooled in her mouth and softened it enough to swallow. Liliya both fascinated and terrified her, and Halya didn't dare disobey.

When Liliya went to fill their water cup, Halya asked the question that had been turning in her mind for the last few days. "I'm very grateful, but why are you both so good to me? Sharing your food, your sleeping spaces. You have each other to lean on and you barely know me."

It felt like the most words she'd said in a row in days, and pink tinged her cheeks by the time she finished.

Slavko thought for a moment. "Liliya is one of the best people I know. Kind and fearless. She's lost a lot, but she's still brave. Everyone loves her." He chuckled. "Especially the boys back home. She may be slow to warm up to you because she's afraid to let people in, but don't give up on her."

Halya absorbed his words, letting the truth of them ring inside her. She'd seen all that and more already in Liliya. It was nice to have someone confirm her assessment, but he hadn't answered her whole question. She needed to know both of their reasons for helping her.

"And for you?" Halya held her breath, waiting for his reply.

Slavko's jaw tightened, and for the first time, a crack of emotion glimmered through his bravado. "I think it's because you remind me very much of my little sister. Sofia. She's about your age. She loves to read, like you. If I can't protect her anymore, maybe it will help me feel better to protect someone like her. That's what I hoped, at least."

"Did it help?" Halya asked.

"Maybe. I don't think anything will keep me from missing her, but I'd like to think that if she were in your spot, someone would look out for her like we are for you." He cleared his throat. "Now, if we can stay together, I think we'll be just fine."

His words, so like what her father had told her, sent warmth coursing through her, and for the first time since she'd left home, she felt a glimmer of hope that she could endure this. They sat in amicable silence until Liliya returned, then together, they found a spot on the ground along the wall and settled in for a long night.

"At least there are no bed bugs here in the grass," Slavko said.

He lay on the other side of Liliya, but Halya could see his impish smile in the moonlight.

Liliya ruffled his stubbled hair. "Thank goodness for small favors."

Halya closed her eyes. She wanted to cross the divide between them, to join in their easy camaraderie, but she didn't know what to say. Ever since she'd lost her poetry book, words escaped her. The right saying or perfect turn of phrase slipped through her fingers like stewed cherries—slick, with no purchase. So instead of speaking, she scooted closer to Liliya. It was enough to just be here with them for now, but maybe one day, she would find her voice again.

* * *

In the morning, they were lined up in wide rows so businessmen and farmers could walk up and down the aisles, inspecting them like livestock at the market.

"Stand close together," Liliya instructed. "Maybe we can all go to the same place."

A man dressed in a suit walked toward them. When he reached Liliya, he picked up her hands and scrutinized them, then gripped her chin, forcing her mouth open. He turned her head side to side as he looked at her teeth. Halya felt Slavko bristling next to her, but before he could speak out, Liliya elbowed him hard. The man looked over Halya and Slavko the same way, then nodded and waved a hand at one of the guards.

In an instant, they, along with two dozen other people who'd been selected by the businessman, were ushered out of the room and into another train car. This time, the ride took less than hour before the doors opened.

"Where are we?" Slavko asked the guard.

"Leipzig," he said. "From here, you walk."

Their barracks room consisted of three high bunk beds along low-ceilinged drafty walls. Eighteen beds for twenty girls. Liliya grabbed a bottom bunk near the door, then waved Halya over. The thin, straw-filled mattresses on the bunk beds in the barracks would hardly be considered comfortable in most situations, but after days of travel, they were almost a welcome sight.

"We can share this bed and the two blankets," Liliya said as she patted the folded blankets on the bed closest to the small stove. "We'll stay warmer that way when it gets cold."

Halya's insides shriveled at the idea of being in these bleak barracks come winter.

"And see." Liliya pointed to the solitary sink and toilet across the room as she continued her forced, cheerful commentary. "Indoor plumbing. It's almost decadent."

Halya stared at the toilet sitting out in the open. "I'd rather have the privacy of my outhouse back home."

"I have something for you." Liliya pulled a scrap of paper out from under her pillow. She unfolded it carefully, revealing jagged edges and a blank page on one side. But when she turned it over, Halya gasped.

Her parents stared back at her. Smooth pencil strokes outlined their features. Alina's half-smile. Her father's crinkled eyes.

"How did you do this?" Halya took the paper, running her finger reverently down the edges of their faces. "How did you recreate it so perfectly?"

Liliya shrugged. "I have a very good memory. When that guard ripped up your real one, I thought you might like a substitute."

"Thank you," Halya said. It felt so inadequate, so paltry in comparison to the gift Liliya had given her: a window to her past she thought closed forever. She threw her arms around Liliya and squeezed. "I've never had a friend like you."

Liliya stiffened in Halya's embrace, then slowly relaxed. "Well, I suppose you have me now," she said.

* * *

The first day set the tone for their miserable new routine. Surrounded by barbed wire, their barracks—filled mostly with other Ukrainians and some Poles—sat next to a former electroplating and electric motor factory, now repurposed to make armaments used in the Nazi war effort. Halya didn't work in the same area of the factory as Liliya, but she did work with two other girls who slept across from them, Svetlana and Luba.

"We're making the weapons they use against us," Halya said to Liliya after her first day of work. She couldn't stop thinking about the guns the men had wielded as they rounded her and her mother up at the market. "We're contributing to the war against our own people."

Each day after roll call, they walked down the street together, under a guard's watch, to the factory where Halya stood at the end of a conveyer belt as gun cartridge shells spilled into a sectioned box. Her job was to make sure each cartridge shell stood straight and pick out any crooked or disfigured ones. Sometimes, she fell asleep standing there, and, if she was lucky, Luba poked her as she walked by before the *Werkschutz* monitoring them hit her awake. A stout, strong girl, Luba's job was to carry the filled boxes to the next room.

Once, while the *Werkschutz* was away, Luba dropped a box, spilling the shells all over the floor, and the guard, Helga, an overzealous young woman in the BDM, the female Nazi youth group, beat her with the butt of her whip until she passed out. Svetlana and Halya had to practically carry her back to their barracks, where Liliya cleaned her wounds as best she could. After that, Halya carried the heavy boxes while Luba did Halya's former job.

Slavko worked in the section of the factory that produced

Panzerfäusts. Luckily, it was nearby, so they were able to see him on the walks to work and dinner. The long workdays passed in a blur, each one running into the next. Wake up at 5 a.m., stand for roll call, drink ersatz coffee and, if they were lucky, eat a piece of bread on the way to work, start work at 7 a.m., work until 7 p.m., walk home, do roll call again, eat some watery broth and another piece of bread, sleep, repeat. She tried to remember home—the tang of sun-warmed sour cherries plucked off the branches of her favorite reading tree or the taste of creamy milk fresh from the cow; Mama's cool hand caressing her cheek and combing the tangles from her thick hair; Tato's booming laugh and eyes crinkled with mirth as he told her silly stories. She took out those memories, the only things rooting her to her old life, and relived them constantly in her mind until they dulled, losing their power to transport her.

"I miss home so much," she said to Liliya as they walked back to their barracks one night. The cool evening air, a welcome relief after the heat of the earlier hours, smelled of rubber and metal. Industry, not open farmlands. Claustrophobia clawed at Halya.

"Ukraine is in your heart. Your family is in your heart. You will be with them again, and until then, Slavko and I are your family." Liliya wrapped an arm around Halya's thin shoulders.

For a moment, a sense of peace, of belonging, surged through Halya. She wasn't alone. Then they rounded the corner outside their barracks and nearly stumbled over an older woman prone on the ground as a guard beat her with a rubber truncheon. The woman pleaded for mercy, but the guard had none, her arm raising and slamming down again and again.

Blood splattered up from a cut on her face, showering Halya's cheek with the woman's pain.

Liliya wiped the blood off Halya's face with her sleeve and increased her pace, tugging Halya along with her. "I saw her steal a piece of bread at supper," she whispered.

Halya looked back at the woman—her skinny legs splayed out on the ground like broken sticks, blood oozing from her temple, bony hands held up over her face. Of course she needed more bread. They all did. They were expected to live and work on starvation rations. The *Ostarbeiter* workers of the Soviet Union and Reichskommissariat Ukraine had it the worst, followed closely by the Poles. Other western European nationalities—French, Italian, Dutch—received more food. Meat in their soup. Vegetables besides rutabagas. More bread. Still, everyone was hungry all the time.

The labor required of them necessitated a healthy diet, but then, the Nazis didn't care about that. *Untermenschen* were disposable sources of labor, meant to be used up until there was nothing left, then eradicated.

Seeing that woman was a stark reminder. Halya's heart didn't matter in Germany, only her ability to work under impossible conditions. It wasn't a question of if she would crack under their torture, but when.

25

VIKA

July 1943, Volhynia, Reichskommissariat Ukraine

"We have to go!" Maksym burst into the house, letting in a rush of sticky summer air. Beads of sweat dripped down his forehead. "I've already hitched the horses. Grab some blankets and food. I'll get the children."

Vika dropped the *rushnyk* she was embroidering for her sister and stood. "What's happening?"

"The Germans are burning Tulychiv." Maksym shook Sofia awake, then scooped Bohdan and Nadya into his arms. "And they've hit Radovychi and Lityn as well. They may come this way next."

A dull roar pulsed in Vika's ears as she grabbed the loaf of bread she'd made earlier that night for breakfast the next day, some *salo,* and a jar of preserves. Tulychiv was only a few kilometers down the road. They knew of many villages destroyed by the Germans as retribution for partisan actions, but never this close to home.

Maksym took the children outside, and the smell of smoke wafted into the house. Vika threw the food into a pile of bedding and rolled it up. Outside, the horizon glowed to the east, and a dark smear of gray reached up into the sky, covering the stars. She set the bedding in the wagon and gave each child a blanket before tucking the food and extra bedding in the front corner.

"Where will we go?" She climbed up in the seat next to Maksym, and he clucked the horses forward.

"Osa. A Polish man I helped escape across the Buh River last week said we could use his empty house if we needed to flee our village."

Vika didn't know if she should laugh or cry over the ridiculousness of their situation. In the past month, as UPA-led attacks on Polish settlements increased, many Poles had fled or been hidden by Ukrainian families. Now, her family would be hiding in their Polish friend's house, a prime example of how so many people, Ukrainians and Poles alike, still helped each other despite the friction between the two groups.

This wasn't the case in every village, though.

Vika abhorred violence against innocent civilians of any ethnicity, and now, the battle between the Ukrainians and Poles looped in a vicious cycle of atrocities in the name of what should have been good causes—freedom for each nationality and unity against the Nazis and Soviets. She didn't know if the greater tragedy was the missed opportunity for the two groups to work together to defeat the foreign invaders and end this war sooner or the senseless deaths themselves. The ugliness of war was something she'd given up on understanding long ago.

"The UPA are gathering to fight the Germans in Tulychiv," Maksym said. "I saw Oleksiy riding through on his way."

"Do you think they can stop them before they get here?"

"I don't know," Maksym said. "If the UPA can get men there quick enough, maybe."

Maksym drew the reins up as a pregnant woman with a small child in her arms crossed the road in front of them.

"Do you need a ride?" Maksym called out.

The woman shook her head. "My husband built me a bunker in the woods. I'm going there."

"With the baby?" Vika said. "Come with us. We're going to a house."

The woman hesitated, then shook her head again. "He won't know where to find me. I want to stay close."

She hurried into the woods without waiting for a reply. Vika saw other villagers doing the same further down the road, escaping into the cover of the trees and brush, hoping the Germans wouldn't look farther than the village buildings for retribution.

"Her husband is probably fighting," Maksym said.

Vika shook her head. "I don't recognize her from the village."

"We've had a lot of people displaced with the increase in German attacks. I'm sure she's staying with family."

"What will we do if they burn Maky or come to Osa next?" Vika asked. "Where will we go?"

"I don't know," Maksym said. "But I've been thinking, maybe it's time we consider leaving."

Vika turned in her seat to stare at him, but he wouldn't meet her gaze. The moonlight filtering through the trees highlighted the dark bags under his eyes and the deep lines etched into his forehead. The worry and fatigue of his job as village elder had aged him, but so had working at the stable under the Germans while passing gleaned information from his jobs on to Oleksiy in the UPA. Maksym walked the fine line between the oppressors and oppressed daily, and the toll it took was evident.

"Leaving our home?" Vika whispered.

He shook his head once. "Leaving Volhynia."

"But how would Liliya and Slavko find us? We can't leave without them."

"We have to protect the children we have here, too, Vika."

"I know that, but that doesn't mean we can abandon the others."

Maksym kept his eyes on the road, his face expressionless. "Instead of waiting for them to come to us, we can head toward Germany and find them."

Vika slapped her hands against her thighs in frustration. "What if we pass by each other? Or what if they're transferred? We'll have no way of knowing. Tell me you're not serious!"

He didn't answer, his movements calm and steady as he guided the horses forward, and she realized with a jolt that this wasn't a spur of the moment suggestion. Her husband had been contemplating this momentous decision for some time.

She grabbed his arm and squeezed hard. "How long have you been thinking about this?"

Maksym finally looked at her, but only for a moment before dropping his eyes and clucking the horses along faster.

"Since the moment I became a village elder."

* * *

Maksym rode out the next morning to check on things back home, leaving Vika and the children in the abandoned house to wait.

As she fed the children the loaf of bread she'd grabbed when they fled, she pondered what they would do if Maksym came back and said their house was gone. Would they be able to stay here in Osa? Would they have to live in their wagon in the woods? Or would they really leave Volhynia altogether?

The morning hours ticked by slowly as Vika waited, turning those questions over in her head, and when Maksym finally returned in the heat of the afternoon, she ran out to greet him.

"Tell me everything!" she said as he sat back and stopped his horse. "Is our home still standing or has it been burned?

"Our village is safe," Maksym said. "The UPA fought them off, but Tulychiv is gone."

"Gone?" Vika gasped.

"Burned to the ground. So is most of Radovychi and Lityn." Maksym swung down off the horse and rubbed its neck as the scent of smoke rolled off him and hit Vika. Sweat and dirt ran in rivulets down his weary face. "It was a big battle, Vika, and so close to home."

"Just a few kilometers away," she murmured as thoughts of her own house burning flashed through her mind.

They returned home later that day, and Vika tried to go about her business like normal—milking the cow, tending the garden—but she couldn't stop thinking about her conversation with Maksym from the night before. How could they leave? How could they walk away from their lives here? Their home?

Their friends? Their chance at Slavko and Liliya coming back to them?

On the other hand, how could she safely raise her other children here? Dark circles framed Sofia's eyes, and she jumped at every little sound. Bohdan, youthfully oblivious of the danger, followed around the UPA men that visited Maksym like a little puppy, thirstily lapping up their war stories, which was dangerous in a whole different way.

Vika understood their need to fight. Ukrainians had always had to fight for the right to exist—against Russians, Poles, Germans, the list went on. Resistance flowed through Ukrainians' veins like blood, but she was tired. She wanted more for her children than the constant battle for freedom. Her love of country directly conflicted with her love of her children, but there was never really a contest. A mother's love trumped all, which was why her biggest hesitation came from Slavko and Liliya.

When the first postcard from Slavko arrived later that week, Maksym brought up his plan again.

"Perfect," he said after reading it. "Now we have an address, so we'll write to them and tell them we're coming."

Vika clutched the paper close to her heart. Nearly half of it was blacked out, but in it Slavko had told them he and Liliya were at a factory outside Dresden in a city called Leipzig, and that they were living like the Gurka family.

"Why does that make you happy?" Maksym asked when she smiled while reading that part aloud to him. "Ihor Gurka is a drunk Nazi lover, and his family lives in squalor. If he says he's living like them, he's suffering."

The smile fell off Vika's face. "It doesn't make me happy. It infuriates me, but I can't help being pleased by how clever my son is at finding a way around the censors. He's a smart boy, our Slavko, and that helps me believe he'll survive."

"Still nothing from Liliya?" Maksym asked.

"No," Vika said. "Slavko says she sends her love, but I think she's afraid to write us. I think she feels guilty."

"That's ridiculous," Maksym said. "She shouldn't."

Vika shrugged. "If she hadn't been here, Slavko wouldn't have been taken."

"But that's not her fault! You don't blame her, do you?"

Vika thought for a moment. After it first happened, it had been easy to hold Liliya responsible, but deep down, Vika knew it wasn't her fault. More importantly, she knew they would have hidden Liliya all over again if given the choice. "I know that, but it doesn't absolve her of her own guilt."

"So, what if we write to Slavko, encode it somehow, and tell him and Liliya not to come home? We'll tell him to wait there till we find him. Then, would you consider leaving?"

Vika nodded slowly. The idea of finding Slavko and Liliya sooner rather than waiting for them to come home was very appealing. "Maybe, but if I'm going to consider this, I want to talk to Maria. She needs to know."

Every few months, Vika loaded up her wagon with her children and made the two-hour trip down the road to Turychany to see her sister, but nearly six months had passed since their last visit. Traveling far from home carried an inherent danger these days, but Vika couldn't wait any longer. Even now, as she steered the wagon through the burned-out wreckage of Tulychiv, she could hear the faint rumbling of bombs going off in the east occasionally. The

front between the Reds and Nazis shifted constantly, sometimes moving closer and sometimes pushing back, but it was
becoming more obvious every day that its arrival was
imminent.

Vika and the children arrived in Turychany at midday, first
driving past the Orthodox church where Maria's father-in-law
worked as a priest before pulling up to their comfortable parish
house. Maria had kept house for him since his wife's death, as
her own husband, Stepan, a Soviet army conscript, hadn't been
home in years.

As the wagon jolted to a stop, Maria ran outside, swooping
the children up into her arms and kissing their cheeks.

Vika's eyes fell on the large mound of dirt in the front yard
of the house next door. "What happened there?"

Maria gave a slight shake of her head. "Sofia, do your Titka
Maria a favor and check if the chickens left us any eggs in their
coop. Take your little sister along. Bohdan, tend to the horses
for your mother."

The children ran off to do their aunt's bidding, and Vika
called out, "Don't stray!"

Vika stepped down off the wagon and Maria grabbed her by
the arm, dragging her inside the house as she whispered, "Our
neighbors, the Ostrowskis, were killed by the UPA."

"And buried in their front yard?" Vika frowned as she
dropped into a chair. "They were good people."

Maria poured them each a shot of *horilka* and sat down next
to her. "Yes, and dear friends. After those flyers came out
warning Poles to leave, I tried to convince them to go, or at least
let me hide them, but they wouldn't listen."

"The children too?" Vika asked.

Maria gave a tight nod, then lifted her glass, and without waiting to toast, threw the liquor back.

Vika followed suit, wincing as the fiery *horilka* burned a path down her throat and warmed her stomach. She wanted an independent country just as much as the next Ukrainian, and while she couldn't dispute her gratitude at the level of protection the UPA offered her village against the Germans, she would never agree with those that thought the only way to a free Ukraine was to eliminate the Poles.

"The Ukrainians asked the Poles to work with them to fight the Soviets and Germans, but the Poles wouldn't recognize the Ukrainians' right to their own country after the war," Vika repeated what Maksym had told her. "Or, at least, that's what I heard. Some say the Poles deserve it for oppressing us for years, but no one deserves death, especially innocent children. I will never support this."

"I think the whole thing has gone too far," Maria said. "And the Poles won't take it lying down, no matter if they instigated it in past decades or not. They've already retaliated against some in the next village over. How are things in Maky?"

Vika sighed, staring down at her empty glass as she thought how to answer the loaded question.

"We haven't had much trouble between the Poles and Ukrainians. Our village is small, and the people remain close, thankfully. Warning each other of approaching trouble. Maksym has helped several Polish families from nearby villages escape across the Buh River. The Germans are staying mostly in the cities now, and the UPA runs the countryside, so Maksym hasn't had to make another forced labor list. I'm glad for that. The guilt he bore for the first one nearly killed him."

"That's something, I suppose," Maria said. "But the Germans are still rounding up people in the cities and doing raids in the countryside."

"I know," Vika said. "We do still have that danger, but the UPA is fighting back. Bombing German supply trains and fighting against Wehrmacht soldiers."

"Along with the Polish Home Army and the Soviet partisans. They all fight the good fight until they turn it on each other, but the Germans always take out their anger on the villagers, no matter who did it," Maria said. "My other neighbor's son was with the UPA and the Germans found out. The whole family was killed last month, and we had to watch their executions."

Vika leaned over and poured another shot for each of them. "It's too much. I can't keep track of all the fighting." She tossed back her shot, this time savoring the burn. "I heard from Slavko. He and Liliya are settled into a factory near Leipzig, Germany."

"Are they safe?"

"As much as they can be, I suppose."

Maria leaned forward and took Vika's hands. "You must think positively."

"Is that what you do?" Vika said, bringing up a topic she normally shied away from. "How do you keep the faith that Stepan will return to you? How many years has it been, Marichka?"

Maria pulled back, her face shuttering closed. "Three years since I last saw him. Six months since the last letter."

"Yet you believe he'll come home?"

"I do," Maria whispered. "I have to, or I wouldn't be able to get out of bed in the morning."

This time, Vika took Maria's hands. "I understand that faith. Better than anyone now, I understand, but I think you should come with us."

Maria's eyes narrowed. "Go with you where?"

"Nowhere for now." Vika leaned closer, though no one else was in the house. "But Maksym is talking about leaving Volhynia if the front gets any closer. Going west toward the Allied occupied areas and starting a new life in a new country. I want you there with me."

"No." Maria snatched her hands away and shook her head. "I won't leave my husband."

"You don't even know if he's alive!" Vika regretted the words instantly, but she wouldn't take them back.

Two angry pink spots flared on Maria's cheeks. "He is alive. I know he is."

"I'm sorry." Vika tried to take Maria's hands again, but her sister brushed her off. "I don't want to leave you. You're all I have left of my old life, my old family."

Maria sagged in her chair. "I know, Vikusia. I feel the same way, but you can't expect me to leave before my husband comes home. You would never do that to Maksym if it were him gone."

Or would she? Vika wasn't as convinced of her own loyalty as Maria, but then, Maria didn't have children yet. She didn't understand the pull, the gravity that bound a child to its mother like the moon to the earth. Vika loved Maksym, and she would never willingly leave him, but if she had to choose, there would be no contest.

"Besides, what if it doesn't?" Maria went on, so wrapped up in her own thoughts she didn't seem to notice Vika's lack of response. "What if the eastern front never reaches here?"

"The Germans are already retreating, and that means Stalin will be back," Vika said. "I don't want to leave our home, but we can't live here if the fighting between the two armies arrives on our doorstep. It's too dangerous."

"Do you really think it's safer in the west?" Maria asked.

"I don't know, but it can't be worse than here. Don't forget, our family stayed before the hunger, and it didn't work out so well for them," Vika said quietly. "We left, and we survived."

"That's not fair," Maria said. "Those were different circumstances."

"Different circumstances, but the same stakes—survival."

"You can find a way to survive here, Vikusia. People are doing it every day."

"Maybe I'm tired of finding a way. Maybe I want something different," Vika said.

There was the truth. She was terrified to leave everything she knew—her home, her village, her sister—but she needed something else. She needed safety and peace for her children. She needed to not worry which type of soldier would approach her house every day. She needed a new life away from the threat of heavy warfare and Stalin's advancing army.

The only things holding her back were Slavko and Liliya, but talking with Maria had clarified things. Staying or leaving, she'd be risking her children. If she could get word to Slavko that they were coming, then maybe she could take her family away from this danger and reunite with Slavko and Liliya. Maybe she could save everyone.

26

LILIYA

November 1943, Leipzig, Germany

Liliya shivered as she waited in line for roll call. A steady drizzle fell on them, soaking her clothes and hair. The winter weather had leached into the barracks, stealing any bit of joy the women might have possessed, not that there was much to start with.

Halya stood next to her in their row of four, barefoot and without a coat, practically convulsing with cold, as Helga counted them all, stopping each time someone collapsed from weakness or illness and then starting again. Liliya wondered if it was this bad in Slavko's barracks. They hadn't seen him in a few days.

In the last couple of weeks, the guards had been waking them up earlier, drawing out the roll call process, *Appell*, so that now, they woke up at four in the morning in order to get through it and get to the factory by six. It didn't have to take so long, but the cruel guards sometimes left them standing in the elements, swaying as they struggled to stay upright, for no good reason until they began their march to the factory. Well-trained German Shepherds surrounded them along with the guards, so even if they'd had the energy to try, no one dared to escape.

When they came back to the barracks after work, they would repeat *Appell* before they could eat dinner, assuring the guards that everyone was still there and working for the German labor force. These roll calls punctuated Liliya's days, and normally, the time she spent standing, listening as Helga counted in her nasal voice, wasn't unbearable. She'd let her mind wander, listening and watching for birds. Even if she couldn't draw them, she enjoyed seeing them. There weren't as many here near the factory as there were in rural Volhynia, but that was to be expected. She missed the variety of colors and songs from back home, so when she couldn't see any birds, she'd go through the catalog in her mind, flipping through mental pictures of the real bird and the corresponding sheets in her journal. She'd looked through them all so many times they lived in her memory, and it normally felt good to think about them, focusing on the details she might forget if she wasn't vigilant. It was a piece of herself the Germans couldn't take.

But tonight wasn't one of those times. Tonight, at this *Appell*, all her energy was focused on Halya.

"Stay up," she murmured, reaching out to give Halya's arm a light pinch. Her fingers, burned and blistered from her days spent transferring bullets from hot water to a conveyer belt, ached, but she did it again. "Halya? Do you hear me?"

Halya rubbed her arm. "I hear you. I'm up."

"Didn't you sleep last night?" Liliya asked. When they'd first arrived, Halya spent most nights sobbing herself to sleep, but now, the exhaustion of work left no time for emotions.

"Yes," Halya chattered. "I just don't feel well."

Liliya reached out and rubbed her back encouragingly when Helga wasn't looking. Her plan to keep the girl at arm's length had failed some time ago, and now, she couldn't deny her fondness for Halya. The sweet combination of pluckiness and naiveté made the girl endearing, and despite Liliya's initial reticence, Halya had wormed her way into Liliya's hardened heart without even trying.

Helga finished the roll call, but instead of ushering them to the factory, she led them into another building next to their barracks. Uneasy whispers rippled through the crowd, and Halya's hand grasped Liliya's.

"Where are they taking us?"

Before Liliya could respond, they stepped into a large, open room with bins of clothes and coats lined up on one side.

"You will pick out one coat or one sweater," Helga instructed. "If you don't have shoes, you may take a pair of wooden clogs. The cost for these items will be taken from your wages."

Liliya wanted to laugh at Helga's casual use of the word "wages," as if the word was anything but a political tool so the Reich could call them laborers and not slaves. After taking out boarding and now clothing fees, the paltry amount they paid each *Ostarbeiter* barely left them with enough to buy stamps and paper for letters home. Besides, *Ostarbeiters* couldn't shop in German stores, so they were limited to what was available in the camp store.

The women, starving and cold, fell upon the clothes like

ravenous vultures, and, in a way, they were. Liliya dug through the bin and came across a small, thick coat. She thrust it toward Halya. "Here, put this on."

Halya pulled the coat on and buttoned it up. "It's warm."

"Good, now look for a sweater or anything that might fit me," Liliya instructed.

But Halya didn't listen. Instead, she touched a dark stain on the front of the jacket. "Liliya, what is this?"

Liliya glanced up and blanched, then forced her voice to be steady and matter of fact. She couldn't undo the deaths of the prior owners of these clothes, but she could fight to prevent Halya's death.

"It's blood. You don't think the Germans bought these clothes, do you? They may be charging us, but they didn't pay for them."

Halya's face paled. "Where did they get them?"

Liliya held up another coat, then pulled it on. This one only had a blood stain on the sleeve. "I imagine from the people they've put in their other camps. You've seen the Jews brought into the factory to work. Kept apart, always wearing a uniform. These are probably their clothes."

"But they're alive," Halya said. "Why is there blood on these?"

Liliya swallowed hard. "They're not all alive, Halya, and we won't be either if we don't get warm. The poor people in those camps have it far worse than us. I wish to God we could do more to help them, but we can barely help ourselves here and we can't waste these clothes. If I died, I wouldn't begrudge some cold girl my coat and neither would you. Now, let's get some shoes."

27

VIKA

February 1944, Volhynia, Reichskommissariat Ukraine

The ground rumbled as German Panzer tanks rolled down the road. Vika stood in her doorway, watching through the smoke-filled morning air as they moved away from Tulychiv, or the direction of what had been Tulychiv. Nothing remained now of the village the Germans had burned to the ground in July, but Vika and her family had fled two more times since then as Germans attacked neighboring villages—once more to the same house they'd hidden in the first time, and once, when they didn't have time, to a friend's bunker in the woods.

All night, mortars and artillery rained on the countryside to the east. Far in the distance, the hazy glow of fire illuminated the sky, courtesy of the Nazis burning bridges and grain stores as they retreated and implemented their scorched earth policy. Though the threat of decimation by fire was terrifying, Vika remembered all too well the horrors of Soviet occupation, and she wasn't sure that a fiery demise would be much worse than living under Stalin's thumb again. If the Nazis were retreating this fast, the Soviets couldn't be far behind.

The house shook as another mortar exploded nearby, and she closed the door and went back inside, as if that would be protection enough from the war raging all around her.

"It's time." Maksym touched her shoulder. "The wagon is ready, and I don't think we can wait much longer."

The night before, Maksym had brought home an oilskin tarp to cover the wagon, and over the past few weeks, Vika had been drying bread and packing away barrels of food for them to eat on the journey. She'd folded and packed her best *rushnyky*, layering her holy icons, prayer books, and Liliya's sketchbooks in between them, and she'd carefully sewed a pouch for her precious store of dried *kalyna* berries so she could plant them if they settled in a new place. She couldn't imagine not having a *kalyna* bush wherever she lived.

Despite all her preparations, it still didn't seem real—she never truly thought this day would come. She leaned over the table and squeezed the edge until her fingers ached. "We have to wait a few more days. We still haven't heard back from them."

"We can't wait anymore, Vikusia. We've written to them both a dozen times and missed our window during the good weather. We've waited too long. Now the Soviets and Nazis are fighting at our door, and we must contend with traveling in the winter." Maksym pulled a folded paper out of his pocket and opened it on the table. "The colonel at the stable gave me this map. See, we're here."

Vika sucked in a breath. This was it. They were leaving.

Walking away from her home. Her sister. Her chance to see her son and niece return.

"So, what will we do?"

Maksym pointed at their village and traced his finger west. "We will go toward them. If they're alive, we'll find them."

If they're alive.

She wanted to slap those vile words out of his mouth, but a bigger feeling overcame the anger. Fear.

"I don't know if I can." It hurt to say those words. To admit she couldn't do something. Losing Slavko had broken her, and now, she was empty. Hollow. A useless, dried husk, floating whichever way the wind blew, unable and unwilling to do anything to steer her own course, because how could she know? How could she know what the right thing to do was in this mess of a life? Any decision she made had the potential to be catastrophic for her family, and that pressure smothered her until she no longer recognized the woman she'd become.

Maksym put his hand over Vika's. "We will do this together. We have to do this. Don't you understand? If we survive the front decimating our village and the Soviets come, they could arrest any of us for my job as a village elder or for Slavko and Liliya's forced labor in Germany. It doesn't matter to them whether we wanted to do the work or not."

She knew that. She'd cited the same facts to Maria. She'd dreamed about raising her children away from the violence of this war, but to do that, she'd have to not only give up everything, but risk everything.

How would they stay safe while they traveled? How would the thin walls of the wagon cover protect them from bullets and bombs? How would they survive?

She voiced none of these concerns to Maksym because she could ask the same questions about staying. Maybe there was no right answer moving forward, only uncertainty. Maybe she had to accept that all she could do was try to fight for her family.

"Once we leave and find Liliya and Slavko..." Maksym went on, his gaze now lowered, and with that one slight movement, Vika realized he believed them dead. They hadn't had a post-card in months, so Maksym was only perpetuating the idea of finding them to appease her. A piece of her faith in him chipped off, destroyed like so many other things by the war.

He went on, oblivious to her reaction. "Maybe we can go to Bavaria. I've heard you can get work on the farms there. Or maybe, if we get far enough, we can get into an Allied-occupied zone . . ." He trailed off as he stared at the map. "I don't know where we'll end up. I only know we can't stay here."

Despite Maksym's disbelief, or maybe because of it, a spark of hope flared in Vika's heart. *Stubborn to the core*, as her mother used to call her, she knew this was her opportunity to fix one of her biggest mistakes and prove him wrong: she would find their son and niece, and in the process, get her other children out of harm's way. If she clung to those ideas, perhaps she could find the strength to do what was necessary.

An explosion sounded in the distance, shaking the walls of the house. Sofia squealed and jumped onto her bed.

Vika exhaled slowly, then turned and walked away without another word to Maksym. She sat at the table and began to write.

Dear Slavko & Liliya,

If you come home and find this, know that we have set off to find you. We won't rest until we do.
Mama

She copied the verbiage onto two more postcards to be dropped in the mail to the last addresses she had for them, then put the original note on the table under the vase of now-dried poppies that always sat where Slavko had originally put them.

* * *

Vika prepared the last meal they would eat in this house—plum preserves smeared on a slice of bread—and set it in front of Bohdan and Nadya. She wanted everything and everyone ready so they could leave as soon as Maksym returned from collecting his pay from the stables.

A girl's voice rang out in the yard.

"Is that Sofia?" Bohdan asked.

Vika set down her knife, thought for a moment, then picked it up again, clutching it tight in her trembling hand. "I'll see."

She pulled open the door just in time for Sofia to run through it.

"They took them! Our horses are gone!"

An anger Vika had never seen before flashed in her daughter's eyes, but she didn't have time to dive into that emotion now. She grabbed Sofia by the shoulders. "Who?"

"The Germans. Two Wehrmacht soldiers came and took them. Said they needed them for the army." She hiccupped back a sob as her bravado faded into fear. "I told them Tato was friends with the German soldiers at the stable, but they just laughed at me."

Even as her heart sank over the loss of the horses, Vika cringed to hear those words about Maksym roll so easily off her daughter's tongue. "He's not their friend, Sofia. And it's not by choice. He'd never work for the Germans by choice!"

"I'm sorry, Mama. I was just trying to help."

"It doesn't matter," Vika said. She didn't have time to get into the nuances of Maksym's choices or lack thereof with her daughter.

"Tato loved those horses," Sofia said. "He brought them back to life."

Vika closed her eyes, remembering the way the two geldings would run up to Maksym in the pasture and rest their heads on his shoulders. His reputation for rehabilitating horses had started when he was a boy. These last two were part of a long line of sad, broken horses Maksym nursed back to health, renewing both their spirits and bodies. He'd been so devastated when the Soviets stole their previous geldings in 1940, he'd left her and the children and followed them.

"I'm going after my horses," he'd announced. "The Russians won't feed them well, and I have to make sure they eat."

"And what about your wife and children? Do you care what we eat?" Vika had yelled as he walked down the road, the scythe he'd use to cut grass for the horses propped on his shoulder.

Three days later, he returned without his beloved horses and refused to speak about it. When the Germans invaded, he talked a local officer into giving him a lame draft horse about to be shot. After six months, Maksym had it galloping and working in the fields, then he traded it for two sickly, half-starved ponies—the ones stolen today—that could pull their wagon.

"What will we do, Mama?" Sofia cut into Vika's memories, and she opened her eyes.

"I don't know, Sofia. I need to think."

* * *

An hour later, the thundering of hoofbeats coming down the road pulled Vika to the window. Her eyes strained to identify the approaching rider, then she heard the familiar voice shout out.

"Vika, I found your horses!" Oleksiy drew up his horse in front of her, his face creased with dust and weariness.

She ran outside, then stopped short as she took in the two chestnut geldings. "Those aren't our horses."

Oleksiy bent and handed her the leads. "They are now."

"How did you even know ours were gone? Where did you get these?"

"It doesn't matter. Just take them and leave. The fighting draws too close, and the Nazis are taking their scorched earth policy very seriously."

A bomb went off in the distance, making the ground rumble and punctuating Oleksiy's statement.

Vika barked out a sharp laugh. "How many different armies want to scorch our earth?"

Oleksiy's jaw tightened. "If you find Liliya, give her my love. Be safe, Vika." He turned his horse to go, then looked back. "Will you tell her I'm sorry? About everything?"

"I will. You could come with us, you know."

Oleksiy shook his head. "I can't leave now. I won't leave. But Liliya was always destined for more. I hope she finds it."

"What will you do?" Vika called out as he turned his horse.

"What I've always done. Fight for Ukraine until I can't fight anymore."

28

HALYA

February 1944, Leipzig, Germany

My dearest Halya,

Your father and I miss you very much. It's not the same here without you. I keep expecting to find you perched in your tree, reading a book. Every time I don't, I feel like I've lost you all over again. I'm glad to hear you're faring well there, though many lines of your previous postcards were blacked out. I worry about what you wrote there. Be smart, my little one.

All my love,
Mama

Halya had read the letter so many times she could recite it by heart, which was what she often did on the long walk to dinner after work. She liked to imagine Mama sitting at the table, writing letters to Halya while Tato sat next to her, leaning over her shoulder to add in his thoughts. It was better than thinking about her life here.

"Time to eat!" Svetlana said, breaking into her thoughts as they each picked up their small ration of food. "Maybe your friend will be back tonight."

Halya shook away the vestiges of home and tried to smile. "Maybe so."

Slavko hadn't met them at dinner for five days in a row.

Halya tried not to worry. His shift could have changed, like Liliya's, who was now working nights in a different part of the factory. She and Halya barely talked lately—one was always asleep when the other left or arrived. Or maybe he'd been reassigned. Neither would be uncommon. She dunked her bread into the watery soup and scanned the room again. An odd-colored carrot, or what appeared to be a carrot, bobbed in the center of the bowl, the lone vegetable in her broth. Around her, the girls she worked next to every day chattered, but none of it registered with her.

When he could, Slavko sat with her, Liliya, and the other girls for dinner. They'd teased her about it, but she didn't care. The only thing that mattered was him showing up. He'd never gone this long without being there.

She locked her gaze on the door, willing him to appear with his easy grin and smart mouth.

"Did you hear me, Halya?" Luba nudged her. "Your friend isn't coming. I heard tonight that he got arrested a few days ago."

Halya swallowed the last bite of her food, the brown carrot. Sweet and slick, it slid down her throat and landed in her stomach like a rock, anchoring her to her seat. She turned to Luba, her fingers white as she gripped the bowl.

"What do you mean?"

Luba shrugged. "I don't know what for, but the Gestapo shoved him and four other men into the back of a car and left."

Images of Slavko in a dank jail cell somewhere, hurt, alone, flashed through Halya's mind, and she hunched over, her arms folding over her middle as she fought to keep down her meager meal.

* * *

The next morning, after a night of fitful sleep, Halya woke up when Liliya stumbled into their shared bunk. Normally, she rolled over and continued sleeping for the extra half hour, but today, she sat up.

"Slavko's been arrested," she said.

Liliya jerked upright. "How long?"

"A few days. Luba saw him get taken in by the Gestapo. Him and a few other men."

"He's not a man," Liliya muttered. "But he gets into trouble like one."

"What do we do?" Halya had thought telling Liliya would make her feel better, that sharing this burden of knowledge would somehow make it less painful, but it hadn't.

Liliya pushed herself up from the bed. "You go to work. I'll go see what I can find out."

* * *

That day, Halya worked in a daze, waiting for any crumb of news about Slavko. Boxes of cartridges stacked up and the *Werkschutz* hit her five times in one shift for laziness.

"Work harder! You're falling behind!"

She hadn't known Slavko long, but he'd inserted himself so firmly into her life that she felt his presence like a missing limb. Maybe it was because he'd been the first kind person to her on this journey, or maybe it was because he made her feel like the only person in the room when she talked.

As she walked back to her barracks that night, a boy sidled up to her. "Hey, aren't you Slavko's friend?"

Halya grabbed him by the arm. "Yes. Do you know what happened to him?"

The boy frowned and extracted himself from her grip. He was older, closer to Liliya's age, if Halya had to guess, and she vaguely remembered Slavko introducing him to her some time ago.

"People were plotting to sabotage the factory." He lowered his voice and stepped closer. "Set off the explosives. You know."

Halya smothered a gasp. "And Slavko was part of it?"

He shrugged. "I don't know. Maybe he was, or maybe he was in the wrong place at the wrong time. Either way, he was arrested with them."

"What will happen to him?" She was afraid to ask the question, afraid of the answer, because why else would this boy take the time to seek her out?

"I don't know that either. They're being interrogated, so if they survive, it won't be pretty."

29

VIKA

February 1944, Volhynia, Reichskommissariat Ukraine

"I'm sorry I wasn't back sooner." Maksym ran into the yard, his chest heaving, but jerked to a halt when he saw the new horses hitched to the wagon. "Where are my horses?"

Vika let Sofia climb in the wagon, then set Nadya in her arms. Everything was ready. She'd already loaded the final items while waiting for Maksym to return.

"The Germans stole them, but Oleksiy brought us these."

Maksym's cheek twitched as he rubbed his jaw, the only slip of distress he allowed for the loss of his old horses before he folded her into his arms. "All right. I'm here now."

She rested her cheek against his chest and breathed him in —the tang of his sweat and the musk of hay and horses that always clung to him.

Nothing was certain. Nothing was safe. But for that brief

moment, enveloped in his warm embrace, she could almost pretend it was.

But it wasn't real. Nobody could protect them.

She pulled back, shocked to find tears leaking from her eyes, but she couldn't tell if they were tears of relief or fear. The two emotions played on such an exhausting loop in her head lately, they'd nearly become one.

"Where did Oleksiy get these horses?" Maksym asked.

Vika brushed the back of her hand over her face, hoping Maksym wouldn't notice her momentary weakness. "I don't know how he got them, and he told me not to ask."

Maksym eyed the skinny geldings. "They need to put weight on."

"Lucky for them they have you, then."

He nearly smiled before climbing in the back of the wagon to hug the children. Vika got into the seat and took up the reins. Veins popped out on her arms as she gripped them, praying they wouldn't slip through her hands. "Whoa, boys. Not yet. Easy now."

The geldings snorted and tossed their heads, not appeased at all by her attempts to soothe them in the chaos. Another explosion sounded, and they lurched forward, jerking the wagon along behind them. Nadya began to cry, and Sofia tried to shush her while Bohdan scrambled to the back of the wagon to stare out behind them. Despite the cold, sweat trickled down Vika's temple as her body tensed.

Maksym climbed up front next to her, and Vika urged the horses on, flicking the reins against their backs. She didn't look back at her dear little house, but with each creak of the wagon's wheels, a piece of her slipped away. Her parents. Her brothers.

Her sisters. She was leaving her country, and she had no idea if she'd ever come back.

As they passed by their neighbor Yaroslava's house, she dashed out into the yard.

"Where are you going, Viktoria Petrivna?"

Vika didn't slow the wagon. "Don't you hear the fighting? The front is just down the road. We're leaving, and you should be, too."

Yaroslava scowled. "I have nowhere to go and neither do you."

"You're wrong. I have family waiting for me. Besides, anywhere will be safer than here," Vika called over her shoulder without turning around.

You've done this before, she reminded herself as memories of their frantic flight across the Soviet border into Volhynia flashed through her brain. She, her sister, and Maksym had left with nothing but the clothes on their backs and one satchel of personal items—her mother's holy pictures and a few precious family photographs. Hiding in the woods and crossing the border in the dark of the night, they'd risked everything to escape Stalin's rule, but it didn't matter. He'd found them again when he'd made his deal with Hitler and invaded and annexed Volhynia into the USSR. Now he was coming for them a third time.

That trip, though just as dangerous, had felt less daunting because they had a goal: Maksym's sister's house in Volhynia. Now, a new war raged around them and their destination was a big city in another country they'd never seen. They could only move forward until they found someplace safe and hope that brought them closer to Slavko and Liliya.

* * *

They traveled southwest initially to skirt away from the bulk of the retreating Wehrmacht soldiers. Maksym wanted to avoid as much conflict as possible. But three days into their journey, two Soviet soldiers appeared in the distance, riding toward them. Maksym had gone in the opposite direction with one horse to see if he could find water nearby.

"Who are they, Mama?" Sofia asked.

"Red soldiers. I'm not sure why they're out here. Maybe partisans. Either way, it's bad for them to see us fleeing west. They'll assume we have something to hide. Here, take the horse and don't say a word. If they talk to you, pretend you don't understand even if you do."

Vika passed the reins to Sofia, then crawled back to the wooden box she kept tucked under their clothing and pulled out their identification papers. She folded them and pushed them deep into the dried bread barrel.

"Mama, they're coming over here!"

Vika scrambled back up to the front of the wagon. "Children, stay there, and don't speak," she said under her breath as the mounted soldiers approached. She took the reins back from Sofia and pulled back, her knuckles white as they squeezed the leather. "Go sit by your brother and sister and keep your head down."

The remaining horse, glad for the break, began to graze on the dried-out grass along the road, oblivious to the fear Vika felt churning in her stomach.

"Where are you going today, Auntie?" The younger of the two men smiled as he pulled up alongside their wagon. Peach fuzz adorned his upper lip, and ruddy circles flushed his baby smooth cheeks. The older man, a grizzled, tanned soldier in a dirty, khaki-colored jacket, stayed back, watching as he lit a cigarette and took a long drag. Both reeked of vodka.

"The Germans burned our village," Vika lied, her tongue slipping easily into the Russian he'd used and she'd heard growing up from the Russian implants around her village. "We're heading to stay with friends in Kraków."

Or maybe it wasn't a lie. Maybe her village had been burned by now. She would never know.

The young soldier drew closer, peering at her with hard, flinty eyes that contrasted sharply with his baby face. "Then you won't care if we check your wagon."

"For what?" Vika asked.

"It's standard procedure," he said. "Who knows what we'll find? Now get out and line up next to the wagon."

Vika and the children stepped down and stood in a row as the men dismounted and began rifling through their things. They tossed what they didn't care about, and bundles of clothes, photographs, and holy pictures sailed out of the wagon and landed on the ground.

Please don't touch the food, Vika prayed.

The young soldier popped open the lid of the dried bread barrel and grabbed a chunk. It broke into pieces as he shoved it in his mouth, scattering bits on the ground in a shameful waste. He laughed as he stumbled back toward her and pulled out his pistol.

Sweat broke out on Vika's forehead, but she kept her back ramrod straight and stared ahead, her anger at seeing them carelessly rifle through their things bolstering her.

The young soldier spat crumbs into her face as he gestured to his comrade with his free hand, but still, she wouldn't look at him. "Enough of this. Let's shoot them."

The older man climbed back onto his horse. "Why? They're not causing any harm."

"So? They're not doing any good either." He pointed the gun at Vika's face, then at each of her children. "Who wants to go first?"

Vika's mouth went dry as her mind raced. They had not come this far to be randomly killed on the whim of some drunk teenage Russian boy. Her lips started moving before her mind had time to think, and the Russian words flowed out of her. "Why shoot your fellow Soviets? Women and children, no less. Fine, if that makes you feel like a big, brave man, then do it. I can't stop you."

The young man quit chewing as he appraised her.

She shrugged, as if she were indifferent, though her knees were knocking together under her skirt. "But I hope nobody ever treats your mother or grandmother like this."

He slapped his leg and laughed. "You remind me of my mother! A good Slavic woman! Fine, fine. We'll let them go like you wanted, Yuri."

The older soldier turned his horse away. "Come on then. We've got a long way to go yet."

As the soldiers rode away, their packs now filled with food from the wagon, Sofia burst into tears. "I was so scared, Mama."

"You did very well to hide it, Sofia." Vika smoothed her daughter's hair. "You did what we must always do. Hide our fear and be brave."

"I don't want to be brave anymore. I just want to go home."

"We can't go home, my love. We can only go forward."

"But where are we going?" Sofia stared up at Vika. Tears trembled on the edges of her long lashes, and Vika winced at the fear and uncertainty in the eyes of her child. "How will Slavko and Liliya find us if we aren't home?"

Vika swallowed the lump in her throat and forced a smile. "We will find them, then we will make a new home."

Sofia balled her fists and stamped her foot. "I don't want a new home! I'm tired of this, and I want to go back to our home!"

The frantic emotions of what had just transpired welled up in Vika, and she reached out and slapped Sofia's cheek before she could stop herself. Regret flooded through her immediately, even before her hand began to tingle from the contact, but she didn't give voice to it.

Sofia stepped back and pressed her palm to her cheek, glaring. Vika wanted to throw her arms around Sofia, tell her it would all be fine, and they would be safe, but she couldn't. She didn't know if any of that was true. So, she said nothing as they stared at each other—an exhausted mother and a frustrated child locked in a battle neither of them could win.

Vika finally turned her back on Sofia and began picking up their belongings. "Come help, children. We need to get this cleaned up."

They had to be ready to keep moving as soon as Maksym returned.

30

LILIYA

March 1944, Leipzig, Germany

Three weeks after he'd disappeared, Slavko showed up at breakfast one morning like it was a normal day, slipping into the cafeteria with a group of other workers. Liliya, now back on the day shift, saw him first as he carefully lowered himself into the chair next to them.

Without thinking, she flew from her seat and wrapped her arms around him, then drew back when he winced.

"I'm sorry! I didn't mean to hurt you."

"You didn't hurt me." His rough voice scratched at her ears. "They did. I'm glad to see you, too."

"I thought you were dead." Halya stood at her seat. Her big eyes brimmed with tears as she stared at Slavko.

Looking at him made Liliya want to cry, too, but she swallowed the lump in her throat, sat back down, and kicked Halya under the table. She hadn't protected him from this torture, and her efforts to help him had fallen on deaf ears, but she could at least prevent him from feeling worse about it all by crying in front of him.

Halya blinked fast and nodded once as she met Liliya's gaze. Pride surged through Liliya, and she gave Halya a little smile. Halya was toughening up.

Burn marks, maybe from a cigarette, peppered Slavko's neck like polka dots. His cheeks, hollow under his swollen eyes, were lined with slices. Rope burns encircled his wrists. Dried blood leaked out from rags he'd tied around the tops of his fingers, and Liliya wanted to ask if they'd ripped off his nails or sliced off the tips, but she didn't.

He moved stiffly, lifting his bowl to his mouth and barely opening his lips to let the broth pour in. He did this two more times, finishing the bowl as if he hadn't eaten in weeks. He probably hadn't.

"Am I not dead? I feel like I am."

His attempt at humor heartened her, but Liliya didn't smile.

"You didn't write to my mother about this, did you?" Slavko asked. "I wouldn't want her to worry."

Liliya shook her head, averting her gaze. She didn't want to tell Slavko that she never wrote to Vika. What could she say to the woman who took her in like a daughter, then lost her son because of it? Her guilt over Slavko's presence here was still too raw, and now, his arrest and torture had only made it worse. Instead, she leaned closer. "I can help you eat. Want me to?"

He grunted, and though he probably didn't intend it as such, she took it as a yes. She broke her bread and his bread into tiny pieces and let it soak in her soup until it was soft, then lifted the bowl to his lips. He pushed her away.

"That's yours."

"It's not now. I want you to have it, just like you've done for me so many times."

"Mine, too," Halya said. She ripped up the rest of her bread and dumped it into Liliya's bowl.

Even under his bruises, Slavko's face reddened. "Fine, but I can lift it myself. I'm not totally helpless."

Liliya slid the bowl closer and watched as he gulped it down, letting the bread slide down his throat without chewing.

"Why did they arrest you?"

He set the bowl down and stared at them. "They thought I was sabotaging the ammunition I worked on."

Liliya glanced around and lowered her voice. "Were you?"

He chuckled, a dry, raspy sound. "Not that time."

They'd all done it in small ways, men and women both. Not filling the cartridge with enough gunpowder or not heating the shells to a high enough temperature in the oven. Little acts of rebellion that brought great satisfaction, but you had to be careful. If too many faulty products came out of one group's line, the Germans would investigate and trace the serial numbers back to where it was made.

"The other men were doing more, though," Slavko went on. "Planning to set off explosives and destroy part of the factory. They finally convinced the Gestapo that I was a dumb kid with no idea what was going on."

"What will happen to them?" Halya asked.

Slavko lifted his chin in the air and took a deep breath. "They're being sent to a concentration camp."

Liliya shivered. Rumors were rampant about the lives of the Jews and political prisoners housed at the concentration camps. Some people called them "death camps," and spoke of mass executions and gas chambers. From what Liliya had seen of the skeletal people transported in to work in some parts of the factory, that assessment didn't seem far off. Surviving as an *Ostarbeiter* was difficult enough, but surviving in one of those camps seemed nearly impossible. "Thank goodness they let you go."

"No." Slavko shook his head, anger flaring in his eyes. "Don't you see? They're doing something. Fighting back, like Oleksiy and Filip. I'm doing nothing useful here but helping the German war machine. I hate myself for making weapons the Germans are using against my own people."

A small shudder rippled across Slavko's shoulder, and he ducked his head, but not before Liliya saw the tears hovering on his lashes.

"You sabotage what you can, don't you?" Liliya asked quietly.

When both Slavko and Halya nodded, Liliya went on. "Every small act is important. Every bullet that doesn't fire or bomb that doesn't explode is a win for us here and for those fighting the Germans. We can't help that we were brought here as workers, but that doesn't mean we have to do good work, right?"

Liliya nodded along with them this time. Remembering that was the only way she could sleep at night.

31

VIKA

March 1944, German General Government of Poland

All around them, glowing orange fires flickered in the fields along the road, and next to those fires sat other refugees going west, away from the fighting. German tanks and soldiers rumbled past in both directions as the rippling front rolled across the land. Vika refused to look at or think about the deep bomb craters carved into the earth north of the road.

After two weeks of travel, the damp, cold air had settled into Vika's bones. Her joints ached, and she couldn't get warm, even standing over the fire as she cooked their simple dinners or bundled up under the blankets surrounded by her family.

Nadya let out a deep, bark-like cough, and Vika's breath caught. She bent over her daughter, taking in the damp hair curling around her flushed face and the glassy eyes. Terror, a different kind from the one causing her to flee her homeland, seeped through Vika's limbs. This fear was familiar and ancient, born of the helplessness of watching a beloved child suffer.

For the next few days, they stayed at their camp by the river as Nadya's fever raged. Vika barely slept. Doubts assailed her. If they'd stayed, would Nadya have gotten sick? Had she made the wrong choice in leaving?

On the fourth morning, Nadya's fever still hadn't broken, but Vika's resolve did. When Maksym came to check on Nadya, Vika pulled him aside. "Did we make a mistake putting our children through this? Maybe we would have been better off taking our chances and staying."

Maksym stilled, his handsome features—only seconds ago soft and kind—now hard. "I'd rather watch my daughter suffer, even die, from an illness in our care, than see her sent to prison or a labor camp in Russia."

Vika gasped. "You don't mean that!"

"I do," he said harshly. "At least here with us, there's a chance she'll survive. She'd have no such thing in a labor camp. We didn't leave only for Slavko, and we're not trading one child's life for another, Vika. It's about survival for all of us. When will you see that?"

"All I see now is my sick child," she snapped as he stomped off. She rubbed her hands over her weary face, plastered on a smile, and turned back to Nadya.

"One more bite, now." She smoothed Nadya's damp hair and held out the spoon filled with preserved *kalyna* berries and honey—her standard treatment for all ailments. Nadya opened her mouth and swallowed dutifully, wrinkling her nose at the tangy berries. Vika said a silent prayer of relief that she was eating.

By late morning, her fever had finally broken. Vika wanted to lie down next to her and let exhaustion overtake her, but Maksym wanted to travel through the afternoon.

Warmer temperatures the day before had given them a glimpse of the spring weather to come. Vika hoped that trend would continue and the worst of winter's assault had ended, just as she hoped Nadya would continue to feel better. She wasn't completely healed, but for now, she was stronger, and that was enough for Vika to be thankful.

Their pace had slowed after those first few frantic days of flight to get away from the front. Now, they moved cautiously, going through empty, burned-out villages, passing by abandoned homesteads, and circumventing bomb craters, but it was hard to tell if it was Nazis now or the Soviets a few years ago who had committed the crimes. The two warring armies had wreaked havoc on the land as they moved back and forth across it, leaving a swath of destruction in their wake.

The days blurred into one another as they moved deeper into Poland. When they came across farms or inhabited villages, Maksym and Vika bartered labor for food so their stores would stretch longer. When they were lucky, kind farmers let them bed in their barns, but most nights they all slept in and around the wagon. Maksym and Bohdan outside, on the ground; Nadya and Sofia curled up near their food; Vika next to them, one hand always resting on each girl—a constant reassurance that she still had these children with her. She hadn't lost them yet.

The further west they traveled, the more refugees they encountered—some roads were nearly jammed with the writhing masses of humanity fleeing the advancing Soviet army.

As they rode or walked alongside the wagon, a myriad of languages filled the air. Some she recognized, like German, Russian, Polish, and the strange blend of Ukrainian-accented German that the *Volksdeutsche* spoke, others she didn't. Sometimes the crowds grew thick, and the foreign words became an incessant racket buzzing in her ears. The battles, the bombs, the sea of refugees lying in the path between her and Slavko and Liliya—thinking of these obstacles made her stomach knot up until she retched, but she never let her children see her falter.

These days, she didn't think. She just moved, sharing driving duties with Maksym as they traveled away from the sunrise each morning and toward the sunset in the afternoon. Away from her homeland. Away from everything she'd ever known.

Toward her son and niece.

Maksym thought it a lost cause. Vika could see that, in the pinch of his lips when she mentioned their firstborn or the way he never spoke of him, but she'd not given up, and she had enough optimism for the both of them.

"Mama, I'm starting to forget Slavko's face," Sofia admitted one morning, her eyes brimming with tears. "It's been so long since I've seen him."

Vika hugged Sofia and tucked her head under her chin. "I know, little one. We must cling to the good memories we have until we can see him again. Why don't you tell me your favorite memory of Slavko?"

Sofia pressed close to Vika. "I remember, when I was very little, Tato would put me and Slavko up on the tall horse and walk alongside us as we came back from the fields. I was so high up on the horse that I could pat the top of Tato's head." She sighed. "Slavko always kept his arms around me so I wouldn't slide off. When we'd get to the barn, Tato would swing us off the horse, then take turns tossing us in the air until we laughed and laughed."

Vika closed her eyes. She could see Sofia's memory as clear as day, and it hit her like a punch to the gut.

"That's a lovely memory. Can you feel him? Feel Slavko's arms around you and his smile shining on you?"

Sofia nodded, her tear-stained face damp against Vika's neck.

"Hold tight to that, Sofia." Vika squeezed her daughter close. "For in your memories, we are all together again. If we stay together, we will be fine. And when we see Slavko again, you can tell him about your favorite memory. I'm sure it's one of his, too."

Sofia sat back, her earnest face hopeful. "Do you think so, Mama?"

"I do," Vika said. "How could it not be?"

* * *

Vika set the pieces of dried bread in the pan so they could soak up the grease from the *salo* she'd fried. The bread and pork fat, warmed over the small fire, made for a filling dinner, but despite Vika's careful rationing, the barrels of dried bread and *salo* and jars of preserves and sauerkraut were all nearly empty. Thankfully, now that the earth had come back to life with the warm weather, Vika would soon be able to forage for greens and mushrooms to supplement their dwindling dry goods.

Orange and red light spilled out of the sunset and across the field they were camped in, painting the landscape in a soft glow. Tucked next to the woods and a small creek, tonight, the stars would be their roof. After a string of nights staying in barns, Vika almost felt exposed out in the open like this again, but she enjoyed the fresh air.

Similar fires from other refugees glimmered in the distance. Their presence gave Vika a small measure of comfort; they weren't alone in this journey.

"I think we'll make it to Kraków in the next day or two," Maksym said.

"Good. We need to replenish our food stores."

"All right. I'll get up early and fish tomorrow morning. I can catch us some breakfast." Maksym tickled Nadya under the chin, and Nadya gave a rare squeal of joy.

Vika's heart warmed to hear her youngest child so happy, even if only for a moment. The evidence of this journey's toll appeared in the faces of all her children—Sofia's brow bore a permanent furrow as she worked tirelessly to help her parents every day. Bohdan, much like his older brother—normally easygoing and happy—now jumped at every little sound, his face always twisted into a perplexed expression. Even Nadya seemed far more sober than a typical two-year-old. Vika wondered what the long-term impact of a life like this would be. How did child's personality develop if they never felt safe?

She didn't speak of it to Maksym, for there was nothing to be done, but in those moments, as she observed the changes in her children, doubt crept in. At least back in their village, they had a roof over their heads and a garden outside. But then, she'd think of the way the Germans took most of their produce for taxes, stole people for labor, slaughtered innocents, and

burned villages, or how the Soviets arrested all the intelligentsia—Ukraine's teachers, priests, scholars, politicians—and
killed or deported them. She'd remember the constant fear, the
pitting of neighbor against neighbor, the seeds of distrust sowed
among the villagers by both the Germans and the Soviets as
they spread their vile propaganda.

No, they were right to leave. Ukraine would always be in her
heart, but she couldn't keep her family safe there now. Leaving
was the only option.

32

HALYA

June 1944, Leipzig, Germany

Halya ripped open the package from home, her mouth watering already. Mama had done her best to make sure Halya always had food, even now. During the hunger under Stalin's rule and later, when the Germans came and taxed everything—taking food, livestock and even people—Mama had found a way, even if it meant she'd eaten less.

Halya didn't remember the resistance to Soviet farm collectivization and the resulting forced famine that had stolen so many of her family members, but her mama did, and she'd sworn she'd never let Halya go hungry again. Now, she sent postcards and packages whenever she could, like this one, with small loaves of bread, dried plums or apples, and rolled tobacco leaves that Halya could trade for clothing or more food. Still, it was never enough to quell the gnawing hunger inside her.

"I've heard they're going to let us leave the factory on Sundays soon," Slavko said as he leaned over to inspect the contents of the package. "Trying to appease us so we work harder for them, I suppose."

"Or so we don't fall down dead so fast," Halya said.

"Why, Halya, this is a side of you I haven't seen before." Slavko grinned. "When did you become so jaded?"

They sat together under a tree outside Slavko's barracks, enjoying one of their rare afternoons off work. Halya shrugged as she ripped apart the bread and pushed a hunk into his hands.

"Thank you, but you don't have to share with me," he said. "You should save it."

"Just eat it," Halya replied, her mouth already full of bread and her hands still unwrapping things. He hadn't received any packages or postcards in months, and neither had Liliya, so Halya shared whatever she could with them. They never voiced their worries about why the communication with home had stopped, but Halya could tell it bothered them.

She dug into the bottom of her package, and a squeal of excitement slipped past her lips as she opened the dried plums. She swallowed the bread, then popped a plum in her mouth and let the sticky sweetness sit on her tongue. She offered one to Slavko.

"So, where would we go? If we went out on a Sunday, I mean."

He took one and chewed on it, savoring it for a minute, then smiling appreciatively before answering. "We could walk into the city. Look at the shops."

"We hardly have any money left after they take their share

for board, food, and taxes. I'm left with two, maybe three Reichsmarks a week, and I have to use most of that to buy post-cards, stamps and soap." She plucked at her ratty skirt, faded and worn from daily use. "I also need to get a needle and thread to mend these rags."

"It would still be worth looking, don't you think?"

Halya saw him drag his eyes away from the last dried plum, and she pushed it into his hands. "Take this. I'm full."

"You are not," he replied, but he took it and bit half, then offered her the rest.

Halya popped it in her mouth. "I'm nervous to leave."

"I know." Slavko patted her shoulder with his big hand. Somehow, despite the lack of food and sleep, he'd grown taller in the year they'd been there. He stood a head above Halya now, his long skinny limbs stretching as his feet and hands enlarged. Like Liliya, he wore the uncomfortable wooden shoes available to buy, but he took them off whenever he could to let his toes uncurl.

"Liliya won't be able to go," Halya said. "She's working the night shift again."

"She'll miss all the fun then," Slavko said.

Halya laughed. "She would think it's a terrible idea and wouldn't want us to go."

Slavko picked at the hole in the leg of his pants. "Did she ever tell you about her family?"

"Not really," Halya said. "Only that her parents are dead."

"Her mother was killed by the Germans, her brother was killed by the Soviets, and her father was killed by the Poles. Every part of this war has taken something from her, yet she's still the fiercest person I know."

"She has to be," said Halya. She understood Liliya's strength perfectly; she only wished she could emulate it more. "She's the last one in her family."

* * *

The next Sunday, Halya picked at a piece of skin on her shredded hands, ignoring the grumbling of her empty stomach. Most of the blisters she'd developed from carrying the cartridge boxes had healed over, toughening into callouses, so they didn't pain her as much. Her stomach, on the other hand, was a constant reminder of her hunger. She was glad she didn't remember the first time she'd nearly starved to death when she was a baby. This time around was hard enough.

Slavko finally arrived, swinging around the corner of the barracks building as if he didn't have a care in the world. Halya supposed today, of all days, that made sense. This warm Sunday, the first time they'd been allowed to use their one free afternoon of the week to leave the factory campus, they were finally going to stray outside the boundaries and walk around the town.

"Are you ready?" Slavko bent low and gave her a quick hug, then pulled back and assessed her. "You look hungry. Here." He fished a small piece of bread out of his pocket.

Halya's hands trembled, but she clenched them tight to her body. "No. You eat it. I can get my own food."

She hadn't eaten breakfast this morning—the guards said that since they weren't working a full day, they didn't need rations—and she'd given half of her bread from the night before to a sick girl in her barracks.

Slavko shrugged and pushed it toward her. "I know you can. You shared your food from home with me last week. Now it's my turn to share. Eat it. Please."

His earnest green eyes bored into hers, and before she could stop herself, she snatched the bread and shoved the whole thing into her mouth, her teeth crunching into the dried crust with ferocious gusto.

"There." He nodded, satisfied with himself. "That will give you the strength for our walk."

She swallowed, the food sliding down her throat along with her pride. "Let's go."

With their OST patches prominently displayed on their shirts, per the law, they went through the guarded checkpoint at the barbed wire perimeter of their camp, then set off down the street. Halya thought it so odd that an entire city, Leipzig, existed in its own world just on the other side of the fence that held her captive, and now, she'd finally get to see it.

The sun warmed their backs, and when Slavko paused to pick a rock out of his shoe, Halya turned her face up to it and let the trace of a smile curl the corners of her lips. She closed her eyes, imagining she was in her cherry tree back home, a book in her hand and "her head in the clouds," as her father would say. The memory, the wish, tugged so hard at her she nearly toppled over with longing. Would she ever see her home again? Her tree? Her parents?

"What are you thinking about?"

Slavko's voice broke into her thoughts, shattering the images in her head, but for some reason, she didn't mind. She felt a level of comfort with this kind, earnest boy and his cousin—a connection she'd never experienced before. She opened her eyes and looked at him, and his cheeks reddened.

"I didn't mean to pry. I've just never seen you smile like that."

Her mouth slipped back into its normal downward curve. "Home. I was thinking of home."

"Which part?" Slavko asked as they resumed walking. "What do you miss most?"

"My tree," Halya answered quickly. "Well, my parents, of course. I miss them above all else, but I had a tree. A sour cherry tree. My mama made the best *varenyky* from its fruit, but I loved to climb into the branches with a book and read. As soon as my chores were done, that's where I'd be. My father said I perched in that tree like a bird."

Slavko grinned. "My mother is the same way with her *kalyna* bush. She tends to that thing as if she gave birth to it, even though it was Liliya's mother that planted it. She's always pruning it and talking to it. My father says she loves it more than him."

"My mama has a *kalyna* bush, too," Halya said. "A big beautiful one by our door. She makes me eat a tincture of those bitter berries when I'm sick."

"Same," Slavko laughed. "Mama says it will fix anything."

Halya's mouth twitched, and before she could help herself, a full-blown smile stretched across her face. Her cheek muscles creaked as they pulled her lips upward into the unfamiliar arc, but it felt good to smile. To be happy with Slavko in this one moment.

"It's good to see you smile so much. I thought you'd forgotten how," Slavko teased.

Halya's smile turned into a scowl. "Has anyone ever told you how ridiculous you are?"

He laughed. His smiles still came easily, even as they arced above the scars on his neck from his time in the jail. She envied his resilience.

"I've been told that a lot, actually," he said.

"Are you always this happy? Even when life seems so bleak?"

Slavko hesitated, and his smile slipped, just for a moment, but enough for Halya to catch a glimpse of his real emotions: fear, exhaustion, worry. Guilt shot through her. She shouldn't have teased him about his happy mood. In fact, she should be taking notes from him. Wallowing in her own self-pity wouldn't get her anywhere. How many times had Tato told her that she needed to face life head on, rise to the challenges in front of her, and be strong? He would like Slavko.

"Never mind, you don't have to answer that," she added. "I'm sorry. I'm just having a hard time adjusting to this life. I'm not myself."

"You are exactly who you need to be right now, but it doesn't mean it's who you have to be forever. We all wear masks to get through the day." Slavko gave her a friendly poke with his elbow. "That's what I tell myself, at least. Now come on, let's look around this town we live in now."

Halya followed, wondering if Slavko ever took his mask off. Did she really know him? Or was it just the Slavko he wanted her to know?

A few blocks from the factory, they came upon a crowd gathered around two young people. The girl, a blonde-haired, blue-eyed waif with a large "P" sewn on to her shirt—much like their OST patches—didn't look much older than Halya, maybe fourteen or fifteen. A man wearing a self-righteous smirk hacked away at her hair with scissors, cutting it to the scalp. The boy, a few years older than the girl, but not yet a man, hung his head in shame next to her, his own hair already shorn. Halya touched her head, her own ragged hair tucked under a kerchief, as sympathy swelled in her chest. The people jeered and laughed as the girl stared straight ahead, her chin trembling. The boy tried to reach out and take her hand, but another man hit his hand away, then punched him in the face. The boy fell to his knees, and the crowd dragged him back up.

Halya stood, rooted to the ground, as the mob hung signs written in German around the couple's necks, then pushed them down the dirt road. A group of young people with instruments began playing a rousing march, and everyone clapped and shouted as the couple walked.

Slavko grabbed Halya's hand and tugged her away from the scene. "Let's go back."

"But why are they doing that to them?"

Slavko ignored her, pulling her along at a fast clip as he moved in the opposite direction of the raucous group. When he finally stopped, Halya yanked her hand back and leaned forward. "Tell me what that was about."

Slavko rubbed the back of his neck. "They were together. A Polish *Ostarbeiter* and a German boy. It's illegal, so they're being punished."

Of course. Halya knew the laws. They'd been drilled into every *Ostarbeiter* who came into Germany. She just hadn't seen any enforced in person. "What will they do to them? Besides what they've already done, I mean."

"I doubt they kill the German boy. He's too useful to them as a Nazi youth. As for the Polish girl . . ." He trailed off and shrugged.

Halya thought of the girl's trembling chin and realized her own had followed suit. She clenched her jaw, speaking through her teeth. "They told us the penalty was death."

"Maybe it will just be prison if she's lucky," Slavko said.

"Whoever thought we'd wish for prison as an alternative?"

"Anything is better than death," Slavko said. "Living is a choice, and you must always fight to live."

"My father said something similar to me once." Longing pierced Halya, making her eyes fill with tears. She'd give anything to see him again.

"He sounds like a wise man." Slavko put his arm around her shoulder, and she leaned into him, letting him help her carry the weight of her grief as she pondered his words.

Living is a choice.

Had she been choosing to live, or had she been floating along just trying to survive? Letting life push her down, crying in her bed all the time, escaping into sleep. She was surviving, but was she living? But how did one find the energy to do anything more than survive with an empty stomach, aching muscles, and crushing despair hanging over them?

"You're right. He is a wise man," Halya said softly. "I should try harder to remember his advice."

33

VIKA

October 1944, Breslau, Germany

Vika's breath clouded into misty puffs as she glanced at the low gray clouds hugging the horizon. From the back of the wagon, Nadya coughed—a deep, phlegmy sound that made goosebumps stand up on Vika's arms. They'd stopped several times on their journey, when Nadya had fallen ill again and to work a few months during the harvest to earn food and money, and now, they needed to find a temporary shelter and more supplies before winter reared its ugly head in full. The delays made Vika sick, but there was nothing to be done about it.

"I spoke with a farmer, and he said we're just outside Breslau. Once we're there, I should be able to get work or trade for food until Nadya is feeling better," Maksym said, as if reading her thoughts.

"Where will we stay?" Vika asked. "She needs shelter. The

wagon was fine in the warm weather, but she can't live in it when it gets cold."

Maksym clucked at the horses, urging them on. "I'm sure we'll find something."

"Maybe we can make it to one of the refugee camps set up in the west eventually, but we can't press on further than Breslau until she's well," Vika said.

"Do you want to stay through the winter?" Maksym asked.

"What else can we do?" Vika snapped. The stress of their journey compounded with Nadya's illness had pushed everyone to the edge. "We can't travel with her this sick. We need to find a doctor and somewhere safe for her to heal."

She wouldn't consider the alternative.

The gray sky cracked open, drizzling a cold rain on them and shutting out the possibility of a fire. As if on cue, Nadya began coughing in the back of the wagon.

"I think we'll eat dinner in the wagon and huddle together for warmth. Just like the little piglets we used to have, remember, children?" Vika tried to sound cheerful, tried to make a fun game out of it, but the excitement of travel had worn off long ago, and exhaustion plagued them all.

As Maksym tended to the horses, Vika scraped the last bit of *salo* they'd worked for at a nearby farm out of the jar and spread it on the two remaining pieces of dried bread she had. This was it. They had no more food after tonight.

"I'm hungry," Bohdan said.

"Then it's a good thing we're eating now." Vika didn't look at her son. She didn't want to see the pale cheeks and sunken eyes —the hallmarks of hunger—on the face of one of her children.

Sofia's clothes hung off her frame in loose folds, and she sat hunkered down next to Vika, wrapped in blankets. Vika cut the bread slices into five even pieces, then pushed the plate of food to her. "Here. Take one."

Sofia wolfed the bread down, then used her finger to wipe up every crumb left on the plate where her slice had sat. Vika set one aside for Maksym, handed a piece each to Bohdan and Nadya, then cut her piece into thirds and gave one to Sofia.

Sofia snatched up the food, then paused. "No, Mama. You need to eat, too."

"I'm not that hungry," Vika lied. Her stomach growled and twisted, but it was a feeling she'd grown very used to in the past. Now, she filled her stomach with rage and fear, two opposite yet still oddly connected emotions, and it fueled her just fine.

Besides, a few more nights of hunger until they got to Breslau wouldn't kill her. She couldn't take that chance with her children.

* * *

The next afternoon, a large city appeared on the horizon. *One more day.* Vika wearily shook the thoughts out of her head as she spotted three small farmhouses in the distance.

"Let's stop up here," Maksym said. "Maybe one of them will trade me labor for food."

"That one, Tato." Sofia pointed to the house on the left. "See, it's got a stork's nest. That means it's lucky."

A glimmer of hope flared in Vika. "Yes, let's try that one then. If it's good enough for a stork, it's good enough for us."

Maksym nodded and urged the horses on.

As the last bits of light trickled out from the sinking sun, the wagon rolled up to the house. Poppies struggled to grow among the forgotten flower gardens flanking the ramshackle fence. Homesickness tugged at Vika's heart. Her poppies back in Maky probably looked just as ragged.

A tired-looking woman, so weathered and worn down she could have been anywhere from thirty-five to fifty-five, came outside. Her pale blonde hair, faded into a dull gray, matched the sallow complexion of her skin.

"You can use my well and my barn for the night but I don't have food to spare," she said in Polish.

Vika patted Maksym's arm, then stepped forward. They'd learned that women on their own often responded more positively to her than him. "Thank you. If you do have anything, just for the children, we'd be happy to work for you. We can do whatever you need."

The woman sniffed, staring off into the distance, then she glanced at the wagon where three sets of hungry eyes stared back at her. Her gaze softened. "I suppose I could use some help with the last bits of my harvest. It's not much, but if you stay and work a few days, I could probably spare some food for them. Maybe for you two, as well, depending on how hard you work."

The knot in Vika's chest loosened, and she bowed her head. "We're grateful. When can we start?"

"Tomorrow morning. For tonight, I have some bread and butter. My sister works at a dairy, and she brings by food sometimes since the Germans took my cow."

As Maksym tended to the horses in the barn, the woman led Vika and the children inside and directed them to sit at the table. The small loaf of bread and a mound of butter made

Vika's mouth water, but she averted her eyes. No sense in hoping for more than she'd been promised. If the children could eat, Vika would be happy.

The woman, who'd instructed Vika to call her Agata, sliced off a thick piece of the dark bread, slathered on butter, and passed it to Bohdan. He murmured a polite thank you, then shoved a huge bite into his mouth.

"Go easy." Vika placed a hand on his shoulder. "Savor it."

As Bohdan forced himself to chew slower, Agata handed similar pieces to Nadya and Sofia. She glanced at Vika, then sliced off another, smaller piece and passed it over.

"Oh," Vika gasped. She didn't want to accept this charity for herself when she needed it more for her children, but the smell of the bread made her dizzy with longing. Her hand curled around it instinctively. "Thank you."

Agata shrugged, her frail shoulders barely lifting under her threadbare dress. "If I don't give it to you, soldiers will probably take it. They make their rounds here."

"Your sister works at a dairy, you said?" Vika said.

"Yes, just west of Breslau."

Vika swallowed her pride, like she'd had to do so many other times on this journey. "We're hoping to find work for the winter and a place to stay. Do you think she could help?"

Agata shrugged again. "Maybe. She's supposed to come by this week. We could ask."

* * *

Two days later, when Agata's sister, Inga, arrived with a basket of cheese and butter and two jars of milk, Vika wasted no time in asking about a job. Older than her sister, but still a nonde-script, war-hardened age, Inga eyed the newcomers warily, then warmed to Bohdan's sweet smile and offered him a glass of milk. Where Agata was flighty and deflated, Inga was sharp and strong. Despite the fatigue ringing her eyes, her worn clothes were clean and pressed neatly, her hair tucked into a tidy bun.

"Why are you wanting to stay here?" Inga's shrewd glance took in Vika and left her feeling lacking. She reminded Vika of her mother.

"We're not. Not permanently, at least. Our daughter is sick, and we need a warm, dry place to let her heal. Just for a short time and we'll work to make some money while we're here. We need more food and supplies if we're to keep moving west."

Inga peered down at Nadya, asleep in Vika's arms, and her face softened the slightest bit. "What is your goal?"

"I'm going to find my eldest son and niece. They were taken to work in a factory in Germany."

Inga's hand faltered, and she nearly dropped a jar of milk. Her voice came out tight and pained. "And you hope to find them?"

"I will find them," Vika corrected. "And we couldn't stay in our village. The front drew too close."

Inga battled back whatever emotions brewed under her surface and gave Vika a once-over, as if inspecting livestock. "The dairy always needs strong workers. I have a spare room in my apartment. I'd have to charge you rent, of course, but you could stay with me. Your children can stay there during the day if your oldest can watch them or they can accompany you to work. As for you . . ." She turned to Maksym. "I don't have a job for you, but I know someone who might."

Vika gripped the woman's hands. "I can't thank you enough."

Inga's lip raised up on one side, a forced effort that seemed out of place on her stoic face. "I am alone now. Some company might be nice."

* * *

Wehrmacht soldiers scuttled about Breslau like rats—lingering on corners and in doorways, scurrying in and out of shadows, waiting for their opportunity to feast. They sauntered, two or three abreast, down the sidewalks and moved over for no one. The whole city reeked of their rot, a pungent smell of arrogance, cruelty, and brash indifference.

"Just avoid them as much as possible," Inga instructed. "There are more here now than before. Hitler has declared Breslau a fortress city, and he's reinforcing it so the Reds can't take it. Our apartment building is only eight blocks from the dairy on the edge of town, so you shouldn't have to interact with them too much. But make sure you always have your papers with you because they will stop you."

Vika nodded as she shifted Nadya in her arms.

Inga unlocked her door and waved them in. "It's not much."

Two high windows framed the opposite wall, and a small table sat next to a stove on the left side of a large, open room. Just past the sofa, a door in the right corner led to a tiny bedroom.

"I'll move this bed out to the main room for me," Inga said. "I don't have another bed, but you can make a pallet on the floor with your blankets. And there's a community bathroom at the end of the hall."

Vika and Maksym followed Inga to the table. "I don't mean to sound ungrateful, but I'm curious. Why are you being so kind to strangers?"

Inga's gaze drifted over to the children, and her features softened into a completely different countenance. She blinked fast, as if pushing rising memories back down. "I had a daughter once. Maybe if someone had helped us back then, things would have turned out differently."

Vika put her hand on Inga's arm. "Was she taken to the labor camps as well?"

Inga gave a tight nod. "Back in 1942. I got postcards at first, but I haven't heard from her in over a year."

Vika ignored the shiver that ran through her at Inga's despondency. She hadn't heard from Slavko or Liliya since the fall of 1943, months before they began their journey, but she didn't let herself dwell on that. She couldn't if she wanted to keep pushing forward.

"That doesn't mean anything," Vika said. "You have to maintain hope."

Maksym stiffened next to her. "Sometimes hope is too painful."

"Maksym . . ." Vika reached out to her husband in surprise, but he pulled away.

Inga laughed—a dry, brittle sound that made Vika wince. "Don't worry about me. My hope died long ago."

* * *

Later that night, as Vika tucked the children into bed, someone shouted in German, then a gunshot rang out. She ignored it, making sure each child had enough blankets before sliding in and wrapping her arms around them. Love and worry made her chest ache. They depended on her to keep them safe, but when she stopped to think about their precarious situation, she grew nauseous. If she couldn't even promise them they'd make it through the night, how could she dream for their futures? Nothing was guaranteed in this life; no one was safe from the Nazis or Soviets.

She smoothed back Sofia's hair, then pressed a kiss to her forehead. She did the same for her younger children, said a prayer for Slavko and Liliya's safety, and let her eyes drift shut.

34

LILIYA

October 1944, Leipzig, Germany

The old man sat under the sprawling oak tree, his back pressed against the bark, a notebook resting on his propped-up knees in front of him. Liliya's fingers twitched as he began to move his pencil. She could almost hear the scratch as it glided along the paper, and the sudden desire to draw made her knees go weak.

Ever since they'd been allowed to leave the barracks on Sunday afternoons and shop in the local stores—or at least the stores that wouldn't turn away *Ostarbeiters*—he'd appeared here on Sunday evenings, and every night he drew, Liliya watched him.

She wanted to ask him which store had sold him the notebook, how much it cost, and how he'd managed to buy it with the paltry wages they received, but she couldn't make herself approach him. She hadn't picked up a pencil since she'd forced herself to draw Halya's parents, but even then, she hadn't poured her soul into the drawing like in the past. She'd pushed herself to create it for Halya while the image was fresh in her head. It wasn't meaningful to her the way her old drawings had been, but even that effort had still gutted her.

"I see you there," the old man called out in Ukrainian.

Liliya gasped and stepped backward into the doorway behind her.

"You watch every week." He didn't look up from his sketch-book. "You may as well come over."

Liliya hesitated, then shouted back, "I don't want to."

"Suit yourself." The man shrugged. "I thought maybe you'd want to join me."

Despite her initial reticence, intrigue propelled her closer. One step. Then two.

"Why would you want me to do that?" Another step.

"I've seen the way you watch me draw, the yearning you keep tamped down." He dropped his gaze to his paper and continued drawing. "It will make you sick to deny that part of yourself."

"That part of me is dead." By now, she was nearly at his side, her gaze following the swoop of his hand as he drew. She twisted her hands into a knot to keep them from reaching out for the pencil, surprised by the urge, the longing swelling up in her chest.

He finally looked up at her with kind blue eyes. Wrinkles fanned out from his deeply tanned face, and his hair had more gray than brown in it. Up close, he was even older than she thought—maybe in his sixties—probably one of the oldest

Ostarbeiters she'd seen. She wondered how he kept up with the work.

"Along with everyone you love?" he asked.

His simple words unleashed a barrage of grief so thick it momentarily stunned her. She nodded.

"I know that feeling." He flipped over the page so a new, clean sheet sat on top. "But you can't stop. Here, give it a try."

"I don't think I can." Liliya took a step back, the initial compulsion she'd felt to get close to this man now shifting into fear. "I don't think I want to."

"Fine." He dropped his offering and began to draw again. "But you will, and when you do, you know where to find me."

* * *

Liliya thought about that man all week, and by the time Sunday came around again, she'd decided she would talk to him more. It didn't mean she had to draw, but she wanted to know more about him. His name, where he was from, how he knew she'd lost so much. That last one bothered her the most. She strove to keep herself together, to keep her pain concealed, but he'd seen right through her facade.

This time, he didn't acknowledge her at all, and she stood, waiting next to him for nearly a half hour while he finished sketching a picture of a beautiful young woman.

"Who was she?" Liliya finally asked.

The man looked up at her, startled. He hadn't noticed she was there.

"You're back," he said simply.

"Was she your daughter?"

He nodded as he ran his hand down the cheek of his drawing. "She was killed when the Soviets invaded our village in 1939."

"And drawing her makes you happy?" She thought of the sketch of her brother she'd done after returning from finding his dead body. Recreating him on paper had made her feel closer to him, but somewhere along the way, maybe when her dead loved ones began to outnumber her living loved ones, that act had lost its appeal and merely become a painful reminder of all she'd lost.

"It makes me remember," he said with a sad smile. "I don't know that anything will make me happy again but drawing her the way I want to remember her helps."

The brutal truth of his statement stole Liliya's breath.

"I remember, too," she whispered. "I can still see them all. How they looked when they died. But that's not what I want to remember."

Nina.

Tato.

Mama.

Mykhailo.

Their names, a constant chant in her mind, a pulsing beat in her veins. It reverberated through her, throbbing down her arm until her hand trembled. She dropped to her knees next to the old man as he held out his pencil and sketchpad.

"Then draw them the way you want. Bring them back to you on your own terms."

She stared at the proffered items and slowly reached out. Her fingers flexed, then tightened around the pencil, and she let it fly, arcing it across the paper, now propped in her own lap, in strong, decisive strokes. As Nina's countenance emerged from the blank page, a surge of emotion swelled in Liliya's chest. She didn't realize tears were falling from her eyes until they splashed down on to the paper, smearing Nina's sweet smile.

Liliya jerked her head back and dragged a sleeve across her face as the old man patted her shoulder.

"See, you can't keep that inside of you. It sours your art and your spirit alike. You must channel it and release it. Put your pain out into the world so we can share the burden with you."

He rustled in the bag at his feet and pulled out another sketchbook and pencil. "I knew you'd come back, so I got you this."

Liliya shook her head. "I can't accept that. It's too much, and I can't pay you for it."

"It is a gift." He pushed it into her hands. "From one artist to another. I have no one left, so let me help you. Now go release your pain."

* * *

Liliya drew for hours, the images pouring forth from her hand, from her soul, like a swollen spring stream rushing downhill. She could no more stop their flow than she could stop breathing. She drew her mother, her father, her brother, and she drew so many images of Nina she lost count. They all hurt, but Nina's loss bore an element of guilt that pierced her like a barb, and she couldn't heal it.

But it helped. The old man was right. Every drawing she did purged a shard of jagged pain. It scraped and burned as she pushed it out, taking small pieces of her with it, but she felt a little better afterward—less a vessel of grief and more human again. A survivor.

Her next drawing surprised her—evolving slowly, more thoughtfully than the previous portraits. A strong jawline, high cheekbones and wide-set eyes. She didn't stop until Filip's face stared back at her, his lips quirked in a grin. Her finger traced the outline, and she imagined him there with her, not a flat drawing, but a living, breathing man. He'd wrap his arms around her and tell her it would be all right, that she would be all right. He'd carry the pain with her, along with his own, and they would work together to heal.

But he was back in Volhynia, and she was here in Germany. They had armies between them.

She couldn't recreate the way his touch felt on her skin or the thrill of anticipation the sound of his voice gave her, but she could draw his likeness. It would have to be enough, for now, and someday, it might be all she had left of her past. She and Slavko hadn't had news from home in over a year. Slavko believed it stemmed from the unreliable mail service. Liliya feared a more dire reason for the silence, for she knew better than anyone how cruel and fleeting life was.

35

VIKA

January 1945, Breslau, Germany

Vika stood, her knees creaking. Pain throbbed in her hands and back, but there were still five more cows to be milked before she could go home after her evening shift. She moved her stool to the next one, an ornery, ginger-colored cow who liked to kick over the bucket if you didn't pay attention. With the stool in place, Vika ignored the ache in her fingers and began milking, squeezing from the top down in one fluid motion.

Laughter rang out across the aisle, where other women milked different cows, but Vika didn't join in. She kept her distance, putting in her hours without talking to anyone. During the first few weeks, several women had tried to befriend her, but they'd quickly given up when Vika only nodded or grunted in return. She didn't have the energy to make new friends she'd only be leaving. The dairy farm provided a solid job for her, which, along with Maksym's job delivering large bags of mail parcels to nearby towns, provided bread and money enough to keep them housed with Inga for now.

Blackout curtains closed tight on every window created a velvety darkness that engulfed Vika when she walked home that night. Her legs ached as she climbed the stairs to Inga's apartment. They'd been lucky to find her when they did. Refugees overwhelmed the city now. People laid bedrolls out wherever there was open space, sleeping in makeshift tents and under wagons. Camps spilled over into empty fields around the city and popped up in public spaces.

Inga greeted her from where she sat drinking a cup of tea at the table. "Your children are in your room. Your husband said he had more deliveries to make, so he went back out."

Vika slipped into the tiny room and bent low over her brood. Bohdan stretched out in a wild tangle of limbs, and Sofia curled in a ball, her arms around Nadya. Vika leaned over and kissed each of them, but her hand stilled as she brushed the hair off Nadya's face. She pressed her lips against Nadya's forehead and gasped.

"My God, she's on fire again."

Suddenly, the air-raid sirens blared. Vika's heart leapt into her throat, and a cold sweat popped up all over her, like it always did when they went off. The horrible, droning noise instigated a fight or flight reaction in her she couldn't control no matter how many times she heard it. Inga told her she'd grow immune to it eventually, but Vika had her doubts.

"Come, children. We must go."

Bohdan scrambled to his feet, and Sofia groaned, but Nadya barely moved. Vika scooped her up.

Her arms ached by the time they made it to the cellar, where a handful of other people from the neighboring apartments had already staked out spots. Inga and Vika sat on a bench against the far wall, Bohdan and Sofia between them. Vika kept Nadya on her lap, rocking and murmuring to the girl who'd only just now opened her eyes. Nadya's fevered body scorched Vika's skin, almost a welcome relief from the bone-chilling cold of the January night if Vika didn't let herself think about what it meant.

"Mama? Is it different this time?" Bohdan asked, just like he did every time they made this trek.

"No. Everything is fine. I'm sure the all-clear signal will sound in no time."

Vika prayed this was true. How many times had they hidden in this bomb shelter only to emerge unscathed a few hours later? Sometimes, she didn't want to bother hiding. The risk seemed so low in comparison to the allure of a full night's sleep, but she couldn't risk her children like that.

So, she forced a smile and exuded cheer while the worry, the fear, the fatigue all pressed on her night and day, rubbing her soul raw until all she wanted to do was scream.

It was exhausting. She was exhausted.

"My head hurts," Nadya said.

"I know, my love. Try to go back to sleep. We'll be back in our bed in no time."

"What about Tato?" Sofia asked.

"I'm sure he's in a bomb shelter somewhere, too," Vika said, though she was sure of no such thing. Maksym rarely had time to stop if he wanted to complete his route. He hadn't said as much, but Vika suspected he ignored the bomb sirens more often than not.

Suddenly, the cellar walls shuddered behind Vika as a bomb hit, and the woman from the apartment below them screamed. Vika shifted Nadya to one arm and pulled Sofia and Bohdan closer with the other. Several more bombs fell, and dust and dirt thickened the cellar air. The woman who'd screamed earlier began to cry, but a strange numbness fell over Vika. None of this seemed real—her sick daughter, her missing husband, the bombs falling overhead—but with three sets of young eyes watching her, she didn't have the luxury of falling apart. They needed her to be brave and strong, and so she was.

She cuddled her children close, covering them as much as she could with her arms and torso, and sang softly to them. Infused with the strength and beauty of Ukraine, the old folk songs from her childhood surrounded them like a blanket. Nadya, her fever still raging, dozed off, and eventually Sofia and Bohdan did the same. After nearly ninety minutes, the all-clear signal blared, and the weary group crawled up from the cellar.

In the west, the oil reserves near the Oder River glowed orange, the flames reaching up into the sky like bony fingers grasping for purchase against the night. The street around them was untouched, but closer to the river, gaping holes in the skyline showed where the bombs had found their targets. A voice crackled over the citywide siren system, and Vika strained to listen, thankful that she'd picked up enough German working in the dairy here to understand most of what he said.

"The civilian populace must evacuate every district of

Breslau east of the Oder immediately. The Oder bridges in the city are being prepared for demolition by engineers. Proceed on foot to the western side of the city, where every step has been taken to prepare for your arrival."

"That's us," Inga breathed. "Where will we go?"

Vika choked down a shrill laugh. Where *would* they go? It was a question Vika had asked herself far too often, and now here she was, asking it again. Where could a family find safety in the middle of a war? Where could a mother promise her children a peaceful night's sleep on this bloody continent?

Fatigue pulled at Vika from every direction, but she hefted Nadya higher in her arms and started walking back to their apartment to pack. "Anywhere but here. If the Reds are that close, we must prepare to go anywhere but here."

* * *

The two women made quick work of packing, and all the while Vika kept one eye on the door, willing Maksym to walk through it and trying not to wonder what she would do if he didn't.

Inga gave Vika an old suitcase to use, and she carefully placed her holy icons and *rushnyky*, Liliya's sketchbooks, and the dried *kalyna* berries at the bottom, then layered her children's clothes over them. She filled the rest of the space with food, a few tin bowls and cups, and a pot.

"How can I leave everything else behind?" Inga cried as she clutched a plate to her chest. "This is all I have left in the world."

"Your life is more valuable than anything here," Vika said. "And if the Soviets get here, you may lose that."

Inga nodded and set the plate down. "What about my poor sister?"

"She's probably already on her way." Vika rolled up an extra blanket. "Maybe we'll meet her along the road."

"I hope so," Inga said as the door burst open, and Maksym stepped inside.

Vika let out a shaky breath. She dropped the blanket and threw herself at him so hard she nearly toppled him over.

"It's madness out there," he said. His arms wrapped around Vika.

She took a moment to gather her thoughts, to breathe him in, and when she finally spoke, her voice wobbled. "I didn't know if you'd make it here."

He pulled back, his hands gripping her arms. "I will always come back to you, Vikusia."

A rush of tenderness for her husband warmed her cheeks. With so much stress over Nadya's re-occurring illness, Slavko being taken, and traveling, she'd nearly forgotten what it was like to feel his love. To remember the spark of heat in his eyes when he looked at her this way.

"The horses and wagon are gone," he finally said when they broke their embrace. "The Bürgermeister took them."

Vika glanced at her children and thought of the deep snow she'd trudged through to get home earlier. Panic fluttered in her chest, and the relief she'd felt at Maksym's return dissipated. "All right. We'll figure it out. The children can walk, and we'll take turns carrying Nadya."

"I'm not going," Inga announced.

Vika whipped around to stare at the other woman. "What

do you mean you're not going? You have to go! They're evacuating!"

"I'll leave, but I won't go west with everyone else." Inga crossed her arms. "I'm going east toward my sister. She's all I have left in the world, and I won't lose her."

Vika thought about her own sister, Maria, and guilt made her stomach knot.

"Inga—" she began, but Maksym touched her arm.

"Let her be, Vikusia. She's made her decision."

Vika bit her lip and shook her head. "Fine. If that's what you want."

"It is. And I want you to take my handcart. For her." Inga ran her knuckles down Nadya's smooth cheek. "She can't walk in this."

Vika threw her arms around Inga. "I will never be able to repay you for your kindness."

Inga stiffened, then slowly brought her arms up and encircled Vika. "Find your boy and heal your family," she whispered. "For all of us who couldn't."

"Come on." Vika glanced at the mass of people in the street. "We need to get moving."

The cold air bit at Vika's bare skin, and she pulled her shawl tighter around her face and neck as she took in the scene before her—crying children, stoic mothers, naïve teenagers hauling carts much like hers filled the street. They trudged alongside the residents of Breslau and the refugees still fleeing the Red Army even now, after they'd thought they were far enough away. Deep snow pulled at her boots, making every step laborious. Still Vika welcomed the work, because it created heat in her body to fight the unbearable cold.

Every so often, a truck drove by with someone shouting over a loudspeaker about the evacuation. As they marched closer to the Oder River, the group slowed to funnel onto the narrow bridge. Vika took the break to check on Nadya. She slept peacefully, so Vika shook her awake. She knew all too well the dangers of falling asleep when you were cold.

"Get up, Nadya. Walk along with me for a bit."

"I don't feel well, Mama." Nadya pushed her mother's hands away and curled into the blankets.

"I don't care." Vika pulled the girl out of the cart. "You must fight through it and get up."

"She's sick," Maksym said. "Let her rest."

"That's how you die when it's this cold," Vika said. "You should know that! She has to move every so often."

"Surely they'll have something set up for us once we cross the river. A camp or building where we can warm up and get food. They said every step has been taken to prepare."

"I don't believe anything a Nazi tells me, and you're a fool if you think crossing the river will save us," Vika said. "We need to keep moving west."

"That's where Slavko and Liliya are anyway, Mama," Bohdan said. "Now we'll just get there sooner."

"That's right, Bohdanko." Vika paused to give her son a small smile.

For a moment, she let her imagination soar as she dreamed of what it would be like to put her arms around her sweet boy and tell him how much she loved him. How sorry she was that she hadn't fought harder to keep him safe. Tears welled in Vika's eyes at the prospect, then froze to her cheeks as they spilled over. She flicked them away and walked on.

The question was, now that they didn't have horses and a wagon, should they try to get on a train? The stations would be overflowing with people desperate to get out of the city. What were the chances they, refugees without German citizenship, could get a coveted spot on a train?

Perhaps they should go as far southwest as possible, marching along with this crowd, then catch a train outside the city. This seemed like the most logical option, but when she looked back at her children huddled under a mass of blankets in the cart, fear swelled in her throat.

"What should we do? Are we going to keep walking?" Vika asked.

"I don't think we should go to a train station here," Maksym said, echoing Vika's initial thoughts. "They'll be too busy, and we won't get a spot. We should keep walking and catch a train in a smaller station somewhere further along. What do you think?"

Vika didn't reply. Around them, the throngs of people pressed closer as more joined in the evacuation. Alongside the road, two women had stopped. One held a quiet infant, and the other was trying to pull the baby out of the first's arms.

"You have to leave him! He's gone, Elsa!"

"No!" The woman holding the baby turned away, clutching the still form to her chest. "I can't leave him here."

"If you don't, your other children might not survive either." The other woman gestured toward three small children crouched near their feet. "Come on, we have to keep moving."

The first woman gave a wretched sob, then let the second woman take the baby from her arms. She set it in the snowbank next to the road, crossed herself, then hauled the first woman up by the arm.

Vika dragged her eyes away from the scene and looked at her own children, huddled in the hand cart. "I think we need to do whatever it takes to get on a train as soon as possible."

* * *

Vika couldn't feel her hands. She thought maybe they'd frozen around the handles of the cart in the hours since they'd crossed the Oder River. She stamped her feet hard with each step. Her toes tingled, but they hadn't gone numb yet, which was a good sign.

All around them, people marched west. Mothers carrying babies and children perched in carts or plodding alongside them. Old men and women clutching their bags while taking tottering steps through the snow. The wind whipped across Vika's face, reminding her that it was nearly twenty degrees below zero. She pulled her shawl tighter around her head and tilted her face down, watching each foot push into the snow and hit the ground.

"How much farther until the train station?" she asked.

"The Freiburger Bahnhof is only a few blocks away," Maksym said. He motioned for Vika to move over, and he took up the cart handles. "We can see what the situation is there, and if we need to move on to a smaller station or not."

Vika rubbed her hands together, then pressed them back under her arms. A few more blocks. She could walk a few more blocks. Before Maksym started, Vika pulled her children out of the cart again so they could walk, too. Sofia and Bohdan grimaced as their feet hit the ground, but soon they were plodding along.

"Just a bit longer, children." Vika forced cheer into her voice. "Walking will keep you warmer. You can make it."

As the station came into view, a scene of chaos unfolded. Masses of people wandered around piles of discarded luggage, prams, and carts. Patients from the recently evacuated hospitals hobbled around on crutches. Mothers carrying heavy loads yelled for children to stay close and not wander.

Two children stood next to a pile of bedding, crying and tugging at their collapsed mother's arm. Another woman came over, pulled the woman up, and motioned for the two children to follow her as she led them all out of the station.

A woman walked by holding two suitcases, frantically shouting, "Franz? Where are you? Franz!"

"What happened to her, Mama?" Bohdan asked.

Vika jerked her eyes away. She didn't want to witness this woman's pain; it was far too familiar to her. Instead, she searched the terminal, looking for a small boy. The crowd was too thick to see much, though, and the woman passed by them, slipping into the tangled mass of bodies. "She lost her child. You three must stay very close to me! Do you understand? Don't let me out of your sight!"

The children nodded solemnly.

Maksym scanned the crowd. "It's foolish to wait for a train when only the wealthiest and most important people will be let on. We need to keep walking."

"Let's just wait a little bit here out of the wind," Vika said. "Maybe something will open up."

Maksym frowned, but he sat down next to the cart and pulled Bohdan and Sofia close.

* * *

They rested for an hour at the station, watching as trains filled up with Breslau's elite and middle class, waiting for their chance to jump in a car.

Nadya sat in Vika's lap. Her fever had broken, finally, but exhaustion still racked her tiny frame. She took a shuddering breath, then pulled the blanket Vika had tucked around her over her head, trying to block out the noise. Vika rubbed her back and took Bohdan's hand.

"I think it's time we get moving again," Maksym said. "Can you do it, children?"

Sofia and Bohdan nodded grimly. They climbed into the cart, and Vika lifted Nadya into Sofia's arms, then they merged back into the masses walking west.

They walked for hours with Vika and Maksym taking turns pulling the cart. Every so often, Vika made everyone get out and walk to keep their blood moving. Maksym slowed his pace with the cart, and Vika fell behind to watch them, ensuring no one stopped or got lost. When she helped them back into the cart and rubbed their arms and legs, they didn't even cry or flinch like they had at the beginning of the journey.

The relentless cold tore at Vika with ragged claws, enticing her to sit and let it devour her completely. Whispers of words swirled past her ears on the wind.

Give up. Close your eyes and go to sleep, and all of this will disappear.

The temptation pulled at her, and she squeezed her eyes shut and walked blindly for a few steps, contemplating the lure of a dreamless sleep. No more hunger. No more freezing. No more loss. It would be so easy to slip away from this fear and uncertainty, to let the cold curl around her, embrace her.

"Mama!" Sofia slapped Vika hard, her thin fingers stinging as they connected with Vika's face. "Wake up! Don't go to sleep! Please!"

Vika stared at her daughter in shock, her cheek throbbing. She touched it, clinging to the feeling of pain, so different from the passivity the cold produced. In her self-imposed darkness, she'd veered right, away from Maksym and the cart, and fallen to her knees on the side of the road where, in a ditch, lay the bodies of six children and their mother. The mother stared up at the sky, sightless, as the wind whipped her scarf out from under the baby at her breast. Her other children clustered around her, all asleep. Or dead, most likely. None of them moved.

Vika sucked in a breath and jerked away from the sight, her eyes already focused ahead again.

"I'm sorry I hit you," Sofia said. "I tried shaking you and yelling, but you wouldn't answer me. I was scared."

"You did well." Vika gripped her daughter's arm. Not once had Sofia complained or fallen apart. She'd cradled her siblings as they cried and encouraged them to walk with kind words when they had to move for warmth. Shame washed over Vika for her weakness, for forcing her daughter to be the responsible one, even for one moment. "You did very well."

* * *

By the time they reached Kanth in the early hours of the morning, Vika had lost count of the frozen corpses alongside the road. Her initial shock at their presence had faded; her emotions numbed like her fingers and toes. An open-bed truck passed them by, filled to overflowing with cold bodies retrieved from the snow, but the dead still accumulated like fallen leaves, along with discarded carts, bundles of clothing, and suitcases.

The crowd had thinned as people gave up next to the road or spread out in search of shelter, fanning out to nearby villages and farms. Vika and Maksym finally veered toward a farm-house tucked at the end of a lane, and there, they found a surprisingly helpful old couple who offered them warm milk and a place by the fire to warm up.

Vika unwrapped each child and rewrapped them in dry blankets, rubbing their legs, feet, and hands until they finally did cry from the tingling sensation of their blood flowing again, then set the wet clothes by the stove to dry. She felt Nadya's head and said a silent prayer of thanks that her fever hadn't come back.

Slowly, the color returned to their pale cheeks, and Vika sat next to them, the last reserves of her energy completely spent. If she closed her eyes for a long blink, she'd fall asleep and not wake up for hours, and she couldn't do that until the children were safe and settled.

The old woman bustled around them, pouring heated milk into cups and slicing up the remains of a loaf of bread. "You need to eat this, then rest. I don't have any extra beds, but you can sleep by the stove tonight."

"We can't thank you enough." Vika stood and gripped the woman's arm. "You saved our children's lives tonight."

The woman stilled, then placed her gnarled hand over Vika's. Her watery blue eyes shimmered with unshed tears. "Too many children have died in this war already. Mine included. If I can help save even one, I will do all I can."

36

HALYA

January 1945, Leipzig, Germany

Never elusive after the long shifts of work, sleep was Halya's release. Most of the time, it enveloped her deeply, sucking her into a dark void of nothingness, a far preferable reality than her days. When she was lucky enough to dream, it was always of home. She'd climb her favorite cherry tree and read her books or help Mama knead bread or listen to Tato's stories. Alone, on the wooden slats of her bed with her thin, lice-infested blanket tucked over her shoulders, she was closer to home than anywhere else.

She'd worked the night shift the previous week, which meant more time being ushered into the bomb shelters under the factory than working. The guards at the factory made sure everyone went down, but in the barracks, there wasn't easy access to a bomb shelter. You had to run down the street to the ones under the factory, and after a while, the guards stopped rousing the sleeping workers and forcing them to go. Bomb sirens went off so often, they'd become a familiar nighttime lullaby. Most girls in the barracks were happy to ignore them and kept sleeping. Today was no different.

But Halya had switched back to the day shift yesterday, so when the first explosion echoed through her barracks, she'd just begun dreaming about eating one of her mama's potato *varenyky*—rich and creamy on her tongue with the thinnest of dough wrappings. The dream was so real, so tangibly delicious, that when her eyes snapped open, she had to wipe the line of drool hanging from her mouth.

"We're being hit!" the girl across the aisle screamed. She'd only arrived yesterday, and Halya had already forgotten her name. Hunger and weariness did that to a person. It made you forget who you were, and if you couldn't remember who you were inside, how could you be expected to remember who anyone else was?

"Where do we go?" The nameless girl ran up and down the aisle between the bunks, her bare soles smacking the wooden floor.

Halya sat up and slid her feet to the ground, thankful that she'd decided long ago to sleep in her precious boots, both to keep warm and to ensure nobody stole them. She patted her pocket, making sure Liliya's drawing still rested there, then grabbed her identification papers and the bundle of letters from home. Mama sent one or two nearly every week, but Halya was only allowed to send two a month. She'd been so exhausted last night she hadn't even read the newest one yet.

An older girl who mothered the younger ones tried to calm

the new girl. "Be still. You can run down the street to the factory if you like, but there's nowhere to go here. They don't care if we get hit while we sleep. We just wait here and hope."

Another bomb crashed into the far side of their building, and the explosion threw Halya back into the wall. She banged her head on the bunk and stars danced in front of her eyes. The barefoot girl landed next to her, her neck bent at an odd angle, her hands splayed out in front of her.

Hania. That was her name, Halya thought dimly.

Halya's ears rang, but she pushed herself up and stood on trembling legs. She was supposed to remember something, but thoughts slipped through her mind like silky grains of wheat. Slavko had said she was always like that lately—forgetful—but it had gotten so much worse this winter. Cold and hunger dulled her.

Slavko. Liliya.

That's what she needed to remember: her friends. A tiny glimmer of life flickered in her chest, propelling her forward as her mind began to turn. What had Slavko told her after the last bombing had taken out one of the barracks?

"If we get hit again, we should run. Nobody will notice in the chaos. We can meet behind the mess hall. There's a place where we can get through the fence."

"Yes," Liliya had agreed. "We'll get through the fence and meet at the edge of the woods just outside the barracks."

But Slavko's barracks were down the street, and Liliya was working the night shift. She would have to do this part alone. Heat pulsed all around her. The far end of the building was on fire, the flames dancing toward her. Girls ran screaming, pushing at the door in a riotous mass. Exiting that way would take too long.

Halya grabbed her filthy blanket and climbed to the top bunk. She wrapped the blanket around her hand and punched through the dirty, brown glass until cold air blasted her face. She spread the blanket over the sill, then turned back and yelled, "You can get out this way!"

Several girls heard and ran in her direction, but Halya didn't wait. She climbed through the broken window and jumped into the night, landing on her feet with a soft thud. Outside, fires raged in the main factory where she worked, in her barracks, and in two more barracks buildings, including Slavko's.

Would they remember the pact? She'd nearly forgotten. What if the bomb hit Slavko's bed? Or the room where Liliya worked? Halya had been lucky that her side of the building hadn't been struck. She didn't want to think about how many girls on the far side had died without even waking up. She hoped they'd been dreaming lovely dreams of potato *varenyky*, too. It would be a pleasant way to go if one had to die— instantly in your sleep, drifting on thoughts of your old life.

People rushed around in a chaotic mass. Halya made herself as small and invisible as possible and ran toward the mess hall.

Smoke filled the air as sirens wailed. Another bomb exploded further down the compound. Halya prayed it hit the officers' quarters. Was that wrong? Praying for someone to die? She didn't think so. How could it be when they'd tried their best to make her suffer to the point of near death every day?

Slavko saw her before she saw him and grabbed her arm. "This way!"

Relief made her giddy, and she followed him to the base of

the fence with renewed energy. Slavko moved the brush blocking a shallow hole someone had dug and pushed her under. "You go first and don't stop for anything. I'll follow."

"What about Liliya?" Halya asked.

"We can't wait for her here. We'll have to find her later."

Halya slipped through the opening and ran. She glanced over her shoulder, expecting to see Slavko right behind her.

He wasn't.

Halya slowed, torn. She could go back into the danger, the uncertainty, and look for him so they could run away together like they'd planned. Or she could keep going.

You must always fight.

Her father's words reverberated through her head as if he'd just spoken them in her ear.

Fight for what? For her freedom from the Germans? Yes, of course that was worth fighting for. But wasn't friendship worth fighting for as well?

She'd never had such close friends, who could read her emotions like an open book or make her laugh when she really wanted to cry. Slavko and Liliya had become so much more than friends.

They were family.

Here, in this terrifying foreign land, they were her constant. And her father had said she must fight to stay with her family, no matter what.

She stopped running and turned back.

37

LILIYA

January 1945, Leipzig, Germany

When the first bomb hit, Liliya jolted, the fog of sleep instantly dissipating. She'd fallen asleep sitting on the toilet again, her head resting against the side wall, still fully clothed. She always tried to nap for a few minutes after she used the water closet and before the guard came around beating on the door. It was her only respite from the exhausting switch of day shift to night they were forced to endure weekly in her building.

She fumbled with the doorknob, bursting out into the now-empty factory. She must have slept through the sirens and been overlooked in the bathroom when everyone went to the shelter. She was completely alone.

Run.

The thought flashed through her mind, unbidden. They'd talked about it so many times since the bombings had increased during the fall—she, Halya, and Slavko—and now, here was her chance. Three more explosions sounded as she slipped out of the door and sprinted down the eerily empty street to the fence surrounding the barracks. The gate hung open, probably forgotten by some guard quick to abandon his post and get to the bunker, so she ran in, her heart skipping a beat as she took in the smoking ruins of what remained of the northern half of her building. Inside, pushing past the last few girls straggling out, she screamed Halya's name, but their bed was empty.

A body crumpled on the floor made Liliya's breath catch. She bent and turned the girl over, praying it wouldn't be Halya's face staring back at her, then shuddered out a sigh of relief when it wasn't.

Back outside, Liliya pushed her way through the injured workers emerging from the destruction of the barracks and moved toward Slavko's building. As the drone of the receding planes faded away overhead, she saw them in the distance— Slavko and Halya, slipping through the small hole at the base of the fence where they'd agreed they'd escape if possible. Liliya ran across the open field between them, both wishing they would stop and wait and urging them forward to freedom.

She didn't see the guard until he was swinging his club at her, and the sharp pain of it connecting with her head dropped her to her knees. The last thing she saw before everything went black was Slavko on the ground just outside the fence, another guard pointing his gun at him.

* * *

The truck jerked to a halt, and Liliya's head banged into the side of it. She tried to twist away, but the press of bodies around her made it hard to move. She remembered waking up, trying to run again, and a guard grabbing her, forcing her into the back of this truck, but she had no idea how long ago that had been or where they were now. Her head throbbed, and her mouth tasted like sawdust.

The truck door opened, and the crowd shifted, spilling outside. She pushed through the throng of people, falling hard on the frozen ground. It tilted under her as she pulled herself to her feet, and suddenly the image of Slavko with a gun pointed at his head flashed through her mind. Was he here too?

"Slavko!" She scanned the crowd wildly as the German soldiers, guns drawn, herded the group toward a ditch along the side of the road. "Halya!"

Four other trucks had stopped nearby, and Liliya shoved through the crowd, shouting their names over and over. She couldn't see far past the sea of people, but when the first round of shots went off and the screams rang out, she froze.

The crowd shifted, revealing the source of the gunshots: a row of seven German soldiers, their guns already pointed again at another group of forced laborers perched on the ledge in front of the ditch. A soldier shouted the order, and the guns released a volley of bullets. The people—men, women, and children of all ages and ethnicities—fell backward into the ditch on top of the first round of victims. Liliya watched the process one more time, trying to understand why this was happening, before she was pushed forward to the ditch.

She slipped her hand into her pocket and grabbed the nightingale Filip had made her, pressing her fingers so tight

around it they ached. It seemed unbelievable that after all she'd
been through, after all she'd seen, this was how it would end for
her—in a ditch alongside the road, dying at the whim of some
Germans. Not because she'd fought back and was caught or
because she'd done something heroic.

Because she'd been in the wrong place at the wrong time.

She couldn't accept that.

When the Germans raised their guns, Liliya moved on
instinct, falling back into the ditch as the woman next to her
took a bullet in the chest, the nightingale still clutched in her
hand. She waited for the sting of pain, for the gush of blood, but
it never came. Instead, she lay there with her eyes closed,
holding her breath as much as possible while the next row of
forced laborers was shot.

She bit the insides of her cheeks raw, muffling any sound
that might have escaped her mouth as a body fell on her. Blood
soaked her then, but it wasn't her own. She held her breath
under the crushing weight as one more layer fell. Two bodies
lay on top of her—one on an angle and one almost fully lined
up head to toe with hers. Her heart pounded so loudly in her
ears she thought they'd surely hear it as they walked around
shooting into the pile, making sure they didn't miss anyone.

But they missed her.

Again.

38

HALYA

January 1945, Leipzig, Germany

Halya found Slavko huddled on the ground near the escape hole, his foot tangled in wire.

"I thought you were right behind me!" She dropped to her knees and started pulling at the tight knot around his ankle. "What happened?"

"I'm fine!" He pushed her hands away. "I've almost got it loose enough. Keep going. I'll catch up."

"No, I can help." She scrabbled through the brush around him, looking for the source of the wire so she could pull more slack. Smoke stung her eyes, but the glow of the fire gave her better vision than the moon alone. Others who had seen their escape poured out of the opening under the fence, bumping into them in a frenzied panic and undoing their tenuous progress with the wire. It was only a matter of time before a guard noticed the mass exodus.

"I said go!" Slavko's voice cracked. "I'll find you!"

"I'm not leaving you!" she snapped. "So shut up, and let me help."

He pressed his lips tight but didn't fight her again, and together, they finally loosened the wire enough for him to slip his foot free.

"Can you run?" Halya stood and held out her hand.

"Yes, I'm not hurt. It was just stuck."

As he gripped her hand and pulled himself up, a shot rang out.

"Stop where you are!" A guard had slipped through the hole and stood over them. His gun pointed in the air, but as they watched, he lowered it and aimed it at Slavko. "Don't even think of running away, *Ostarbeiter*."

* * *

The guards gathered up the displaced laborers and put them in an old schoolhouse down the street from the factory for the time being.

Halya recognized some familiar faces, but many were missing. She hoped they'd made it farther than she had. She pressed her back into the wall and closed her eyes.

"You're a fool," Slavko muttered, but he leaned his head against her shoulder. "You shouldn't have come back for me."

"I would never leave you," Halya said.

"You will stay here until further notice," a guard interrupted their conversation. The room stilled as he spoke. "Don't bother trying to escape. Armed guards are stationed around the perimeter, and we will shoot."

The cold consumed Halya. She huddled close to Slavko, shivering and wishing she'd kept her lice-ridden blanket.

"Do you think the factory is destroyed?"

He grunted. "Doesn't matter. They'll just ship us somewhere else to work."

"I hope they feed us before they do."

"The food is terrible, anyway," he said.

"Where do you think Liliya is?" Halya finally voiced the question on both of their minds.

Slavko didn't answer right away, and when he did, Halya barely heard him whisper.

"I don't know."

* * *

As darkness fell, more survivors trickled out of the bombed buildings, burns and gashes gaping open on their sooty bodies. Each time the door opened, Halya held her breath, part of her hoping it would be Liliya walking through the door and the other part hoping Liliya had escaped and made it far away from here.

"We will be reassigning some of you to go with us to another camp," a guard announced that night. "This one is too full. Those who go will be given better rations."

Halya felt her hand moving upward at her side. She wanted to raise it, to offer to go and get food for her empty belly.

Slavko elbowed her. "Don't you know by now that you should never volunteer for anything they offer?"

Halya's stomach tightened. "They said they'll have better food at the next camp."

"I don't trust them," Slavko said.

"I don't either, but what choice do we have?" Halya asked. "Do you want to sit here and starve?"

"We'll get away, like we were supposed to."

"We can't run. They said they would shoot us," she whispered.

"Only if they catch us," Slavko said. "Let's wait and see."

"Fine," Halya said. The food was so tempting, but staying with Slavko was more important, and if he wouldn't go, neither would she.

The guard went through his list, and Halya held her breath, praying they wouldn't call her name, or if they did, that they'd call Slavko's, too. She could face the unknown if he was by her side.

The selected people moved out the door and into the open-bed trucks lined up outside. Halya recognized two sisters who'd occupied the bunk next to hers. The older one limped as she moved, and her younger sister, only eleven years old, held her up.

Through the window, Halya saw the guards counting and assessing how many fit in the trucks, but they were already half full when they'd arrived. One guard pushed the people in tighter, creating more room, then waved angrily back at the building. Another guard nodded his head and made his way back inside. Realization dawned on Halya as she observed the people who had been chosen. All bore injuries or were older. The people remaining in the room had avoided being maimed in the bombing. Most stood, milling about as they waited for further instructions. A few of the weaker ones sat against the wall, their eyes closed.

"Stand up!" Halya snapped as she scrambled to her feet.

"What?"

"Just stand!" Halya pushed at Slavko. "Look strong."

"I am strong," he muttered.

"We need five more people for the new camp!" the guard announced. His long finger floated in front of him, following his eyes as he scanned the room. It paused on three young women huddled together on the floor. "You three!"

He resumed his perusal. "I should mention, the new camp has a doctor, so if you have any ailments, come along and you'll be treated faster."

Lies! Halya wanted to scream. Everyone knew the Germans didn't care about the infirm.

Maybe not everyone.

The guard's beady eyes landed on Halya and Slavko. His mouth parted, and Halya's blood turned to ice. He was going to point at them. He was going to choose them. She felt Slavko stand up straighter and puff out his chest.

Yes. Look strong. Strong survives.

She did the same.

Suddenly, an older man stood up. "We'll go." He limped forward, dragging a young man with flushed cheeks behind him. "My son is feverish. He needs to see a doctor."

The guard's finger dropped, and the breath Halya had been holding rushed out as the guard turned away from them.

"Perfect." The guard grinned, his smile oddly boyish under the cruel glint in his eyes. "I'm sure we can get your son all the help he needs."

"I have a bad feeling about this," Halya whispered to Slavko. "If the factory is in shambles, what will they do with all of us?"

"Move us to another factory, I'd guess."

"But thin the herd first," she replied. "They took all the injured and weak people."

He frowned. "Not just the injured and weak. They took those three healthy sisters, too."

Halya could see his mind working. "Don't you think we should run?" she asked.

Slavko finally nodded. "Before dawn."

They waited until the guards were preoccupied with the arrival of another group of *Ostarbeiters*, then slipped out a back window of the old schoolhouse. They melted into the velvety darkness, running in the wheel ruts left behind from the first truck and jumping into the thick snow on the side of the road whenever they saw headlights. When they couldn't run any further, they walked until their legs wobbled. As the first hints of sunlight peeped over the edge of the world, they finally slept, tucked under a pile of pine boughs and snow.

When Slavko woke her hours later, Halya opened her eyes slowly, disoriented for a moment. She crawled out from their makeshift shelter and stood next to him. The sun sat low in the sky. They'd slept through most of the day, and evening was upon them again.

"Where should we go now?" she asked.

"Away from here. Look what we slept next to!" Slavko's jaw flexed, and he wouldn't meet her eyes. He grabbed her shoulder and spun her around. "Do you see them?"

Halya's eyes widened as she took in the view, and she shuddered. She saw them. She saw all of them. Dozens of bodies stacked in a shallow pit. Bloated and stiff.

"It's everyone who left for the other camp," Slavko said. His words bounced off her frozen body as the scene came into focus.

The sisters. The older man and his fevered son. Their lifeless eyes staring up at the dusky sky.

"They shot them," Slavko said. His fists clenched and unclenched as he stared down at the corpses. "Look at the way they're lying all in one direction. I bet they lined them in a row, one group after another, and shot them all."

He vocalized everything they were seeing, but Halya couldn't form any words. They'd all fled from her mind, leaving only a burning anger throbbing in their place.

"Do you see them? Why aren't you saying anything? We were right. They lied to get people away so they could kill them and be done with it!"

Where her emotions consumed her from the inside out like a hot fire contained in a stove, Slavko's raged like a roaring inferno racing through the forest, his anger radiating off him and pummeling into her in scorching waves.

She reached up and gripped the OST patch sewn on to her jacket. With a vicious yank, she tore it off, then reached over to Slavko and did the same to him. He turned to stare at her.

"I see them," she finally said. She barely recognized her own voice with its quiet, seething tone.

Slavko's pinky finger reached out and hooked onto hers for one second, the touch grounding her—and him, she suspected —before he pulled away. "Come on. We should go."

He began walking away, but a flash of movement caught

Halya's eye and she froze, staring. It moved again, and she saw it was a hand at the edge of the pile, reaching out, scrabbling against the ground.

"Slavko, wait! Someone is still alive!"

Halya ran to the pile and grabbed the hand. "We're here. We'll help you get out!"

Slavko came up next to her and began moving the dead bodies, clearing a path for the person buried underneath. He grunted with the effort, and Halya knew she should help him, but the hand gripped hers so desperately she couldn't let go. As Slavko dragged a body off the pile, something broke loose and rolled into Halya's lap. She picked it up and gasped.

"This is Liliya's nightingale! Liliya is in here!"

39

LILIYA

January 1945, near Leipzig, Germany

The scent of death lingered in Liliya's nose. Sweat, urine, feces, rot. Every time she took a breath, she was there again, trapped under the pressing weight of the dead bodies.

Slavko put his hand on her shoulder, and she jumped away like a tightly coiled spring.

"I'm sorry." He stepped back, eyes wide. "I didn't mean to startle you."

"It's fine." Liliya wanted to reach out and embrace him easily, like she had so many times before, but she couldn't make herself touch him or anyone else. Something fundamental inside her had ripped apart while she lay there for so many hours, leaving her numb and cold, and she didn't know how to weave it back together.

"I'm going to go get some water from the creek. Maybe

someone will let me borrow a cup," Slavko said. They had set up camp near another group of refugees while they decided what to do next.

"Maybe you just need some time," Halya said hopefully as he walked away.

Liliya hated the way Halya looked at her with a mixture of fear and pity. She was supposed to be taking care of Halya and Slavko. They shouldn't be worrying about her, but she couldn't make herself care enough to do anything about it. Part of her wished they'd never found her in the pile; part of her wished she'd been shot with all the other laborers deemed unworthy of saving.

"Maybe," she said dully.

Halya gave her a tentative smile. "I'm sure that's it."

Liliya hated the hope in her expression. She hated the part of herself that wanted to extinguish it even more, but she couldn't stop it.

"Or maybe this is just who I am now. Broken and cold, but somehow, for some reason, still alive." The words fell out in a torrent, like an unleashed dam. "Do you know how many people I've watched die? How many dead bodies I've held? They all died so easily no matter how hard they fought, yet I persist, even when I don't care if I live or die. Why do you think that is?"

Halya's eyes widened. "I don't know."

"Maybe not caring is the secret." Liliya rubbed someone's dried blood off her arm, letting the remnants of the person who died next to her flake away into the air as if they were nothing. And they were—nothing but another casualty accumulating in this war. How many could you count before it stopped matter-ing? "Maybe being unable to love or be loved is the key to surviving. Maybe I've found the secret. I'll survive, but I'll never be who I was again."

"I don't believe that," Halya said.

"I don't have anything to believe in anymore," Liliya replied.

The distant drone of an airplane stopped their conversation cold.

"What's that noise?" Halya asked.

"The Germans are strafing us again!" a woman up the road shouted.

Panic broke through the apathy cloaking Liliya and yanked her upright as visions of her mother flashed through her mind. "We need to get off the road. Now!"

People pressed around them on both sides as the droning grew louder. On the horizon, three planes came into view. Staccato bursts of bullets rained down on the road a few kilometers ahead. Screams pierced the air.

Halya froze.

"Get on the ground!" Liliya pushed Halya to the side of the road and screamed, "Slavko! Where's Slavko?"

Blood pounded in Liliya's ears, but it didn't drown out the buzzing drone of the engine or the pop of the bullets as the Luftwaffe planes swooped down over the road, shooting at the refugees.

Her body acted of its own accord, launching herself on top of Halya, covering the young girl's body. Halya's small shoulders trembled with fear, pressing their bony points into her chest, but Liliya could offer no comfort. Panic rendered her mute. In reality, she lay on top of Halya, waiting for a bullet to pierce her back, but in her mind, she lay pinned under her mother's lifeless body, crying for help as Mama bled out on top of her.

The planes passed them by, their buzz fading as they moved on. Liliya finally stood on shaking legs and pulled Halya to her feet.

"Are you all right?"

Halya's chin quivered, but she gave a tight nod.

Liliya scanned the hectic scene in front of her. Bodies strewn on the ground, some pushing up on unsteady limbs and some eerily still. People crying. A wagon overturned; the horse hitched to it lying on the ground bleeding.

"I don't see Slavko!" Halya's voice took on a frantic note, and Liliya grabbed her hand.

"He's probably gone on ahead to get away from the mess. I'm sure he's fine." Liliya moved through the crowd, pulling Halya along as she tried to squash down the panic rising in her chest. "Come, we'll find him."

"There!" Halya pulled out of Liliya's grasp and ran toward a boy hunched over on the road. Slavko looked up, then opened his arms and caught Halya in a hug.

Liliya exhaled a tremulous breath. He looked fine. She hadn't lost anyone today. A surge of emotion left her shaking. Slavko waved her over, and she rushed in to join their embrace, surprising herself.

"You're all right, Liliya. It's over now," Slavko said.

"It was just like before." Liliya closed her eyes.

"This has happened to you before?" Halya pulled back to stare at Liliya. "When?"

"At the beginning of the war, when the Germans first

invaded Ukraine," Liliya said haltingly. "Strafers killed my mother."

"You had to be so scared, but you threw yourself on top of me so I was protected." Halya wrapped her arms around Liliya again and squeezed tight. "You saved me, Liliya."

Liliya's throat ached from the tears she held back. "Anyone would have done the same."

"No. Only someone who loves me would have done that. You're not broken, Liliya." Halya turned Liliya's prior words back on her. "Please don't give up on yourself so easily, because I'll never give up on you."

The dull ache that lived permanently in Liliya's chest swelled into her throat. Faces flashed through her mind: Nina, Mama, Tato, Mykhailo. She touched her nightingale, now safe again in her pocket.

Filip. Halya. Slavko.

Maybe she did have something to live for.

40

VIKA

February 1945, Kanth, Germany

Just as Vika feared, Nadya's fever came back. Vika had expected the elderly couple to push them out, but instead, they'd allowed them to stay on the floor in their spare room.

"Stay until she feels better," Pani Nowak said. She'd finally introduced herself the next morning at breakfast. "Our daughter suffered a similar affliction when she was younger. The doctor said she was prone to chest infections."

Vika wanted to kiss her. So many refugees had been turned away, the residents of various villages locking their doors against the migrating souls. But this kind Polish couple welcomed them. Grateful, Maksym and Vika did everything they could to make life easier for them. Vika milked their cow and did all the barn chores while Maksym chopped wood and hauled water. Whenever Pani or Pan Nowak rose to do something, Vika and Maksym rose faster and did it for them.

They stayed for a little over two weeks, and if Pani Nowak had her way, they would have stayed indefinitely.

"You've been a blessing," she told Vika repeatedly. "You've made life easier for us, and we want you to stay as long as you like."

But they hadn't gone far enough to be safe. Stopping now wouldn't further protect the children they had with them, and Vika wouldn't lose sight of her mission to find Slavko and Liliya. So, on the morning of February 13, Pan Nowak drove them to the train station in his cart, where Maksym sold their handcart and used a few of their precious Reichsmarks earned in Breslau to buy passage to Dresden. From there, they could travel by foot or find temporary work and save up to buy tickets to Leipzig, where Slavko and Liliya's factory was.

Through the train car window, Vika watched the countryside roll by. The bucolic villages still appeared whole, as if the war hadn't touched this part of Germany like it had ravaged Ukraine. But every now and then, they'd pass a series of giant bomb craters or piles of rubble where homes had once stood, a sharp contrast to the rolling hills and quaint cottages.

When they finally stepped off the train in Dresden, they were immediately swallowed up into the sea of war-torn refugees and writhing humanity. A cacophony of different languages echoed throughout the high domed station. Vika stared up in wonder at the vaulted glass ceilings and arched doorways.

"Let's go there." She finally pointed to a Red Cross tent after gathering her bearings. "Maybe they can help us."

They moved through the crowd, and at the tent, a kind woman offered them broth, coffee, and milk. A sigh of near pleasure escaped Vika as the first sip of weak, but hot, coffee passed her lips.

"Why are there so many refugees gathered here?" Maksym asked the woman.

"There's an influx from the east," she replied in Polish. "But it's gotten worse since Breslau evacuated; most of the population came here."

"Is there a place to look for missing people?" Vika asked.

"Yes, but first let's get you to a shelter. Go with that group there." She pointed to a crowd gathering near the entrance. "They'll get you registered."

After the destruction of so many villages and cities in Ukraine and Poland, the untouched beauty of Dresden shocked Vika. "It's as if the war doesn't exist here," she said to Maksym.

His eyes narrowed as they scanned the pristine streets. "Yes. The Nazis don't mind destroying other countries, but this city seems to be doing just fine."

A boy darted out of a side street and crossed their path. The way the boy moved, long limbed but graceful, the strong cut of his jaw . . . Vika's heart jumped into her throat, and without thinking, she dropped her things and sprinted after him. In two bounds, she'd grabbed his arm and spun him around.

"Slavko!" she cried, but her voice trailed off as she took in the strange face. Her free hand flew to her mouth. "I'm sorry, I thought you were someone else."

The boy gave her a dirty look and wrenched his arm away.

"I thought it was our son," she whispered as Maksym came up next to her.

"Slavko wouldn't be in Dresden." Maksym took her hand. "Vikusia, you see him everywhere. Kraków, Breslau, here. The last address we have is further west in Leipzig, so we must start there."

"But what if he escaped? What if he's headed home and we pass right by him?"

Maksym didn't respond, but Vika saw the expression on his face. She clawed her fists into her skirt so she wouldn't hit him. "I don't need your pity, Maksym. I need your support in finding our son."

"You have my support!" Maksym spoke low, into her ear, so the children wouldn't hear. "Do you think I don't want to find Slavko? I'm only being realistic, Vika! We have three other children to worry about."

"I'm well aware of that!" Vika took Nadya from Maksym and pulled Bohdan closer, but doubt sent sticky tendrils into her. Was she losing her mind? Seeing Slavko's face on every teenage boy she passed? Or was Maksym so sure that his son was dead that he'd given up on the possibility of finding him?

Which was worse?

Their group was led to what looked like a school. Blackboards still adorned the front walls, but the desks had been removed and replaced with pallets on the floor. Other refugees already lay sleeping as Vika and her family picked their way across the room toward an empty spot near the window.

Vika set Nadya down and covered her with a blanket just as a low-pitched siren echoed through the night air.

41

HALYA

February 1945, Dresden, Germany

Air-raid sirens pierced the night air, and Halya's mouth watered. Far past the normal reactions of fear and surprise, her body's response to the ear-splitting sound was now salivation.

They'd adapted quickly to life on the streets of Dresden since they'd arrived four nights ago under the cover of darkness, jumping off a slow-moving train as it approached the city. They knew from their travels that air-raid sirens meant empty houses as the native populations retreated to their bomb shelters, and empty houses meant they could finally eat.

Two nights ago, they'd found a half-eaten roast chicken sitting on an abandoned table. Three plates situated around it held a few boiled potatoes and assorted, picked-over bones.

That was the last real food they'd eaten.

They weren't the only ones at this game, risking death by

Allied bombs to fill their stomachs. Other bands of homeless refugees moved stealthily through the dark streets, slipping in and out of homes in search of anything that would help them survive another day, but when the sirens went off this late, usually dinner had passed, and they were left scavenging around the kitchen for whatever dry goods they could find.

Tonight, it was just Halya and Slavko. Liliya had run into an old friend working as an *Ostarbeiter* in a hotel who'd said she could help, so they'd split up in hopes of finding more food and planned on meeting later at the train station, where thousands of refugees lingered.

They didn't dare register with any of the Red Cross workers there in case the German authorities checked those records and forced them back to work in the factories, and they were undecided on whether they should try to make it home through the fighting or wait. So, for now, they lived on the streets and scavenged.

"In here!" Slavko waved Halya forward.

She stepped up next to him and peered inside the kitchen. A large pot sat on top of the stove. Her stomach growled as she twisted the door handle. "It's locked."

Slavko looked around, then grabbed a stick off the ground from under the tree in the front yard. He smashed it through the dirty windowpane, and ran it around the edge, clearing out broken glass shards. Halya barely heard the splintering glass over the shriek of the siren still blaring. If planes really were approaching, she'd have no idea they were there until they hit her.

He took off his coat and laid it over the sill, then boosted Halya into the room and scrambled in behind her.

The walls muffled the siren slightly, but Halya paid it no attention either way. All she could see was the soup pot.

Slavko ran over to the stove and peered inside. "I think this soup is rotten."

Halya grabbed a spoon and bowl off the table and handed it to him. He wrinkled his nose as he shoveled a scoop into his mouth straight from the pot.

"It's terrible!" He took another bite, then handed the bowl back to her.

Halya dipped the bowl into the pot to fill it, then lifted it to her lips and drank. A rancid, sweet smell wafted into her nose, but she ignored it and gulped down several mouthfuls. The potatoes hadn't fully turned yet, but they were well on the way. Still, she ate, because the soup filled the gaping hole constantly gnawing inside her.

She set the bowl down and wiped her mouth off with the back of her hand. "It's not much worse than the soup we got in the labor camp."

"That's true," Slavko said. "There are real vegetables in this soup."

Halya took a few more swallows while Slavko continued to eat out of the pot. When they'd finished, they scoured the cabinets for any other food they could take with them.

"Three tins of sardines!" Halya whooped with joy. "And two apples!"

Brown spots littered the wrinkled skin of the old apples, but Halya's fingers handled them with reverence as she slipped them into her pocket.

"Nothing in this cupboard." Slavko pushed the doors shut as the sirens went silent.

Halya handed him the sardines. "Here, put these in your pocket. We should get moving."

They'd been caught only once by a man who ventured up from the cellar to find two skinny children eating the dinner his wife had left on the table. He'd chased them out with a broom, swinging it and cursing at them. It was an experience Halya would rather not repeat.

Outside, she searched the sky for any signs of airplanes approaching. Sirens didn't always mean planes, but it always meant dinner, and that was a risk worth taking.

But tonight, in the silent lull after the air-raid siren's final note, a distant, buzzing drone filled the air.

"Slavko." Halya grabbed her friend's arm. "I hear something."

Slavko cocked his head, listening. "It's airplanes."

"We need to find Liliya. It's almost ten o'clock."

"There's no time. We need to get to shelter first," Slavko said. "We'll find her afterward."

Without another word, they took off running.

The drone intensified, drawing closer, and suddenly, Halya stopped and pointed. "Look!"

Glowing red balls floated down from the sky, brilliant against the darkness of Dresden.

"I think they're targets," Slavko said. "So they know where to bomb."

Other colors illuminated the sky as they ran. Bright blue, orange and a vivid green, all hypnotically beautiful and terrifying at the same time. Halya had never seen anything like them, and she wished she could stop and watch. Instead, she tugged on Slavko's hand.

"This way! The tunnels in the park!"

Halya said a silent prayer for the animals as they ran past the zoo. She and Slavko had walked through the zoo once, and Halya had quickly decided the majestic giraffe was her favorite animal. Slavko liked the tigers, though. What would happen to the animals, she wondered. Would the Allies bomb them, too?

They scrambled down into the tunnel and pressed into the crowd already huddled there, just as the first bomb hit.

42

VIKA

February 1945, Dresden, Germany

"Where do we go?" Sofia's voice snapped Vika into action.

She'd frozen at the sound of the sirens, foolishly lulled into a false sense of security after weeks of quiet respite with the Nowaks. But she should have known better. Nothing was safe, and she could never let her guard down.

Maksym grabbed their suitcase, and she stood, pulling her children with her. "It's fine. I'm sure they won't bomb here, but we need to find shelter to be safe."

The other refugees were doing the same, grabbing important items and shuffling out of the building. No one moved with a particular sense of urgency, their fear dulled by the repetition of this drill in the cities they'd fled from all over Europe.

Out on the street, the sirens screamed louder, a low dull whining that scratched at Vika's ears like nails on a chalkboard.

Bohdan tugged on Vika's hand and pointed up. In the sky, a myriad of colors flickered, illuminating the city. Greens, oranges, blues. The crowd stopped for a moment, dazzled by the light display.

"What is that, Mama?"

A man next to them answered in a rush. "They're lighting up the city with flares and marking it to find their targets."

Despite the frigid winter air, sweat beaded on Vika's forehead, and she scooped Nadya's slight body up into her arms.

"Should we go back to the railway station?" Sofia stood close, her hands on Bohdan's shoulder.

"No," Maksym said as he grabbed Bohdan's hand. "I think the railroad station would be a target."

"Then what do we do?" Vika asked.

The throng of people pushed against them, but no one seemed to know where to go. Then the same boy who'd led them here shouted, waving his hand in a motion to follow. Vika tucked a blanket tighter around Nadya and fell in line with everyone else.

The boy led them across the street to a municipal building. Amid the din of sirens and frantic buzz of terror, the crowd funneled inside and down a narrow staircase. At its base, the cellar split in two, one hallway veering left and one veering right. A man stood at the bottom, trying to stem the chaos and usher people to the left, including Maksym, Bohdan, and Sofia, but when Vika moved to follow them, the man barred their way and pointed to the right, gesturing that Maksym's room was at capacity.

"Maksym!" Vika shouted.

He met her gaze over his shoulder. "It's fine, I'll find you when it's done! Just get to safety!"

Vika let the man push her into the room on the right. A dim lightbulb illuminated the open area. People spilled inside, finding seats around the perimeter and in the middle of the floor.

Vika set Nadya on the ground as their young German guide shouted more instructions, but his words were lost as the first bomb landed.

The walls shook, pushing dust and plaster into the air. Nadya screamed, and Vika curled over her daughter, covering her with her body as best she could as another bomb hit.

43

LILIYA

February 1945, Dresden, Germany

Liliya hurried down the streets of Dresden, hoping to find Halya and Slavko before taking shelter, but when the glowing orbs started falling from the sky, she realized she was out of time. Most people were already in shelters, but a few stragglers and bands of newly arrived refugees still sought safety. She slipped in with a group of people as they moved into a cellar under a church. The space continued to fill even as the first bomb hit, rumbling through the old stone structure. Liliya tucked her head down and tried to block everything out. The noise, the smell of sweat and fear, the screams of young children terrified by the ordeal, all of it became background noise as bomb after bomb fell.

Time stretched on in an eternity of terror, but questions pushed through the fear and into Liliya's mind. Where were

Halya and Slavko? Were they safe? Would the next one take out the building above her? Would it collapse, trapping her underneath to suffocate? Or would she die instantly, buried in a barrage of brick and mortar? Would the building catch fire? Would she burn first? Or would the smoke kill her slowly? And if she survived, how would she ever find Slavko and Halya now in this destruction?

They tumbled through her mind so fast she couldn't focus on any one of them long enough to think of an answer.

Most people sat silently, struck dumb by the intensity of the bombs, or perhaps pondering the possibilities like Liliya, but the young boy next to her kept up a steady stream of chatter, talking to no one in particular. Liliya tuned him out, lost in her own thoughts, until she heard the words, "Polish Arabian horses."

A spark flickered to life in her numb heart, and she turned on him, grabbing his arm.

"What did you say?"

He stared blankly at her. "I don't know. I just ramble when I'm nervous."

"What about the Polish Arabians?"

"They're on their way here tonight from the east. They're being sent west to avoid the Soviet front."

"To Dresden?" She could barely believe it. "Do you know where?"

He nodded. "The army barracks. My father works there."

"Where is that?"

She listened intently as he gave her directions, all previous thoughts of peril falling away as a new purpose formed in her mind. She would claw her way out of a fiery pile of bricks with her bare hands if she had to, just like she'd scrambled out from under the pile of dead bodies on top of her that day in the woods, because if it was Filip's Polish Arabians in Dresden, maybe Filip was there, too. And, once she found him, they could look for Slavko and Halya together.

* * *

"You can't go up yet, Fräulein! It's not safe!" The earnest young boy tried to grab for her arm, but Liliya pushed past him. After over two hours in the bomb shelter, she could wait no longer. Her head ached, and she couldn't get enough air in her lungs with each breath. Lethargy tugged on her limbs, and she knew she had to get out of this place before it sucked out what remained of her will to live.

Filip might be here, and if he was, she had to find him. After all these months, all this time, she had another chance, and she wouldn't squander it.

His name, along with Slavko and Halya's, became a chant in her numb mind as she picked her way back to the street. The church she emerged from was largely untouched, but the building next to it was in shambles. Hot wind swirled around her, picking up speed as it whipped through the shattered streets. To the south, fire raged, towering up into the dark night and filling the sky and her lungs with smoke. She moved north, and in the next block, ravaged by a direct hit, crumbling buildings spilled their broken stones into the street, leaving only the skeletons of former structures still standing. She stopped at the intersection and looked around, her eyes straining to find any clue to what the boy had told her about the Polish Arabian transport, but all she could see was fire.

An old man stood staring up at the smoking rubble of what used to be a building. Tears and soot coursed down his grooved face. His lips moved wordlessly.

She ran to him and shook his shoulder. "Do you know where the army barracks are? I'm looking for the horses."

She had to shake him again before he turned to her. His bushy eyebrows scooted high on his wrinkled forehead, and he cocked his head, confused. "Horses? The barracks are that way." He gave a half-hearted jab of his finger, pointing down the street, then resumed staring at the building. In another time, she would have asked if he was all right. She would have helped him find his family or get to safety, but now, all she could think about was getting to Filip.

She ran down the street, dodging broken bricks on the ground and falling embers as she went. Limbs protruded from piles of rubble. An arm. A hand. A foot. Tiny clues to the loss buried underneath the wreckage of Dresden.

The dense smoke burned Liliya's lungs and eyes, and the heat of fires raging around her scorched her skin. The world glowed with an orange, smoky haze, and Liliya thought that this was surely what hell must look like.

A man with a handheld air-raid siren ran past her, the sound of his alarm barely audible over the noise of the imploding city, but it sent a fresh wave of terror through Liliya. How could there be more coming? What was left to destroy here?

The second round of bombs fell as she came upon a long line of horses. The fire hadn't reached here yet, but its glow illuminated the scene in front of her. Mounted men each led another unmounted horse alongside him. Their sleek muscles rippled as their hooves clopped on the street.

"Move, men! The barracks are just ahead!" the man in front shouted as a bomb hit a few blocks over. Airplanes droned overhead, and Liliya froze. Filip had to be here, somewhere in this line of horses and men.

Unless he was already dead.

The thought crystallized in her mind before she could stop it. This whole thing could be for nothing. He could have died months ago, and she'd never know. And why should she? She had no claim on him. No reason to be a part of his life. This was a fool's errand, and she was the fool.

"No!" The word came out of her mouth of its own volition, a violent plea and fervent prayer in equal parts. He was here somewhere, desperately trying to get to safety.

Like she should be doing. But her feet wouldn't move as her eyes searched up and down the line for him. She was close. She had to be, and she couldn't miss her chance. She would find him, then she would find Halya and Slavko.

The air grew so hot it swirled up into fiery, tornado-like spirals, licking at the sky and pulling at her hair and clothes. A woman clutching a baby screamed as a gust of searing wind sucked the child right out of her arms and into the inferno.

People trying to slog through the streets fell onto all fours, crying as their shoes, then their hands, sank down into the melted tar.

Another bomb exploded, this one much closer, and the horses shrieked with terror. All down the line, the riderless horses pulled away from their leads and stampeded off into the night.

Men shouted as the remaining horses reared. A few riders were thrown off, but most held their seats then urged their horses forward. The street began to clear out as Liliya pressed back into the wall of a former building, the bricks hot against her back, her eyes still searching. Another bomb hit, and smoke billowed over the street as flames lapped at the buildings across the way.

She didn't know where to run, where to hide, because the whole world was on fire.

A runaway horse charged past her; the whites of its terror-filled eyes bright in the gray night. It stopped and reared, and for one hauntingly beautiful moment, Liliya stared, mesmerized, at the contrast of the magnificent animal silhouetted against the backdrop of fire, smoke, and utter devastation.

The horse landed and a man approached it, then grabbed the loose lead rope dangling from its halter. With gentle words, he stroked the horse's sweaty neck.

"Hush now, I've got you. You're safe with me."

Her heart stopped.

That voice. The same she'd been soothed with months ago.

She'd know it anywhere.

Filip.

She stepped forward and shouted for him, her words disappearing into the blistering night as the building she'd taken shelter by, already half decimated after being hit earlier, collapsed.

44

HALYA

February 1945, Dresden, Germany

As soon as the bombing stopped, Slavko and Halya left the press of people in the tunnel, weaving through the crowds gathering in the Great Green Park.

"Where are you going?" Halya bent over to catch her breath. Slavko moved so fast she could barely keep up.

He whipped around. "We have to get out of here."

"But it's safe here," Halya said. Around them, though the smell of smoke lingered, the air was clean and cool. The big trees offered a tangled roof of protection from the tragedy outside the park. She dropped to the ground and rested her back against a chestnut tree, turning her face up to the icy drizzle falling from the sky. "We should rest for a few minutes before going back to find Liliya."

Slavko squatted next to her. "We have to leave the city. We

can't go back. Didn't you see as we left? That hotel is gone. If she survived, Liliya will be making her way out of the city and looking for us, too. We'll find her, but not in there."

"How could you say that?" Halya tried to yell at him, but her throat was raw from the smoke. "We can't just leave her! Besides, the bombing is over!"

"The fires will only get worse, Halya." His expression was harsh and unyielding. "And what if the planes come back? I don't want to hide underground again, like a sitting duck just waiting to be shot. We need to get out to the country."

"Surely they won't come back." She rubbed the soot and ash out of her eyes. "Look around you. They've already destroyed the city. What's left?"

"We can't be sure about anything." He took her hand and tugged at her. "Please, Halya. Let's go."

She let him pull her up and drag her past the zoo, where the animals were still shrieking in terror. Halya wanted to rush in and open their cages so they, too, could have a chance to run free and escape the fires. She hoped their keepers were doing just that.

They moved carefully through the streets, stepping over corpses burned to a crisp and people emerging, dazed, from cellars. Walls of fire and rubble redirected their route again and again. The heat of the fires negated the cold February air, and sweat dampened Halya's back. Ashes rained down, along with floating embers. One fell on Halya's jacket, and she batted it away before it ignited.

"Here." Slavko pointed to a water barrel behind a house. "Let's wet our clothes. It's so dry out here, we're lucky we haven't gone up in flames already."

Despite the heat, Halya shivered. She'd seen a woman running down the street, her clothes and hair on fire, screaming until she keeled over, sinking into the soft tar.

They scooped the warm water into their mouths, then dunked their arms and splashed their clothing until they were drenched. Fifteen minutes later, their clothing had already dried, and their throats ached for more water.

As they crested a hill, Halya turned to look back at the carnage. Hot wind swirled around them, coaxing the separate fires into one twining beast. Soaring high above the city, it jabbed into the sky like a beacon. Twisting and roaring, it grew thicker, stronger. Halya could feel it pulling on her, drawing her back to it like a siren's song.

Slavko jerked on her arm, breaking the fire's hold on her. "We can't stop, Halya!"

She gave the roaring beast one more look, then followed her friend.

45

VIKA

February 1945, Dresden, Germany

The lights flickered as part of the ceiling near the staircase collapsed into the room, blocking the exit and the doorway to the other cellar where the rest of Vika's family was. She pulled Nadya close as the building groaned around them.

"We can't get out!" a Polish woman screamed. "We'll die down here!"

Panic pulsed in Vika's veins. She struggled to take a breath, to think through the cloud of dust rolling over the room.

"Mama? Will we die?" Nadya's wide eyes stared up at her, inches away from her face. Vika drank them in, their tranquil, blue color, their implicit trust, their love.

A strength she'd never felt before surged through her. They would survive this. She would find her family. She would rise from these ashes and make a new life for them away from the heartache and loss of this brutal war. She had to believe that.

"No, of course not." She stood and hefted Nadya on to her hip. "There must be another way out."

She searched the room and found a second door in the back. When she pushed it open, a rush of cool, damp air washed over her. She turned to the teenage boy next to her. "Where does this go?"

He shook his head, not understanding, and she repeated herself in stilted German, then Polish.

He spoke German slowly back to her. "The homes on this block are all linked by a series of tunnels. Some even lead to the riverfront. We can move through them until we find a way up."

"I think we should wait here," an older, German woman said. "Surely someone will come help us."

Vika ignored her and stepped into the tunnel. A few people followed, including the boy, but the rest stayed behind.

"I've been down here before. I think that's the way to the river," the boy pointed.

She gave a tight nod as she pictured the cool, running water of the Buh River back home. Imagined sliding into it, letting it wash over her body. The river was the answer. The river would save them.

They wove through the narrow passageway, twisting and turning. People flowed with them and against them, searching for their own way out of the maze, and Vika soon lost track of the boy. Every so often, a flickering light bulb illuminated their path, and Vika checked on Nadya, who clung, red-faced and wide-eyed, to her neck.

But the closer she moved to the river, the hotter the air

became, as if the river exit was sucking in the heat from the buildings and tunnels behind her.

Suddenly, the man in front of her jerked to a stop, and Vika ran into him.

"What's happening?" she shouted. The press of people around her thickened as bodies bumped into each other, trying to move forward. Claustrophobia choked Vika, the dark, tight tunnel squeezing in around her until her breath came in short gasps.

"The door is stuck!" someone up ahead yelled. "Everyone needs to move back!" When no one responded, these words were repeated in several different languages. Still, no one yielded.

Vika didn't wait to see the outcome of the stuck door. She turned around, shoving back the way she'd already come. Her foot landed on something soft, and she stumbled into the wall, nearly dropping Nadya. Below, the lifeless face of an old woman, bloodied and trampled, stared up at her. Vika swallowed a scream and lurched ahead into another branch of the tunnel.

That too, was filled with people, but Vika jostled her way forward, fighting her rising panic. She had to get out of these tunnels, out of this underground maze. Opening the next door she passed, she entered a small cellar. A light bulb still burned in the center of the room, revealing half a dozen people slumped over. Vika imagined they'd run out of air or succumbed to the heat, just as she'd feared would happen, but she didn't stop to check. Her eyes fixed on the stairway leading up, and she strode toward it. She had to see the sky. Breathe fresh air.

She clomped up the steps, drove her shoulder into the door at the top, and stepped into a kitchen, fully intact. Through the blown-out windows, she could see the fires raging outside. No sky was visible. No fresh air available.

Still, they were free of the tunnels, and the bombing had stopped. She could loop back around to the cellar where she'd been separated from Maksym, Sofia, and Bohdan, find them, then get out of the city.

Vika walked out into the burning night. She clutched Nadya close as they moved down the street, which remained largely untouched despite the fire roaring around it.

"What now, Mama?" Nadya asked.

"We're going to find our family."

Nadya pressed her face into Vika's chest. "I'm scared."

"I know," Vika said. "Just close your eyes and hold on to me."

Vika searched up and down the nearby blocks for an hour before she found the building they'd gone into. Or what she thought was the building. It was nearly impossible to be certain —she'd had so little time to take in her surroundings before going underground, but she thought she remembered the red front door and matching shutters of the structure in front of her now. Half of it had collapsed, and the other half stood gaping open, giving everyone who walked by a view of the destroyed rooms.

Nadya slept in her arms, so she set the child down next to her, then fell onto the pile of rubble—all that remained from the left side of the building—and began digging. The hot bricks blistered her hands, but it didn't register. Nothing registered other than the fact that her family was buried under this building, but after thirty minutes of digging, she seemed no further in than when she started.

"Mama! I hear it again!" Nadya sat up, her voice cutting through the fog of Vika's determination.

Vika straightened and wiped her bloody hands on her skirt. The low buzz of airplanes sounded in the distance. Before she could answer Nadya, the whistling screech of a falling bomb pierced the night air, followed by another. And another. A second round had begun. Vika grabbed her daughter and ran to find shelter.

When Vika and Nadya emerged from the second cellar, hours later, she could barely see. Her eyes ached, and she moved down the street in a daze until someone ushered her into a field hospital. There, medics used special eye drops and a thin metal tool to scrape the ash and soot from her lids. She held Nadya as they did the same to her, unwilling to let the nurse take her away. The nurse offered them a small cup of water with an apology that they hadn't received their supplies yet to offer them more, but Vika didn't care. She gave almost all the water to Nadya, only taking one sip to quell the burning in her dry throat. When she could see, and Nadya had finished her water, she went back out on the streets.

Dresden burned for days, and as it did, Vika searched. When Nadya slept, she set her on a blanket on the floor of a field hospital room and helped there, hoping that her family would appear. She tipped cups of water into parched, burned lips, hoping with each sooty face she wiped that she would reveal Sofia or Bohdan or Maksym. She held dirty hands and listened as women and men both cried for their losses, but as time went on, fewer survivors trickled out of the carnage, and her hopes of finding her family faded. Still, she searched the streets every day, covering Nadya's eyes as they walked past concrete water reservoirs filled with the bobbing corpses of those desperate enough to seek refuge from the heat of the fires in their depths, only to find they couldn't climb back out as the water boiled them alive.

One evening, she held the lights up for a crew as they pried open the door of a cellar, but they rushed right back out only minutes after entering.

"What is it?" Vika grabbed a young boy's arm. "What's down there?"

"You don't want to know." His sooty face shimmered with sweat.

"Tell me!"

He wrenched away from her and vomited into the charred remains of a bush.

Vika looked up at the building, a two-story building similar to the one she and Maksym had taken cover in, then ran down the stairs.

She jerked to a stop halfway down when the smell hit her: an indescribable thickness that singed her nose hairs and made her stomach revolt. She clutched Nadya close and buried her face in her daughter's head as she took the remaining steps down.

A lantern hung near the base of the stairs, and around the perimeter of the room, bodies lay wilted over where they sat. Heads, shriveled and dried out, perched precariously on shoulders as if they'd just nodded off for a quick nap. A desiccated woman—discernible only by her still coiffed hair—slumped over a pram containing a tiny husk of a child. A layer of ash covered the entire room, as if a horrific giant had seasoned the people with salt and over-baked them in this oven-like cellar.

Vika held her breath as she looked at each body, searching for clues to their identities, and when she recognized no one, she raced back up the stairs. She walked away from the building, relief and horror warring inside her, then slowed as she approached an intersection where a large bonfire raged. Around it, SS officers pulled charred bodies from a giant pile and tossed them into the fire, finishing the job the British and Americans had started.

The smell of burned hair and flesh choked her. Images of Sofia and Bohdan's little faces, blackened beyond recognition, or Maksym's strong body, withered and scorched, played on a loop in her mind. She set Nadya down and, just like the boy, retched in the street.

* * *

Vika had walked through all of the hospital tents countless times and scoured the streets and neighborhoods near where they'd taken shelter. Rescue missions had shifted to body recovery missions, and that night, as she slept next to Nadya under a big willow tree along the river, images of the death and destruction she'd witnessed haunted her dreams.

Vika couldn't ignore the futility of her search amid such destruction. Maksym or Sofia or Bohdan's charred forms could be right in front of her, yet unrecognizable. The terrible truth was, she might never find out what happened to them. But still, somehow, she maintained her hope, sustaining it like a small plant in her garden, each happy reunion she witnessed a drink of water helping it grow and flourish so it filled her broken heart.

On Friday, three days after the first bombing, Vika began her daily routine of searching the field hospital. By now, the nurses knew her and stopped to point her toward new patients or offer Nadya a treat. Walking slowly up and down the aisle, she peered down at each victim. Wrapped in gauze, some were unidentifiable, but easily ruled out as Maksym or the children based on other physical features.

"Viktoria!" a nurse called out to her, then waved her over to the far side of the tent. "Hurry!"

Vika grabbed Nadya and ran down the aisle, skipping around bustling volunteer nurses and trays of medical supplies. A girl crouched in the corner, her eyes wide and vacant.

Vika's heart lurched. She dropped to her knees so her face was in Sofia's line of vision. Sofia stared back as she blinked awake at the familiar face, then burst into tears.

"Mama?" Her sweet voice was raspy and raw. "Is that really you?"

"Yes, my love, it's me." Vika set Nadya down and wrapped her arms around Sofia. She smoothed her daughter's hair, the burned pieces at the ends of her blonde braids disintegrating as Vika touched them, turning her fingers black and floating into the air in a powdery haze.

The hair would grow back. Sofia had survived, and that was all that mattered. But that small action, after all she'd seen, finally broke Vika and a flood of tears erupted from her eyes.

She clutched her daughter tighter, wishing her embrace would remove the pain and fear haunting the little girl.

"Poor thing hasn't spoken a word since they brought her in," the nurse said. "But I remembered your description, and I wondered if this could be her."

Vika had forgotten anyone else besides Nadya was with them. She wiped her eyes and struggled to find the words, to force them out of her mouth, because she wasn't sure she wanted to know the answer. "Did she come in alone?"

"No, there's a man and boy with her. They're being seen over there. I can take you to them if you'd like."

46

LILIYA

February 1945, Dresden, Germany

Bright light seeped through Liliya's closed eyes. She didn't recognize the voice speaking to her or all the German words, and she didn't care. She wanted to sink back into the blackness because something terrible awaited her if she opened her eyes. She didn't know what, and she didn't know why, but she was certain that the blissful ignorance of her sleep was better than the alternative.

A cold, damp cloth pressed against her forehead, followed by more German words. Her head rolled away from the pressure as memories began to flit into her mind.

Germany.
Dresden.
The bombs.
Oh, God, the fire.

Filip.

Halya. Slavko.

Her eyes flew open.

"Where am I?" Her voice rasped, and she clutched a hand to her throat as she glanced around the big room. A hospital room. Rows of beds fanned out around her, filled with bandaged and sleeping patients. She stared up at the woman standing next to her.

"You're at a hospital west of Dresden. You were taken here after the bombing."

"Where's Filip?"

The nurse clucked sympathetically. "Perhaps he's in another hospital somewhere."

"How long has it been?" Liliya wheezed. A thousand knives stabbed into her chest with each breath she drew.

"Two days." The woman smiled, her face feathering into wrinkles. "I'm Nurse Venhaus."

Liliya stared at the smiling woman, trying to reconcile her memories with the situation in front of her now, but the cruel impossibility of it stunned her. How did this happen? Filip had been so close she could have touched him, and what had happened to Slavko and Halya?

"No! That can't be right! I have to go!" Liliya tried to get out of the bed, her pulse throbbing in her aching head, but her legs wouldn't support her.

"You'll need to build up your strength first."

"I don't have time for that! I have to find them." Tears sprang to her eyes as the bone-deep certainty that she'd failed stole her breath. Were they even alive? Had they died in the bombing, waiting for her?

Nurse Venhaus frowned. "You won't get anywhere if you can't walk. Now, it's almost time for dinner, so sit back and rest. I'll leave you alone for a bit to get your bearings."

The nurse scuttled off as Liliya contemplated the word.

Alone.

She'd lost her parents. She'd lost Slavko and Halya. She'd lost Filip.

She was alone.

If we stay together, we'll be all right.

The mantra Maksym had repeated to the family and she had repeated to Slavko and Halya so many times taunted her. A tear slipped down her cheek.

Alone.

How had she failed so miserably?

Her hand flew to her pocket, searching for Filip's little bird that had comforted her so many times on this journey, but even that was gone.

The woman in the next bed spoke up in Polish, interrupting Liliya's thoughts.

"The Reds are still coming." Her voice was coarse, probably from smoke damage, like Liliya's. She peered over at Liliya with one eye. The other was wrapped up in white gauze that encircled her head. "I've heard they're only weeks away."

Fresh terror bloomed in Liliya's chest at the thought of the approaching Soviet army. Not only was her family missing, but the war was still raging around her. It seemed the world had ended that night in Dresden. How could they still be fighting?

She remembered the brief moment of victory she'd felt when she'd seen Filip. The surprising surety that she'd been through the worst, and that it could only get better. A bitter chuckle slipped past her lips. She was a damn fool.

"I'm going west," the woman said. "As soon as I can get out of here, I'm going west. You could come with me, if you want."

"I can't," Liliya said. "I have to find my family first."

"Were they there with you?" the woman asked. "When the bombs hit?"

Liliya didn't know what to say. She'd been with Filip, but he hadn't seen her. Slavko and Halya had been with her earlier, but who knew where they were now?

She gave a small nod.

The woman shook her head, and her face creased with sympathy. "Then they're probably all dead. You need to move on."

47

HALYA

May 1945, Dresden, Germany

Nearly three months passed, along with more rounds of bombing in March and April, and Halya and Slavko still had no clues as to what had happened to Liliya. They'd lingered in the countryside, loath to leave without knowing for certain and circling back into Dresden every so often to search for her, but then the Reds arrived. Rolling into the city with tanks and trucks in a flurry of smoke and dust, the Soviet army invaded as it freed. Oppressed as it liberated.

Whispered rumors of their vicious assaults on women soon became widespread facts, but Halya and Slavko still searched. Slavko grew angry whenever she did it, but sometimes, when he slept and she couldn't, Halya would slip away, wandering through the skeletons of broken buildings, looking for Liliya.

Halya ignored Slavko's protests, comfortable with the protection of a slender knife she'd found in the rubble, her wits, and her rage.

That night, only three blocks from the abandoned building where she and Slavko normally slept, a scream echoed from the apartments across the street. Halya squinted, trying to see what was happening under the pale moonlight. Suddenly, a dark figure flung itself from the second story, her dress billowing around her waist, and landed with a thud on the street.

A shout rang out, this time in angry Russian.

The woman on the street tried to stand, then groaned. Halya ran over and grabbed her arm, yanking her up, surprised to see a much younger face than she expected. Thin as a rail, like they all were, the girl couldn't have been more than twelve.

"It's the Reds," she sobbed. "They're in there! They've come for the women!"

Without a word, Halya threw the girl's arm over her shoulder and dragged her down the street.

"My mother is still up there," the girl said. "She pushed me."

"You can't help her now, and this is what she wanted—to save you. We'll come back for her."

The girl leaned on Halya, crying. "There'll be nothing left of her. They'll rape her until she's dead."

Halya didn't reply because the girl was probably right. Evidence of the Reds' brutal occupation was on display all over the city—disfigured faces, growing bellies, haunted eyes.

"How many were there?"

"Only two this time."

Halfway down the block from the apartment, Halya pulled

the girl in between two buildings and pressed against the wall, holding her breath until she heard it: boots clipping on the ground, a Russian voice cajoling them to come out. She counted the steps. Just one man.

What would Liliya do in this situation?

The question calmed Halya. Liliya wasn't afraid of anything. Liliya would be brave and strong. So, tonight, Halya would be Liliya.

"No matter what, stay here, all right? I'll keep him away from you," Halya whispered to the girl. She reached into her boot and pulled out the knife. Pressing it tight against the inside of her wrist, she stepped out into the street.

The Russian man grinned. "Ah, you wanted me to find you?"

Pain ripped across Halya's scalp as he grabbed her by the hair and threw her on her back. He dropped to his knees and yanked up her skirt with one hand and started to work on his belt buckle with the other.

With her skirt covering her trembling hand, Halya flipped the knife upward so it pointed at the Russian. Terror crystallized her thoughts, pushing everything into slow motion. She'd thought about a moment like this before—what she would do, how she would react, but her imagination never accounted for the raw fear thrumming through her body. She waited, her heart pounding in her chest, her thumb tracing the grooves in the knife handle as he pushed down his pants. The steel, cool against her hot skin, calmed her as she pondered the best place to stab him. She wasn't strong, but she was smart, and she knew there were places where she could do more damage than others.

When he leaned over to lower himself, she pulled her skirt off her hand, then thrust her arm upward with all her might, plunging the knife into his neck.

He froze, his eyes wide with shock, as she yanked the knife sideways, ripping open his throat. Blood spilled out of his neck, running down the front of his body and onto Halya. She scooted back, staring as he pitched forward where she'd just been lying. Shock pulsed through her. But no remorse.

She plucked the knife free, her breath coming in fast gulps, then wiped the blade against his drab green tunic and straightened.

"You killed him!" The girl came out from behind the building, favoring her left leg as she swayed. She stared at Halya, awe replacing the fear on her face.

"I did." Halya looked down at the motionless body, still not quite believing what had just happened. Was this what it felt like to actually do something? To successfully fight back? To finally save someone? She'd expected to feel strong and brave, and she did, but she also knew this victory was temporary. Hollow. It didn't make up for all she'd lost. Nothing would.

Halya emptied her pockets again, even though she knew the result would be the same. In the two days since they'd left Dresden, she'd searched a million times. She hadn't had the courage to tell Slavko yet, but she couldn't put it off any longer.

She took a deep breath. "They're gone. My identification papers."

"You're sure?" Slavko asked. "When was the last time you had them?"

"The day before we left."

"So, the night of the attack?" Slavko frowned. He'd been so upset when Halya had returned, covered in blood, but he'd helped her wash it off with a bucket of cold water, then held her while she'd shivered to sleep.

"Don't ever scare me like that again," he'd told her over and over.

That was when they'd decided to move west toward the occupied American and British areas. With the Soviet presence in Dresden and everywhere in the east, it wasn't safe to stay or go home.

She patted her pockets one last time. "Yes. Maybe they fell out of my skirt when he pulled it up."

Slavko grimaced, then rubbed his hands over his face. She'd reassured him so many times that she hadn't been hurt, that she'd defended herself, that she was fine, but she knew he hated to think about it.

She was fine, though. She'd witnessed far too much inhumanity to harbor any sadness or regret for the death of a man who'd wanted to do her harm. But sometimes, late at night, she mourned for herself, because taking that step, taking a life, as necessary and justified as it had been, would now always be stain on her soul.

"So, you think your identification papers are lying next to a murdered Soviet soldier?" he asked.

Halya nodded miserably. "I think so."

"All right." He took her hand and squeezed it. "Let's think on it. We'll figure it out together. We always do."

* * *

They traveled west and spent their nights hidden in barns, squirting milk straight from the cows' udders into their mouths and stealing vegetables from German root cellars. Some areas looked untouched by the ravages of war, and a bitterness rose within Halya at the sight of full larders and plump housewives with two cows each. When she compared it to what she'd lost, who she'd lost, the urge to scream and destroy their happy farms nearly overwhelmed her.

Sometimes, as they pilfered the gardens, they were caught and chased away by angry housewives. Sometimes, they were caught and brought inside for full meals and a warm place to sleep by the fire. One never knew which type of woman would emerge from her kitchen—an angry, red-faced shrew or a kindly, repentant angel. Mostly, it was the former.

They finally saw their first American soldiers in a small village outside Leipzig, almost back where they'd started in the factory before they'd initially gone east toward home. Strapping young men full of confidence and smiles, the Americans offered her and Slavko kindness and chocolate bars.

She learned how to say, "Do you have gum?" in English from a displaced Polish boy, and her efforts were rewarded the next day with a whole pack for her and Slavko to share.

In that moment, Halya thought the war was finally over. Two hours later, as dusk descended on the small farm they were currently camped at, a piece of gum wadded in her mouth, she saw the hanging man.

The body spun in lazy circles, a macabre dance moving in time with the sound of the creaking branch it dangled from—

the purple face, the protruding tongue, and the grotesque bend of the neck exhibited from all angles, for everyone in the village to see. A dirty white bandage, reminiscent of a time when he had hope enough for his future to treat his wounds, not cause them, fluttered out from behind him, waving in the wind like a flag of surrender.

He couldn't have been much older than her father, Halya thought. And he'd been kind to her. Giving her food yesterday morning when she had none, and directing them to an abandoned barn where they could sleep without being accosted by the barrage of Soviet soldiers who'd arrived in the last few days and talked of repatriating people back to the Soviet Union.

"I will never go," the man had declared to a large crowd the night before. "They will kill us all, or at the very least, send us to labor camps and work us to death there. Even if we had no choice in being sent to Germany as forced laborers, they'll think we were traitors."

Halya stared at the man, waiting to feel something. Sadness, perhaps? Maybe regret that she hadn't stopped him? It should be anger coursing through her, propelling her to fight against the fate this man had given his life to avoid.

But there was nothing. No emotions. No thoughts. Just a cold hardness knotted tightly in her chest and a crystal-clear realization: if this grown man was so scared to return to Soviet-ruled Ukraine that death proved a better option, she and Slavko were right to be heading west. She could never go back home, especially after what she'd done.

Halya didn't know how long she stared at the man hanging from the end of the rope. As the blue sky faded into twilight, the breeze picked up, making him sway and sending the dirty white bandage trailing from his head into a frantic flutter.

"Halya, what are you doing?" Slavko appeared silently at her side, his gaze fixed on her, not the man.

"He was afraid to go back," she said. "He was so afraid to go back to the Soviet Union that he chose death."

Despite everything she'd lost, everything she'd been through, Halya hadn't contemplated taking her own life. Maybe because she'd experienced what it felt like to have that hole in your heart when someone you loved was gone, or maybe because she had Slavko by her side, reminding her she was not truly alone. She reached out and took Slavko's hand, relishing the feeling of comfort that flooded her when he squeezed her fingers.

"I wanted to talk to you about that." Slavko shifted in front of her, blocking her view of the hanging man. "If we get into this camp tomorrow, you have to lie about where you were born."

They'd finally arrived at the outskirts of a displaced persons camp and planned on entering the next day in hopes of regular food, shelter, and the possibility of finding their families.

"I spoke with a group who left the Mannheim area. They said the Soviets are forcing repatriation. The group left their American camp in the middle of the night to avoid being transferred to a DP camp in the Soviet zone. Four hundred of them walked away. And aside from that, if the Soviets do have your papers, they could be looking for you." He dropped his gaze. "About the incident with the soldier."

"I know. But what if my parents escaped and came this way? How will they find me if I don't say who I am?"

Her mind, foggy with hunger and fatigue, couldn't make sense of what she should do. Even if her identification papers weren't found next to the dead soldier, if the camp officials knew she was born in Soviet Ukraine, they'd send her home. Separate her from Slavko, who'd been born in Polish-occupied western Ukraine, and was, at the moment, exempt from the aggressively enforced Soviet repatriations back east.

And, according to the rumors sweeping through the refugee community, if she went home, the Soviet government would consider her a traitor to the people for working in Germany—even though she'd had no choice—and she could be sent to the gulags.

"Maybe you can still give your real first name and patronymic, then use my last name and my village since it was considered to be in Poland," Slavko said. "We can say we're cousins, like me and Liliya. My friend told me as long as you say you were born in Poland, you'll be classified as a Polish-Ukrainian and you won't get sent back. Even if your parents can't look for you, you can still look for them. And, if you're listed as coming from a different village, the Reds won't know it was you who killed that man since that village won't match your paperwork."

Halya thought of the millions of refugees wandering the countryside, the long lines of bereft people waiting to process into the camps. Finding her family would be like finding a needle in a haystack, but she could search for them as much as she wanted without exposing herself. Besides, for all she knew, they could still be back in the Kyiv Oblast, and if she went there to find them, she could be sent away to the gulags anyway. At this point, all she could control was her own fate.

"You're right. I have to lie," she said. The decision sat like a brick in her gut, a betrayal of all she'd fought to live for, but it was the only way to continue to survive. "I won't be from Soviet Ukraine. I will say I'm from Maky, Volhynia, Poland. Just like you."

48

VIKA

June 1945, near Prague, Czechoslovakia

"Come on, Bohdan!" Vika waved at her son. "We need to get home."

Home was currently an abandoned barn on the farm where Maksym had found work in a small village outside Prague. After they'd been reunited in Dresden, they'd traveled to Slavko's factory and found empty, bombed-out ruins. Since then, Vika hadn't pushed to travel onward. She didn't know where else to go now.

Bohdan clutched the loaf of bread they'd just bought at the market and ran to his mother. "I saw some kids playing over there. I thought I could maybe go say hi. Please, Mama?"

Vika walked back down the street and peered into the alley. Against the far wall of a building on the next street, a group of boys around Bohdan's age were huddled together, looking down at something on the ground. Vika couldn't see what it was, and she didn't have time to check.

"No. Not tonight."

Bohdan's mouth pursed into a pout, but he walked along next to his mother without any complaint. Suddenly, a loud boom echoed around them. As the sound faded away, children began screaming. Vika grabbed Bohdan's hand and ran back to the alley they'd just passed. This time, she had to look through the veil of smoke and debris permeating the air. A woman's shout rang out and, as the smoke cleared, a group of adults descended upon the cluster of children, one of whom now lay inert on the ground.

One woman grabbed a wheelbarrow and pushed it up to the child, then hefted him into it. She gripped the handles and ran straight at them through the alley. Vika pushed Bohdan back against the wall as the woman approached.

Vika stepped forward to offer help, but when her eyes fell on the wounds of the boy, the words stuck in her throat. Burns scorched his face and upper body so thoroughly she couldn't make out his features.

"I need a doctor!" The woman ran past them, screaming, and turned into the street on her search for help.

"What happened to him, Mama?" Bohdan's grip on Vika's hand was so tight her fingers ached.

Before Vika could respond, a Red Army soldier walking past them paused and answered. "Those fools found an unfired *Panzerfaust* and shot it. That boy was standing behind the shooter, and the backblast coming out of the tube hit him."

"What's a *Panzerfaust*?" Bohdan asked.

Vika jerked Bohdan's hand, willing him to be silent. No one

engaged with Red Army soldiers voluntarily. Drawing that kind of attention never ended well.

"A tank killer. The Germans shot those at our tanks and—" He made a whooshing sound as his hands balled up, then expanded in a simulation of an explosion. His lips curved up into a gruesome smile, but it didn't reach his eyes, which had settled on Vika.

"Anything else I can help you with?" The predatory gleam on his face reminded Vika of the foxes that lurked near their chicken coop back home.

"No," Vika murmured. She turned on her heels and, pulling Bohdan along, walked back to their campsite as fast as they could go.

* * *

"These children run feral," Maksym said after she recounted the story later that night. "Their parents are dead, in camps, or not home yet from fighting. And the parents who are around are so busy trying to stay alive, they don't have time to deal with these things. That's why we need to get into the American zone and find a refugee camp as soon as we can."

"If we do that, we're admitting we'll never go home. I'll never see my sister again or find out if our son made his way home. Do you realize what you're asking of me?"

Maksym threw his hands up in the air. "I've told you before! If we go home, I'll be arrested, and so will you and the children. We shouldn't even be here in the Soviet zone. They've already begun repatriating people."

"You chose to be the village elder and make transport lists! Not the children and me!" Vika yelled.

"I chose?" Maksym's voice went deadly quiet. "You know very well I had no choice in the matter, but even if I had, I would choose to protect my family every time. I lowered the quotas and saved who I could, but it killed my soul to send people away from Ukraine. That 'choice,' as you call it, saved our other children. It saved you!"

All the anger drained out of Vika in a rush. She sat down hard on the ground, her hands shaking, and stared at the fire. The commitment to proclaiming yourself a refugee with no home felt too great, even if it was true.

"I don't mean it, Maksym. I'm just scared."

Maksym sat down next to her and pulled her close. She let her head fall against his shoulder.

"I am, too, Vika. But you know, the camps may surprise you. What if Slavko made his way to one? What if we find him there?"

They sat in silence as Vika let that idea turn over in her mind. It rolled slowly, clinging to what little hope she had left. She needed something to believe in, something to propel her forward out of this stagnant limbo. This could be it.

"Fine, Maksym. We'll leave for the camp tomorrow."

* * *

At sunrise, they walked west down the railroad tracks, Maksym carrying the suitcase that contained all their worldly possessions. Even little Nadya walked, her small hand tucked into Vika's so she wouldn't stumble over the wooden ties. Bohdan skipped ahead, somehow still excited for the adventure to come, while Sofia kept looking backward toward the rising sun, toward Ukraine. Vika understood. They were leaving behind nothing and everything all at once.

At the processing center in the camp, Vika bit her lips with shame as she was deloused and as her children were labeled "malnourished." She'd done everything in her power to protect her family, to provide for them, but it was never enough. She hadn't been enough.

"Don't say that," Maksym whispered in her ear when she cried that evening in their new bed in the communal barracks room. With only a sheet between them and the next family, Vika did her best to muffle her sobs. "We saved them, Vika. This is the beginning of our new lives, and who knows where it will take us? We must stay positive."

She'd never thought that her own failures would rise up so spectacularly in the face of such kindness. The bowls of hot soup and slices of thick bread provided by the camp had instigated tears, as had the clean sheets and solid roof over her head. In the nearly year and a half since they'd left home, she'd never given herself time to grieve what she'd lost, but now, she couldn't stop.

"Do you think they'll be all right? Our children?" she asked.

"Of course they will," Maksym replied. "Bohdan already made friends with a group of boys in the barracks. I saw them playing ball out in the field. Do you realize we're safer here than we have been since the war started six years ago? Safer than we were in our own home?"

"You're right." Vika nodded slowly as the realization dawned on her. "It's been so long since I've let my guard down. Since I didn't have to worry about soldiers killing or taking my children. I don't know how not to worry. War is almost all Bohdan and Sofia know, and Nadya doesn't even remember our home."

"Now they'll learn a new way of life, just as we will. You'll see." He took her hand and pressed it to his lips. "This is our fresh start."

49

LILIYA

July 1945, Bomberg Displaced Persons Camp, Germany

"Name?"

"Liliya Yaroslavivna Shums'ka." The words scraped out like rusty nails against her raw throat.

The uniformed woman, with her neatly curled hair framing a smooth, young face, checked a box on the form and plowed on. "Nationality?"

"Ukrainian."

The woman pursed her freshly painted lips. "Soviet-Ukrainian or Polish-Ukrainian?"

A surge of anger rolled up in Liliya, and she paused, tempering her words. "Why can't I just be Ukrainian?"

"I'm sorry, I need to clarify where you were born."

She closed her eyes, picturing the poppies waving in the yard of the small house she'd lived in with her parents, and then with Maksym and Vika. What did it look like now? Had the Soviets burned it? The Germans? Maybe the Poles or the Ukrainians?

"Maky. Volhynia. In Poland." She swallowed down the questions, pushing them into the pit of despair already boiling in her stomach.

The woman's pen began scratching on the paper. "I'll mark you as Ukrainian-Pole, then."

Liliya barked out an unexpected laugh, startling both herself and this ignorant woman, at the irony of her identity being both Ukrainian and Polish now. Perhaps it was better this way. Maybe if they'd united long before instead of fighting each other, they would have been better able to fend off the Germans and Soviets occupying their land.

"I am not Polish or Soviet. I am Ukrainian."

The woman stiffened at Vika's response. "I understand, but as Ukraine is not a real country, we have to label you by where you were born instead of how you ethnically see yourself."

How do *I see myself?* Once upon a time, that question wouldn't have merited much thought. Daughter. Cousin. Friend. Scholar. Artist. But one by one, those things had been taken from her. Some by Stalin. Some by Hitler. Some by her friends and neighbors. Where did that leave her now?

What did it matter anymore? She could never be that girl again.

"I am Ukrainian, so that's how I see myself. But if you can't write that, then put down Ukrainian-Pole," Liliya said.

The woman sighed. "So, you did not live on Soviet land before 1939, correct?"

"Why?"

"If you resided on Soviet land before 1939, we have to repatriate you back to the USSR."

Liliya sucked in a breath. Go back? To what? Her decimated village? A sea of death and loss?

Home.

Maybe she would go back one day and fight for Ukraine, but if she did, it would be on her own terms, not the Soviets'.

"I was born in western Ukraine. Polish ruled." It was the truth, but she couldn't prove anything if they asked. Her papers were destroyed long ago. "What else do you need to know?"

The woman gave Liliya an appraising look, as if deciding how much to press her, then moved to the bottom of the paper and resumed her interrogation in fast bursts.

"Religion?"

"Orthodox."

"Languages spoken in order of fluency?"

"Ukrainian, Polish, Russian, German."

"Parents' names?"

The questions rattled on, and Liliya answered. Little pieces of her past clawed up out of her memories and spewed out into the void of her empty world, each one a poisoned barb of grief.

Liliya stared down at her hands. Strong, but shaking. Scarred, but with streaks of new pink flesh growing up from her burn wounds. A symbol of her life. A window to her battered soul that she wasn't ready to face. She interlaced her trembling fingers, locking them together.

Together.

She'd promised Halya and Slavko they would stay together, that they would survive together. She'd promised Filip they would see each other again.

The woman tapped her pencil as she looked over the sheet, then poised it back at the top of the paper, ready to ask the question she'd put off earlier. Sympathy softened her face.

"Do you have any family here with you?"

The fragile strands of self-control Liliya had clung to snapped. She choked out the answer, the sting of failure scorching her like the fire she'd battled in Dresden.

"No. I am alone."

50

VIKA

October 1945, Neumarkt Displaced Persons Camp, Germany

After a few months of decent meals and a roof over their heads in the camp, Sofia, Bohdan, and Nadya finally had meat on their bones and smiles on their faces, but a new threat had appeared.

Vika pulled her children close as the crowd of Ukrainian men swarmed around the car holding the Soviet repatriation soldiers. They pushed against it, rocking it back and forth while shouting, "We'll never go back!" and "I'd rather die than live under Stalin again," until the Neumarkt Displaced Persons Camp director and police force made them disperse.

The Soviets got out of the car, their eyes shooting daggers at the mass of angry Ukrainians, still shouting and waving their fists. They huddled with the camp director for a moment, then got back in their car and drove away.

Vika knew it wasn't over. The agents would come back, slithering through the crowd like snakes, spreading their lies and trying their best to lure people back under the yoke of Stalin's brutal rule. Luckily, the Soviets couldn't use their normal, violent techniques here in a camp in the American zone, and the DPs knew it.

She'd heard that the last time they'd come, a group of Ukrainian and Polish men, united in their hatred for the Soviets, had found one of the Soviet repatriation soldiers alone, outside the camp, and beat him nearly to death before slipping away in the darkness to avoid punishment. Now, the Soviets always made sure to travel in groups.

"Come, children, we must go back to our room. Your father will be waiting, and we need to prepare."

Tomorrow, they would be boarding a train to transfer to another displaced persons camp, this one in Aschaffenburg, Germany. As the United Nations Relief and Rehabilitation Administration, the group in charge of the camps, worked to organize the millions of refugees, families were relocated to different camps to more evenly distribute them and keep them from getting too comfortable. The UNRRA hoped they'd choose to return to their countries, but for the vast majority, they had no homes to return to, their countries were in ruins, or they feared punishment by the Soviet government.

Refugees also willingly applied to move as they desperately searched for lost family members, but Vika and Maksym hadn't asked for this move. Still, Vika hoped for more space and privacy at Aschaffenburg.

Sofia, Bohdan, and Nadya followed along behind her as she walked back to their "room," which consisted of four sheets hung up for privacy around their two beds in a massive open room filled with other refugees. A latrine building stood in the middle of the sleeping quarter buildings, and they received all of their food from the camp mess hall down the road. It was a nomadic, difficult life, yet the few months they'd spent here were the most stable they'd had in a long time. The children attended a school run by a group of Ukrainian teachers, church services were held in one of the open halls, and recently, groups had started distributing Ukrainian newspapers.

"Oh, excuse me!" A tired-looking woman, roughly Vika's age, apologized as she stepped backward into Sofia. She'd been searching the wall filled with scraps of paper listing the names and villages of those searching for family members. Vika knew, because, along with registering her search with the camp and the Red Cross, she'd filled one out for Slavko and Liliya two weeks before, pressing the pencil so hard into the small piece of paper it had broken three times. Each time, she sharpened it with a knife and resumed writing.

Stanislav Maksymovich Melnyczuk
    Age: 16
    Maky, Volhynia, Poland-Ukraine

Liliya Yaroslavivna Shums'ka
    Age: 19
    Maky, Volhynia, Poland-Ukraine

The woman stared at Sofia, then drew a shaky breath and forced a wobbly smile. "I'm sorry," she apologized again. "I don't mean to be rude. My daughter would be close to your daughter's age, I think, and I imagine I see her in every girl I come across. But, deep down, I know it's a lost cause. We were told she died in a bombing. I look because I have to, you understand? Not because I expect anything."

Sympathy, and the shared sisterhood of loss, pushed Vika forward. She placed her hand on the woman's arm. "Of course, I understand. I'm looking for my son. I wish you luck in your search ..."

"Katya," the woman smiled sadly, placing her hand over Vika's. "My name is Katya. And I wish you the same."

51

LILIYA

November 1945, Bomberg Displaced Persons Camp, Germany

The man limped as he walked, his left leg dragging behind him the tiniest bit. Liliya watched him from under her lashes as he moved past her. He'd lost weight—his cheeks gaunt, his once wide shoulders now stooped—but there was no mistaking who it was.

"Oleksiy!" His name erupted from her lips in a mix of laughter and tears.

He froze, his head slowly turning to where she sat on a bench next to her barracks.

"Liliya?" His voice had a new rasp to it, his eyes wide with shock as he took her in. "Is that really you?" In seconds he was next to her, his arms wrapped around her as she stood on tiptoes to kiss his cheek.

"I never thought I'd see you again," he murmured into her hair.

"How did you get here?" she asked, pulling back so she could look closer at him. A wicked scar slashed across his cheek, and she could feel his hands trembling against her back.

"I was captured as the Germans retreated," he said. "In our last skirmish with them. They sent me to Auschwitz."

"Oh, Oleksiy," Liliya breathed. "How did you survive?"

He laughed, but it was bitter. "Luck, I suppose. We lost quite a few good UPA men there, but the fight carries on."

"What are you talking about?" Liliya shook her head. "How can you keep fighting?"

A flash of anger passed over Oleksiy's eyes. "How can we not? Ukraine is under the Soviet chokehold again. The Germans are gone but our oldest foe still occupies our land. We must fight."

"So you're going back?"

"I have to," Oleksiy said.

"With the Soviets in power, it will be more dangerous than ever," Liliya said.

Oleksiy shook his head. "The danger doesn't bother me. I will die for Ukraine before I let her fall without a fight, and I'm still standing."

"But this is your chance! You could move on. Stop fighting and live a normal life."

"I can never live a normal life after the things I've seen. The things I've done." He dropped his head. "I'm broken, Liliya."

"We're all broken, Oleksiy." Liliya ran her hand down his cheek and tugged his chin up. "Now is our chance to heal ourselves."

"I don't think I'll ever heal," he said. He pressed her hand to his face, then turned his lips into her palm and kissed it. "I've made my peace with that. And with losing you."

He let go of her hand, and Liliya let it fall to her side, an ache of sadness welling in her chest. She'd never loved Oleksiy the way he wanted her to, but she'd always loved him.

"Are you with anyone?" he asked.

"No. I was separated from Slavko in Dresden. I came across someone from our village, and she told me Vika and Maksym came this way."

Oleksiy nodded. "They did. They left before the Reds arrived. It was a good thing too. Their house, your house, is gone."

A surprising jolt of pain pierced Liliya. Her home. The last place she had lived with her parents and brother was gone, another casualty of the war. "What happened to it?"

"The front settled in the village for some time. Most of the houses were destroyed in the fighting."

"So that's it. There's nothing left of me there anymore."

"Ukraine is there," Oleksiy said. "I'll be there, too, living in a bunker and continuing my work with the UPA as we fight for a free Ukraine."

"But my family is gone. My home is gone. Ukraine is my heart, Oleksiy, just like you will always be. But I have to move on. I have to build a life for myself outside of this war."

He gave her a small, sad smile. "What will you do now?"

"I'm thinking of leaving. Finding a new home in a new country, far away from this. Maybe America. I have to do the things I promised myself, my parents, I would do, but first, I have to keep searching. I have people I promised to help, and I lost them."

"And if they're dead? Or you never find them?"

She took his hand, weaving her fingers into his. "Then I find myself."

"Do you remember when I left you that special pencil in the willow tree?"

"Of course. It was one of the nicest gifts I've ever received. You must have worked for months to earn the money to buy it."

He nodded. "You drew a picture of me with it."

"Yes, and you asked me to add me to the picture, so I drew myself next to you."

He reached into his pocket and pulled out a yellowed piece of paper. Carefully, he unfolded it. "I've kept this with me for all these years. Ukraine is my heart, too, Liliya, but you've always been my soul."

52

LILIYA

April 1947, Wildflecken Displaced Persons Camp, Germany

Liliya stared at the wall, the narrow bunk lumpy under her stiff back. Her home for the last few months, the Wildflecken DP camp was, at its core, just like every other DP camp she'd been at. Bomberg, Regensburg, Neumarkt. The names became a blur as she moved from one to the next, always searching, always longing to find a clue to her missing family.

She'd long ago given up hope that Halya, Slavko, or Filip had survived Dresden. She still didn't know how she'd managed not to die in the angry firestorm. For a long time after she'd reunited with Oleksiy, a tiny seed of hope for Vika, Maksym and the children took root in her chest, nurtured daily by the stories around her of families reuniting, of lost husbands returning home, of *Ostarbeiters* finding their parents again. It was what compelled her to check the wall of names daily, to follow every rumor she heard, to switch camps as often as possible.

But as the months wore on and turned into years, that tiny seed of hope grew dormant. It stopped pushing shoots up to her surface, propelling her out of bed each day in search of more answers. It shriveled, dying under the dark shadows of her despair.

Late at night, when she couldn't sleep, she wondered if she'd made a mistake not pushing Oleksiy harder to stay with her. Maybe if she'd lied and told him she loved him how he wanted her to, he would have remained with her, safe in the DP camp, instead of going back to Ukraine and fighting the Soviets.

For all she knew, he was dead now, like everyone else from her old life.

She couldn't go on like this forever. Soon, she would have to decide: continue to search or put in paperwork to be admitted to a new country. Forge ahead and make her new life on her own, or dwell in the past.

"Liliya! Are you home?" A woman's voice broke through her musings, echoing in the large room set up as a women's dormitory. Liliya rolled over and pulled aside the sheet she had hung around her single bed.

"What do you want, Yaroslava?"

Yaroslava, her old neighbor from Maky, had seen Vika and Maksym leaving their village, fleeing the approaching Soviet army. Somehow, she'd managed to keep her family together and reconnect with Liliya here in the chaos of the DP camps, but Liliya couldn't find her own flesh and blood? Every time Liliya thought about it, her body trembled with fury. It wasn't Yaroslava's fault, but Liliya couldn't help hating her for it.

Hate. Liliya's most readily available emotion. She hated waking up each day alone. She hated the pitying looks Yaroslava and the other women in the barracks gave her. She hated the helplessness of being stuck in these camps, relying on the administration to try to find her family. She hated the wall filled with names and addresses scribbled on scraps of paper, because none of them were ever for her.

Anger, which had once been her ever-present companion, paled in comparison to the hatred now transforming her into a bitter, shriveled woman. Gnarled and thick, it twisted around her heart like a tangled vine.

Her only solace was the education she'd been receiving from refugee professors and scholars who'd organized a school and higher learning opportunities for young adults. In the chaos of the DP camps, she studied biology, art, ornithology— all the classes she'd dreamed of before the war, and other basic college-level classes to further her education. But, while they provided a temporary reprieve, a place for her to immerse herself in another world and forget the troubles of her present, they didn't take away the hate festering inside her, and it always reared its ugly head again as soon as she closed her textbooks.

"Your name is on the list." Yaroslava pulled back the curtain, letting in the sunlight.

Liliya squinted and raised her hand to shield her eyes. "A list for what?"

"They're shipping a group to Aschaffenburg. It's one of the biggest camps in this area. Your family could be there."

Liliya heard the hopeful excitement in Yaroslava's voice and wanted to hit her. Once upon a time, she'd had that same hope, that same idealistic dream of what her future could be in this post-apocalyptic war zone. But not anymore. Reality, and the drudgery of moving through nearly half a dozen camps already in search of her family, had slaughtered any vestiges of hope she once harbored.

"I brought you this, too." Yaroslava set a book on the bed and gave Liliya a gentle smile. "Poems from our homeland!"

Liliya stared down at the Lesya Ukrainka poetry book, then let the pages fall open to the most well-read poem. Her breath caught when she recognized the poem Halya had recited to her, "Against All Hope, I Hope," while they huddled together under their thin blankets at the factory.

The words blurred before her, and Liliya slammed the book shut, unable to finish the poem. What were the odds that this book, that this poem, would appear to her now? Was this a sign? Maybe she had given up too soon.

"You need to go prepare," Yaroslava said. "This could be it."

The tiny seed of hope inside her glimmered with a small pulse of life, and Liliya nodded. How could she not have hope? How could she give up, ever? This *could* be it. Maybe, finally, after all this time, this could be it.

53

LILIYA

May 1947, Aschaffenburg Displaced Persons Camp, Germany

Aschaffenburg overwhelmed Liliya. By far the biggest of the camps she'd been in, the LaGarde Kaserne, a Ukrainian camp, teemed with life and culture. Newspapers and flyers, all in Cyrillic letters, advertised church times, dance classes, and community meetings. It seemed a whole thriving microcosm of Ukrainian culture existed here in this camp nestled along the Main River.

At her intake session, she answered the questions and signed her name where applicable. When the woman, who told Liliya her name was Margaret, asked if she was looking for anyone, Liliya gave her all the names of her family. Recited them like a mantra.

Viktoria. Maksym. Stanislav. Sofia. Bohdan. Nadiya. Halyna. Filip.

The last two names weren't blood, but they were family.

"I'll go through my files and see what I can find. Come back tomorrow and check in with me again," Margaret said.

Liliya forced a nod. She'd heard this promise before, but nothing had ever come of it. Still, she'd return tomorrow, and the next day, and the next, and every day until Margaret grew tired of her and sent her away. The truth was, these poor workers were dealing with an unparalleled humanitarian crisis. They did what they could and tried to reunite families whenever possible, but logistically, they usually spent far more time worrying about feeding the masses of hungry displaced persons or securing more supplies or finding countries to accept these lost souls and new citizens.

On the way to her barracks, she passed an open field filled with children playing some game with a ball. They laughed and ran, and Liliya stared, trying to remember the last time she'd seen such unbridled joy. Next to that sat a large barracks building set up like a fancy department store. A woman walking by saw Liliya gawking and, in Ukrainian, told her if she needed new clothes, she could go in there and try anything on. "They're all international donations. Free if you need something."

She bustled away before Liliya could ask her anything further, and Liliya trudged on to her room in another barracks building. Situated off a long corridor with a stove at one end and a bathroom at the other, the room housed six other single women. Some beds had a sheet curtaining off their little section for a modicum of privacy. A pile of sheets sat on the foot of a bare bed, and Liliya sank down next to them, wishing—not for the first time—that she at least had Filip's carved nightingale to remember him by.

Liliya laid her head down on the pillow and clutched the book of poetry to her chest. Would this camp really be any different? Or just another flavor of the same dish, long soured and rotten like the food she'd forced herself to eat to survive during the war?

As she drifted off to sleep, only one coherent thought flitted through her mind: she couldn't let any seed of hope grow into something too large, because she couldn't bear to have it trampled again.

* * *

Margaret didn't look up from her papers as she shuffled through them. Then, she stopped on one and read it over. In her strange American accent, she said, "Here it is. I have a Maksym Melnyczuk, Viktoria Melnyczuk, and their children. All from Maky, Poland." She looked up. "Is that who you're looking for?"

Liliya couldn't reply through the sudden well of emotion clogging her throat. She held out her hand, demanding the list with a breathy, "Please."

Margaret handed her the paper, leaning forward to point out the names written in English. "Can you read that? Here they are." Her finger traced each name, and Liliya's eyes followed along, tears blurring her vision.

"Is there a Slavko?" Liliya asked. "A Stanislav?"

Margaret took the paper back and scanned it. "No, no Stanislav. But there is a Sofia, Bohdan, and Nadiya."

They survived. And they're here.

She swallowed hard and stood. "When can I see them?"

Margaret stood with her. "I can take you right now if you'd like."

"Please," Liliya said, her mind whirling at this sudden turn of events. It was everything she'd hoped for, everything she'd dreamed about, and now it was actually happening.

It didn't feel real.

"This is one of my favorite parts of the job," Margaret said over her shoulder with a grin. She proffered an elbow to Liliya. "Come along now, no need to stay back there."

Liliya wanted to pinch herself, to shout with joy, but she pressed her lips tight and walked silently with Margaret. What if Margaret was wrong? What if it was the wrong family?

Dinner distribution was well underway, and they passed women carrying tin buckets of soup from the cafeteria to their own communal stoves in their barracks. There, they would doctor up the food with extra bits of meat they'd procured on the black market and vegetables from the small gardens they managed to grow.

They entered a three-story barracks building on the far end of the open field and climbed two flights of stairs. Margaret strode down the long hall, then paused to check her paper before knocking sharply on a door. She gave Liliya a wide smile.

"Are you ready?"

How could she feel so terrified, yet want to barrel through the door at the same time? She knotted her hands together and nodded.

A man opened the door, and the smell of cooked cabbage and wet laundry wafted out.

"Can I help you?"

Liliya's heart sank. She didn't know him. It *was* a mistake. This wasn't her family.

But Margaret pressed on. "I'm looking for Maksym and Viktoria Melnyczuk?"

The man pulled the door open and ushered them into the small room. "Yes, they share this room with us. Come in."

The room was divided into three sections, two closed off with sheets hung across from wall to wall on either side and a large open section in the middle. A clothesline of drying laundry hung behind a table and chairs, around which a large group had gathered for dinner. A dozen faces peered up at them.

"Liliya!" Sofia's voice was the loudest, her feet the fastest, as she threw herself at Liliya and hugged her. "Where have you been?"

The same sentiment and hugs were repeated over and over, from Bohdan to Maksym to Vika. When she'd hugged everyone and wiped the tears from her eyes, she saw Margaret had slipped away and someone else stood in the doorway.

His dark, wavy hair, now neat and styled, curled around a leaner face. His jaw hung open and the loaf of bread he'd clutched near his chest swung down to his side. Sofia swooped forward and grabbed it before it fell as the room went silent, watching.

Liliya took an uncertain step forward, wanting to fling herself into his arms, but she was afraid that he'd moved on, that he'd push her away or that his girlfriend or wife was right behind him. Her heart hammered in her chest, and she gave him a tremulous smile.

"Hello, Filip."

Her words released him from his trance, and he strode forward, his rough palms cupping her cheeks, then weaving back into her hair as he tilted her face and kissed her, full on the mouth, in front of everyone. The children whooped and hollered, but the world faded away for her. All she could feel was Filip. His lips, his hands, the urgent press of his hard body. His kiss ravaged her, filling the empty spaces in her soul and drawing every shred of doubt, every speck of worry, from her.

When they finally separated, the room exploded in cheers, and Filip swooped Liliya up into his arms and twirled her. She wrapped her arms around him, just as she had that day so long ago when he'd given her a ride on horseback, but this time, she didn't let go.

* * *

Liliya flipped through one of her old sketchbooks. Like her, it had traveled across the continent. Hidden with Vika's belongings and kept safe, it opened a window into a life Liliya barely recognized. Her childhood dreams—carefully drawn out in pictures of birds, animals, and the faces of those she'd loved—were now more of a mobile monument to all she'd lost than an example of her skills. Her new sketchbook, a continuation of the one the old artist at the labor camp had given her years ago, highlighted a different view on life. With harsher lines and raw beauty—images of battered doves perched on bombed-out buildings or a mother cradling her sick child in a makeshift refugee camp—her current work not only provided a cathartic release for her, it documented the true horror of this war. She'd taken courses in the DP camps—to fulfill her parents' desires for her just as much as for herself—but she was no longer so sure of what she wanted to do with her life.

"I can't believe you thought to bring my old sketchbooks all this way," Liliya said. "Thank you, Vika."

"I had every faith we would be reunited, and I knew you'd want them." Vika twisted her hands in her lap and dropped her voice. "Liliya. You told us about losing Slavko in Dresden, but I want to know more. What was his life like? Did he grow into a good man? What happened to him when he was away from us?"

Liliya took a deep breath and started at the beginning, telling her of Slavko's bravery during the transport and in the camp, of his dedication to protecting their young friend, Halya, and his arrest and resolve to continue sabotaging Nazi weapons despite the punishments he'd already received. She told her about Slavko's escape from the factory during the bombing and their reunion in the woods after he helped save her.

"We made it to Dresden, and we separated to look for food." The pain of Slavko's loss sliced through her again, as sharp as the night it happened. "We were supposed to meet up. Then, the bombs started falling. But he wasn't alone, Vika. He and Halya were together. They were always together."

Vika hung on her every word, and by the time Liliya stopped talking, Vika was on her feet, walking over to her.

Liliya stared up at her aunt, unsure how to react to her approach. Vika's eyes were glass, her face like stone except for the tiny wobble in her chin. Suddenly she threw her arms around Liliya.

"Thank you for telling me everything." Vika wept on Liliya's shoulder. "It makes me feel closer to him, knowing how he spent those first years apart from us. Even the hard parts."

Liliya crumpled under the weight of her guilt. "I'm sorry, Vika. I'm so sorry he was forced to go because of me. I'm sorry I didn't take better care of him." Liliya's voice caught. "I'm sorry I lost him."

"Shh." Vika sat up and smoothed Liliya's hair, her face wet with tears. "You did everything you could, my girl. I don't blame you, and I'm so glad you found us again."

Liliya couldn't hold back her own sobs then, and the two women clung to each other, their tears washing away the years of remorse and regret like a spring rain cleansing the land. And Liliya knew that now, like after the rain, new beginnings would grow between her and her aunt.

Just when Liliya thought all her hope was dead, her reunion with her family after all this time resurrected it. Maybe Slavko and Halya *were* still out there. Once again, she let herself dream of hugging Slavko and telling him she was sorry for not meeting him in Dresden. Of telling Halya that she'd been wrong. It was all right to love and be loved, to let yourself feel joy even in the direst of circumstances. It was the only way to survive.

Being with Filip again reminded her of that more than anything. In the weeks after their reunion, they spent every waking moment together, and when he proposed with a ring made of braided grass, Liliya nearly knocked him over with her enthusiasm in accepting.

Liliya threaded her fingers through his as they walked through the camp together.

"I still can't believe you saw me in Dresden," Filip said. "I wish I'd heard you shout my name. Everything could have been different." He paused and glanced at her. "I went there for you."

Liliya turned to stare at him. "I thought you went for the horses."

He shook his head. "After you left, the Germans wiped out most of my resistance unit. I still don't know how I survived." He closed his eyes for a moment and took a deep breath before going on. "The horses were all I had left. I threw myself into taking care of them, into ensuring their survival for Poland while I worked out a way to get to you. When the orders came to move them west, I volunteered because I knew you were near Dresden. I wanted to make sure they survived, yes, but they were my way to find you." He swung her hand up to his lips and kissed it. "It was always for you."

The thought of the time wasted as they searched for each other still pained Liliya, but Filip's presence next to her removed the sting. It was almost perfect. After so many years of heartache and devastating loss, she'd found love. Now, if she could only find Slavko and Halya.

Every day, they checked the walls at the various camps in Aschaffenburg, picking through the layered mess of pinned-up handwritten notes scrawled in various languages.

So many lost souls searching for their loved ones. Every scrap Liliya touched scorched her fingers, as if the pain of the writer, the uncertainty and fear, could seep into her and bring her back to those painful years when she, too, had been alone. But now, Filip's steady presence at her side reminded her she wasn't alone, and she never would be again.

Then, one day, she found it. The simple letters painstakingly written out.

Stanislav Maksymovich Melnyczuk
Maky, Volhynia, Poland

She didn't remember running back to the room they all shared, but she remembered the look on Maksym's face, the way he dropped to his knees in front of the window, the threads of gray, now prevalent in his dark hair, shimmering in the sun, as she showed him the paper. And she remembered the way Vika had only nodded once, then quietly wiped her eyes on her apron, as if she'd known all along that Slavko was fine and would be found.

As if she'd never doubted.

54

HALYA

June 1947, Aschaffenburg Displaced Persons Camp, Germany

Halya tied the fishing line to the end of a stick, then threaded the thin line through the hook. When the makeshift pole was set, she cast it out into the flowing water of the Main River. A German woman walking by glared at her, and Halya glared right back. In the three weeks since she and Slavko had transferred to the LaGarde Kaserne in the Aschaffenburg DP camp, she'd learned many of the locals didn't appreciate the refugees fishing in their river or living in their city, but she didn't care. The Germans had taken plenty from her, so she didn't feel bad taking their fish.

Life wasn't much different here. Just like at the two previous camps they'd been at, they slept in the old army barracks filled with other refugee orphans, ate three meals a day, and even attended the makeshift school. When they ventured out into the city, they collected random, abandoned bicycle parts so Slavko could cobble together a whole bike from the rusted remains of many. His skill at fixing them gave them the opportunity to earn a little spending money, and with that, they bought line and a hook so Halya could fish. What she caught and cooked on the hotplate in her barracks supplemented their meals nicely.

And each day, Halya and Slavko checked the wall where refugees pinned up papers offering information or begging for it. Names, ages, villages, any clue to connect someone to life before the war. Life before the forced migration of millions of people. Life before the forced death of millions of people.

But finding one person in this vast sea of lost souls was daunting. The administration tried, documenting names and searching for missing loved ones, and the walls at the various camps always overflowed with scraps of paper covered in people's life stories, but none of it was foolproof.

When Halya filtered through those papers—some wilted and despondent, others crisp and hopeful—she ended each session by touching hers, confirming it was still there, offering up her life story in a false, partial summary. Her real first name and patronymic name, Slavko's last name and village, and her parents' real names. She hoped it was enough both to keep her safe and to reconnect her with her parents, but she never stopped worrying that neither would be true.

Halyna Mykolayivna Melnyczuk
Maky, Volhynia, Poland
Searching for Kateryna Bilyk and Mykola Bilyk

The International Refugee Organization woman who'd registered Halya said she would continue to check with other camps and notify her if any of her family members turned up, but with each day that passed, each month that flipped over on the calendar, Halya's hope dwindled.

"There you are!" Slavko plopped down next to her on the riverbank. "I've been looking all over. Mrs. Smith wants to see me."

"About what?" Halya pulled the line in, checked her worm, then recast.

"She said she may have found my family." Slavko kicked at the dirt, sending a clump tumbling into the water. It melted away, dispersed down river by the current. "And I wanted you to come with me."

He said it carefully, and she could feel him holding back his own excitement, watching her reaction instead of rejoicing.

Halya's grip on the stick tightened until her fingers ached. She was happy for Slavko. Truly. He mourned the loss of his family, just as she did hers. But what would happen to her if he reunited with his family? How could he be her surrogate family if he had his real family back?

"Why do I need to be there?" The question was harsh— her emotions raw. She'd admitted, only once, late at night while they sat under the stars, that she feared she had no one left who wanted her in the world.

"I'll always be here for you," he'd told her. "You and me, we're a team. No matter what."

"No," she'd said. "One day your family will show up, and I'll be alone again."

Now, that day was here, and she felt the familiar doubts

creeping up again. The worry that he'd abandon her as soon as his flesh and blood appeared.

"Come on, Halya." Slavko nudged her shoulder with his knee. "Let's go see what she's found."

"You should probably go alone." She stared out across the river. "I don't want to intrude."

"Well, too late for that. We're a package deal now, and my family, if they've even been found, will understand and love you just like I do." His face flushed, and he cleared his throat before turning on his sunny smile and offering her his hand. "Now, come on."

55

VIKA

June 1947, Aschaffenburg Displaced Persons Camp, Germany

When Liliya barreled through the door, Vika jumped to her feet, her needlework falling to the ground in a forgotten pile of thread and cloth.

"He's on his way! I finally found Margaret, and she's going to fetch him and bring him here!"

Vika's heart banged against her chest so hard she thought it would crack open. "You're sure? You're sure it's him? Let me see that paper again."

Liliya dug into her pocket and held out the paper. "Look! Everything is right. His name, the village, his age. It has to be him!"

Vika stared at the familiar handwriting, and a great shuddering sob tore through her. "I thought maybe I'd dreamed it."

Liliya guided her aunt back to a chair. "I saw Bohdan and told him to find Maksym, but Slavko might beat him here."

A few minutes later, Maksym burst into the room, his chest heaving. "Is he here? Did I miss him?"

"Not yet," Vika murmured. Her eyes were fixed on the door, her stomach twisted into knots. "Tell me again."

Vika had heard the brief story of Liliya's discovery of Slavko's note a dozen times in the twenty-four hours since Liliya first came home with it, but she'd never tire of it. As Liliya finished, a knock echoed in the room.

Vika didn't remember opening the door or speaking to Margaret, but suddenly, he was there in front of her. Her first-born. Her Slavko.

She threw herself at him, shocked to find him so much taller than she was. He hugged her just as tightly as he used to, but now his head towered above hers, his thick arms encircled her, and he stood eye to eye with Maksym. He'd become a man. And even as Vika took in the scars on his face and wariness in his eyes, she still saw the same sweet boy she'd lost so long ago. She couldn't stop the tears of joy pouring down her face or take her hand off his arm as he greeted everyone else. She had to touch him, to reassure herself that he was really here after all these years.

After Slavko and Liliya embraced—Liliya crying nearly as much as Vika—Slavko went back to the door and pulled in a quiet young girl with startlingly large blue eyes. Liliya shrieked and swooped the girl up into a hug. When they separated, Slavko grabbed the girl's hand and brought her in front of Vika and Maksym.

"Mama, Tato, this is my dear friend, Halya." He glanced at

Liliya. "*Our* dear friend. We met on the train to Germany and have been together every step of the way since. Even when I was separated from Liliya, I had Halya with me. She hasn't found her family yet, but I assured her mine would welcome her."

He put his arm around Halya's shoulder, love radiating from him, and Vika realized she might have gotten her son back, but he wasn't just hers anymore.

"Hello, Halya." Vika stepped forward and embraced the girl, a waifish package of skin and bones, and whispered in her ear. "Thank you for taking care of our Slavko."

As she pulled back, Halya's face broke into a dazzling smile. "Thank you for raising such an amazing son," she said shyly, and Vika, just like her son, fell in love.

56

HALYA

June 1948, Aschaffenburg Displaced Persons Camp

Halya smoothed her hair. The nearly eighteen-year-old woman staring back at her in the mirror looked nothing like the girl she remembered from home. Her mahogany hair, long again finally, was curled into soft waves around her face. Her cheeks, not hollow from hunger as much as from the high arch of her bone structure, were pinked with a flush. But if she looked close enough, she could see the faint lines of grief etched on her forehead, the shadows of fear in her eyes, and the stubborn tilt of her hard chin.

She walked, along with a bevy of laughing teenage girls, through the field between the barracks to the large building where the dances were held. People from all around the camp, making the same trek, chatted as they migrated.

"Halya? Is that you?"

Halya paused at the entrance to the building and let her friends go inside without her. The loud music—a polka— trickled out into the night through the propped-open door.

"What? I take a shower and put on a clean dress and you don't recognize me?" She spun in a circle, letting her skirt flare around her calves as her anxiety melted away. Slavko always had that effect on her.

"I recognize you." His green eyes swept up and down, taking in her new hairstyle, makeup, and dress. "I just can't believe it's you."

"I think that's even more insulting." Halya ran a hand over her curls, suddenly feeling very silly in allowing her friends free rein in doing her hair and makeup.

"No, that's not what I mean." Slavko rubbed his jaw, his eyes still on her. Inside, the band switched to a slower song. "Will you dance with me?"

"Shouldn't we go in first?"

"It's more private out here." He held out his hand. She placed hers in it, then let him pull her close, his other hand pressing against the small of her back.

She swayed with him, her feet barely leaving the ground. It surprised her how intimate it felt to be held by him when they'd slept next to each other under the stars or in abandoned barns countless times.

Something about this was different, but Halya couldn't place it.

"For the record, you don't look like yourself either," she said, gesturing to his new clothes. Slavko was a great favorite with the ladies at the dances. Always a good-looking boy, he'd grown handsome—long limbed and strong with bright green eyes and dark blond hair—and his sunshiny disposition and easy grin didn't hurt either. In the sea of gray post-war sadness, Slavko stood out like a tropical flower. "Have you fancied yourself up to catch a girl?"

Slavko shook his head. "I'm not interested in catching a girl."

"Oh." It was one syllable, but it hung between them, charging the air.

His palm pressed a little tighter on her back, and she stepped closer to him.

"Then why do you come to these things so much?"

Slavko shrugged. "They're fun. It's nice to feel normal." He looked down at her through the thick fringe of his dark gold lashes, his stare suddenly intense. "Why are you here, Halya? I thought you hated dances."

Halya grinned. "I promised my friends I'd give it a try now that we've finished the last of our classes. And they were so excited to gussy me up." She lifted her hand from his shoulder for a moment to wave at herself. "I couldn't disappoint them."

"They did a fine job. I mean, they had a great base to start from." Slavko cleared his throat and glanced upward before dropping his gaze to meet hers. "That is, what I mean to say is, you look beautiful, Halya."

Slavko's cheeks flamed so much that Halya almost touched one, just to see if it was as hot as it looked. His palm dampened in hers, his gaze trailing down from her eyes to her lips. He leaned in, his face so close she could feel his warm breath on her cheek. Suddenly, his lips were touching hers. Soft and sweet. Gentle, but with intention. With purpose.

With desire.

In a heartbeat, everything Halya knew to be true shifted. It wasn't a big shift, but an infinitesimal slip, a locking into place of a puzzle piece that had always fit but was turned the wrong way, and suddenly she could see the whole picture. See her best friend in the world, her dearest found family member, as something she'd never considered.

A man.

Slavko rested his cheek against her hair. "My family is applying for admittance to America through the new Displaced Persons Act."

Halya's heart stopped in her chest. She tried to form words, to ask questions, but she couldn't move. The thought of Slavko leaving struck pure terror into her heart. The silence stretched on, and she swallowed hard, then forced her mouth to work. "Have you heard if you've been accepted?"

"No. We start the paperwork this week."

Suddenly, she couldn't breathe. The night sky spun overhead, and Slavko's hand tightened on her waist. He called her name, but his voice sounded so far away and tinny. Then, she heard his words, let the emotion infused in them draw her back to the present.

"I want you to come with me." He let go of her hand and gripped her chin, tilting her gaze up to meet his. "Do you hear me, Halya? I'm not interested in catching a girl because I'm in love with you. Will you marry me?"

Her eyes locked on his, and she sucked in a deep breath. Her greatest fear and her greatest wish colliding so closely left her stunned. She didn't have to be alone. She could be with Slavko and his dear family forever.

But marrying him meant moving to another continent. It meant giving up on finding her family here and now.

Slavko rushed on. "I know you don't want to leave in case your parents are still alive, and if you want, I'll stay back with you. We can keep looking for them here."

She knew he meant that. In the three years since they'd entered the camps, Slavko had been with her every step of the way in her search. Even after he found his family, he still scoured the walls with her and made inquiries wherever possible.

She stared into his earnest green eyes, absorbing the sacrifice he was offering to make.

"You would give that up for me? This chance to go to America?"

"I would give up anything for you, Halya. I love you and having you at my side is all that matters to me. You make me want to fight for a better life, no matter where we are."

After a brief hesitation, he went on, "But if you want to go, we have to marry now so we can put in the paperwork together."

Halya drew in a shaky breath. Suddenly, she was a little girl again, snuggled up on her father's lap, listening to his stories and life lessons.

Promise me you will be brave and always fight, no matter what happens. Fight, because life is always worth fighting for.

Tato wouldn't want her to stay, stagnating in this camp when she had the opportunity to go to America.

He would want her to move on past the grief and pain.

He would want her to love and be loved.

To experience joy and fulfillment.

To fight for a better life.

She cupped Slavko's cheeks in her hands, his ever-present stubble prickling her palms.

"You are my family, too. Your family is my family. I love you, Slavko. I will marry you, and we will go to America together."

57

VIKA

October 1948, Aschaffenburg Displaced Person Camp

Vika and Maksym held their breath as Nadya received her chest X-ray, part of the bevy of medical tests required for immigration. She hadn't relapsed with her cough in almost a year, but any spot on her lungs would mean she didn't qualify and they couldn't leave.

When that test, and all the others, came back clear, Vika finally allowed herself to think of what this could mean—a new life for her family, away from the pain and devastation of the war. It was almost too impossible to fathom.

A soft knock echoed on her door, and Vika knew exactly who it was. Slavko had delivered the news about his engagement to the family last night, and ever since, Vika had expected the girl would visit. She understood the decision weighed heavily on Halya, but not because she didn't love Slavko.

Vika ushered her into the room and offered her a seat at the table. Halya took it, mumbling a hello as she chewed at her lips, so Vika didn't mince words. Maksym and the children would be back at any time, and she wanted a chance to talk to Halya alone.

"I thought you might come by. How are you handling all of this?"

Halya blinked, probably surprised at Vika's bluntness, but then, if she was to be a part of the family, she'd have to grow used to it.

Halya answered slowly. "I love Slavko with all my heart, and I want to marry him, but it's hard to leave without knowing what happened to my family."

Vika shook her head. "It doesn't have to be a choice between the two. You've searched for years, living in limbo in these camps, but even from America, there are ways to still search. We can help you."

Halya lowered her voice, as if admitting a secret she didn't want to share. "I saw someone from my old village, and he told me everything was destroyed. My house included. He thinks my parents died."

"I'm so sorry, Halya." Vika sat down next to her, searching for the right words, but nothing was adequate. "What is your heart telling you?"

Halya's expression softened. "To marry Slavko. To try to find happiness. But it still feels wrong."

"Because in doing so, you feel like you're letting them go," Vika finished. She understood all too well.

"Yes," Halya whispered.

"Then don't. Hold on to your parents—their memories,

their love, and bring it with you. Let them live on in you and your children. Choosing Slavko, choosing a new life, doesn't mean you have to give them up."

Tears welled in Halya's eyes, and she blinked them back. "Did Slavko ever tell you that I lost my real mother when I was very young?"

Vika stilled. "No, he hasn't said much about it."

Halya took a deep breath. "My mother died when I was a baby, and her sister—my aunt—married my father to help raise me. I don't remember my birth mother, but she's always been such a presence in my life."

"I'm sure she'd be so proud of you," Vika said. "As would your aunt."

"My mama," Halya said. "She loved me like her own, and I love both her and my father dearly. They didn't have children together, but our home was filled with love because they knew the pain of loss. So, you see, in leaving, in admitting that she and my father are gone and moving on to America, I've now lost two mothers. And as happy as Slavko makes me, that's a hard thing to accept."

A surge of protectiveness shot through Vika, and she took Halya's hand. "If you'll let me, I'll be a mother to you. I know you're grown and you don't really need a mother anymore, especially after all you've gone through, but it would be an honor for me to call you daughter."

Halya's face broke into one of her breathtaking smiles even as tears welled in her eyes. "You really mean that?"

"I do." Vika pulled Halya into a hug. She could feel each bone in the girl's back, but she was in better condition already than when they'd first met her. "We already think of you as a daughter. This will just make it official."

"This means everything to me," Halya said.

"Family is everything," Vika said. She sat back and wiped the tears off Halya's cheeks with her thumbs. "And you've gained a new one. That doesn't mean you ever have to forget your original family."

Halya pulled a piece of paper out of her pocket and unfolded it. "Liliya made this for me years ago. I had a picture of my birth mother and my father, but a guard ripped it up. Liliya had only seen it once, but she drew them for me so clearly. I spent so many nights staring at this picture as I fell asleep, but really, it was always my aunt, my mama, that I missed the most."

"She raised you. She was your mother, too." Vika peered down at the drawing. "Though it seems you favor your birth mother."

"I've been told that a lot," Halya said. "I only hope my strength resembles my mama's as much as my looks resemble my mother's."

"I think you are the best of both of them." Vika hesitated. She didn't want to ask, but she had to know how deep this loss ran, how close her connection was to this fragile yet indomitable girl. "Was it the famine that took your mother?"

"Yes," Halya answered. "Though a Soviet bullet ended the inevitable sooner, I was told."

A wave of longing washed over Vika, and she closed her eyes, remembering. "I lost my parents then as well. And almost all my siblings to the labor camps or the hunger. I escaped with Maksym and one sister before they closed the borders, but I think of them every day."

This time, Halya reached out to Vika. "So, you know," she said simply.

Vika opened her eyes and met Halya's clear gaze. "I know what you're giving up. I know what you've lost. And I love you all the more for it."

58

LILIYA

February 1949, USS Ernie Pyle, *Atlantic Ocean*

Filip kissed Liliya's cheek, and she gripped his hand. His solid, steady presence had moored her this past year. Through their short engagement and jubilant wedding to the chaotic birth of their daughter in the DP camps, Filip had become her rock. Theirs was a love story Liliya had given up on because she'd given up on herself. But now, as she stared at her handsome husband and beautiful daughter, their old lives fading in the distance as they sailed toward America, she felt a fullness in her chest she could barely contain.

I think this is what happiness feels like.

It was such a foreign concept, an elusive ideal, that she'd forgotten how to accept it. Sometimes, she tried to think back to the last time she could remember being happy. Perhaps it was sketching birds with her mother under the cherry trees. Or walking with her father down to the pond to fetch water while they practiced languages. But those memories were so distant, so far back, they seemed to be from another life, from another person.

She wondered about Oleksiy but feared she'd never learn his fate. He'd probably gone back like he intended and was still fighting for Ukrainian independence, especially now with Stalin reasserting his dominance over western Ukraine. The same battle with another generation carrying on the torch. The world had stopped fighting, but Ukrainians could not.

She felt guilty walking away from that fight, but now, her focus had to be on her daughter and finding the best life for her. Maybe if she'd never found Filip, never had a baby, she would have eventually gone back and fought for Nina, for her parents, for all the lives needlessly wasted, but now, she had a new purpose.

That new purpose waved her chubby little arm in Liliya's face and squealed.

"I think she wants you," Filip said, laughing. He held out young Nina to Liliya.

"That's good," Liliya said. "Because I very much want her, too."

59

VIKA

February 1949, USS Ernie Pyle, *Atlantic Ocean*

Vika smiled as Slavko and Halya, the young, newly married couple, embraced. One could almost imagine they were carefree, just a happy pair on their honeymoon traveling to America. But despite the love arcing between them, Vika could read the pain in Halya's eyes, the uncertainty she would carry forever about this decision to move on without concrete answers.

Further down the rail, Liliya and Filip cuddled their daughter. Born without a home, without a country, young Nina would shed her birthright as a displaced person and adapt far quicker to their new life than any of them. She would be an American, unable to remember the violence and horror her family endured, but the marks would always be there, affecting her throughout her life even though they hadn't touched her personally. Family shaped a person, and none of them had come out of this war unscathed. So, battle worn and weary, they would shape Nina as best they could.

They would tell her about her namesake and the years the family spent apart. They would tell her of the epic journey her honorary Baba and Dido—Liliya insisted Maksym and Vika take up those roles—had made to escape Stalin and Hitler and reunite the family. They would sing the songs of her people so that she, too, would never forget where she came from, even though she'd never seen it.

They were lost to Ukraine, but they would always carry their homeland in their hearts.

Vika slipped her hand into her pocket, running her fingers over the dried *kalyna* berries. This powerful symbol of Ukraine would join her in her new life as both a reminder and a promise. It would take time for a *kalyna* bush to take root and grow, but eventually, it would thrive. Just like her and her family.

She stared east toward Ukraine. She had to leave now, for her family's safety, she knew that, but her homeland still tugged at her. It always would. Perhaps, someday, Ukraine would throw off the Soviet noose tight around its neck and rise again as a free country. Perhaps, someday, she could return and see her dear sister, Maria, meet Maria's children, and their children. Perhaps, someday, Slavko and Halya's grandchildren would come back and meet their cousins from the old world and see the beautiful land Vika loved.

The words of the old Cossack song her father always sang, the anthem of the famous Sich Riflemen of World War I, danced on her tongue, and she sang them, soft and clear.

Oy u luzi chervona kalyna pokhylylasya

Chohos' nasha slavna Ukrayina zazhurylasya
A my tuyu chervonu kalynu pidiymemo
A my nashu Slavnu Ukrayinu, hey, hey,
    rozveselymo!

Maksym took her other hand and pressed it to his lips, paraphrasing the song into her skin. "Yes, our red *kalyna* is bent low now, but our glorious Ukraine shall rise up and rejoice again."

"Yes." Vika smiled at him. "Someday."

ACRONYMS & TERMS

AK: Armia Krajowa (Polish Home Army), the official name of the Polish Resistance that eventually absorbed most Polish partisan and underground forces.

NKVD: Narodnyi Kommissariat Vnuntrennikh Del (People's Commissariat for Internal Affairs), the Soviet secret police from 1934–1946, which later morphed into the KGB.

OUN: Orhanizatsiia Ukrains'kykh Natsionalistiv (Organization of Ukrainian Nationalists), Ukrainian political group dedicated to the establishment of an independent Ukraine.

UPA: Ukrains'ka Povstans'ka Armiia (Ukrainian Insurgent Army), Ukrainian military group (mostly in Western Ukraine) that fought from 1942–1949 against the Germans, the Soviets, and the Polish Resistance with the goal of an independent Ukraine.

Schutzmannschaft/Schuma: collaborationist auxiliary police battalions of locals in Nazi occupied countries.

Ostarbeiters: Eastern workers. Laborers taken from Nazi occupied countries in the east and forced to work in German factories and farms for the war effort.

UNRRA: United Nations Relief and Rehabilitation Administration, provided economic assistance to refugees during WWII and ran the DP camps until 1946.

IRO: International Refugee Organization, an intergovernmental organization formed to deal with the refugee problem after WWII, it ran the DP camps from 1946 until it disbanded in 1952.

AUTHOR'S NOTE

The line between fiction and family history in this book is so blurry it's sometimes hard for me to remember where it begins and ends. From little tidbits and scenes to a full storyline, this novel is in large part inspired by the Ukrainian side of my family. It's the book I've dreamed about writing since I was a little girl.

My great-grandparents were from the historic region of Volhynia, located in what was then eastern Poland and is now western Ukraine. In 1939, at the start of World War II, the Soviets invaded. They enforced collectivization, tortured and executed civilians, and conscripted 150,000 young men into the Red Army. The NKVD arranged purges of political threats—Polish military veterans, civil servants, policemen and their families, including the elderly and children.

As the Soviets retreated from the Nazi invasion in 1941, they slaughtered their political prisoners and enforced a scorched earth policy in their wake. Life under Soviet rule had been so brutal that many Ukrainians welcomed the Germans as liberators, but when another horrific occupation commenced, they soon learned that the Nazis were no different.

Like many before, the Nazis wanted Ukraine's land. Its bounty was an integral part of Hitler's plan for an eastern empire, and they intended to use the existing collective farms to starve the local populations just as the Soviets had done—shipping food out of Ukraine to Germany and planning the deaths of tens of millions so they could colonize it. The Nazis also solved the problem of the workforce deficit in Germany by taking laborers from their newly occupied territories across Europe—rounding up many of the same people who had survived the Holodomor in markets or as they came out of church, stealing them from their homes, or sending notifications to report to the labor department for their assignments.

By November 1943, the required age minimum for laborers had been lowered to ten years old. If people refused or ran away, their homes were burned and their families punished. Village elders and local governments were forced to create labor lists, and while some simply complied, others found various ways to subvert the Nazis, such as working to increase local labor quotas to keep people in Ukraine with their families.

The food, housing, medical inspections and treatment of *Ostarbeiters,* Eastern Workers from Reichskommissariat Ukraine and other occupied eastern territories, varied depending on their location—farm, factory type, etc. All the situations Liliya, Slavko and Halya experienced—daily roll calls, sabotaging equipment, backbreaking work schedules and bombings in the barracks—are drawn from a myriad of first-hand accounts.

Those who rebelled or escaped, if caught, were either

executed immediately or sent to death camps such as Auschwitz or Dachau.

At its height, the forced labor program employed over 7.6 million workers, roughly 2.2 million of which were Ukrainians. Near the end of the war, *Ostarbeiters* were marched to other camps and factories, forced to dig trenches, and sometimes killed in mass executions when camps and factories closed, as Liliya experienced.

Back in Volhynia, Ukrainians were members of the Soviet army (mostly conscripted), the Ukrainian Insurgent Army (UPA), the Nazi auxiliary police forces, and, more rarely, the Soviet Partisans. It's a sad and baffling truth that, while the Nazis considered Ukrainians and other Slavs "sub-human" and murdered, deported, and enslaved millions of them, other Ukrainians served in the German army and in the auxiliary police. When it became clear the Nazi promises of a free Ukraine after the war were lies, many Ukrainians left German service to join the UPA and fight the Nazis, Soviets, and Poles.

Fighting raged between the groups. The UPA attacked Polish settlements. The Polish Resistance reciprocated. Both groups fought the Nazis, and for every strike against them, the Nazis executed innocent civilians and burned villages to the ground in retaliation. My great-grandparents and their children were forced to flee their home and hide three times as Nazis burned nearby villages, uncertain if they would find their home still standing when they returned. As the Eastern front shifted, rolling back over Ukraine and Poland again, waves of refugees moved west away from the turmoil in their homeland, including my family.

The stories of my family traveling through Europe, on a

wagon, in the middle of a war are the ones that first piqued my interest in this history at a young age—particularly the story of my great-grandmother saving her family with her bravery and quick thinking after Russians robbed them and lined them up to shoot them. But asking questions about that history led to so many more stories: how my grandfather was so hungry he happily ate rotten soup a woman offered him or how he witnessed a young boy maim himself after playing with a loaded *Panzerfaust* he found. My great-uncle recalls, among many other things, his parents crying over the graves of murdered Poles, dear friends of theirs, when they visited family in their old village before leaving Volhynia.

As the Soviets continued pushing the Nazis back, the front approached Breslau, Germany (now Wrocław, Poland), and Hitler evacuated the civilian population and the many refugees passing through there, including my family. Thousands of people died as they fled through sub-zero temperatures and snow, and in a cruel twist of irony, many of those who survived the frigid flight from Breslau ended up in Dresden just in time to experience the fiery apocalypse of the Allied bombing.

From February 13–15, 1945, eight hundred bombers dropped roughly 2,700 tons of explosives and incendiaries on Dresden in several waves. Thankfully, my family was not in Dresden, but they were close enough to hear and see it in the distance. The ensuing fires twisted together into a horrifying firestorm that sucked people and debris up into it, killing roughly 22,000 – 25,000 people. They asphyxiated or essentially baked in cellars; they sought refuge in water reservoirs, then boiled to death when they couldn't climb out; they sank into the melting roads; and in the middle of the second wave of bombs, Polish Arabian horses being evacuated from the approaching Red Army in the east arrived in the city.

Filip's journey with the Polish Arabian horses is based on a true story. The Germans prized these valuable horses and there were several confiscations and evacuations of the horses from eastern Poland at various times. One group from the Janów Podlaski stable ended up arriving in Dresden on February 14 as the second round of bombs fell at approximately 1 a.m. Many of the horses bolted and ran away; many died. One young groom, Jan Ziniewcz, famously held the lead lines of two stallions, Witraż and Wielki Szlem, his hands bleeding as they bucked and reared while explosions and fire raged around them. But, he never let go, and those two stallions were instrumental in rebuilding the nearly decimated Polish Arabian bloodlines after the war.

I was especially intrigued by this account of the Polish Arabians because my great-grandfather was an avid horseman. While he didn't work at a Polish Arabian stable, he did dote on his own horses. At one point, he saved a lame horse the Germans were going to euthanize and nursed it back to health, only to have the Germans steal it back again when it healed. Another time, he propped a scythe on his shoulder and left his wife and young children so he could follow his beloved horses —stolen by soldiers—to make sure they ate well as he tried to get them back. He was unsuccessful, but I loved the idea of weaving in this fascinating Polish Arabian history to pay tribute to his passion for horses, which has trickled through the generations down to my daughter.

As the war ended, Ukraine was left in shambles. Roughly 7 million Ukrainians had died, and 2.2 million had been shipped off as forced laborers. Of the 36 million remaining Ukrainians, 10 million were homeless. Nearly 29,000 villages and cities, including the village where my great-grandfather was born, were decimated.

Those who'd left Ukraine—whether forced or voluntarily—fell under the "Displaced Persons" (DP) umbrella, a phrase that encompassed a spectrum of people across Europe—forced laborers, concentration camp survivors, prisoners of war and refugees. While it is difficult to land on an exact number due to the post-war chaos, researchers estimate up to 10–12 million DPs existed in Europe. Initially, Allied forces repatriated many DPs back to their own countries. Those returning to Soviet countries were considered traitors to Stalin, ostracized for life, and often arrested and sent to gulags. By the end of September 1945, the remaining 1.2 million DPs—mostly from Poland, Ukraine and the Baltic States—refused to go home, justly fearing persecution at the hands of the Soviets. The scene in which Halya sees a man choose to hang himself rather than go back to the Soviet Union is based on something my great-uncle witnessed, and it was not an isolated incident.

Initially run by the United Nations Relief and Rehabilitation Administration (UNRRA), then taken over by the International Refugee Organization (IRO) in 1946, the Displaced Persons camps typically grouped people by ethnicity, not country of origin. Stuck between their broken pasts and uncertain futures, DPs tried to piece their lives together by searching for lost family members, marrying, and starting new families. In the old army barracks often repurposed for their housing, community groups opened their own schools, churches and businesses, and organized dances, plays, and elections for governing committees. In Aschaffenburg, my grandfather went fishing in the Main river and, always mechanically inclined, collected broken bicycles and their parts to cobble together whole bicycles to sell.

Very slowly, the DPs—often presented inhumanely as an untapped labor force—found new homes in Belgium, Canada, Great Britain, France, Australia, Brazil, Argentina, and Chile as farmers, miners, domestics, and factory workers. In the United States, mounting pressure to help more led to the Displaced Persons Act of 1948, which allowed 200,000 DPs to apply for resettlement in the United States. Sponsored by the United Ukrainian American Relief Committee, my family was able to participate in this program. Later amended and expanded in 1950 and 1951, in total, the Displaced Persons Act helped almost 400,000 DPs resettle in the United States.

In researching my Ukrainian family history, I have found relatives embroiled in nearly every aspect of this upheaval. While none of the characters in this book are exact matches for members of my family, I drew inspiration from all of them to influence many of my characters' arcs. Vika's family's flight from Ukraine and their time in the DP camps, while fictionalized, is inspired by my great-grandparents' journey and infused with memories from my great-uncle and grandfather. I was also able to use my family's actual DP camp intake records, obtained from the Arolsen Archives, to create the scenes where Liliya goes through the interview process of entering the camps, and where Vika laments that despite everything she did, her children were marked down as malnourished, as were my great-grandmother's children.

My family eventually moved through two different camps,

Neumarkt and Aschaffenburg, and managed to find and reunite with a lost nephew before emigrating to America on the USS *Ernie Pyle* in 1949, three years after their arrival in the camps. My great-grandmother left a sister behind in Volhynia; she never saw her again or met her children and grandchildren. They still live in Ukraine. I hope one day soon to bring my children there, to show them the village where my grandfather—a man they knew and loved—was born, to introduce them to their cousins, and to finally reconnect the ties WWII severed in my family.

This story—much of it dealing with painful, brutal history and with my own family's trauma—was difficult to write. But even in the midst of the darkness, I found glimpses of light. Against the backdrop of Polish-Ukrainian conflict in Volhynia, Poles helped Ukrainian families, Ukrainians helped Polish families, and groups of Polish and Ukrainian partisans united toward the end of WWII to fight Soviet occupation.

Those instances of strength and unity, rather than hatred and division, carry Ukrainians and Poles forward today. Despite years of Nazi, Soviet, and ongoing Russian propaganda exploiting the history to sow discord, Poland was the first country to recognize Ukraine's independence from the Soviet Union, and it has been not only a staunch ally during the current Russo-Ukrainian War but also a generous haven for millions of Ukrainian refugees. The Polish-Ukrainian relationship is a testament to the power of learning from the past, finding the good, and choosing a better path forward—a sharp contrast to the continued aggression and brutality coming from Russia now. It is a lesson of which the world should take note.

For more information on this complex history, I suggest

reading a wide variety of resources and materials. Here are a few books I used:

Bloodlands: Europe Between Hitler and Stalin by Timothy Snyder

Harvest of Despair: Life and Death in Ukraine under Nazi Rule by Karel Berkhoff

The Last Million: Europe's Displaced Persons from World War to Cold War by David Nasaw

The Long Road Home: The Aftermath of the Second World War by Ben Shephard

The Wild Place by Katherine Hulme

The Culmination of Conflict by Stephen Rapawy

The Reconstruction of Nations by Timothy Snyder

Wearing the Letter P by Sophie Hodorowicz Knab

OST: Letters, Memoirs and Stories from Ostarbeiter in Nazi Germany from Memorial International

Genocide and Rescue in Wolyn by Tadeusz Piotrowski

Volyn and Polissia: The German Occupation, Books One and Two edited by I.E. Shtendera from the Litopys UPA Library

Thousands of Roads: A Memoir of a Young Woman's Life in the Ukrainian Underground During and After WWII by Maria Savchyn Pyskir

The Fire and the Darkness: The Bombing of Dresden, 1945 by Sinclair McKay

Hitler's Final Fortress: Breslau 1945 by Richard Hargreaves

ACKNOWLEDGMENTS

I often think of the trials my ancestors endured to give me the life I have now, and I'm endlessly grateful to them. For me, learning their history is the best way to honor their memories. While this deeply personal and often complicated book wasn't always easy to research or write, it is my tribute to those who came before me, to those who made me.

I am eternally grateful to fellow writers Amanda McCrina, Marina Scott, and Andrea Green for reading this manuscript and providing invaluable insight, advice, and friendship. To my agent, Lindsay Guzzardo, thank you once again for plucking me from the slush pile and helping to make my dreams come true. Taryn Fagerness, thank you for working so hard to help my stories reach countries I never imagined possible. Thank you to my endlessly supportive editor, Tara Loder, who was always there to answer my questions or brainstorm ideas with me. To the rest of the Boldwood team—Amanda, Nia, Claire, Caroline, Sarah, Jenna, Ben, Megan, Sue, Marcella, Isabelle and everyone else behind the scenes, thank you for your tireless efforts to bring my books to life. You guys are wonderful!

Families are the backbones of my novels, and I am so fortunate to have the complete support of an amazing one. Thank you for always believing in me.

This book wouldn't have been possible without the stories

passed down from my great-grandmother, grandfather and great-uncle. I've lost two of them already, but I am so fortunate to still have my great-uncle here. Uncle Bohdan, thank you for always being ready and willing to talk with me. Ukraine is in my heart, as you so often tell me, but you are helping me keep our family's Ukrainian history alive, and that is everything.

Last, but certainly not least, I am so thankful to my readers and the reading community—bookstagrammers, bloggers, librarians, and book clubs. Every message, every email, every review you write means so much to me. Thank you for using your precious time to give my books a chance. I hope you enjoy this new one as much as I enjoyed writing it.

BOOK CLUB QUESTIONS

1. Did you realize Stalin made a pact with Hitler to invade Poland? Why do you think that part of history is often overlooked?

2. Each of these three women, Vika, Liliya, and Halya, are facing the war at a different point in their life. Which of them did you connect with most? Why do you think that is?

3. Liliya blamed herself for Nina's death and for Slavko being taken as a forced laborer. Do you think any of it was her fault? Should Vika have not allowed Liliya to hide in their barn?

4. Forced laborers often found themselves in the position of helping the German war effort against their will. What would you do in their situation? Would you sabotage weapons and supplies if the punishment was death or a death camp?

5. We all face choices every day, but many of the choices these characters made had life and death

consequences. Were there any choices the characters made that you disagreed with?

6. To survive in Dresden after escaping the factory, Halya and Slavko broke into homes, stole food, and didn't feel bad about it. Do you think they were wrong to do that?

7. Many people in the Displaced Persons camps were able to reunite after the war, many weren't. Which of the characters' reunions moved you the most? Did any surprise you?

8. Oleksiy chooses to go back to Ukraine and fight while Liliya chooses to stay in the camps to search for her friends and family. Would you have gone back to Ukraine? Or would you have taken your chance in a new country?

9. Vika met Katya, Halya's aunt, at one of the camps, but didn't realize who she was. How many missed opportunities like that do you think occurred? How important was "found family" for forced laborers and people who couldn't reconnect with their blood families?

10. Halya couldn't find her parents after the war, so she chose to marry Slavko and go to America with him and his family. Do you think she made the right choice? What would you have done?

MORE FROM ERIN LITTEKEN

We hope you enjoyed reading *The Lost Daughters of Ukraine*. If you did, please leave a review.

If you'd like to gift a copy, this book is also available as an ebook, large print, hardback, digital audio download and audiobook CD.

Sign up to Erin Litteken's mailing list for news, competitions and updates on future books.

https://bit.ly/ErinLittekenNews

The Memory Keeper of Kyiv, another powerful historical novel from Erin Litteken, is available to buy now...

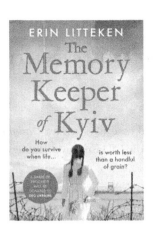

ERIN LITTEKEN

The
Memory
Keeper
_of_ Kyiv

How
do you survive
when life...

is worth less
than a handful
of grain?

A SHARE OF PROCEEDS
WILL BE
DONATED TO
DEC UKRAINE

ABOUT THE AUTHOR

Erin Litteken is an international bestselling author with a degree in history and a passion for research. At a young age, she was enthralled by stories of her family's harrowing experiences in Ukraine before, during and after World War II. Her historical fiction draws on those experiences. She lives in Illinois, USA with her husband and children.

Visit Erins's website: https://www.erinlitteken.com

Follow Erin on social media:

facebook.com/erin.litteken
twitter.com/ErinLitteken
instagram.com/erinlitteken

Boldwood

Boldwood Books is an award-winning fiction publishing company seeking out the best stories from around the world.

Find out more at www.boldwoodbooks.com

Join our reader community for brilliant books, competitions and offers!

Follow us
@BoldwoodBooks
@BookandTonic

Sign up to our weekly deals newsletter

https://bit.ly/BoldwoodBNewsletter

Made in United States
North Haven, CT
21 February 2024

49009968R00233